Heartscale

Lola Ford

Cover by Enmanuel Martinez, 2019
Map by Niklas Müller, 2019

ISBN: 9781070326726 (paperback)

For everyone who has ever wished for a dragon of their own.

CHAPTER ONE

Graith

Graith was tending his wheat fields when the news arrived. A dragon had been sighted flying over the nearby lands. Lord Arish had sent out heralds announcing that there was to be a hunt. Graith hadn't minded all the commotion in the following days, as he was just a farmer. He continued to prepare for the harvest and the approaching winter. In his mind he had one duty, and that was to continue to provide his tithe to his lord.

Over the following days, as he moved from one field to the next, news about the dragon continued to circulate. Men from the other nearby villages started to group in town, and Graith couldn't help but wonder just how many men were needed to slay a dragon. He couldn't remember a time when so many people had gathered in his small town. Graith lived in Lord Arish's outermost lands where few bothered to travel.

In Graith's experience, the only visitors who would travel this far out were tax collectors and the tradesmen who came by twice a year. They normally brought with them the kinds of specialty parts that the local blacksmith, while capable of making, simply didn't have time for, as well as special treats and foods that the villagers wouldn't get to experience otherwise.

As Graith finished harvesting his fields, the number of men camped around town continued to grow. His duties done, Graith decided to visit the town pub. He figured he'd be able to catch up on the news he'd missed over the last few weeks.

The pub was located in the heart of the small town. A single-story building, the pub wasn't much larger than the few houses nearby. The door was kept open, and the hearth lit all hours of the day. On nice summer evenings, tables would even be brought out into the front lawn. The only notable features were a well out front, and a small three stall barn out back for visitors' horses.

While he had never been on the best of terms with his neighbors, Graith didn't really have a problem with them either. He simply liked to do his job at his own pace, in his own fields. Graith couldn't understand why they would volunteer to help, and then expect the same in return. It was never something that interested Graith. The first year he'd owned the farm they had come rushing over, but when Graith hadn't returned the favor they'd snubbed him. Since then he'd only had his friend Ralph and the occasional trip to the pub for the day-to-day news.

Having no wife to gossip while doing the washing or shopping left Graith at another disadvantage. Another way that his neighbors decided meant he wanted nothing to do with them. Plenty of them had sisters they were looking to marry, but Graith was too busy for a wife.

Upon entering the pub, many of the locals appeared quite shocked at his appearance. The times Graith did visit the pub were usually the quiet nights. Ignoring the looks, he sat down at the nearest table with an open seat. With so many new people in town, the pub was quite full, and the only opening was nearest to the kitchen - which at this time of day was putting off quite a bit of heat. Three of the visitors sat there, slightly red in the face and uncomfortably warm.

They nodded in acknowledgment of him and waved the serving girl over.

"Haven't seen you lot around here before," Graith said as a way of greeting, while the serving girl filled his mug. The visitors consisted of an older man, with a bent neck but sharp eyes, and two youngsters who looked fresh from their own fields. All looked at him in surprise.

"We've been in town for nearly two weeks!" the younger looking of the two boys said.

Graith flushed slightly. He hadn't realized it had been that long since he'd come for a drink.

"What brings you to town?" Graith asked, at the same time trying to get the serving girl back over so he could order some stew. "I'd noticed people arriving, but I've been busy harvesting my crops."

"Lord Arish sent us all to hunt a dragon," the older man said with a frown. Graith did recall the man who'd tried to recruit him a while back.

"Never seen a dragon around here before," Graith said. "Don't reckon I would recognize one, even if I saw it."

"Not recognize a dragon? A great flying serpent, all fire and wrath? Death on wings and you wouldn't recognize it?" The older boy asked him bewildered.

"Did I notice you lot arriving?" Graith asked. "What makes you think I would recognize a dragon then?"

"Well, you'd likely recognize it from not having ever seen anything like it before." The older man shrugged, then continued with what he had been saying, "A couple of months ago, a soldier came through our town looking for recruits. Told us to head to the village closest to the mountains and wait for the rest to arrive. We've been gathering supplies and weapons. Last I heard we're to head out next week, scouring all the caves between here and the Eastern Reach for this dragon."

"What's so special about the dragon? Why hunt it down?" Graith didn't understand what all the fuss was about.

"Are you serious? It's a danger! A hazard! Takes our livestock, burns our villages! It has to be destroyed," the younger boy said with vehemence, very nearly standing from his seat to lean towards Graith as he spoke.

"There were villages destroyed?" Graith asked, not remembering hearing news of such.

"Well, not yet. But in the past, other dragons have!" the boy admitted.

"What about the livestock?" Graith asked.

"Huh? Well a few sheep and a cow have been taken," the other boy said.

"Over the last couple months? That's as many that die from their own stupidity in that amount of time, no real hurt there." Graith was getting annoyed - all this hullabaloo, for what? A possible threat?

"Look man, dragons are dangerous. They need to die as soon as we know about them. Think of the damages more than one could do. It's your responsibility to your lord to root them out."

The young men seemed angry at Graith's lack of fervor, while the older just shook his head. He obviously didn't think that was true, but he was here to hunt down the dragon, which was more than Graith was doing.

Graith snorted. "My only responsibilities to Lord Arish are to harvest my crops and pay my taxes. He asks nothing more of me."

"Bah! We're good men of our lord, and we'll hunt this dragon in his name," the older of the two boys said, dismissing Graith with a wave.

That seemed to signal the end of their conversation. The recruited soldiers went back to their meal and seemed content to ignore Graith. Graith on the other hand, got up and roamed about the tables while sipping his ale. As he walked, whispers and rumors about the dragon floated through the air.

"It's said to be as big as a castle!"

"Fire breather, as hot as any blacksmiths forge!"

"Scales harder than the hardest plate steel, but twice as thick!"

Shouts and boasts joined them from those souls who thought that they would be the one to bring down the mighty dragon.

"I'll land my lance right through its eye! Straight into the brain!"

"I'll cut off its tail and then its head!"

"I'll land an arrow in the back of its maw as it tries to breathe fire!"

To these boasts Graith just shook his head and continued onward. Had he been a younger man, maybe joining a mercenary group might have interested him, but he thought not. He'd never wanted to go on adventures or explore before settling down. No, he had grown up on his farm, and harvested wheat his whole life. When his father had passed, the farm had become his.

He was rather proud of the fact that the only change he'd made was to go over his finances and find that he had the means to annex two more acres of land and purchase a new horse.

He was content with his lifestyle. He worked, he cooked, he slept, and he lived his own simple life. That suited him just fine.

That night, Graith sat down at his hearth in his favorite leather chair. It was a commodity he'd rewarded himself with a decade ago, when he'd had an especially abundant year. As he faced the small fire, he thought about what he'd heard at the pub.

The last time a dragon had been seen on these lands, he'd been a small boy. He could still remember the feast that had been held by Lord Arish's father, Lord Derk. It had lasted three days, and his own father had even taken him into Dunlaith to celebrate. While the feast had been a fantastic affair, Graith couldn't help but think about the poor beast who'd died for it to happen.

Graith sighed as he stood, preparing for bed. He'd always wanted to see a dragon alive, but none had ever flown over his farm.

***

Several weeks later, long after the men had left town, Graith went to the pub again. It was empty now, except for the serving girl and the owner. He drank an ale and listened to the fire in the hearth crackle and found himself wondering if the hunt had been successful. Though he thought not, as he was sure there would have been news if it had been.

When Graith went to sleep that night, he found himself dreaming of a dragon.

The dragon was indeed massive, but not as large as some had claimed. It was a dark navy blue, not black like he had expected. Its wings shimmered in moonlight and Graith couldn't help but want to touch the fine gossamer webbing. Its head was nearly as tall as his whole body, and he was not a short man. It had wicked white fangs that looked more than capable of rending a sheep, cow, or even a man, apart in seconds. Tiny pebble scales formed around its nostrils and eyes, gradually getting larger, until by the neck they were as large as his hand. The scales on its back were as large as the spade of his largest shovel.

It had a crest of horns wreathing its face, a bright white in contrast to the dark scales. All along its back, following its spine, were long spikes which created a crested effect for its whole body. The spikes continued down to its tail, which was curled around its body, not unlike a cat.

But more than anything, it was the dragon's eyes that captivated Graith. Large and iridescent, they were an icy blue, with slits from top to bottom, again reminding Graith of his barn cat. They held an intelligence that surprised Graith - and a deep sadness.

He reached out wanting to comfort the beast, but even as his fingers went to brush the tiny scales of the nearest nostril, he awoke.

He laid in bed for several long minutes, thinking about his dream. Graith was not known for dreaming. In fact, it had been many years since his last one, a fact that didn't bother him. It left him feeling rested in the morning, unhindered by what might have been, or unrealistic fantasies others seemed to dream of.

But why would he be dreaming of a dragon? A *sad* dragon? Why did he care that it was sad? Not being able to answer these questions left Graith lying in bed far longer than normal. When he finally sat up, he scrubbed at his face.

It didn't matter.

He bathed and dressed for the day and went to his kitchen to make breakfast. After eating, he sat and tried to figure out what he had to do today.

He was having a slow morning and just couldn't seem to keep his mind from wandering back to his dream. He paced around the small house before finally deciding that he needed to take stock of his harvest for the year.

He had finished storing away the wheat to dry the day before, but he still needed to bundle and transport it all to the wheat grinder. Wheat was fine and all, but it was flour that the lord needed. Graith had a large barn where he stored the wheat to dry, with distinct locations for each field harvested, as well as a place to bundle it and then pack the bundles onto his wagon.

He grabbed his ledger then headed to the barn. He thought this year might make his top five largest harvests, but he wouldn't know for sure until he had finished bundling the wheat.

He fed his chickens as he crossed his small fenced yard. He carefully set his ledger aside and pumped water for his horse and cow who both were roaming the small paddock. Picking the ledger back up, he resumed his walk. He thought about riding his horse to the barn but decided the walk would help clear his head.

He could see his barn, which resided on the north side of his property, well before he reached it. While not situated for the easiest access from his home, it was centered between his best fields. It was also in the direction of town. A dark mahogany from age, the barn was two stories tall and had large, sliding doors on both ends, and windows propped open along the sides high above. A normal sized door was inset within the larger, locked sliding door which Graith opened to enter the barn.

Inside Graith turned to his immediate left, towards his small office he'd built for the exclusive purpose of keeping his past ledgers, and his small safe, which contained his life savings. The barn was dark, with no lanterns to possibly set his precious harvest on fire, but Graith didn't need a lantern as he maneuvered around his office to open the shuttered window. His office faced away from the rising sun, but the window provided enough light for him to see by to unlock the nearest set of large sliding doors.

He lifted the iron latch and started to slide the door open. As he did so, he heard a slithering sound behind him. Having gotten the door open about two feet wide, he turned to look around his feet for a snake, annoyed. Sometimes they were able to get in from under the floor. He'd tried to have the barn built as securely as possible, for rodents eating away at his harvest was bad for his profits. Unable to find a snake, though surely he knew what he'd heard - he turned back to the large doors. Now too far apart to push from the middle, he grabbed the left door and pulled it open.

As he headed to the right door, he heard the slithering sound again, but this time it was accompanied by a sharp tapping noise. Stopping again, he turned to investigate the now illuminated barn. There was nothing on the first floor, but the sound, still audible, was coming from above.

Damn snakes, he thought as he went to the nearest ladder and started climbing to the loft. Focused on the rungs before him, he did not immediately see the source of the sound. But as he reached the second floor and stood upright, he saw it.

It was quite hard to miss, as it was the midnight blue dragon from his dreams the night before.

CHAPTER TWO

Nerie

Nerie and Raana raced through the streets, headed to the royal hatching ceremony. Young girls from the middle district, they were well dressed for the special occasion. Raana wore a burgundy dress, while Nerie wore a navy vest over a white shirt and a long navy skirt. Both laughed in excitement as vendors sold colorful candies and savory treats. On any other day they would have stopped to sample the wares, but not today. They were on their way to the palace.

It was an exciting time for everyone in the kingdom. All across the city of Roria, golden and navy banners hung from every window. Flowers laid in baskets waiting to be thrown into the air. The market bustled as the kingdom waited with bated breath to celebrate. As the girls wove their way to the palace, they discovered line after line nearly backed up to the lower district.

"This way!" Raana said as she pulled Nerie through streets she hadn't even known existed. Raana had told Nerie the night before that she had a friend in the palace who'd said that he could get the girls inside to actually see the hatching.

As they made their way from crowded street to crowded street, Nerie felt lost. But Raana was confidently leading them from one turn to the next. When she brought Nerie to a small back door on the far side of the palace, Nerie held her breath anxiously. She'd never been inside the palace before. Not many commoners had, as it was only opened for the hatching ceremony and for coronations - neither of which had ever occurred in her lifetime.

Raana knocked sharply twice before a handsome young man with dark hair and dark eyes pulled it open. She leapt into his arms and started kissing him. Nerie was shocked, as she'd had no idea that her friend had such a *friend*.

"Raana! What would your mother say!" Nerie asked with a giggle, as Raana and the man separated.

Raana just rolled her eyes.

"I'm Zaid. And I intend to find out what her mother has to say as soon as I save up enough to ask for her hand in marriage," Zaid said with a wink, then led them inside.

It turned out that the back-door led to the nearly sweltering kitchens. Zaid grabbed two aprons and handed them to the girls.

"I couldn't just get you in for free. We need more hands than we have here in the kitchens today. Just for a while - we all want to be at the hatching too," Zaid said apologetically.

Raana and Nerie spent the next few hours helping prepare for the feast that would follow the hatching. Nerie was tasked with folding bread while Raana started turning a boar over the fire. Nerie was a little annoyed that Raana hadn't told her in advance - even with the apron she was getting flour on her new outfit. While the kitchen was crowded and hot, no one was rushing. The way the staff were acting, it seemed like there was a while yet to wait for the hatching to start.

After Nerie finished with the dough, she was dusted off and given a tray to carry to the front of the palace. She had no idea where she was going but was told that she just needed to head down the main corridor and that one of the servants was expecting her. She felt incredibly self-conscious at first but calmed herself down by thinking how lucky it was that the outfit her mother had bought was nice enough to pass for a royal servant. She walked slowly but with determination as she tried not to slosh the liquid around. As Nerie stepped out of the kitchen Raana shouted to her she would catch up in just a few minutes, because she was waiting for Zaid.

As Nerie approached a large set of double doors, one of the king's personal servants came to her aid, taking the refreshments directly to a group of waiting nobles. Through the doors she could see that they had tents erected around the hatching grounds on one side, and the far side had tiered seating where commoners were already funneling in. She walked slowly towards the door, mesmerized by the scene in front of her. Between all the nobles' tents there was one that was clearly for the royal family.

They were sitting on a dais behind where two dragons were curled around an egg. The one that the hatching was all about. A bright green dragon rested on the roof above the dais, his head drooping down, watching his soon to be hatched sibling with keen interest. Nerie was glad the tray had been taken from her, for if it hadn't been, she would have dropped it in surprise.

She had never actually seen a dragon before.

The three dragons looked like jewels in firelight, the midday sun causing them to glow as they shifted slightly. Everyone in the kingdom knew that Soros was the dark-purple dragon and Eras was the bright fire-orange dragon. That meant that the acidic-green dragon must be King Soren's dragon, Ilex.

The egg nestled between Soros and Eras was a pale yellow. Nerie stared at it with interest. She could already imagine the little dragonling clearly. She would be a creamy yellow like fresh turned butter, but as she aged, her scales would darken into the purest gold. Prince Aldis or Princess Astra would be more than lucky, Nerie thought wistfully. Soros looked over at Nerie, her purple eyes calm and deep. She blinked, and Nerie blinked in response.

A servant, rushing on some unknown errand, collided with her and she was jolted back into reality. She needed to join the waiting crowd. So many people were already cramming themselves into the stands overlooking the dragons that at first Nerie hesitated. Then she thought about how long she had waited to see the little dragon hatch and shoved herself into the crowd. There was a railing surrounding the warm sands that the egg was nestled into, and Nerie shimmied her way around it so that she was directly opposite the royal family, and directly in front of the large egg.

Soros watched her for a moment longer but turned her attention to her bored son who had started huffing smoke rings above the crowded arena. A slight growl from Soros and he curled into a tight green ball. Nerie couldn't help but smile at the sight. Twenty-one years old and Ilex was still basically a hatchling himself.

Nerie's eyes were drawn once again to the royal family, waiting on the dais patiently. They were known for keeping to themselves. As far as Nerie knew, they only left the palace for matters of diplomacy. She'd only seen King Soren a few times, from afar on crowded streets. She'd only ever seen Queen Alaena once, when she'd been very small. Looking at them now, she saw that the king and queen were regal and poised, sitting on two thrones and watching the dragons themselves.

Nerie had never seen the prince or princess before. She looked at them while the crowd continued to shuffle in. The egg had begun to wobble slightly in the sand and the prince and princess were standing, waiting to walk forward when it hatched. Princess Astra looked to be nearly twenty, conceived directly after her father ascended to the throne. Her eyes were locked on the slowly rocking egg. Prince Aldis was younger, barely into his teens. There had been rumors when Nerie was young that Queen Alaena could bear no more children for the king. Nerie remembered vaguely when the kingdom had celebrated Aldis being born. She'd been about four years old and a kind woman had given her a bouquet of yellow roses, telling her that each petal was a year the prince would live.

As the egg rocked a little more fervently, a herald stepped forward and started to recite the history of the ceremony to the crowd.

"Dragons have been extinct in the wild for generations. Our kingdom of Situra and the royal family of Therius gave a home to the last mated pair, Soros and Eras. It is clear from our history that they first came to Situra during the Great War and pledged themselves to General Kyre, who became our first king. Shortly thereafter, Soros and Eras laid their first egg, and the dragoness Wyla was hatched. She chose to Kyre, reaffirming his right to rule, and starting our tradition of the hatching ceremony.

Since then every twenty-one years, they have laid a single egg. An egg that determines the future of Situra when our future king or queen is chosen by the young dragonling."

The man took a deep breath before continuing, the crowd nearly silent as they listened.

"When King Soren Therius was chosen by the dragon Ilex, our kingdom celebrated for weeks on end. It has been twenty-one years since that day, and Soros and Eras have once again laid an egg. This time the hatchling will choose between Princess Astra and Prince Aldis."

The stands had become even more crowded while the herald spoke, and Nerie was now shoved into the railing as people pushed in behind her. A sharp crack could be heard from the sand and screams of joy echoed from the crowd.

Astra and Aldis both stepped forward to greet the soon to be born hatchling.

As the hatchling emerged from her shell, Nerie couldn't help but think, *Oh I was right!* As pale as the roses from so long ago, with glistening wings of gossamer, the young dragoness stepped forth. She looked to be made of gauze, but her eyes shone of a strength of steel.

She raised her little head and looked Astra right in the eye. They stared at each other for a long moment before the little dragoness turned her head to look at Aldis. He didn't even get to look her in the eyes before she had passed him over.

The hatchling seemed unwilling to choose between the prince and princess. She paced restlessly around the large enclosure, and as she neared Nerie, Nerie wanted with all her soul to reach out and touch the hatchling. The small dragon looked at Soros and Eras before stalking farther away from the prince and princess.

She headed directly towards Nerie.

Nerie couldn't look away from those golden eyes. She didn't even realize how close the hatchling had gotten until she nudged Nerie's hand that rested on the railing. There were screams and yells from the crowd, and someone shook Nerie - but she still couldn't look away from the large golden eyes.

The king stood, pointing at Nerie, yelling for guards. Before she even knew what was happening, she was surrounded by guards, with the crowd being forcefully shoved away. The guards were demanding Nerie follow them, but she was still lost in golden eyes, not able to focus on what was going on.

Kiriga hissed and screamed in defiance that Nerie was being touched. All Nerie could think was that the dragonling was so tiny, and that she couldn't look away from her.

The hilt of a sword collided with the back of her head, and the last thing she saw before darkness was Eras, his giant fire orange body surrounding her and the golden hatchling, roaring.

CHAPTER THREE

Graith

Graith blinked. Unable to comprehend what he was seeing. There was a dragon - a *big* dragon - inside his barn. A living, breathing, *dragon*. And it was watching him.

He took a step back, his heel colliding with the top of the ladder, and he glanced behind him. A fall from this height could kill him. That's when he felt it - the tail had shot out and wound around his waist, pulling him away from the edge.

Oh, good lord it was going to eat him! Graith, who had always considered himself a calm and cool-headed man, started screaming. Shrieking really. He was being pulled nearer to a dragon. A dragon with long, sharp fangs and talons large enough to pin him down. His eyes squeezed shut, and the screaming increased. He tried to run, but the tail held him firm.

When it released him, eyes still shut, he collapsed into a moaning pile on the ground. He knew what was coming, knew his life was about to end.

In fact, he felt warm blood seeping under his hands.

Had it already bitten into him and he was in shock and had not felt it? His hand slid in the hot slimy mess as he pulled it to himself frantically. He started patting his body all over, sure that there was a mortal wound somewhere. His eyes opened, and he saw that no, his body was intact.

He glanced up and came eye to eye with the dragon. It

had those sad eyes again, the same as he had seen the night before. It was watching him. Not attacking, not hunting, not even looking moderately interested in eating him.

Graith looked down again, and it hit him that the blood was not his. And there was a lot of it. His eyes followed the trail of blood, and it led back to the dragon. Pale and withdrawn, the dragon was a faded shadow of the one in his dream.

The realization calmed Graith. It was obviously wounded and not trying to eat him. Then why had it grabbed him? Was it worried he was going to fall?

That made little sense. It was a beast. Wasn't it?

Those eyes, however, held an intelligence that he had noticed before. Maybe it *had* known he was in danger of falling.

He got to his feet and took a shaky but deep breath. He took a step towards the dragon. It watched him as he watched it. He took another. Again, nothing but watching. His stride lengthened, and he briskly walked to the dragon's side.

With that much blood, the beast must be grievously wounded. He decided that since it had tried to help him, he would help it. He didn't like to see animals in pain.

He'd had a horse break its leg once, and as a result he'd had to put the beast down. There'd been no way to set the leg and keep the horse healthy while it healed. But other animals, they got minor injuries and he always took the time to heal them to the best of his ability. This would be no different.

The dragon simply watched as he approached and when he reached out and felt along its hard body, it rolled, allowing him to look. He sighed in relief when he found the sources of the blood. It was three smaller wounds, each bleeding slowly, but not life threatening. The first was a long, shallow cut on the inside of the dragon's front right leg, along the seams of softer, protected, skin-like scales. The second - the tip of the dragon's tail was cut off. It looked as if an axe had been used, for it was a clean and even cut. The remaining tip of the tail was quite wide.

The third injury seemed to be the most dangerous. The

gossamer membrane of the left wing was in tatters. Punctured by arrows, and perhaps cut by a sword, there was no way the dragon could fly.

Feeling distraught even looking at the creature's wing, Graith muttered, "Oh dear, oh dear. I'll be right back. We'll get this taken care of."

Moving away from the dragon, Graith moved back to the ladder and shimmied his way down as quickly as he could without falling. Reaching the bottom and looking around, Graith swore. He had nothing in the barn to treat the animal.

He glanced back up at the loft and shouted, "I'll be right back!" before running as fast as he could back to his home. He cursed himself for building the barn so far away but didn't dare stop to catch his breath until he had reached his small home.

Rushing inside he immediately grabbed clean linens, his sewing kit, and a pair of large kitchen shears. He also thought to grab a bucket for water. He had another pump near the barn to fill it. Shoving his supplies in the bucket, he glanced around, thinking as quickly as he could about what else he might need for the dragon. His eyes alighted on the leftovers of his previous night's dinner and thought that the dragon might be hungry. However, he thought if it was like other injured animals, the dragon would not want to eat, and it could be dangerous for it to eat so soon after being injured.

What else did he need? Again, he looked around the room, this time his gaze landed on the spare belt he had. The tail! He wouldn't be able to sew that injury shut, but a belt would make a good tourniquet. He grabbed it, threw it in with the supplies, and decided he had everything he would need.

He hurried back outside, grabbed the reigned halter of his horse, and quickly mounted bareback. It would be much quicker to ride back to the barn, and if need be, back to the house a second time.

Urging the horse into a quick trot, he headed back to the barn. Upon his arrival, he tried to bring the horse inside to its stall, but in abject terror the creature screamed and reared away from the door. Graith didn't blame it, as he had felt the same way when the tail had pulled him.

Leading the horse to the shaded side of the barn, he tethered the animal to the water pump. He then went inside. He would be unable to climb up and down the ladder with the bucket in his hands. He took the belt, looped it through the handle of the bucket, then fastened it in a wide loop, slipping it over his shoulder.

The bucket bumped against his buttocks as he climbed. Reaching the top, he made his way back over to the dragon. Its eyes had been closed when he had crested the top of the ladder, but as he approached the nearest eye opened, saw Graith and closed again. It looked paler than it had before, though it could have been the barn was now well illuminated from the open door. However, it was not illuminated enough for Graith, not for what he was about to do. He fully opened the nearest window to allow more light to spill directly onto the beast. It was *much* paler now, he saw.

He went to work.

Unstrapping the belt from the bucket handle, he applied the tourniquet to the tail first. Not much else he could do for that. The bleeding slowed and had all but stopped by the time he had gotten to the front of the dragon and had it roll to its side for him to examine the arm wound. The whole time Graith talked to the dragon, just as he would one of his animals. Low soothing tones, not really words so much as sounds and gentle meanings.

"Ahh, you'll be all right, I know you will. A beauty such as yourself must live. Ol' Graith's got this, just let me do my work."

The dragon panted and Graith took one of the sheets and cleaned the wound. The blood there had started to coagulate. There was dirt and muck in it.

"This'll hurt little one," *Did he just call a dragon little one?* "but it'll be over quick."

Pulling his sewing kit out, he quickly threaded the needle and went to work stitching up the injury. Long minutes went by with the dragon occasionally shuddering in pain, Graith leaning along its hard belly to support himself as he sewed the awkward injury.

"There, there. That part is all over now," Graith told the giant. It opened its eyes and inspected the injury. Now the hard part. Graith cleared his throat.

"I uh, hope you can understand me. You seem to have an intelligence about you," he said.

His throat went dry when he heard, not with his ears, but in his head, *Yes, I understand you.*

It was an alien sounding voice. Feminine, and wholly inhuman.

That was unnerving, but Graith continued after clearing his throat again, "I - well, I need to sew your wing. It - well it's going to be painful, and I - uh, need you on the first floor. I need to be able to clean it as I go, and I can't carry a full bucket of water up here."

The dragon studied him for a long moment, then the voice sounded in his head again. *Of course, Graith.*

She, for after speaking he knew it was a she, lifted her large body, being careful of her arm and wing and *hopped* to the first floor. Graith scrambled down the ladder, rushing to follow the creature, the handle of the bucket roughly digging into his arm. He set the bucket down, emptied it, and ran out to the pump to fill it with water.

The horse, still tethered there, gave a terrified winnie but was unable to pull away from him. Graith reeked of dragon blood.

After filling the bucket and heading back inside, he instructed the dragon to stretch out her wing. She obliged, and Graith nearly cried looking at the damage. If he bungled this up, she might never fly again.

It's alright Graith, I trust you. You took care of my tail, and my arm. You can do this too.

She seemed to know what he was thinking, and that outright terrified him. But he had to try, had to at least attempt to fix her wing.

First thing he did was remove the remaining arrow shafts, and then he started cleaning. Straw, dirt, and blood caked the wounds, which had slowed to a sluggish bleeding. He worked top to bottom, left to right. He darned the punctures as if he were he repairing a pair of holey socks.

The holes were the easiest part. It was the tattered mainsail that caused him to pause. He laid a sheet on the ground, to protect the cleaned wing from getting dirty, and started to untangle the mess.

It looked as if a sword had found entrance through an arrow wound and was able to slice down the mainsail in an S shape. She'd probably felt the cut and turned away from the attack, her own momentum doing more damage than the attacker's strength.

Once Graith had the mess untangled, he started at the top of the wound and sewed down the length. He went slow, afraid of misaligning edges and wrinkling the membrane in an irreparable way once it healed. He constantly checked to make sure that everything was even, flat, and clean.

After what seemed like ages, he found himself at the bottom edge, both parts meeting up perfectly. He let out a sigh of relief. At least the stitches were in place, and the wing could start healing.

Graith worried an infection might set in, but being unable to do anything about that currently, he simply stood, stretched, and moved to the other wing. Having only taken two arrows to this one, with both making a clean exit, he simply darned the holes shut.

He was exhausted and soaked in sweat and dragon blood. He glanced around, realizing that the noonday sun had come and passed. It was nearing dinner time, based on the position of the sun. He stood and rushed outside. He'd left the blasted horse tethered to the pump with nothing to drink.

He took his now dirty bucket, emptied it, and walked to where the horse was. Once again, the stupid beast reared but was unable to escape. Graith ignored it, pumped a small amount of water in the bucket to rinse it out, and filled it full for the horse to drink.

Honestly, the horse was no worse for wear from having been in the sunlight for the last few hours. He walked slowly back to the entrance, not caring if the horse did in fact drink from the bucket or not.

Reaching the door, he just stood and looked at the monster before him. She was resting now. Her dark blue scales still looked pale. Her eyes were closed, and she seemed exhausted. But her breathing was normal, and all the bleeding had stopped.

Why had he helped her? She was a *dragon*. He should be hunting her down with the rest of the men.

But he wasn't.

He had helped her, healed her.

For a beast that could bite him in half, she looked fragile, and all he wanted to do was protect her.

"Dragon."

Graith.

That still unnerved him.

"How do you know my name?"

That's simple, you muttered it, while you were helping me.

Graith supposed he had, he didn't really remember. He had been too focused on getting the bleeding to stop. All right then.

"Dragon," he started again, but she cut him off.

It's Azelia. My name is Azelia.

"Oh, all right then Azelia," he continued feeling flustered, "Um, how did you get in my barn?"

Graith had been thinking about this for a while, and it confused him. He had been the one to open the doors, and the second set, he could see from here, were still locked. All the windows had been closed, and simply, there were no other ways in. Even for a flying dragon.

One of the top windows was unlatched.

"What?"

The one at the far end.

"Oh. All right then," he was saying that a lot, but what else did you say to a dragon? "But why my barn?"

It was the first I found. I was injured and needed a place to heal. You just sped up the process.

It was true, the areas he had sewn shut were already scabbed over. He was glad that he had gotten the wing clean and laid out correctly before it had started to heal itself. No saying how badly it would have healed otherwise.

"How did you fly on that wing?"

I made it worse climbing through the window. Now Graith, thank you for all your help, but I must *be going,* she said, even as she tried to stand.

"Going? Going where? Those men are surely still wherever you came from. They won't stop until you're dead."

I must go. My clutch - my eggs - are alone. Unprotected. They need me.

"You can't fly! You still look so weak. Your color hasn't returned at all!" Graith said in a panic. He knew she would be killed if she left the barn. "Do the eggs, uh, need you to sit on them? Like chickens?"

No, she sounded amused, *They can survive on their own. But those men. If they find them, they will destroy them. And I can't let that happen.*

"I'll go with you." It was out of his mouth before his brain could catch up.

"I'll go with you," he repeated - this time aware of what he was saying.

But why?

"You are injured. You can't fly, and you can't travel fast, I'm willing to bet. There are men after you, and maybe, just maybe I can help you. You'll need to move your eggs anyways. Your cave is no longer safe. What if you brought them back here? I could keep you safe," he said, feeling overwhelmed, but at the same time sure that this was the right thing to do.

What was he doing? This was a living, breathing, dragon. The monster of legend who would eat him if he displeased her. But it felt right - what he had to do.

Azelia just looked at him for a long moment, then between one moment and the next, was standing - towering over him. She leaned down and gently licked his face. He almost fainted of fright but was more intrigued by the texture of her tongue. Not what he would have expected. He thought it would be like a cat, since so much of her reminded him of one. Instead it was velvety, much more like the dog he'd had for hunting.

All right. Let's go.

CHAPTER FOUR

Graith

Graith stood, staring at Azelia in shock.

She had agreed? What world did he live in now? Mind reeling, he just continued to stand there.

Until Azelia gave him a gentle shove with her snout and asked, *Now what?*

That was a good question. Now what?

He looked around until his eyes landed on his wagon. Then his mind shot into action before his body could catch up, his mouth even behind his body.

"We'll take my wagon. It's how I normally transport my wheat. But..." he trailed off, thinking about the horse. It just wouldn't do. He would have to get another, calmer beast. If such a thing was possible.

He walked over to the wagon. It was small enough to be pulled by one horse, but it should be big enough for the dragon to rest in if she were to get tired. He inspected it, for he hadn't used it yet this year, and it would do him no good if his cotter pins rotted while they sat. He was making a mental list of things he would need. He knew he would need food, mostly dried, and at least two pouches of water. He didn't know what the dragon - no, *Azelia* - would need, but he would cover that after he finished getting what he needed first.

He went into his office where he had left his ledger and opened his safe. He had come a long way from that first year after he'd inherited the farm. Since he had no wife or children to spend money on, and he patched his own clothes and repaired his own tools, he simply didn't spend much money other than what he spent on food that he couldn't provide himself. Mostly meat. So, he had saved and saved, and now had a pretty copper to his name. He gathered it all into the travel pouch he kept for such an instance and closed the safe.

He went out to the horse, the stupid beast was tired at this point, only pulling away in fear, not rearing. Graith untethered it, mounted, and rode back to the house. He passed his milk cow, and feeling generous, decided he would feed it to Azelia. If she wanted it, that was.

He reached the cottage, and this time tethered the horse to the pump there, which had a water pail set under it, and the horse drank gratefully. He went inside and started collecting things he would need. Graith had no idea how far away Azelia's clutch might be, but he liked to always be prepared.

He grabbed his largest saddlebags and started packing. In went his fire-kit, a small cast iron skillet, a little crock of grease from his larder. Hard cheese as well, wrapped in an oiled cloth to keep it fresh. One of his utility knives and a slate cutting board went in too. It continued on, thing by thing, until the bags were as full as he could stuff them. He had packed his clothing last, changing into clean clothes in the process.

It wasn't enough. He still needed things such as a new sewing kit, bread, as well as the meat he would need on the trip, and a new traveling cloak. One that was rainproof. He rarely traveled farther than the village, and never on nights that it rained. It was an item he hadn't ever needed before. He sighed, all of that would probably fill another pack.

The whole time he wondered what Azelia was doing. She hadn't followed him from the barn, even though she had been up and moving. Once he was done, he grabbed the bags and his saddle, and rode back to the barn. She was there, in the back of the wagon, sleeping. Watching her, he wondered how long it had been since the attack, and how far she'd had to fly before finding his barn.

He removed the saddlebags from the horse's withers and placed them in the back of the wagon with the dragon. As he did so, the sound and motion woke the sleeping dragoness. Lifting all three of her eyelids to watch him, she had no interest in moving.

"All right, Azelia, I'm headed into the village. I'm going to trade in the horse and see about getting the rest of the things that I need. Is there anything you need before we leave here?"

I need rest, she said wearily.

He had a feeling that she would be able to fly now if she needed a quick escape.

Other than that? Food. Water. I need no clothing or tools. Once I fill my belly, I'll be good for several days.

"Speaking of days, how far is your cave from here? Just so I can get an idea of where we are going."

I live a half day's flight from here, but that is many, many miles. I would guess that it will take us at least four days to traverse on foot. But I have not done so, I may be vastly wrong.

Graith nodded. He had half expected her answer, as he knew that the foothills leading into the mountains were filled with caves. While he had never gone himself, he knew many people who had made the trip hunting.

Thinking about what she had said about food and water he told her, "You may have my cow to eat. And you should be able to work the pump near the house with your claws, they are similar enough to a hand. There is a bucket there to collect the water or you can drink it as you pump it. I'll be back late tonight, and we'll leave tomorrow morning."

The dragoness hummed her approval and Graith went - for the last time - out to the surly horse. It had gotten some water and food in while Graith had packed and its poor attitude had returned. He waited for it to stop bucking away from him before mounting and heading into the village.

***

The trip to the village took half an hour, and he made his

way straight to the general store. The traveling traders only made their way this far out a few times a year, and if anyone would have the supplies he needed, it would be the general store.

The old man who ran the store sold his wares at a marked up price to the people of the village. It was unfortunate and unavoidable as this was where he hoped to get a cloak and a new sewing kit. He entered the shop as the rays of light from the setting sun blazed through the front windows. The owner squinted up at him. Recognizing Graith, the man frowned.

"Aye, what'd 'ya need Graith?" he asked, his voice grave. Graith ignored the man's tone and continued into the shop.

"I'm looking for a new traveling cloak and sewing kit. Oh - and a handful of cotter pins," Graith said, thinking about his mental list.

"A traveling cloak? Don't have too many of those at the moment. I'll see what I can do."

The man was first and foremost a salesman. He went into the back of his shop and started rummaging around. He returned shortly with three different cloaks. One was a dark satin material. Not good for traveling at all, but it would make quite a statement. The second was wool. It would have been nice, but it was not treated with beeswax to keep the rain out. The final cloak was also wool, but it had been rain proofed. It had also been dyed a lovely black, and Graith knew it was the one he wanted as soon as he saw it. The shopkeeper knew too, seeing the way he eyed it. He smirked, and Graith knew it was going to cost him.

"Alright, I'll take the wax treated one. I also needed the sewing kit and oh, six cotter pins," Graith said.

He decided right then that he would pay whatever fee the man asked, in order to get out of the shop as quickly as he could. The man was obviously going to try and up-sell him. He had never liked Graith, and Graith had no idea why. Maybe it was how infrequently he visited.

The shopkeeper opened a couple of drawers behind his counter and quickly pulled out the pins and sewing kit. Those were much more commonly sought-after items. He turned and placed them on the cloak and folded everything up into a bundle.

As he named the price, with a smirk on his face, Graith almost sputtered out how outrageous it was but kept silent. Instead, he simply handed over the money. Grabbing his purchases, he headed out the door. The shopkeeper seemed almost disappointed that Graith had paid the ludicrous amount instead of arguing. He kept looking at the small fortune in his hand and apparently decided it was best not to say anything.

Carrying his bundle, Graith mounted his horse and rode to the farrier. The man always had extra horses on hand, and Graith's current beast was no laughable specimen. He arrived after a short trot and knocked on the farrier's door. It opened and the one person in the village who seemed to like Graith stood behind it.

"Ah Graith! Long time no see, my good man!" Ralph nearly shouted.

Ralph was a big man, bigger than Graith even. Six foot five inches and all muscle. He worked with horses all day and his body showed it. He also had the most calming aura about him - no matter how frantic an animal, Ralph could settle it in moments.

"Come in!"

Graith shook his head and motioned to the stable. "Let's head out back, I need a horse."

Ralph stepped outside frowning. He had sold Graith his last horse only two years before and it had been a good work animal. As they reached the side of the house, he saw the horse. It was still in good health and looked strong. Ralph wondered what Graith needed a new horse for and asked as much.

"I got a new animal. Horse can't stand it or its scent. I need one that won't blink an eye at it."

"Hmm. I think I have one who might be solid enough for you."

Ralph led Graith to a gelding that was part draft horse

and all muscle. Graith walked over and examined him. He pulled out a cloth from his pocket and showed it to the animal. The horse sniffed the fabric with interest and flicked its tail but showed no signs of duress. Graith smiled and turned to Ralph.

"I think you're quite right, my friend. He didn't react to the scent at all. If he takes issue with the animal when it is in front of him, I'll simply put blinders on him."

He reached up a hand and gave the horse a scratch on one of its long ears.

"I also need a new saddlebag, if you have a spare."

Ralph nodded and they both headed back to his house, where he kept all the tools of his trade.

"Come inside and have a drink with me Graith," Ralph said, but Graith shook his head.

"Nah, I have work to be done and more places to go before it gets too late."

The sun had set and Graith still needed to visit both the baker and the butcher.

"At this hour? You know everyone's gone home and is enjoying their supper."

In fact, that's what Ralph's wife was doing now, finishing up the evening's stew.

"Come on in. Join us. Sarah would love to see you."

Graith grimaced but agreed. He didn't want to rub anyone else the wrong way - let alone the two people who treated him kindly. He sent a mental apology to Azelia and entered the house.

What are you apologizing for? came the voice he had heard for the first time this morning.

He choked on the ale that Sarah had just handed him.

You… You can hear me?! he thought, still sputtering on his drink.

Ralph slapped him on the back.

Yes? This is how my kind communicates. And over long distances. Now what were you apologizing for?

Graith took another sip and looked at Ralph. He was speaking, but the words were not penetrating Graith's mind.

32

I was apologizing for not arriving back at the farm tonight. A friend, Ralph has offered for me to stay with him for the night, and I will finish getting my supplies in the morning.

That's all right, as you had already said we would be leaving tomorrow morning.

It was true, but Graith had intended to get everything he needed tonight and to head back before morning.

I... he paused, I just don't want your eggs to be in danger for any longer than necessary.

They're safe enough. Higher in my cave system. Not as easily reached as my sleeping cavern.

Graith sighed in relief. He still didn't understand why he cared about the dragon - he should want to kill her.

I'll be home as soon as I can.

All right, Graith.

Graith turned his full attention on Ralph and Sarah. They had handed him a bowl of stew and a large chunk of bread. He thanked them and as they ate, they talked about the year's harvest, the upcoming winter, and the foals that would be born come spring.

They joked with Graith about why he had yet to get married, and if he would ever choose a woman to help him with that farm of his. Not long after finishing their meal, the fire was banked, the dishes done, and a spare sleeping mat and blanket were brought out for Graith. He thanked Sarah and Ralph and laid down to sleep.

Graith? He heard that voice again. This time there was a strange aura in his mind. The best way he could conceptualize it was as a pale gray cloud oozing from her mind into his. She sounded scared.

Yes Azelia? Is everything alright?

Yes. It's just, I was thinking about my eggs.

What about them? You said they'd be safe.

They are... I guess I'm just worried.

There was a long pause and then, *Graith, why do men hate dragons?*

He lay there, silently thinking of a way to answer.

Honestly, he wasn't sure. *He* didn't understand. It seemed men reacted to dragons in fear only. He thought she was a beautiful creature, and just wanted to see her and her hatchlings flourish.

They are scared, Zel. They think they're the best hunters, and then dragons come along. You are capable of killing me, of many men, if you so choose.

Zel? Why did you call me that?

Graith blushed in the dark. He hadn't even realized he had done it, let alone think she would have noticed.

Ah, well, friends have nicknames, and we are going to be spending a lot of time together, so I thought it would be all right. I won't do it again.

No, it's okay. I want to be your friend. Zel. I like it. What should I call you then? Gray?

You can call me whatever you like, Zel.

With that, Graith drifted off to sleep.

CHAPTER FIVE

Graith

Graith woke as the sun crested the eastern horizon. He folded the bedding and washed his face at Ralph's water pump.

It was going to be a long day.

When he re-entered the house, Sarah greeted him with a lump of cheese and a chunk of yesterday's bread. He sat at the table eating while Ralph went to check on the horses. As he finished eating, he stood and hugged Sarah. Thanking her for the food and bedding, he headed out to see Ralph.

"So, what do you want for the gelding?" he asked as he rounded the corner to see Ralph.

"Just the male you brought back with you, I take it you didn't want him any longer?" Ralph said.

Graith stared at his friend, then shook his head.

"The gelding is a much finer horse than the beast you saddled me with last time! I insist I pay you the difference!" he said.

"I think not, Graith. You've kept him fit and well fed, and I don't understand the temperament issues you were talking about."

He was standing, petting the nose of Graith's horse.

"He became downright mean about my new animal."

"What is it? A wolf?"

"Something like that."

Ralph gave him a inquisitive look but left it at that. He

would accept no more coin for the gelding, nor for the saddlebag or hospitality.

"You're my friend. I will not charge you for a favor!"

Graith shook his head but pressed it no further. He had things to do, places to be.

"Thank you, Ralph."

He moved his saddle to the gelding, needing to tighten the girth much less on this horse than his last. It just watched him in interest out of the corner of its eye. Graith did not mount, as the baker lived in walking distance, so he led the horse by its halter.

"Morning, Gloria!" Graith greeted the woman.

She merely looked up at him and continued kneading the bread she was making.

"What do you need, Graith?"

"A little more than the usual. I need several days of travel bread."

At this she looked at him - interested - but still continuing her work.

"Aye, I have some. Maybe a dozen loaves, will that be enough?"

"Should be. As long as I don't break the outer crust it'll keep for quite a while, right?"

She nodded, "Aye, close to two weeks."

"That'll do then."

She motioned to the shelf behind her where the loaves were cooling on a rack. He took the whole tray, went out to his saddle bag and carefully loaded them in. He returned the tray, thanked Gloria, and set off for the butcher. He mounted this time, the butcher's building being on the outskirts of town. The smell of blood in the summer could be overwhelming so it had been built with consideration for the rest of the village in mind.

The butcher was outside, gathering a pig he was about to slaughter. He looked up when he heard the sound of the gelding's hooves on the packed dirt as Graith approached. He frowned, as he was another one of those people who for some reason just didn't like Graith.

"What can I do for you?" he asked before Graith was able to dismount.

Once he was on the ground, Graith answered, "I'm here for some of your dried meat, Byron. About five pounds."

He knew it wasn't much, but with the bread and cheese, it should last him if he only ate a little a day. The butcher sneered but led Graith inside. He went straight to the back where he kept the dried meats.

"Going on a trip are ya?" he asked as he sat a sack on the counter, pulling out dried pieces of meat and adding them to his scale. Graith looked up in surprise.

"What makes you ask?"

"You come in like clockwork every week for meat. Today is not one of your normal days. And you are asking for dried meat, not fresh."

"Well, yes, I am. A very short one. Only a few days," Graith answered, looking around the shop nervously.

It was really none of Byron's business. The butcher finished weighing out the meat and pulled out a second sack for the meat that was going with Graith.

"That'll be a gold and three silver," he tallied up.

Graith simply handed him two gold. The man started to get the change, another seven silver, but Graith waved him off. The man, even though he was no fan of Graith's, still grabbed the bag he held and tossed in several more good-sized pieces of dried meat. Nothing more was said, and then Graith was on his way out the door.

Graith mounted his new horse, turning to make his way back to his farm and Zel.

He had been quite embarrassed when she had asked him about calling her that. He hadn't meant to, but Zel was just so much easier for him to say. Or in that case, think.

He did so now, thinking out at her, mildly wondering how far away they could communicate.

Zel, I'm on my way back. I need to replace one of the cotter pins in the wagon, and then we can be on our way.

All right. I ate your cow - like you suggested. I'm feeling much better.

I'm glad. You were a mess yesterday.

Others have seen worse, she told him. *But I thought I had gone far enough away that I would be safe in the mountains.*

You were seen and men wanted you dead. They weren't going to stop until they found you, no matter how far out you had gone. I'll be home soon - within half an hour.

Good. I'm going to stretch my wing and leg by walking around.

Don't go far from the barn, my land is large, but not so extensive that you can fly without being seen.

I wasn't going to fly! he heard her pout.

Silence, other than the clip clop of the gelding's hooves, filled the short trip.

It wasn't very long before he saw his barn - and the outline of the dragon flapping her wings. Her motion looked more like a harassed chicken than a dragon. He looked around worried but saw no one in any direction.

I'm back.

Oh good! I thought I smelled a horse. Is this one better tamed than the last?

We're about to find out.

For as he said that, he rode the gelding toward the dragon, and waited for him to react.

Nothing.

He rode directly to Zel's side. She reached out and sniffed the horse. The horse sniffed back and then put his head down looking for grass. Graith let out a breath he hadn't realized he'd been holding.

"Alright Zel, I have the rest of the supplies. You ate and drank enough while I was gone?" he asked as he dismounted.

He removed his saddle and new bag.

I did. Can't you tell?

He looked over at her, she was indeed a much darker navy than the last time he saw her. More like the dream he'd had of her. She almost twinkled where the light reflected off the tips of the largest scales on her side.

"I can. You look much better."

He placed the saddlebag in the wagon with the others and threw the saddle over one of the half-wall partitions on the inside of the barn. No need to bring it when he had the wagon. Any other riding could be taken care of bareback.

He replaced the single cotter pin that had rotted since the wagon's last use the year before and hooked the horse to the front. Again, the gelding did nothing more than watch and look for food on the floor around him.

"All right Zel, we are ready," he said.

The dragon's long tail lashed in excitement. She was still missing the tip, but it did look as if it were going to regrow. She hummed her pleasure and gave him another lick like she had the day before.

Let's go get my clutch!

She seemed ecstatic and relieved to be moving. As they left the barn, Graith had to wonder how well hidden her eggs actually were - and if there were men still looking for her in the caves or mountainside.

With that thought his mouth turned downward. He was not a fighter. Not even a hunter.

"Zel, I have no way to protect you or your eggs if we encounter other men."

She looked at him and gave an uneasy huff.

I will do so then. I'll protect us all. If something happens to me, just promise me you'll get my clutch to safety?

"Aye, I'll do that."

They were passing his house when he sighed, halting them.

"One moment. I'm useless with it, but I have a bow and a few quivers of arrows. I'll bring them, just in case."

He pulled the gelding to a stop, and it again just looked for food. He ran inside the house to retrieve the bow. As he stepped out of the house, he locked the door. He looked at the chickens and reckoned they could take care of themselves. He only kept them in a slightly gated area, and they could get out - had gotten out on more than one occasion - if they so chose.

He hopped back onto the wagon seat and urged the

gelding forward once more. With that, they were off. Zel trotting in front of the gelding - looking back at Graith every so often and making what he could only imagine was a draconic smile.

CHAPTER SIX

Graith

They were in the woods, heading towards the base of the mountains. The nearest mountain was a full day and a half from Graith's farm, but Zel had informed him that they would then need to go north along the ridgeline to reach her cave system. They had been traveling all day at a brisk trot, and between the tree cover and the shadow of the mountains it was fast approaching full dark.

Zel, we need to stop for the night.

Her tail gave a lash of annoyance, but she responded evenly, *I smell water. I'll lead the horse to it, and we'll camp there.*

She had been walking in a straight line this whole time but now veered off to the left. The gelding - Graith really would need to name him soon - followed her without the reins to tell him so.

While they trundled through the underbrush, Graith decided to broach a subject he had been thinking about all day.

Zel, tell me about yourself? Graith asked. He had given up speaking aloud several hours ago, as it only made him hoarse and honestly there was no need.

I am a dragon! she said quite proudly but did not elaborate.

In the minutes it took to reach the bubbly little stream and clearing, she still did not answer.

As Graith unhitched the horse, it meandered over to the stream to drink. Zel was wading in, flapping her wings like a bird in a birdbath.

Deciding to push the conversation some, he said, *Well imagine that. I meant about your life. Do you have a mate? Why are you here alone with your clutch?*

She was silent for a long moment. Her movement in the stream stilled as she looked at Graith, her eyes an icy blue.

We dragons are quite similar to you humans. We can take a mate for however long we like. We can have trysts or romances for the ages. I thought I had found a dragon mate who would love me the same way I loved him.

While Zel talked, Graith turned away, setting himself the task of preparing a fire. He walked around the clearing, picking up dead fall and rocks to build a fire ring.

We mated. Dragons know when we will have a clutch, and we knew as soon as we mated that we had conceived. Not a full moon later, he left me. He said he was not prepared to be a father.

She paused again, leaving Graith to wonder if she was finished. Unsure, he returned to the clearing with his small collection of rocks. As he arranged them to make a decently sized circle, she started speaking again.

I was hurt - angry, and quickly growing big and full of eggs. I ran away.

Another pause, Graith turned his focus to the wood. He didn't want to rush her as she was obviously struggling to tell him this. While the dead fall would be sufficient for starting the fire, it would burn quickly and need to be tended often. As he searched for more substantial fuel for the fire, she started speaking again.

There are stories about why our kind does not live in the northwestern mountains. I ignored them. I thought they were just stories, why would a human be able to hurt me, or my clutch? Why would they want to? So, I flew and flew, exhausted but seeking out a cave to call my own, to raise my hatchlings alone.

Graith thought she might be done speaking as she had

finished in the water and was curled up near the soon to be fire pit. The gelding had positioned himself back in between the bars of the wagon, and promptly went to sleep. When she spoke again, it was much quieter.

I was heavy with eggs so I flew much lower than I normally would, which is probably why I was seen.

Her tail lashed, and she was silent. Graith knew this time she was done.

Graith finished stacking the wood and went to fish his fire-starter out of one of his bags. Before he found it, however, there was a fire crackling behind him. When he turned to look, he was surprised to find Zel with a little smoke curling from around her lips and grinning her strange smile.

Not in the mood to cook, Graith cut off a chunk of his hard cheese and took out a loaf of travel bread and a piece of the jerky.

He was getting ready to sit on the opposite side of the fire when Zel asked, *Do you not want to sit with me?*

Startled, he jerked back upright and moved over next to her. She patted the ground behind her foreleg with her tail, motioning for him to lean against her. He hadn't been that close to her since he'd tended her wounds - now that she was looking healthy and powerful - he had a moment of hesitation.

She noticed, and told him solemnly, *I'll not harm you Graith. You've shown me more compassion than anyone, save for my grandfather.*

He slowly sank to the ground, then very gingerly leaned back against her. She was warm - almost as warm the fire from his current spot. He ate and listened to the sounds of the woods. It was unusually quiet, but that didn't worry him, as he was with a dragon. They were the top of the food chain after all, no creature in its right mind would come poking around.

He gradually snuggled up against her and drifted off to sleep, using her forearm as a makeshift pillow. He'd thought about getting his new cloak, but between the fire and her body heat, it wasn't needed.

He awoke slowly the following morning, more comfortable than he was used to. He had yet to open his eyes, but he smelled something he couldn't quite place. It was a musky smell, with the smell of fresh grass, and smoke… Smoke!

His eyes popped open, but all he could see was a luminescent navy blue. He turned, the navy lifting off him, and he was almost blinded by the bright morning sun.

It had been Zel that smelled of smoke. His heart calmed from its frantic racing, and he noticed that Zel had used her tail to tuck him against her body, covering him with her wing. He vaguely wondered if that was how she watched her eggs. He stood, and she watched him, for she was already awake.

Zel, you could have woken me when the sun was rising, he admonished.

I could have, however, you seemed like you needed the rest.

He sighed. He had. He'd not slept well the night before at Ralph's home.

Let's continue our journey then.

He led the horse - who he'd decided as he fell asleep last night to name Mero - back to the water to drink before hitching him to the wagon.

They set off, once again in a straight path for the nearest mountain.

***

They reached the mountain around noontime that same day and then turned north for the next several days' journey. They continued their pattern of stopping to camp when the sky darkened and moving when the sun rose.

The third morning of their trek Zel became anxious. She rustled her wings, lashed her tail, and swung her head from side to side. She was in a state of constant vigilance for nearly an hour.

Zel… Graith started, finally unable to deal with the yellow cloud of anxiety oozing from her mind any longer.

She cut him off, *They are near.*

Who?

The men who attacked me. I can smell them.

Graith pulled Mero to a stop and listened, however, he couldn't hear a sound. No dogs barking, or the sound of wagons being pulled through the underbrush. No yells or shouts from men.

You smell them? he repeated, unsure.

Yes.

Is it a smell from them passing or…?

She cut him off again, *No, I smell them now. They are probably a few minutes' flight north of here.*

As she said that, her wings rustled again, and it looked as if she were preparing for flight.

Zel! Graith was desperate to calm her, *Are we near your cave?*

Her eyes - normally an icy blue - were dark.

Yes. At this speed, we are only a few hours away. The men have left it and are near enough for me to smell them. I will go to them, burn them!

Zel! NO! Graith shouted with his mind.

She looked at him, her anger looking for a focus, and for a moment he was scared she would turn on him.

Why? she asked, looking angrier by the moment - smoke was now roiling from her nostrils.

Think about what they did to you before! You don't want that again. You won't be able to protect your eggs!

Graith realized he was going to lose the argument as soon as he mentioned her eggs. She reared back and launched herself into the sky, raining down branches as she broke through the treetops.

Cursing, Graith motioned for Mero to follow under her, trying to keep her in sight through the thick trees. He wouldn't leave her by herself, even if he had no skill with a weapon. She needed his help, even if it was only as his skill as a healer. He privately vowed that he would heal her as many times as she needed until they were able to retrieve her eggs.

Within minutes of her abrupt departure, he heard the

screams start.

CHAPTER SEVEN

Graith

It felt like forever as Graith tried to get to the source of the screams. In reality it was closer to ten minutes - but within five - the screams had stopped.

Then the roars began.

Graith had never heard anything quite like the noise Azelia was making now, but it couldn't be good.

He broke through the underbrush into a clearing and stopped.

The ground was littered with charred bodies.

Even Mero started to back up in panic. The smell of burnt flesh and hair was overpowering, nauseating.

Graith launched himself to the ground and ran for Zel. She was on the ground, curled around something that Graith couldn't see.

Her roars were maddeningly loud, so he clapped his hands over his ears.

Zel! Zel! Look at me! Graith said as he neared, wanting her to acknowledge his presence before he got any closer.

She didn't look up.

Azelia! Look at me!

This time she looked up and Graith nearly ran in the other direction.

Her normally icy blue eyes were a molten orange. She had smoke pouring from her mouth and nostrils.

She looked like a wild animal.

THEY MUST ALL DIE.

The smoke thickened, and a lash of flame escaped her maw.

Graith retreated - terrified of the beast before him. There would be no reasoning with her at this moment. He backed all the way up to Mero, never turning his back on Azelia for fear that she might strike at him. He was afraid of her for the first time since the barn.

Once he reached the horse, he mounted the wagon and continued his retreat. He found a creek he had crossed in his haste to reach Zel and started setting up camp. He had started a fire, and it was well into the second round of logs when the roars finally died down.

However, they were immediately followed by a sharp high-pitched tone that made the hairs on the back of Graith's neck stand up.

The keening continued for the next several hours, far after the sky grew dark.

***

Zel?

Graith had tried repeatedly to reach out to the dragon in the long hours after his retreat. The sun had disappeared far below the horizon, and the sky was a pale gray quickly fading to black.

This time though, a response came.

A voice he nearly did not recognize said, *What do you want, human?*

Taken aback, Graith looked around for some sign of another dragon. The keen had stopped when the response had come, but that made Graith even more uncomfortable.

Zel? Is that you?

Azelia - and yes.

She'd liked that he'd called her Zel. What had happened in that clearing that he hadn't seen?

Graith reached out again, as cordial and gentle as he could be.

I apologize, Azelia. May I ask what happened?

Anger, deep and burning, filled his mind.

48

He had never felt her emotions this deeply before, it seemed she'd lost control of her telepathy. He understood that she had stayed where she was for two reasons, she was protecting *something* there and was protecting *him* from herself.

Azelia, what did you find?

Again, no words came, just more anger, and this time hurt.

Then an image.

A shattered egg.

Graith turned his head to retch. The feeling of hurt was quickly overtaking the anger, and the strange piercing keen started again.

This time he recognized it as a keen of loss.

Zel, I'm so sorry, Graith said, daring to use her nickname.

Unsure of what else to do, Graith decided to comfort her. He thought that if he could feel her emotions, she probably could feel his.

The feeling of devastation he'd felt when she'd shown him the shattered egg, the sickened feeling, the sadness for her loss. He didn't know how to comfort her. He'd never been a father, and her loss left him feeling like his world had been shattered. A feeling that was only an echo of how she currently felt. He desperately wanted her to know she wasn't alone.

Graith ended up staying up all night listening to her keen. Not speaking but staying in contact with her.

***

When the first signs of dawn approached, Graith stood, shaking his weary body into action. He grabbed the saddle bag with his knife and new sewing kit and headed for the destruction filled clearing. He let Zel know without actual words that he was on his way.

Her keening stopped.

By the time he reached the clearing, the sun had fully risen, and Zel was still where she had been when he'd left her the day before.

Or at least he assumed it was her - the dragon laying before him looked nothing like the Azelia he knew. She looked withered, and her scales had paled almost to white. He feared she was dead at first, as her eyes were closed, but he could see she was breathing.

Against her pale scales, Graith could easily see where blood leaked from the few puncture wounds her wings had taken before she'd decimated the group of men. He continued to approach slowly, talking to her, fearful of startling her.

She didn't move.

It was definitely Azelia - surrounded by an aura of grief.

Graith was swept up by her emotions, and tears leaked down his face. While he knew he was being affected by her despair, he truly felt dispirited too.

Zel. I'm here.

I know.

The voice - different from before but still not her normal voice - responded wearily.

He walked up and ran a hand over her eye ridge, simply leaning against her large head to comfort her.

What do dragons do with their dead? he asked gently.

Now that he was standing next to her, he was able to see the tiny body she was curled around.

We burn them, she shuddered out after a long moment.

Not bothering with her wounds, Graith set about finding wood for a pyre. He did so with quiet determination, for every time he thought about the unhatched dragonling, his eyes would well up with tears.

He brought the wood back to the burnt-out clearing and once he had enough, he started building the pyre. The whole time Zel did not move. She stayed curled around her lost hatchling in mourning. Once he had finished building the pyre, he stood next to Zel and cleared his throat gently.

It's time Zel.

She let out a low growl. She did not want to remove herself from around the dead hatchling. He placed his hand on her shoulder, and after another long moment she gave in.

Wobbly on her feet, she reached out with her front claw

to lift the tiny body. Instead of trying to hobble over to the pyre, she simply leapt over to it. She carefully placed her hatchling upon the platform and backed up.

Opening her great maw, she set it ablaze.

Graith followed her retreat, and once he reached her, he once again leaned against her shoulder. They stood together for hours, watching the pyre burn to ashes. Where the heat from the flames brushed against Zel's scales, color briefly returned, but as cool air hit, they paled again.

Once the fire was mere embers and the dragonling long gone, Graith spoke again.

"Will you tell me what happened?"

I arrived moments after leaving you, having flown directly to the men. Of course, I recognized them - their smell alone was enough. I started to attack as soon as I saw them, broad waves of flame.

She shuddered, her massive frame feeling as fragile as a leaf in the wind.

I didn't know they had my egg. They screamed at me to get my attention. Told me to land or they would shatter my egg. I landed - yet they shattered it anyway.

Her scales warmed in anger, and her eyes glowed orange once again.

I killed them. All of them. I wanted to leave no trace of them behind.

Graith thought about what she had said, then very carefully brought up a subject he knew may again enrage the dragon.

This means they found your eggs. They would not have taken only one.

I know, she said - her voice sounding weary beyond words. *The other four are still missing. I know not all the men who originally attacked me were there.*

Graith closed his eyes and scrubbed at his face. He had not eaten or drank anything since before the attack. He was weary and wanted to go back to the camp he had set up but was unsure if Zel was ready to move.

She decided for him as she stood and headed off in the

direction of his camp. He had again forgotten that she simply knew what he was thinking. She was about halfway there when she spoke again suddenly.

If we go after them, they will kill all my hatchlings.

It was a statement of fact.

Yes. More than likely.

What will they do with my eggs?

Graith had been thinking about that for a while.

I think they will either try to sell them, or take them to Lord Arish and see if they can be tamed when they hatch. I don't know if any dragon eggs have ever been taken intact before.

Where is this lord of yours?

He lives in Dunlaith, a two-day journey from my farm.

And he is your peoples' ruler?

Yes and no. He is lord of the province, not the kingdom. That would be King Oron.

They reached the campsite and Graith dug out some food. He took three large chunks of jerky and forcibly put them into Zel's mouth.

You do know that I can eat by myself.

Then chew dammit.

She sighed but started to chew.

After he finished eating his food, Graith heated some water and started cleaning Zel's wounds. None of the punctures were still bleeding nor did he think they required sewing closed.

I'm so sorry for your loss, Zel, Graith told her once again.

He snuggled up against her side, and she curled around him tightly. They drifted off into a restless sleep.

CHAPTER EIGHT

Nerie

Nerie woke to her head throbbing and stars flashing before her eyes. She could hear loud sounds but was unable to determine what they were or where they were coming from. As she blinked the lights away, the world slowly swam into focus. The colors she had been seeing solidified into the shapes of four dragons. She was comforted slightly by the fact that the last thing she had seen and then the first that she had awoken to had been the dragons. The little gold one was sitting in a manner that reminded her of her favorite dog, except its little wings hung limply. She also was staring at Nerie with a strange intelligence.

The noises had resolved into words as well. A deep voice was having a seemingly one-sided conversation. Another, higher pitched, voice was screaming obscenities, and a third came from right next to Nerie's ear.

"Are you all right? Your head was bleeding when they brought you in."

Nerie jumped away at the sound - or she tried to, but her head and neck were the only things that moved. That scared her for a long moment, until she started to slowly wiggle her fingers and toes. Her body didn't move as fast as she would have liked. That momentary scare over, she looked for the source of the voice.

Young Prince Aldis was sitting next to her, looking like he had been crying. His blond hair was matted, and he had dark streaks running down his face where the tears had only just stopped flowing. His beautifully made velvet outfit of navy and gold was covered in sand. Nerie couldn't help but smile at him - he looked so disheartened. She'd always had a soft spot for younger children.

Prince Aldis saw that her eyes were open and looking at him. He leaned forward and asked, "Well, are you all right?"

"I suppose so. Everything hurts."

As she looked around the room, she realized she must be in the royal quarters. Fine silks hung from the stone walls, and artwork and gilded decorations were everywhere. It felt wasteful, as she lived a perfectly happy life in the middle district with none of those things.

The roofing fascinated her, however. It was low and wide, made of large slate panels. It surrounded the courtyard that was situated in the middle. The room they were in was square, the courtyard open to the sky and large enough for all the dragons to lounge in comfortably.

Nerie also saw the source of the two other voices. One was King Soren. He was looking at Ilex and speaking. The large green dragon was sweeping his tail in agitation. The king, now that she was closer, was younger than she expected. She supposed that made sense, as he had been twenty when he was chosen by Ilex, which would put him in his early forties. He had dirty blond hair like his son, but with dark tan skin. He already had crow's feet wrinkles around his blue eyes. Nerie imagined this was from him smiling and laughing all the time. She thought it made him look kind.

The other voice was Princess Astra. She was screaming at the young dragoness, who wasn't even looking at her. She had dark hair like her mother and her father's dark gold skin. Her face was red, and she had yet to stop screaming at the dragonling. Tired of it, great orange Eras finally turned his head to her and let out a low growl. She stumbled backwards, tripping over her own skirt - letting out an ungraceful scream as she hit the ground.

As Nerie continued to look around she saw Queen Alaena sitting off to one side. The queen looked angry, her brows furrowed and arms crossed. She was staring at Nerie with as much intensity as the little dragonling. The dragonling who was now nudging her foot.

Kiriga.

Nerie wasn't sure how she had known her name, but she had the moment the hatchling had touched her hand.

That's because I told it to you, said a voice in Nerie's mind.

She sat up in surprise, pulling the attention of the two royals not currently watching her. Astra, having gotten to her feet, paced over to Nerie. Before she could react, Astra had slapped her across the face.

"How dare you *steal* my dragon! I was to be queen!"

Nerie's face stung, and before she could respond that she hadn't meant to, Kiriga had launched herself at the princess.

"Kiriga! No!"

She hit *you. That is not acceptable.*

"She's the princess!"

As are you!

Nerie stood, looking between the little dragoness - who she'd pulled off the princess - and the king. Horrified.

She had grown up not knowing her father, that was true. Her mother had been flighty when she was young and uninterested in taking a husband. She had always told Nerie that she was the light of her life, and that she needed no one else. Nerie looked just like her mother too - red hair and bright green eyes. *Nothing* like the man standing before her. He, however, was looking at Nerie with familiarity.

"Miss - I'm sorry, I don't know your name," he said, pausing briefly for her to answer.

"Nerie."

"Nerie, we are going to need to summon your mother here. Can you tell us where to find her?"

She numbly told them - of course Myha would be needed. A servant - who Nerie hadn't even seen in the corner - raced out of the room. Kiriga bumped her head into Nerie's back in support.

"Well, while we wait, why don't you tell us about

yourself Nerie?" Soren asked, trying to break the awkward silence that had filled the room.

She didn't know what to say. Did she say, *I'm a commoner?* No, because apparently, she was *not* a commoner, not according to a dragon's voice in her head. Did she say *You must have cheated on the queen to be my father?* That would go over *really* well.

Instead, she just started talking. Telling them all about her life. About Raana, her mother, about the book shop they kept. No one said anything as she spoke, and she couldn't believe she was actually there in the royal palace.

Every now and then a reassuring nudge on her back reminded her *why* she was there - because Kiriga had *chosen* her.

CHAPTER NINE

Nerie

Nerie wasn't sure how much time passed before her mother arrived. She had spoken about herself for a long time. Her friends, her hobbies, her likes and dislikes. When she started talking about her mother, Queen Alaena left the room. She stopped speaking for a moment, but the king urged her on.

Princess Astra was sulking on the opposite side of the courtyard, and Prince Aldis was hanging on her every word. He seemed like the kind of soft-hearted soul that would give away his fortune if presented with the opportunity. He also had no idea what the world outside the palace was like.

When Nerie had spoken about her favorite game of word association - where you say a word that started with the letter that the previous word had ended with - he had immediately wanted to play. His father had shushed him so that she could continue. When she had spoken about her mother and her owning and running a shop, Aldis asked why they didn't just have someone else run it for them. It seemed like he wanted to know more about every part of her life.

When her mother was finally brought into the room, Nerie leapt to her feet. At some point she had slid onto the floor, and had sat cross-legged. Her mother was pale. She was looking around the large room with a cross between wonder and fear. When her eyes landed upon the dragons, she tried to take a step back. However, the man escorting her had a tight grip on her elbow. She shrieked and tried to pull away.

"Mama!" Nerie exclaimed, at the same time that King Soren said, "Vizen, you can release her."

"Nerie! Why are you here? What's wrong?" She took a step towards Nerie, forgetting the dragons at the sight of her only child.

"Myha," Soren said her name softly, but it brought her to a jarring halt. She threw herself into a low bow before the king.

"Myha, you may rise." Soren's tone was weary.

She stood, looking between her daughter and her king. She was as pale as a sheet.

"Now, why am I just learning about the existence of my daughter, Myha?"

"Your highness, what do you mean?" Myha's gaze dropped to the stone tiled floor.

"Myha, don't play games with me. Nerie has been speaking with us since I sent for you. After she was *chosen* by little Kiriga."

Myha's eyes darted to her daughter, then to the dragonling behind her. If it was possible, her face became paler.

"Astra, Aldis. Leave." Soren didn't raise his voice, or even look at his children, but both immediately vacated the room.

"Now, why did you not tell me about Nerie?" His voice was sharper this time, and Nerie wasn't sure how to feel about him talking to her mother like that.

"What was I supposed to do? Come before you and Alaena and proclaim your bastard?" Myha's voice was tight, her eyes still focused on Nerie.

"Yes, that's exactly what you should have done." Soren ran his hand through his dirty blond hair in frustration. "Now the kingdom will think that the next queen is a commoner."

"She *is* a commoner." Myha's voice raised in pride at that, seemingly ignoring the statement that her daughter would be queen.

"No, she is *not*. She's a descendant of the Therius bloodline. Kiriga knew that instinctively and chose her."

The king had started pacing, looking at the woman he had forgotten had even existed until earlier this morning. He had known whose child the girl was the moment he had laid eyes on her. He'd never wanted the guards to harm her, but there was always that overeager young soldier seeking attention. The guard in question would be doing latrine duty for several months. He was lucky it wasn't worse.

Nerie stood awkwardly to the side. What was she supposed to do? Her life was a lie. Her mother *had* known who her father was. She would be a different person if her mother had only told the king. She would have lived a different life. She wanted to fade out of sight, but at just that moment both her mother and well - her father - turned to look at her.

"Queen?" Her mother seemed to have just realized the implications of Kiriga choosing her daughter.

"Yes, queen." Soren's brow wrinkled. "She is years behind in her education. Aldis knows more about foreign policy than she does."

Insulted, Nerie felt the need to speak up, "I have an education!"

Soren sighed, shaking his head. "You do, but not the right kind. Do you even know what Kiriga eats?"

She twisted to look at the young dragon behind her.

"Are you hungry?"

No, I was fed while you were unconscious.

She felt ashamed that she hadn't even thought to ask the hatchling. Kiriga simply rubbed her head against Nerie, purring like a cat.

We have a long time to get to know each other.

"All right, maybe I do have things I can learn, but still, I *am* educated," she told the king.

"Nerie, Myha, you will both have rooms in the palace. We'll send servants down to your home to collect whatever you need. From this moment on, we *need* the people to know that Nerie is my daughter. No matter how that makes you and

I look, Myha. We cannot have people doubting the dragons' abilities to choose their ruler."

He paused for a moment while servants, again hidden in the corners and shadows, ran to do his bidding.

"For now, let's start with dinner. Nerie, I'm sure you'd like to get to know your brother and sister."

Nerie frowned at that. She didn't really want to get to know Astra any more than, she was sure, Astra wanted to get to know her. Not after the way Astra slapped her when she woke. Nor did she want to leave Kiriga by herself.

"Can I just stay with Kiriga?"

Soren's eyes darkened. He wasn't used to people disobeying him, even if it wasn't a direct order. He decided to compromise.

"You will, she can accompany you throughout the palace for as long as she is small enough to fit indoors. Even when she's not," he gestured to the open roof, "many rooms are designed like this. Ilex, Soros, and Eras can move around the palace as they like."

This made Nerie feel a little better. Until she looked at her mother. Myha was still pale and was looking at the floor again.

"Mama, what's wrong?"

"I would *prefer* not to see our queen." She glanced at Soren when she said that.

"No - you will join us as well. Like I said, we need the kingdom to know that Nerie is our daughter. Alaena will not say anything."

Myha nodded, not feeling eased at all.

"Servants will be in to dress you for dinner. There is a feast to be had, as the next queen has been chosen!" Soren put on an air of excitement, but it was easy to see through. "I must speak with Alaena and my children. I will see you both soon."

As he left the room, Myha swept Nerie up in a hug, sobbing. Nerie hugged her back tightly, Kiriga crowded in close too, trying to be involved. When Myha felt the little dragon, she screamed and stepped back.

"Mama, it's all right! This is Kiriga. Kiriga, this is my mother."

Hello, Myha. You have raised a worthy daughter.

Myha's eyes went wide as Kiriga spoke to her. Nerie could hear it too and smiled.

Myha dropped into another low bow.

"Dragoness, I am honored."

You need not bow to any of us, Myha.

If Kiriga's voice was like chimes, this voice was like a gong in Myha and Nerie's heads. Eras had curled up into a ball, his head over his tail, his large left eye facing the two women.

Nerie turned and looked at the great orange dragon. She had not heard him speak before. He blinked his eye, three sets of lids slowly closing over one another. She liked him.

I'm glad. We will be around forever.

This voice was softer but reminded Nerie of thunder. That was Soros then.

"You can hear my thoughts?"

Yes, all three dragons replied.

A knock came from the door, and a servant came in. She introduced herself as Karina. She had brought both Myha and Nerie beautiful silk dresses of the royal navy and gold. She helped them dress, and then led them to the grand ballroom. Kiriga followed behind, her small wings tucked against her body and her long tail dragging on the floor.

As they entered the hall, cheers greeted them. They were seated at the high table, in the seats of honor. King Soren was seated in the middle of the table, to his left sat Alaena, to her left Astra and Aldis. Nerie was seated to Soren's right, then a small dais which had been constructed for Kiriga, then Myha. As the meal was served, Nerie picked up a small loaf of bread, laughing.

What is funny?

The fact that just before you hatched, I made this bread dough.

Oh. May I have a small piece? I've never had bread before.

Nerie broke off a small piece and offered it to Kiriga, who took it daintily. Soren saw this and leaned over to her.

"You know, that will just give her a stomach ache. Like I said earlier, you have a lot to learn. Dragons are carnivores. They only eat meat - and they like it raw."

Nerie flushed with embarrassment. It was too late now, as Kiriga had already eaten the piece.

Oh well, the little dragon laughed into Nerie's head.

CHAPTER TEN

Nerie

Nerie could feel the eyes of the people on her as she sat at the head of the large room. The laughter and cheering were boisterous, but every now and then would lull and she knew they were once again staring at her. Kiriga did the best that she could, whenever Nerie felt nervous or felt like she was being watched, Kiriga would stand up and stretch her tail or wings. The people would *Ooo* and *Ahhh* her, taking the attention away from Nerie. That was, until King Soren decided it was time to make a speech.

"My people! Situra and *I* have both been blessed today. We have learned of Nerie, daughter of myself and Myha. From the moment I saw Nerie, I *knew* she was my daughter."

Nerie's face burned red. She could see out of the corner of her eye that her mother and Queen Alaena's faces were also flushed. One did not simply air their dirty laundry for the masses to see. But the king was adamant in his desire that Nerie be recognized as his daughter. That she be recognized as a descendant of the Therius bloodline.

"Now she is your future queen! Therius blood flows through her, pure. It called to Kiriga. The dragoness has chosen."

While he was speaking, the queen started to slide her chair back, but Soren laid his hand on her shoulder and continued.

"For over a century, the heir apparent has been chosen by

the offspring of the Mighty Eras and the Eternal Soros. Nerie is next in this ever-enduring line. My people, welcome your future queen!"

There were screams and cheers as Soren finished speaking, but after several long moments they faded into silence. The people, so loud before, were now so quiet that when the door from the kitchens opened, it sounded like it had been smashed into the wall. The resounding clatter seemed to be a signal that they may start talking again. This time, it was in hushed tones, and the looks at Nerie became much more frequent.

She tried to focus on her food, but it was richer than she was accustomed to. Her stomach began to ache, and all she wanted was to go to bed.

You know, I've never slept before. Is it fun? Also, my stomach hurts too.

The sudden thought from Kiriga surprised her. The hatchling was twisting her small yellow head back and forth, stretching her neck out. Nerie reached out and rubbed the small protrusions above her eyes and Kiriga calmed a bit. Unsure what to do, she leaned slightly towards Soren and whispered to him.

"Sir, Kiriga isn't feeling well. Will we be excused soon?"

Soren turned his head towards her, smiling. "Of course. I'd forgotten how small they are when they hatch. Ilex is so big now, and Soros and Eras are even larger. I'll have Karina show you to your rooms."

He beckoned and once again, from the shadows, a servant stepped forth. It was the same woman who had brought the dresses for her and her mother. Nerie stood and waved to the crowd who had cheered when she stood. Kiriga tripped getting to the ground, but she kept her head up and perked her wings up. She knew she was being watched and enjoyed it. Myha stayed seated, as she had not been dismissed. Nerie looked back at her, but followed Karina, as she could feel the little dragonling's growing discomfort.

They headed out of the hall the same way they had come in. In a series of turns that she would likely not remember, they ended at a set of doors that were gold plated and easily nine feet tall. Karina pulled them open and bowed Nerie inside.

She couldn't believe her eyes. Inside was the most elaborate sitting room she had ever seen. Each wall contained a doorway to additional rooms. From here, she could see a bedroom, a closet and full wardrobe, and a bathroom that might be made out of jewels. The sitting room itself had several lounge chairs and a table that was ornamented with obsidian and gold. A chandelier hung, with crystals that cast glittering rainbows on the walls. She was frozen for a moment, unable to urge herself to step into the room. It was so grand and extravagant that she felt that she didn't belong.

Kiriga, however, had no such compunctions. She trotted in, looking around. She stood on her hind legs reaching upward towards the chandelier, chirping happily. She toppled over when one wing became untucked from her back and pulled her sideways.

"Kiriga! Are you alright?"

Of course, I am! What are those sparklies! I want them!

"They're crystals, silly."

I want them.

She waved one clawed paw in a feeble attempt to grab them.

Looking around abashed, Nerie realized she'd entered the room to aide the little dragon. Karina stood just inside the door, watching them. She'd said these were to be Nerie's rooms. *Rooms.* The thought of such things wasted on her clouded her mind. She had thought Karina was leading her to the rooms she and her mother would share. A bedroom each.

Feeling the urge to explore, Nerie walked into the bedroom, looking at everything. The largest bed she'd ever seen was in the center. Next to the bed was a large cushion, presumably for Kiriga. Another door on the far wall was open and she could see it led to her own open courtyard.

She could see Eras's orange hide, and curious, she walked across the room. Her feet sank deep into the plush carpet, making her wish she didn't have her shoes on so that she could rub her toes into the soft fibers.

Kiriga had also spotted her father and was making a beeline for his gigantic frame. She reached him and rubbed her little head against his front right leg. His paw was bigger than her whole body. Kiriga herself was the size of a large dog. Eras lowered his enormous head and gently licked Kiriga - in response her little tongue darted out and licked his nostril. Nerie giggled at the sight.

Nerie was mesmerized by them and couldn't seem to look away. She thought that the dragons were the most beautiful creatures she had ever seen. Eras and Kiriga preened in happiness at her thought. Every movement seemed to cause them to shimmer in the fading sunlight. Nerie didn't understand the fear that so many people had shown of the dragons, including her own mother.

That's one of the things that makes you *special, Nerie,* Eras's deep voice boomed in her head.

"I'm not special though," she protested.

You are special because you are mine. Kiriga sounded so earnest that Nerie couldn't do anything but smile.

She walked over to the two dragons and petted Kiriga's little head. Then she reached up and scratched Eras's eye ridge, he groaned in pleasure and almost knocked Nerie over when he rolled his head so she could better reach. She laughed and scratched harder.

He's as easily pleased as any of our hatchlings, Soros' voice thundered in Nerie's mind with amusement.

Nerie didn't know where the great, purple dragon was, but she still asked, "Would you like me to scratch your eye ridges?"

Thank you dear, but no. I am resting in the hatching sands. Gentle laughter rang for only Nerie to hear.

It was like being part of a secret group. Just her and the dragons. She loved them already and wanted to know everything about them. That reminded her of Soren telling her she had so much to learn. It also reminded her that Kiriga's stomach was still upset.

"Kiriga, how are you feeling?"

Tired, and my belly still hurts some. But not as bad.

"We should sleep then. Remember you said you'd never slept before?"

Oh yes!

Nerie led the little dragonling back inside.

"This pillow is for you, love. Just lay down and get comfortable."

The yellow dragon sunk her little claws into the pillow as she climbed up, then walked in a circle three times before collapsing into a crescent moon shape.

Now what?

"Now you close your eyes. Quiet your mind."

Oh. Lie with me Nerie?

"Okay, but just this *once*."

She walked over to her big bed and grabbed one of the soft blankets. She bundled it around herself and climbed onto the over-sized pillow with Kiriga. She cuddled close and found the small dragonling to be quite warm. She used Kiriga's hind leg like a pillow and curled up tight.

"Good night, Kiriga."

Good night, Nerie.

Karina, forgotten, went around the room putting out the small flames that illuminated the space. Once she was done, she shut the door to the courtyard, then quietly exited and shut the bedroom door behind her.

Both Nerie and Kiriga were sound asleep before she left.

CHAPTER ELEVEN

Nerie

Nerie woke the following morning to the sound of thunder. Or at least that's what her sleep-ridden brain told her it was. However, as the sound continued and she became more alert, she realized the sound was coming from much closer.

Right below her ear.

Nerie! You're awake! I'm hungry! Kiriga's little voice chimed crystal clear in her mind.

As she blinked the sleep out of her green eyes, she looked around in confusion. Nerie had forgotten that she had not fallen asleep in her own bed the night before. Instead she was sharing a giant pillow bed with Kiriga. She'd been using Kiriga as a pillow and at some point, her blanket had slid to the floor. It hadn't woken her because of the heat the little dragon was producing.

The thunderous noise sounded again, and it clicked into place that the noise was Kiriga's stomach.

Yes! I'm hungry, remember?

"What do I feed you?" Nerie looked around uncertainly. She wasn't sure what to expect her first morning in the palace.

Food.

Nerie rolled her eyes at the dragonling.

"Yes, food. I even know it's meat you eat. But where do I *get* the food?"

Ask her!

Kiriga's head swung towards the door that led to the sitting room. It was closed, and in the corner next to it was Karina, waiting to be acknowledged by the princess.

"Um. Good morning Karina. Kiriga is hungry…"

She wasn't sure what to say and trailed off. Until her own stomach growled.

She flushed pink and quickly added, "So am I."

Karina stepped forth smiling. "Of course, Princess. Breakfast is on its way."

Turning a deeper shade of red, Nerie looked at the woman. "Oh please, don't call me princess. My name is Nerie."

"I'm sorry, Princess. The king has declared that you are to be addressed as such by all palace staff. I will be obeying his command."

"Oh. What else did he say?" Nerie asked, curious as to what the king was saying to explain her presence - or, at least, if he had said anything more than his speech the night before.

While Soren had insisted that she tell him about her life, he hadn't really spoken to her, other than to ask a few questions. She didn't know anything about him or the rest of the royal family. He was the king. Alaena was the queen. Aldis was the prince and Astra was the princess. Not Nerie. It felt wrong to hear someone address her as such.

"That you are now Crown Princess and that your every wish - within reason - is to be granted. Your mother was also given the title of Heir-Mother. She's also to be obeyed without question."

"Oh, where is she?" Nerie had more than a few questions for her mother.

"She's been given her own suite of rooms down the hall. I can summon her if you would like - after your breakfast."

"I'd like that very much."

"In the meantime, please let me show you to your wardrobe."

Karina bowed to Nerie, who once again flushed red. She

didn't deserve to be treated like this.

Yes, you do. I chose you. And if I deserve it, so do you.

She had forgotten that the little dragoness had access to her thoughts and feelings.

Of course, I do. You're mine. I'm yours.

To get her point across, she pushed thoughts of love and care at Nerie. It was a warm pink and green aura that Nerie could almost see it was so potent. It was so unexpected how fully loved Nerie was that she started crying and hugged the little dragon.

Yes, yes. I love you. You love me. Now - I'm hungry.

Kiriga let out a little whine to emphasize her point.

Karina - once again forgotten - stood waiting on the new princess. When the dragoness whined, she cleared her throat, bringing Nerie's attention back to her.

"Oh! I am so sorry!"

She raced over to the maid, who had pulled the door open to the large sitting room.

"No, I'm sorry for interrupting, Princess. If you are ready, I'll show you your wardrobe now."

"Of course." Nerie had a sudden overwhelming feeling that she was going to be an awful princess. Maybe the worst in the history of Situra.

No, you are not, Kiriga told her sternly. Her force of will, even for a newly hatched dragon, was amazing to Nerie.

Karina led them out to the large sitting room, then through the door to the right. About half the size of the bedroom, but still twice the size of her room at home, the walls were lined with clothing and accessories.

"Princess, do you favor a color? The king didn't know, so he directed me to fill it for the time being with an assortment of colors and fabrics."

Nerie couldn't stop looking around. The fabric of any one of the dresses was worth a small fortune. And the jewels - a single one was worth more than their whole shop. Her mouth fell open a little in awe.

"Um…" She wasn't sure what to say, she would wear anything in the room without question, "No, I'm not partial to a particular color."

I am. Yellow and gold. Just like me! Kiriga's voice was cheerful, but insistent.

Karina whirled around and bowed so low to the ground that her head touched it.

"Oh Dragoness, thank you for blessing me with your speech. If the princess is so inclined, I shall order that color at once," she said without getting up.

She still did not stand and Nerie realized Karina was waiting for her to answer.

"Yes. Yellow and gold sound fabulous."

Karina straightened and bowed a second time to Kiriga, then to Nerie.

"Of course, Princess."

She pulled a golden gown from among the many choices and accessories to match. "Princess, we didn't know your exact size, just an estimation. If you would try this on, I can get it hemmed to your size while you bathe."

"I'm sure it will be fine as is," Nerie said, flustered that her clothing was so important.

"If you're sure. I'll let the queen know that you'll be ready to receive her after your breakfast and bath."

She led Nerie out of the closet. Waiting for them on one of the small tables was a large tray of food. It held juice, pastries, fruit, eggs, and sausage - which only took up a small portion of the tray. The rest was filled with a large pile of meat cutlets.

Oh good! I am starving!

Nerie giggled as the small dragon chomped down on the first large piece that she was handed.

Now Kiriga, chew between bites. You don't want to choke, Eras's deep voice rang out for Nerie to hear.

The statement caused her to start laughing as she picked up an apple to eat. As Nerie sampled a little of each of the foods on the tray, Karina went off to the large bathroom to draw a bath. Once her task was complete, she informed Nerie.

"Whenever you are ready, the bathwater has been drawn

and is hot."

"Thank you, Karina," Nerie said, still embarrassed at how much effort Karina was putting into taking care of her.

"Will you need help bathing my lady?"

The question took Nerie by surprise and she flushed a beet red.

"Oh no. No! Not at all. I'm quite adept at bathing myself."

"Yes, of course, Princess. I'll go inform the queen that you'll be ready to receive her soon."

"Why does the queen want to see me?" Nerie asked worriedly.

She didn't think the woman liked her, in fact she was sure of it.

"She'll be in charge of your political and economic tutelage, as well as etiquette. The king himself will oversee your training in the care of the dragoness."

She had forgotten that the king had said that she was uneducated. It still made her flush in anger, but it was true that she didn't know the first thing about ruling a kingdom, let alone caring for a growing dragon. All she had experience with was running a small book shop.

Nerie nodded to Karina who left to do her bidding, and headed into the bathroom. At first, she was confused how the large tub had been filled with steaming water. Then she saw that there was an entrance for the servants on the far wall. It blended into the tiling and was easily overlooked, but as Nerie investigated, she found that she could lock it from her side.

The tub was some sort of pale stone and had a plug on the long side, at the bottom. Walking around the tub, she found that it drained into a grate that must lead to the sewer system. The public bathhouse that she was accustomed to visiting was drained every few hours and was heated from flames underneath the large pool.

Kiriga had followed her into the bathroom and stuck her large head into the bath. Water splashed over the sides and Nerie could feel Kiriga's excitement.

I want to play in the water!

"I need to bathe first. Once I'm clean, I'll wash you off!"

The little dragon looked crestfallen as Nerie undressed and climbed into the tub.

I could fit in there with you!

"No, you can't, silly!" Nerie said as she splashed water onto the yellow dragon's scales.

Kiriga paced around the tub, sniffing things as she went. Bars of soap lined one side and towels hung from racks on the other. As she scrubbed off, Nerie reveled in the idea of being the only one to use a bath. It was delightfully wasteful. Before too long, the water started to chill, and her fingers became shriveled prunes.

Is it my turn yet?

"It can be. I'm getting chilled."

Nerie carefully climbed out of the slick tub, pulling one of the plush towels around her. As she was wrapping it around her torso, she heard a splash as Kiriga threw herself into the bath. Water cascaded down the sides of the tub and Nerie worried about the mess but was quickly distracted by the hatchling. Kiriga was standing on her rear legs with her forepaws grasping the edge of the tub. Her little talons dug into the stone like butter, leaving long grooves. She beat her small wings, sending more water raining down.

"You are getting water everywhere!" Nerie shrieked as she was soaked once again.

This is sooooo fun!

The aura from Kiriga's mind was pink and yellow and bubbly. She *loved* the water.

Nerie scrubbed the little dragon clean, and they continued to splash the water around. Her laughter rang through the tiled room.

Completely engrossed in playing with Kiriga, the sound of someone clearing their throat loudly from the doorway had Nerie slipping to the floor.

Trying to get to her feet, Nerie grasped her towel tightly around her body. As she managed to get her footing, she saw it was Queen Alaena standing there. Frowning.

"Your Highness!"

Nerie tried to bend over into a bow, but the slick floor caused her to lose her balance again.

As she tried to stand upright the queen glared down at her.

"I will be waiting in the sitting room for you. Do not keep me waiting."

CHAPTER TWELVE

Nerie

Queen Alaena turned and walked out of the bathroom. Nerie pulled herself upright and turned frantically to Kiriga.

"Come on! You heard her! We need to get ready."

Calm down. You are my chosen. *You may go at whatever speed you want.*

"No, I can't! She's the queen!" Nerie said frantically.

She tugged at the little dragon, trying to pull her out of the tub. Kiriga was much heavier than she looked - and she wasn't helping matters. She'd been having fun, she didn't want it to end.

"I'll go without you!"

You wouldn't! Kiriga cried indignantly, throwing herself out of the tub in an instant.

Nerie grabbed two more dry towels - one for herself and one for Kiriga. She wrapped hers around herself, having lost the other in the tub while trying to get the hatchling to move.

She started patting Kiriga dry. At first, she just dabbed at the dragon's head and torso. Kiriga turned herself to allow access to her right wing and tail. There, Nerie hesitated.

You won't hurt my wings. They might look thin, but my skin is much thicker than yours.

Reassured, she continued her ministrations on the dragonling.

Finally done, she looked around the bathroom. There was a large reflective glass on one wall. Nerie had seen it earlier but was more interested in the tub then. Now, she walked over and looked at it.

She'd never actually seen a mirror before. Sure, there were reflective metals and liquids, so she had a somewhat blurry idea of what she looked like. But this - it looked like another person was standing right there - copying her, motion for motion.

Her damp red hair was a dark auburn that hung limply past her shoulders. Her skin, similar to King Soren and Prince Aldis, was an even golden color. Her eyes were a pale green under a furrowed brow. Seeing her expression, she relaxed her face, trying to put that haughty look onto it that Astra had seemed to have mastered.

I don't want you to be like her.

"Why not? She's been a princess much longer than I have."

I don't like her.

"Oh, all right then."

Kiriga turned her head in the direction of the sitting room, *Queen Alaena is getting annoyed.*

That put the rush back into Nerie's movements. There was a brush sitting on the vanity below the mirror, which she pulled through her hair in a few quick strokes.

Karina had hung the gown on a hook, waiting for Nerie to don it. Nerie looked it over with relief, it hadn't gotten splashed on. Pulling it over her head, she dropped the slick sheath down her body.

Ooo I do like that color on you! We will look so good together! Kiriga preened with happiness.

They stepped outside the bathroom to the sitting room - and the waiting queen.

Sitting on the far couch facing the bathroom, Queen Alaena sat with her back straight and her shoulders back. Her long, black hair cascaded down nearly to her hips in gentle curls. She was wearing a dark navy gown that looked like a second skin on her.

Feeling self-conscious, Nerie ran her hands over the soft fabric of her own gown. It hung loosely around her shoulders and hips.

Maybe I should have let Karina hem my clothing.

You look beautiful. Only do it if you are uncomfortable.

I am, looking at her.

"You know, you look just like him when you speak to her," Alaena's tone cut into Nerie's thoughts.

Nerie flushed, looking at the queen. At this point, she felt like that was going to be her eternal state of being in the woman's presence.

"I do?"

She had a tough time believing she could resemble the king in any way. Yet, here was his spouse, the person who probably knew him best in the world, telling Nerie that she reminded her of him.

Her - his bastard child.

"Yes. Now, please take a seat."

The queen gestured slightly at the opposing couch.

Nerie sat. She slouched into the seat, her hands clasped in front of her. Her right thumb picked at the cuticle of the left. Her heels crossed and uncrossed. Waiting had never been her strong suit, and the queen wasn't saying anything.

"I see we have a lot of work to do. I am to tutor you in all political and economic matters. It seems I also need to tutor you in social mannerisms," Alaena said, eying Nerie's posture.

"You are Crown Princess now. Heir of the house of Therius. You have ah -" she paused, thinking on her word choice, "certain expectations to uphold."

Nerie sat up a little straighter. She didn't like where this was going. She didn't know what kind of a teacher the queen was, but she didn't want to ruin Alaena's opinion of her quite yet.

If she had anything other than a negative opinion of her husband's bastard. Honestly, Nerie was surprised the woman would even talk to her.

"What kind of expectations?"

"Royalty carry themselves differently than the common riff-raff. You are to be a paragon of social etiquette and graces. When one looks upon you, you should be exactly what they imagine the princess or queen embodies. You are the physical representation of our kingdom. Not only to our own people, but to all others as well."

Nerie hadn't thought of it like that. She knew that the king was, well, *kingly* - but if she had been asked what made him so, she wouldn't have been able to verbalize it.

"Weakness on your part symbolizes weakness of the kingdom to the rest of the world. That cannot - *will not* - be allowed."

"Oh."

She didn't know what else to say. She would never be able to live up to that high standard. The queen seemed fully aware of it, as did Nerie.

Yes, you will! her ever-present supporter said into her mind.

I can't. Maybe if I had been born into it. Raised that way... I have too many things working against me.

But you have me!

I do. But I have years of practice ahead of me to even have a semblance of decorum.

Everyone has to start somewhere!

Queen Alaena cleared her throat.

"You are always allowed to speak to your dragon of course, however, to do so in front of guests is quite a faux pas."

"I'm sorry. I'm not trying to ignore you. I just - I'm overwhelmed. Kiriga is only a day old. My head still hurts from where the guard bashed me. I haven't seen my mother yet today."

Outright frowning, Alaena cut her off.

"First and foremost - Princesses do not complain. If you are unhappy with something - change it."

"I didn't mean to complain. I just have a lot on my mind!"

"Princesses also do not make excuses. You own your actions. Thus, you must be aware of each of them and make them wisely."

Nerie grimaced. Each statement cut like a knife, and she didn't like to be hurt.

"It's not like I asked to be princess. Kiriga chose me. Not Astra. Not Aldis. *Me*."

Alaena's eyes narrowed and her mouth pursed.

"And if I'm in charge of my actions, then I'm leaving. I'm going to see my mother. We have a lot to discuss."

Nerie shoved herself to her feet and strode to the door. Kiriga's little tail lashed and she followed behind.

Alaena was also on her feet. "You will not leave this room, young lady. We haven't even started your lesson yet!"

"Yes, we did. You told me that I'm in charge of my actions. So, I am doing what *I* want."

"You leave this room and - "

"And what? You're not my mother. You're barely a teacher to me."

Nerie pulled the door open and stepped out into the hallway. Karina was standing there, looking as passive as ever. She must've been waiting for the queen to leave.

"Karina. I want -" she paused, "Take me to my mother."

Karina's eyes flickered to the door and where she knew the queen to be. She nodded and led the girl and her dragon down the hall.

Nerie's bare feet slapped on the floor as she paced behind the woman. Kiriga's talons were a sharp staccato in tandem with the slaps. Another series of hallways that she would someday have to memorize. Then they were at a set of doors.

The doors weren't nearly as ornate as Nerie's and only about seven feet tall. Karina pulled one open and bowed Nerie inside.

Myha was sitting on a large sofa. Her sitting room was drastically smaller than the one in Nerie's quarters. She had a lavatory, but its tub was much smaller and made of what appeared to be copper. Myha's bedroom was also much smaller and didn't seem to have access to a private garden.

The back wall of the sitting room, which in Nerie's room held her wardrobe - was nothing more than a wall, covered by a large tapestry of dragons. In the image, Nerie recognized Soros and Eras, but the other jeweled dragons were unfamiliar.

Seeing Nerie, Myha jumped to her feet and ran to hug her daughter. Karina once again faded into the background. She bowed and stepped back into the hallway, closing the door behind her.

"Oh, Mama! I missed you!"

"You saw me last night!"

Nerie was already in tears. How was she supposed to do *this*? Be princess to a kingdom that she'd only ever known from the depths of its middle class. She tried to say as much to her mother, but it came out a garbled mess.

Pulling Nerie to the soft couch, Myha held her as she cried softly. Stroking her daughter's soft hair, she whispered to her.

"How about I tell you a story? About me, before you were born?"

Nerie nodded into her shoulder, her sobs racking her thin frame. She didn't get to hear about her mother's past very often.

"You know our bookshop? Well, it was my papa's before it was mine. My mother died when I was little. You know as much already. Anyway - Papa would have me run it for him when he was busy - just like I have you run it for me sometimes now."

Nerie tried to quiet her breathing - as her mother was talking very softly - and she wanted to hear. She was only partially successful. Her breathing came in long ragged gasps.

"Well, one day, a man - Oh, he was quite a handsome man - came into the shop. I showed him around. He said he was looking for a specific book. One about dragons."

At the mention of dragons, Nerie's interest spiked. Myha was still slowly stroking Nerie's hair, massaging her scalp and twirling strands of her hair.

"Now, you know how rare the dragons are. We only had one book about them in the whole shop. In fact, you've probably read the book a million times before. It was your favorite growing up. About how Soros and Eras came to Situra."

Trying to nod, a large glob of snot ran down her face. Nerie was an ugly crier. She had snot dripping down her face and her eyes were so puffy she could hardly see out of them. She angrily tore the seam of her dress and used the hem to wipe her face. All she could think was *What would Queen Alaena have to say to* that?

"Unfortunately, that was not the book that the man was looking for. He left, and I thought that was it. A strange man looking for a strange book."

Nerie nodded her head successfully this time, looking at her mother. She wondered what book the man *had* been looking for. She also wondered why this was the story her mother wanted to tell.

"The next day he was back. He actually introduced himself this time - Soren. I didn't think anything of it, as Soren was an immensely popular name after the king had been born. He was looking at the book we did have. He called me over, started telling me how the book was wrong. How it mischaracterized Soros and Eras. At that point, I thought he was *quirky*."

Myha smiled in memory. Nerie smiled back at her. It was good to see her mother reminiscing. She now had an idea of where this was going.

"He came back every day. He always looked at different books. He would tell me about various places."

Myha shook her head, her own red hair tumbling around her heart-shaped face.

"I thought we were in love. I mean - we did things that people in love do - we went on dates, we laughed, we kissed. We - well - you were conceived."

Her smile faded at this point.

"One day, shortly after I'd found out I was pregnant with you, he came to see me. I was going to tell him I was expecting. He chose that day to confess to me - he was the king."

Myha took a deep breath, her eyes unfocused as she

relived that memory so far in the past.

"He wanted me to come live in the palace with him - and the queen. I was mortified. What does one say to that? I didn't tell him about you - instead I told him to leave and never come back."

Nerie was sitting up straight at this point, holding her mother's hand, which was gripped vice-like around her own.

"I didn't know Nerie. Not until right then, that he was the king. I thought the king stayed in the palace all day."

Myha had tears of her own running down her face at this point.

"The rumors about the queen being barren were rampant at that point. I felt used. Betrayed. I told him no, that had I known he was a married man, I would've never agreed to be with him."

She sniffed and rubbed her face. A single tear ran down as she finished her story.

"Maybe I should have been his royal consort. But I couldn't, Nerie. I just couldn't. He said he understood. He left. That was it. And then you were born. So perfect. And I was happy. Happy with our life. Happy with you."

She pulled Nerie's head to her shoulder, rocking them both gently back and forth.

"I'm sorry, baby. So sorry that I never told you the truth before now."

Kiriga, who'd been lying curled on the floor, stood and walked over to the pair. She laid her little head on their laps and nuzzled both women.

CHAPTER THIRTEEN

Graith

Graith and Zel were up early the next day. The sunlight filtered between the leaves, momentarily warming Zel's hide and leaving a trace of color before vanishing again. They made slow progress to Zel's nesting cave. Her eggs were large and fragile, and they hoped that perhaps not all of them had been removed from the cave. Or if they had been taken, maybe they would be able to determine which direction the egg thieves had gone.

They'd been near her main cave the day before. They would have reached it by nightfall but instead had encountered the group of men. Graith briefly wondered if the three men from the pub had been in the group, but since all were unrecognizable after Zel's rampage, he was unsure.

They traveled in silence as the sun moved slowly overhead. Graith simply watched Zel and let Mero follow on his own.

When they arrived at Zel's cave, it was obvious that all the eggs would be gone. Ropes and a pulley system had been constructed and left behind by the men who had raided the cavern. They apparently had felt no need to remove it once their job was done.

Graith dismounted from the cart, unworried that the gelding might wander off. Zel launched herself into the sky, more of a large leap than flight, landing at the entrance of the cave. After studying the lift system for a moment, Graith was able to hoist himself up.

Emerging at the entrance, Graith had to be impressed. The sunlight streamed in behind him, allowing him to see deep to the back wall of the cavern. The space was huge. His barn could've easily fit inside - with room to spare - however, it currently sat empty. There was some discarded rope off to one side and some tattered paper near the entrance.

Graith stepped towards the paper, his feet making deep indents in the soft sand that coated the floor. As he reached down to grab the worn, ragged paper, the tear completed its rip. He picked up both halves and held them together in the sunlight.

A map.

The cave they were in had been marked - along with where he assumed Zel's main cave had been. It also had several towns, including Dunlaith, and even the capital city of Tesia marked. He had to resist the urge to ball the paper in his fist.

Instead, he carefully folded the two halves together and placed them in his pocket.

He looked around the cave a second time. This time he saw where Zel had kept her eggs. Large rocks placed in a rough circle filled a good fourth of the cavern floor. They were spaced far enough apart for a man to walk between, but were nearly as high as Graith's waist. Graith could almost imagine Zel laying inside the circle, curled around the eggs in the same manner that she curled around him at night. His heart ached for her.

Zel, they're gone.

I know.

She wandered over to the ring, sniffing the ground like a hunting dog.

I'll find each and every one of the men that took my clutch.

Graith sighed and headed back to the lift.

I'll meet you at the cart, I found a map. We can decide what to do from there.

Zel seemed to ignore him and continued sniffing the

ground. He was sure she was memorizing every scent, and unlike the first group of men, these ones would probably meet a slower, more painful death.

He reached the cart, patted Mero on the snout and pulled the map back out. It was a large map, showing the entire country of Lutesia, and the surrounding countries Situra and Etria. Graith had never even been farther than Dunlaith, Lord Arish's home.

Well, he corrected himself mentally, he hadn't been before now. Now he had traveled all the way to the western mountains. He frowned, thinking of his crop sitting in his barn. He wouldn't be going back, would he? Zel needed him.

A moment of mental insecurity hit him hard. *Did* she need him? Why had he come along? He had just walked away from his whole life, for what? A dragon he was supposed to want to kill?

Graith? Zel's mental voice, almost back to her normal self, reached out to him.

Zel, why am I here?

She was quiet for a moment.

You're here because you're my friend? Right?

Graith let out a breath he didn't realize he'd been holding.

I am, Zel.

She lowered herself from the cavern and nuzzled his back. He turned and rubbed at her eye ridge. Color returned where he rubbed, but slowly faded back to near-white. Graith had chosen not to ask Zel about her change in color. He assumed it was due to her grief and that her navy would return in due time. Though he didn't know for sure, since she was the first and only dragon he had met.

After a moment, Graith turned back to the map. Zel raised her head above his to look down at it.

I recognize those places! She told him excitedly, seeing the towns that had been marked on the map.

You do? Graith asked in surprise, then remembered Zel had told him that she'd come from a faraway land.

Yes, I flew over several of them on my way here.

Where are you from, Zel? Graith asked curiously.

The south, there are lands where dragons and people coexist, the humans there call it Etria. It's very far from here.

Graith frowned, he'd known that there was a country to the south of Lutesia. He hadn't remembered the fact that it was home to dragons - if he had ever known in the first place. He had never paid much attention in his geography classes when he was young, as he had very little use for them - never intending to leave his home.

He looked back down at the map. Its size was daunting, and there were so many places they could have taken the eggs. He sighed and scrubbed at his face. He felt movement behind him and when he looked again, Zel was pointing ever so delicately with one of her foreclaws to the town where Lord Arish lived.

Dunlaith. We should go there first. The lord there was the one who sent the men after me in the first place wasn't he? Zel asked.

Once again, Graith was surprised.

Zel, can you read?

She scoffed at him and looked annoyed.

Can you talk? Of course, I can read. What kind of uneducated fool do you think I am?

Graith reddened and shook his head.

Zel, you forget, you're the first dragon I've ever met. Men here talk about killing dragons and what horrid creatures they are. I have no idea what you can or cannot do.

She seemed to be a little mollified at that, and once again nuzzled him.

I did forget. Humans in Etria are so very different from the humans here. But Dunlaith, that seems like a good starting point. You, of course, will have to do all the talking since I would be killed on sight.

Graith nodded, deep in thought. He had no hesitations about continuing to help Zel, but he was a planner.

I think we should head back to my farm and travel from there, as I am familiar with the roads. Plus, I'll need a few more things from my home.

He gently folded the pieces of map back together and placed them in one of his bags. Climbing into the wagon seat, he gazed up at the empty nesting cavern and then down at Zel.

We'll get them back Zel.

She didn't answer him, instead she once again leapt into the cavern, where she turned and roared to the sky, issuing her challenge to those who had taken her clutch.

CHAPTER FOURTEEN

Graith

They set off for Graith's home, retracing the path they had made on their journey to her cave in the first place. At one-point Zel flew off, telling Graith she would be back shortly. About an hour after she left, she returned, carrying a few swords and another bow in her forepaws.

What are those? Graith asked, unsure where she would have gone to get weapons.

Weapons from the men that I killed in my cave initially. There were so many, it was all I could do to get away at the time.

Aye, I remember. You weren't much more than a bloody meat sack.

She chuckled darkly at that.

You could have killed me then, I was so weak and exhausted. Or, if you had merely left me, I may have bled to death.

I could never have done that, Graith insisted.

He examined the bow she had brought for him. It was much finer than the one he had currently, made to punch through heavy leather rather than hunting. However, the bowstring had broken, and the one he had would be insufficient for a replacement.

You are sweet, Graith.

He smiled up at her, then looked at the swords she had brought. They were standard issue, all having the same length and general weight. He'd never used a sword before, but it wouldn't hurt to carry one.

***

The journey back to Graith's farm was uneventful. They made it in three days, since they used the trail they had created. Once they arrived, Graith couldn't help but look around and feel like he no longer belonged there. He was a different person than the man who'd found a dying dragon in his barn just over a week ago.

That man had belonged - but now?

There was more of the world that Graith intended to see, and staying here would be like forgetting Zel even existed. Or what he'd promised her.

They went to his house where the chickens were still in the yard. The door was locked, but other than that, he could have simply been away for an hour, not the long week he had been. He opened the door and was surprised to discover a letter someone had slipped under it. Graith looked around, wondering if he was going to see anything out of the ordinary, but everything looked just as he'd left it.

The pile of laundry he needed to wash, the bed, rumpled from the last time he had slept in it. His favorite chair, still sagged in the middle of the seat, as if he had just risen from it.

It was his home, but it felt like a stranger's.

He slowly walked to his chair, looking around him, feeling as if he was walking into someone else's life. He sank into the chair that molded around him perfectly, and mechanically opened the letter.

It was from Ralph. That seemed to pull Graith back into the here and now, and his brows furrowed as he read the letter.

Graith,

I came to see how the gelding of yours was doing. I wanted to make sure he was getting along with your animal that the other was afraid of. I'm only writing this because I didn't find you at the house, barn, or any of your fields - for the last two days. When you return from wherever you've gone, come see me. Sarah is worried about you.

Ralph

Guilt spread over Graith, his face burning in shame.

Of course, Ralph would come check on the gelding.

He was concerned about all the animals he raised. He was also a good friend. Graith should have told him that he was leaving town for a while. Honestly, he'd thought no one would notice or care that he was gone. It's not like he had regular visitors.

Running his hand through his hair, Graith thought about riding into town now to let Ralph know he was home. But that wouldn't do much good, as he was just going to be leaving again. Indecision seized him, and guilt flowed through him for several minutes.

Zel's voice broke through, stopping his mind from racing.

Graith, what's the matter? she asked, sounding worried.

I wasn't a good friend to Ralph. He came to check on me and Mero, but we weren't here.

You were being a good friend to me *at the time. You can explain to him later. For now, you should rest. I know you're not used to traveling, and we've done much of it in the last few days.*

A shadow passed over the window, and Graith looked up to see Zel's large blue eye peering through. He noticed her scales had darkened to the palest shade of blue, and he hoped that it was a sign that she was healing. She might be a creature of legend and feared by all, but she had emotions just as human as he did. He couldn't imagine having his children taken if he were in her place. She was stronger than he could be in that position.

He wasn't sure how to verbalize these ideas to her, so he just sent warm and caring thoughts her way. He received them in turn.

Smiling, he got out of the chair. His knees popped and his back ached as he made his way to the bed that no longer felt like his - though it was much softer than the ground he'd been sleeping on for the better part of two weeks. As he laid among the woolen sheets, he missed having Zel curled around him. She provided such a feeling of protection, without it he felt exposed - even in his own home.

***

The next morning, he took stock of his possessions. Sometime in the night he'd decided that once he left, he would not be coming back.

He carried in his large saddlebags and unpacked them. He planned on repacking only the things that were too important to leave behind. As he dumped the contents of the three saddlebags, dirty clothes and dishes toppled out, along with the small odds and ends that had seemed useful at the time. He set the dirty things aside and sorted through the rest.

He still had a few loaves of bread and a few small hunks of dried meat. He grabbed the oiled cloth his cheese had been wrapped in and set it aside. While tasty, cheese was expensive, and he'd run out of it the night before. Food was going to be the biggest problem while traveling, but he hoped that Zel would share anything that she caught.

Of course, I will, she said in response to the unasked question. *Though, isn't it unusual for an adult, male human to not be able to hunt for themself?*

Graith reddened and scrubbed at his scalp, *I have a hard time bringing myself to kill anything. Even if it is food.*

Looking back down at the pile of items, he saw his fire-starter. It had fallen to the bottom of one of the bags after the first night - Zel had lit all the fires they'd built. It was tossed in the *leave behind* pile.

Next was the quivers of arrows. He'd not had time to practice because of their steady pace to the mountains. That reminded him of the new weapons Zel had brought him. He didn't know how to use them either, but that would need to change. He was going to leave his farm behind - he knew he *needed* to know how to at least protect himself.

Maybe your friend Ralph would be able to help you? Zel said.

Perhaps, but I'm not sure he knows how to handle a sword either. Most of the villagers are just farmers like me.

With a shake of his head, he swiped what was left of the *to be sorted* pile into the *leave behind* pile before grabbing his cloak. It hadn't seen any use during their first trek, as it hadn't rained - and Zel made quite the warm bed. It was set to the side, to go into the bags last. Winter would be coming soon and traveling without it would be a miserable task.

Graith glanced at the window where Zel still waited and saw that she was looking at him. He needed to get moving. She was waiting on him.

Quickly washing and then hanging his clothing out to dry, he returned inside to pack up the household. He stored the quilts and linens, dusted the house, and looked through his remaining foodstuffs. He had several jars of preserved foods, mostly vegetables he'd stored for the coming winter. Graith put them with the items he would be taking. There was no use in letting the food go to waste.

After several hours of cleaning and packing, Graith was done.

He'd decided to take the chickens, the last of his animals to Ralph, when he took him the keys to the house. If he ever returned, he could reclaim the farm, but he doubted he ever would. He found an old tarp to cover the wagon - both to protect against the weather and because the essentials didn't quite fit into the bags.

As he shut the door for the last time, he looked back at the little house. He'd been born here. Lived his whole life here. Now he was leaving. Sometime between traveling with Zel and arriving back the day before, things had changed.

He had changed, and the farm would never be enough for him ever again.

Graith picked up the three fussy hens, setting them in the back of the cart, on top of the tarp. Looking around one last time, he gathered the few of the eggs they had lain and then climbed onto the wagon bench.

Zel, I'm done here. Let's go.

He felt her wordless assent and he picked up Mero's reins. They set off towards the village. Zel was going to veer off to the north and meet him on the far side after he'd met with Ralph.

The short trip seemed to take no time at all after the days of travel he'd recently done. The seat of the cart would soon be more familiar to him than his leather chair he was leaving behind. Reaching Ralph's barn, Graith saw his friend leading a horse inside. He pulled Mero to a stop once Ralph saw him and waved him over.

"Graith! Where have you been? Sarah and I have been worried about you."

Ralph's eyes searched Graith, and his brow wrinkled. He was anxious, and Graith was ashamed to have been the cause.

"I went on a trip - out towards the mountains." Graith waved a hand in the general direction of Zel's cave. "Mero's been a good horse so far. Made the trip smoothly."

Graith reached up and patted Mero on the snout. Mero gave a soft whicker and nuzzled his hand.

"Named him did ya? What took you out that way? I thought you'd have heard a dragon had been spotted out there."

Ralph was frowning slightly, and Graith shuffled his feet. He'd known his friend was worried about him, but he had forgotten the general unease - hate even - surrounding dragons. What was he going to say? He'd been prepared to tell Ralph everything. Even Zel had thought it was a good idea.

But now? He was having second thoughts.

"I did hear. But it was important." Graith looked around, seeing a few curious eyes from neighbors. "Ralph, can I talk with you? Privately?"

He decided to tell Ralph the truth. He deserved it, after all he'd done for Graith. The trip to Graith's farm alone was over an hour of traveling both ways - and he'd made the trip at least three times while Graith had been gone. Ralph obviously cared about him. The least Graith could do was tell him the truth.

Ralph nodded and motioned for Graith to follow him inside the barn. Similar to Graith's, his barn was set up with several stalls for horses and a little office for business.

"Go ahead and have a seat, I just need to get Betty here into a stall!"

Graith went in and had a seat. Ralph came in moments later, as he looked at Graith's face, his own turned from jovial to serious. He pulled his chair around to face Graith and sat down.

"What's going on Graith? Why the sudden trip out to the mountains?" he asked once again.

CHAPTER FIFTEEN

Graith

Ralph seemed extremely worried, and Graith felt uncomfortable for being the cause. He'd abandoned his farm and gone chasing through the mountains with a *dragon*. And here was Ralph, waiting on an explanation. He shifted in his seat, unsure how to broach the topic he was about to share with his only friend.

"Ralph, I'm leaving," Graith said.

It was a starting point, but the worst was yet to come. Graith folded and unfolded his hands nervously. The serious look on Ralph's face, however, changed to one of shock in an instant.

"But - why?" Ralph was grasping for words. "You have the farm. You have Mero, and the cow, and the chickens. I wouldn't be surprised if you produce a third of the town's wheat, Graith."

He spoke rapidly, in denial that his friend was about to up and leave everything behind.

"The cow's gone. I brought the chickens with me. I was hoping you'd take care of them for me. Mero will be going with me. What else am I leaving behind? Hell, look at my life here. I don't have family. You're my only friend. Everyone else hates me."

Graith was growing frustrated with the quaint life he'd been leading. Before now, he'd never even considered leaving. After even a small bit of excitement, he was weary of farm life and he was getting away from it. He'd felt guilt over Ralph's letter, yes, but as shocked as his friend was, Graith thought that perhaps it was a bad idea to tell him about Zel.

Thinking of her brought the gentle touch of her mind to his. It relaxed him slightly.

"I met someone, Ralph. Out in the mountains. She wants to travel. I'm going to go with her."

The worry and shock in Ralph's eyes faded slightly as he took in that bit of information. In fact, a sly smile was spreading across his face.

"Oh, found a lady friend did you, Graith? About damn time."

"Well -" Graith started before Ralph cut in.

"Of course, you would want to travel with her if that is what she wants."

Ralph laughed, and reaching over, grabbed Graith by the shoulder. The anxiety was gone from Ralph's face, replaced by joy for his friend.

"What's her name? And where is she? Sarah would love to meet the woman who captured your icy heart!"

Graith shook his head, blushing red. That was *not* how Ralph was supposed to take that. What was he supposed to say? *Oh well, you see, she's not a human. She's a dragon, so of course she can't come into town...*

Laughter in the back of his mind made him blush more.

Oh, hush it, you. You thought I should tell him in the first place, what if he wants to kill you?

Maybe it's for the best if you let him think I'm your lady love. At least then he won't sic the town on me with pitchforks and torches!

Zel's mental laughter rang loudly in his mind.

Graith cleared his throat and tried to speak, but the lie he was about to tell caught in his throat before he could say it. Instead he decided to go about it another way - tell a partial truth.

"Her name is Azelia, Zel for short. She's meeting me outside of town, so I won't be able to bring her to meet

Sarah."

Ralph nodded along, perfectly happy to accept this information.

"Graith, I'm just glad you've found yourself a woman. Even if it's taking you away from the village. What are you going to do with the farm?"

Graith let out a sigh. The farm. His family's home for the last four generations.

"I'm just going to leave it. It'll be there if I ever decide to come back. I've cleaned everything out except the barn. I wanted to leave you with the keys to the house. Just in case."

He dug the keys out from beneath his shirt and pulled the leather thong they were looped on above his head. Ralph took them carefully, as he knew how much the farm meant to Graith. Or well, how much it had. He didn't know how removed Graith felt from it all now.

"One more thing, Ralph, I've harvested this year's crop, but didn't bundle it yet. It's drying in the barn. It should be ready in another week or so. You can keep the profits from it. But don't let ol' Sal undersell you per pound."

Ralph nodded. Graith knew that it was a lot of work for the farrier, but also knew that it was a lot of extra money for the year.

"Graith, that's a lot of money. You're sure you don't want me to just set it aside for you if you come back? Say something goes wrong with you and Zel? I wouldn't want you to be short."

"I'm serious. Keep it. Even if something were to happen between us, I don't think I'll be coming back any time soon."

With that, he stood. Ralph followed the motion, still unsure about the fact that his friend was leaving their little village forever. Graith reached out, and Ralph grasped his arm. It went from a friendly shake to a brotherly hug as they both realized they might never see one another again.

"Take care, Graith. If you ever need anything just send word. Sarah and I care about you deeply."

"And you, Ralph. You take good care of Sarah."

They left the little office and turned toward where Mero

had made himself comfortable chewing hay. He had pulled the little wagon with him to reach it.

"Oh yes. About the chickens…"

Graith was more than a little nervous about dumping them with Ralph, who already had a menagerie of animals to take care of.

"Yes, yes. They can stay. Are they good egg layers?"

"They are. Well, except the damned rooster. He crows at the morning sun alright though. Some nights I've thought about eating him for dinner."

They both laughed and Ralph helped Graith unload them from the wagon.

Then it was time.

Graith was itching to get on the road, and he could feel Zel in the back of his mind, her feelings echoing his. He walked towards the cart, scratching Mero's ear before getting on the driver's bench.

He carefully backed the horse and cart up until they were outside the barn, near the house. Ralph was following, making teasing comments about how in love Graith must be. Instead of answering, Graith just shook his head.

"You be safe now Graith, you and Zel. The world is a dangerous place. Keep your eyes out for that dragon!"

Graith flushed red again and could only nod and wave as he reined the horse into motion.

That was it - he was on the road.

He was on the way to meet up with Zel, and to help her find her clutch. A sense of anxiety swept over him as he rode through the center of the village.

Don't worry. I can protect you Graith. The voice in his head was soothing.

I'm not worried about my safety. It's more a worry of - I'm not sure - never coming back. This is my home.

It's not. No one there cares for you with the exception of Ralph and Sarah. You don't go to town events or even to the tavern for a drink except on rare occasions. Shall I go on?

As she spoke, Graith relaxed. Zel was right. It wasn't his home, not really. Sure, it was where he had lived, but he was apart from everything that went on. At this point he wasn't even sure he needed a home. The road was going to be his home, and it was going to be exciting.

Zel chuckled but said nothing else. She was still half an hour away. Graith settled in, prepared to ride all the way to Dunlaith.

CHAPTER SIXTEEN

Graith

Graith met up with Zel around noon and they were on their way within minutes. Graith found that traveling on the road was his much preferred method to trailblazing, and the miles fell away beneath Mero's hooves.

For the most part, the road was empty. The afternoon of the second day, they passed a small family that Graith thought he faintly recognized from his village. They did not acknowledge him, so he kept his head down and continued on.

Zel chose to walk parallel to the road, just inside the forest of dense trees. Occasionally Graith could hear her crashing about, but for the most part she was silent. The birds and woodland creatures hid themselves from her, and thus from him. So their journey for the most part was quiet.

By the end of the second day, the road which had been dirt before had become gravel. This signaled to Graith that they were approaching Dunlaith, home of Lord Arish. He had not been here since his father had brought him as a small boy, but he knew they were less than a day's ride out.

He reached out to the now familiar mind of his companion, *Zel, we should stop for the night. The woods get thinner from here on out, and we don't want some traveler to wander by.*

He felt her listen, but there was no verbal response. He could sense that she was about to argue and decided to continue speaking.

We made good time getting here. I'll go into town tomorrow and see if there is any news of the men who took your eggs.

A brief flare of anger was the only response in his mind, but before he could soothe her it was gone. When she responded she sounded despondent.

Of course. I'll just wait outside - she paused, then before she pulled away added, *like a dog.*

Graith wasn't sure what to say. It wasn't like a giant dragon could just walk into the town square. Frustrated, he turned Mero off the road and forged a path straight to the dragon.

When she wasn't in the first two clearings that they reached, he started to get annoyed. She had been right inside the woods all day, close enough that he'd been able to see her at points, her pale hide looking like a patch of sky inside the green foliage.

Zel, where are you? It's going to be dark soon.

A harrumph from inside his mind was the only answer.

If you don't tell me, I'm going to camp at the next clearing. With or without you.

Again, there was no response.

Annoyed, Graith continued on. When he finally broke through to the next clearing, Zel was lying there curled up, tail twitching, and if she weren't so much larger than the cart, she could have passed for Graith's least favorite barn cat.

She did not welcome him or acknowledge his presence in any way. He hadn't left his seat since early that morning, and was quite tired, so he chose not to acknowledge her either.

He untied Mero and dug through his packs for some bread. He'd told himself that he would learn how to use the bow, maybe not to hunt, but to protect. After traveling all day he simply had no energy to spare. Instead he searched for his fire starter - he realized, as he was unable to find it, that he'd left it behind, content to rely on Zel. Sighing, he shook his head and then went around collecting dry wood.

The whole time he collected wood, Zel pointedly ignored

him, even tucking her face under her left wing. After he had built up what would be a more than adequate fire, he turned to the dragoness.

"Zel, would you please start the fire? It's getting quite chilly out."

She slowly pulled her head out from under her wing and turned towards the pile of wood.

Then she huffed.

A burst of fire springing forth, and what should have been a fire that lasted all night was incinerated instantly.

"Are you kidding me, Azelia?" he asked, taking a deep breath in frustration.

She eyed him, her eyes whirling an angry pale white.

You think I'm a dog. Or some animal you can simply train to be obedient.

Graith stared at her, dumbfounded.

"When have I *ever* said that?"

You didn't correct me earlier. And you just use me for my fire.

So angry he couldn't speak aloud, he responded, *You're the one that lit the fires the whole way to your nesting cave and back! I couldn't find my flint tonight. So, I asked. Nicely. I didn't command you or order you. I asked.*

Zel had the wherewithal to look ashamed.

My children are in danger and all I can do is sit in the woods and wait for you - a human - to try to help.

Her eyes had swirled to an anxious yellow. Graith's anger dissipated in a flash. She looked so very distraught.

I know Zel. We'll get them back. But to do so, we must find out where they were taken.

He walked over to her and leaned against her snout, unconsciously rubbing the soot off of a few scales. After a few minutes of comforting the dragoness, Graith went and collected more firewood. This time, Zel obliged and lit a small fire. Within moments of settling down against her, both fell into a restless sleep.

***

The next morning dawned cold and bright, and Graith

was forced to pull his cloak out of his bag after crawling out from under Zel's warm wing.

We should make it to town by noon, he said, unwilling to spend the energy to speak aloud.

About that, she said slowly, *I think I should stay here.*

Why? Graith was startled after her annoyance the night before.

The way I acted last night. Plus, I'm a dragon, in an emergency I can just fly there.

There will not *be an emergency,* Graith said rolling his eyes.

That's why it would be an emergency.

Graith shook his head at her sudden excitability.

All right. You do whatever you need. You'll be able to hear me?

I should. I'm going to hunt today while you travel. I'll stay in touch, that way, if you do get too far away, I can follow you.

She sounded so pleased with herself that Graith nodded along, there would be no convincing her otherwise.

It didn't take Graith nearly as long as he thought to reach the town. Dunlaith, home to one of the five Councilmen of Lutesia, Lord Arish.

Dunlaith was a large castle surrounded by a bustling market protected by low walls. The town overflowed from the walls though, with houses becoming smaller and more bedraggled as they strayed outward.

As he drove his cart through the streets, Graith felt more than a little overwhelmed by the sheer number of people. He'd been to Dunlaith once as a boy, and it had seemed huge then.

He had been expecting it to be much smaller than he remembered, as most things from childhood are. However, faced with the settlement before him, he had trouble even calling it a town. It was easy to see the districts as they rose above him, but at the same time it didn't fit his mental, arbitrary, definition of a city either.

Graith frowned, trying to categorize the place, but his

attention was brought back front and center as a woman screamed at him, saying his cart was blocking her way. Which it *was*, but that was no fault of his own. The town had gated entrances, and the line to enter the town proper was quite long this morning, so his forward progress had stopped.

He gave a brief apology and took a moment to look around. He was nearing the gates and could see that the homes and shops that lined this section of the road looked to be prospering. Not that even the most far-reaching houses had looked that worse for wear. This region of Lutesia was doing well, that much was sure.

Thinking about his harvests over the last few years, Graith's profits had risen and the tithed and taxed portions, while large, had been reasonable. This section of the road was mostly taverns and inns, which he thought about stopping at for information. He decided that something as valuable as dragon eggs would have been taken straight to the castle, or at least the upper district.

Reaching the gate after nearly two hours of slow progress, Graith barely had to urge Mero before the horse pushed his way through. The guards on duty looked bored and relaxed in their black and red uniforms. None of them even gave Graith a second look.

Why would they? The kingdom wasn't at war, and he was coming in on the western road, the only thing in that direction was the mountains.

No one even knew about Zel, and most of these people had probably forgotten that a dragon had been spotted months ago.

Zel's amusement at his thoughts bubbled forward, and Graith found himself calmed. She was still there, even if she was out hunting. At the thought of her hunting, she sent him the feeling of being full. This made his own stomach grumble, as he had forgone that morning's bread. While Graith had been thinking of Zel, Mero had continued onward without direction. When Graith looked around again the surroundings while similar to before, seemed nicer.

Houses had gilded paint, stores had hanging signs, and

the clothing worn was made of slightly nicer fabric. He saw far more silks and satins than cottons or wool.

Graith decided this would be where he started his search, and he started to look for an inn.

CHAPTER SEVENTEEN

Graith

As Graith urged Mero along the crowded road, his eyes alighted on a clean looking inn. It had a large covered stable that pulled his attention. As he drew closer, he saw a young boy attending the few animals already inside. He slowly backed the cart along the far side and once he was done, the boy was waiting for him to unhook Mero. As he jumped down to the cobbled ground, he patted his hip, checking to make sure his gold pouch was still attached to his belt. It gave a cheerful little jingle.

The boy, who could be no older than ten, was looking at Mero with large round eyes. Being the only horse Graith was using, he had forgotten just how large the gelding was. He was nearly a head and neck taller than the other horses stabled. An easy eighteen hands tall. The boy barely came up to his withers. As Graith finished unhooking Mero from the wagon, there was suddenly a lead next to him, and the boy was looking between him and Mero.

"There's a good boy, Mero!" Graith said loudly, patting the horse on the neck.

"Now lad, you take good care of Mero here. He's been traveling nonstop for several days. You clean him up and get him some warm food and there'll be a reward for you."

He winked at the boy, whose round eyes now went from Mero to Graith.

"Yes sir! Though I might need to find a larger stool to

stand on to groom him," he said quickly, his excitement at the thought of his reward showing.

He grabbed the lead and Mero followed him like an over-sized puppy.

The large horse taken care of, Graith turned to the inn. He'd been trying to think about how to ask about dragon eggs in a normal conversation all morning, but everything he thought of just seemed well, like he would end up having questions asked about himself.

He opened the door to the inn, the handle smooth from wear over the years and stepped inside. The inn was bright and warm. A large fire crackled on the near wall, and the tables that didn't have patrons at them gleamed in the light. The ones that were occupied with patrons had large drinks and steaming bowls of food in front of their owners. He'd barely gotten inside the door before a young serving girl had called a welcome and was working her way towards him.

"Good afternoon, sir! Please have a seat wherever you'd like. I'm Daisy, what can I get for you?"

Her personality was bright, and she had a large smile on her face. It was almost infectious.

Almost.

Graith had overestimated how many people would be here this early in the day. It had only taken him a couple of hours to get here from his camping spot and another hour or so to get into the city and make his way to the inn. It just wasn't the kind of atmosphere ripe for rumors or stories. He sighed and made his way to a central table.

He'd just have to wait.

Daisy had followed him to the table and was eagerly awaiting his order. Graith felt rushed but pushed the feeling aside. No need to let his irritations rub the serving girl the wrong way. He was going to be here for a while, and ostracizing one of his hosts right off the bat was never a good idea.

"I'll take an ale and whatever is freshest."

"Oh, aren't you just in for a delight! Pa's just finished cooking shepherd's pie!"

She giggled and was off.

Daisy returned a few minutes later carrying a large bowl and mug. Graith could see the foamy head on the ale just waiting to slide over the rim, and before the bowl was even set in front of him, he could smell the delicious aroma.

With the bowl before him, he saw the most exquisite shepherd's pie he'd ever seen. The potatoes were whipped into clouds and the beef was falling apart. Vegetables had been chopped finely and mixed into the thick brown gravy. His mouth watered and he had to try his hardest not to shovel it into his mouth.

"Thank you, Daisy. I'll be here awhile today, please just keep the ale coming."

He fished out a few coins and gave them to the girl, who grinned at him and did a mock curtsy.

"I'll be around! Just call my name if you need anything else!"

She gave him a wink before turning and making her way back to the kitchen.

Graith looked around. The people currently in the inn were well dressed and either looked like they were guests staying in the upper floor or locals who frequented the place for their midday meal. None of them had given him more than a cursory glance when he first entered, and all had gone back to their food and conversations.

He looked down at his food and picked up the spoon that had been shoved into the soft potatoes. He took a bite and his eyes nearly crossed in delight. He was sure he would never again appreciate eating a loaf of bread with cheese. Hell, he might stay here forever, just to eat more of their amazing food. Waiting for more patrons to arrive now seemed like a trivial matter - all he had to do was continue to eat the food.

Three - no four - bowls of the shepherd's pie, and several pints of ale later, Graith was feeling full, tired, and ready for some news.

He'd chatted with Daisy about the weather, the harvests, and other generic conversation topics throughout the day. In return, she'd been quite attentive to his needs.

He sighed.

He'd never been a city man, but if this was what it was like all the time, well, maybe he should reconsider.

Zel had been silent the whole day, and Graith got the distinct impression she was sleeping her own meal off. Not that she wouldn't wake if he even thought in her direction too hard. The trip had been rough on her.

She was a creature of flight after all, and for most of the time he had known her she had traveled by foot... paw? Claw? He shook his head slightly.

No need to get caught up in the semantics of dragon anatomy.

He felt sad thinking about her situation. He couldn't imagine being left to raise a family by himself only to then have them kidnapped away. He reminded himself that was why he was here.

To help.

People were slowly starting to fill the large space. A musician with a lute had begun to set up, quietly tuning his strings. Daisy was going from table to table bringing out mugs and bowls of what smelled like chili. Graith supposed that the shepherd's pie was more for the high paying customers. He smiled, glad he'd gotten more than his fair share earlier.

He grabbed his mug and stood, walking toward the group of people who were pulling chairs over near the musician. He must be a regular occurrence with the way people were flocking in the door. He had started a mellow but fast-paced song. Graith found himself tapping his foot along to the beat.

While he listened to the music, he also listened to the crowd forming around him. Most were talking about the musician, Dominic, from what Graith could gather. It seemed like many people wanted him to perform at their own taverns and inns, but he would only come here.

A few others were talking about the tail end of harvest season, taking bets on when the first hard frost would hit. Graith even chimed in on that one, saying he didn't see it being more than a week away.

"So, pal, what do you do? Haven't seen you around before."

An arm rested on Graith's shoulder and he involuntarily tightened up. A man, younger than himself, but not by much, was the one with his arm on Graith. He was wearing a brocaded vest and a pair of tights that Graith would've been ashamed to be seen in. The man seemed to be eying Graith's new cloak, which most certainly did not match the rest of his older clothing.

Graith frowned then cleared his throat. It would do him no good to stomp out a conversation before getting any information.

"I'm a farmer from the westernmost village. Doesn't even have a name, it's so small. Finished my harvest and wanted to see Dunlaith for myself."

The man nodded along, smiling a smile that didn't seem altogether friendly. When there was an uncomfortable silence, Graith pushed on, "How about yourself? Are you a local?"

"That I am. I live in the upper district. I'm a personal acquaintance of Lord Arish."

"Oh. That's nice. He's a good fellow then? Last time I was here his father, Dirk, was still Lord."

The man sneered, and Graith could see the man's estimation of him fall lower.

"It's ah - been a while then?"

"Yes."

The conversation had gotten awkward, and Graith did the only thing he could think of. He stood up and walked away. The man glowered at him, but Graith made a point not to look over.

During their conversation the music had picked up its pace, and most of the patrons were now working on their second mugs of ale. The volume had started to rise, and a couple of people were dancing. This was the atmosphere that Graith had been waiting for.

A couple of men roared with laughter, and Graith made his way over to them. They seemed to be well into their third pint by now. Hopefully they would be coherent enough to answer his questions but drunk enough to forget who was asking.

"Hello gentlemen! How goes your evening? Enjoying Dominic's music?"

They looked at Graith and smiled.

The first, a blond man in his early twenties replied, "Yussir! We come just about every night!"

He took a long drink of his ale and grinned at his friend. The second man was also in his early twenties, but dark-haired. Both were wearing finer clothing than Graith, but nothing like the man from before.

"I'm new to town. Just finished up my harvest. I was wondering if you lads had heard anything about a makeshift militia a while back. They came to my village, preparing to hunt a dragon. I couldn't go, as it was harvest season, but I was hoping to find out how their hunt fared."

The two looked at each other, trying to remember past their current pint.

"I do think I remember that. Heard a lot of folks died. Seem to remember a group going up to the keep," the blond replied.

"Bunch of wagons and people went up there oh… a week or two ago. Wanted to speak to Lord Arish. Don't remember anything coming of it though."

The dark-haired man seemed to think hard, but Graith could see him losing concentration within moments.

"Thank you both. Next round is on me!"

Graith waved Daisy over and let her know. The two men slapped him on the back and thanked him.

People continued laughing and dancing in time with the music, but Graith was ready to go. He had his information, and now he needed to use it.

But it was late.

He was sure that the city gates were closed by now, and where was he going to go? He thought he should go visit Lord Arish and see if he could get any more news.

Graith sighed.

It would be a waste to leave the inn that evening.

He waved Daisy over once again. She tried to approach but couldn't squeeze her way through the middle of the crowd. She instead grabbed his hand and pulled him out. Graith was tired and let himself be pulled.

A twang in the music caught his attention, but the crowd's laughter swept the moment away.

"Yes, hun? What can I do for you this time?" Daisy smiled up at him, and leaned in.

"Can I get a room? It's a lot later than I thought. I'll be staying the night."

"Of course! Let me show you the way."

She didn't let go of his hand as she pulled him towards the stairwell. They were about halfway up the stairs when the crowd's volume seemed to increase and Graith realized the music had stopped.

They reached the landing and she showed him in the first door on the left.

"In here, hun. *Anything* else I can do for you?"

She was leaning towards him, completely blocking the entrance to the room. She still had his hands in hers and was pulling him closer.

"No, that's all -"

He never got the chance to finish his statement.

Dominic came rushing up the stairs, and by the time he reached Graith, he had quite a bit of momentum going. When the punch landed, Graith went sprawling across the floor. Daisy screamed and grabbed Dominic, pulling him away.

"What are you doing, Dominic?!"

"I saw the way he was looking at you, Daisy!"

"Looking at me? I was *looking* at him! What's it matter to you anyway?"

"Why do you think I only play here, Daisy? When even Lord Arish is asking me to play for him? It's certainly not because I like this shitty little inn!"

The two continued to fight as Graith's ears rang loudly.

As did a roar from outside.

Graith! What happened? Zel's mental voice was

panicked.

Zel. Hide. I'm fine. Some lovers tryst that I got caught up in, I think.

No. I need to come to you.

No, you don't! I'm fine. Going to have a hell of a black eye, but I'm fine. I'm not in danger.

He could hear another roar. Hopefully people would think it was thunder. But the patrons of the inn, who had been quite loud until now, had quieted.

"YOU!" Dominic roared, pointing at Graith, who had managed to push himself into a sitting position.

"You'll leave Daisy alone. Don't you touch her again!"

Graith just stared at the man. Why would he want to touch Daisy in the first place? She was basically a child to him.

"I have no interest in her. All I wanted was a good night's sleep," Graith said, while trying to stand.

"I *saw* the way you were looking at her. How close you were!" Dominic just wouldn't back off.

"Dom! He didn't do anything. And you're a fool to not have realized before now that I would do *anything* to keep our customers happy."

Dominic was in a black rage but seemed to realize that Graith really was not interested in Daisy. He stomped off and Daisy looked between the two men before following Dominic down the stairs.

Graith rubbed his head and reached out to Zel again.

Stop your roaring. The whole damn kingdom can hear you.

I want to eat that man.

You just ate earlier.

I could eat him if I tried.

Please go hide. I need to go see Lord Arish in the morning, and then I'll meet you on the eastern side of town.

He could feel her discontent but ignored it. She did stop roaring, but the inn - so loud before - was now silent. Graith was left wondering just how many people had heard her. How many knew what a dragon's roar sounded like.

Wearily he opened the door to the room that Daisy had shown him to. Kicking off his boots, he didn't even bother to undress as he thankfully made his way into the soft bed and was asleep before he knew it.

CHAPTER EIGHTEEN

Graith

Graith woke up more comfortable than he could remember being in weeks. It was bright outside and he could hear people in the streets. He was surprised the commotion hadn't woken him up sooner. He stretched as he got out of bed and walked to the window, peering down on to the street.

People were everywhere, but unlike yesterday when everyone had been focused on their own tasks and business, today they were in groups. No one was traveling around the town on their own.

They look like ants down there, Zel sounded in a poisonous mood this morning.

Morning. Are you looking through my vision?

Yes. You have business to attend to. Time to get moving. You need to return to me.

Anxious, are we? he asked as he turned back to the room to change.

You were injured last night!

Graith rubbed his temple carefully. He remembered. His face was sore and he wondered what wonderful shade of purple his eye might be.

That I was.

He could feel her tail twitch without even seeing her.

Get a move on then.

Before he'd fallen asleep the night before, all he'd managed to remove was his belt and throw it onto the small table in the corner, drape his cloak over the back of the accompanying chair, and pull off his boots. His rumpled clothes were less than appropriate to wear before Lord Arish. Pulling on fresh pants and shirt he quickly headed out of the room.

When he reached the dining hall of the inn, a delicious smell wafted from the kitchen. What would it hurt to have breakfast? Daisy emerged from the kitchen at the sound of someone coming down the stairs. Seeing Graith, she immediately turned around and rushed back into the other room. Moments later, an older gentleman with thinning gray hair came out. He was covered in flour and was wiping his hands on his apron.

"Morning there! What can I get ya?"

Graith sat at the same table as the night before, looking around. After the previous evening the large room felt empty. He could still smell appetizing odors coming from the kitchen though.

"Ah well, whatever it is that I can smell, eggs and fresh toast perhaps?"

"Aye we have eggs, but no toast. We do have a specialty pastry, however."

"Sounds wonderful."

The man disappeared into the kitchen and reemerged carrying a plate and bowl. He set it down before Graith and dropped into a flourished bow.

"Enjoy your food, sir!"

The man stood and went to leave but saw Daisy sticking her head out of the kitchen. Graith also saw the serving girl and couldn't help but frown. Not that she had done anything wrong, but he *was* the one sporting a swollen eye.

"I am so sorry about last night, sir. Daisy told me what happened. Sweet lass, my Daisy. Not the brightest, however. I've known Dominic was enamored with her for ages. She didn't. And until last night he intentionally didn't acknowledge that she… ah, enjoyed *fully* pleasing our customers."

Graith blanched a little. In his village, even the notion of such could get a person exiled, at the very least.

"You, uh… don't mind?"

"Why would I? She keeps quiet about it, and guests are always willing to pay more for a room."

"Well, I'm sorry if I caused a disruption."

"Not on you at all, on her. But mostly on Dominic. I don't think he'll be playing here anymore."

The man patted Graith on the shoulder and walked back to the kitchen. Graith turned to his food, his eyes alighting on the pastry. It was round and flat, and looked to be filled with a soft cheese. He took a bite and the flaky dough was sweet in his mouth. This was a luxury he must indulge in whenever he was in a town.

Hurry up and eat. You're running late, Zel was letting her annoyance at him leak through.

Late to a meeting that I'm going to have to force anyway? Not really. Graith didn't care if she wanted him to hurry, his breakfast was too good.

Zel huffed and backed out of Graith's mind. He finished his breakfast quickly though and made his way out to the stable for Mero.

Out in the courtyard, Graith could see Mero happily munching away at the grain in the box next to him. There was also a large bucket of water hung there and as Graith approached, he could see the large horse was impeccably groomed. Graith whistled, impressed.

He'd forgotten to come check on Mero the night before, along with the stable boy who'd taken such diligent care of him. Graith looked around now for the boy, but he was nowhere in sight. That was odd. The lad had looked like the stable and horses were his life.

Graith was surprised that the boy wasn't around, but he had places to be. He opened the stall holding Mero and had to chuckle. There in the straw at Mero's hooves was the boy, asleep and covered with a stable blanket. Graith carefully led Mero out of the stall and over to the little cart. He really should have left the cart with Zel, but Mero was just too big to comfortably ride bareback. After he hooked up the horse, he went back into the stable.

Squatting down next to the boy, he shook him gently on the shoulder. The boy threw an arm over his eyes and rolled over.

"Lad. Come now and wake up."

"Pa, it's too early…" the boy mumbled from under his arm.

"Lad, I'm not your pa. Just trying to pay you for your services."

Little brown eyes blinked up at him. Then the boy was hastily sitting up, pulling straw from his hair.

"Sir, I'm so sorry for sleeping in here. Mero though - he just looked so lonely -"

The boy was nearly twitching, he was so nervous about being caught sleeping.

"Lad. It's alright. I just wanted to pay you for your service."

Graith dug out a full gold coin and handed it to the boy, who looked at it with wonder.

"Sir, you can't give me this. It's far too much."

"I can, and I have. Though if I were you I would either hide it or spend it where you'll get a lot of change. Things like that go missing too easily."

The young boy just nodded before tucking the coin into his boot. Graith ruffled his hair and was on his way.

***

Lord Arish's keep was on a hill overlooking the rest of Dunlaith. A large stone building, it was several stories tall. It towered above all of the surrounding buildings. A small wall divided the keep's gardens from the rest of the town. As Graith made his way through the gate, he looked around in wonder, feeling like he had entered another world.

There was fine green grass that didn't seem to be affected by the oncoming winter. Large trees that were nearly as tall as the manor littered the grounds. Small buildings hid in the shade cast by the trees, including a stable and living quarters for the staff. The road between the stable, manor, and gate - as well as the smaller foot paths between buildings - were covered in fine gravel that hardly made a noise as the wheels of the cart went over it. If the inn in the upper district had been nice, this was the definition of luxury.

There were people stationed along the path directing the flow of incoming guests. Graith was led to the stable, his small cart was parked, and Mero led away within moments of his arrival. A servant seemed to appear next to him, showing him the way to the manor.

A small staircase of stone led to the main entry hall. The floors were stone, with a plush red carpet creating pathways to follow. Directly on the right was the entry to the main hall, where Lord Arish sat greeting his people.

Inside, Graith joined a line of people eager to speak with their lord. As the line slowly moved onward, Graith looked around the massive room. Lord Arish was on the far end, on a dais raised just enough for him to see the whole hall. He was seated on an elaborate throne, gold and ivory glistening in the light that streamed in the large windows. There were tapestries hung between each window, and a large hearth on the far wall, opposite from the Lord. Trestle tables were currently pushed to the sides, so that the hall was open, but Graith had no problem imagining them set up for a meal. Great chandeliers of deer horn and steel hung high above their heads.

As he moved forward towards Lord Arish, Graith continued to worry over what exactly he was going to say. He wanted information, but he couldn't seem too knowledgeable about Zel, and the fact that her eggs had been transported into town, without raising suspicion.

Relax Graith. It'll be fine, Zel told him suddenly, reassuring him.

Oh, will it? I don't even know what to say to him. Just...

Before Graith could hear Zel's suggestion the line shifted a final time, and he stood before Lord Arish. The man looked down from his throne, and Graith froze.

"Yes? What business brings you before me today?"

Eyes wide, Graith couldn't bring himself to answer.

What was he doing here? This was a mistake and he was just going to get Zel killed.

"Well, man? What's your name?"

Graith's mouth opened and words started to come out. Words that *he* was not thinking.

"My Lord, I'm Graith Tresker, a wheat farmer from a local village. A few months ago, men came through town looking for volunteers to hunt a dragon. I couldn't volunteer at the time, as it was the middle of my harvest. They never returned to my village, so I came here to offer my services to you. If you have a need for me."

"Ah, yes. The *dragon*. We thought perhaps it had perished, but just last night its roars shook the windows of Dunlaith. This does not surprise me. We have taken its clutch. No doubt it is in search of the eggs."

"It had eggs? It's female then? Where are the eggs going?"

Lord Arish's eyes narrowed at the rush of questions.

"Aye, we believe so. As to your request. I currently do not have any need of your assistance. The men who are taking the eggs onward are trusted and well vetted. You are neither. I thank you for your diligence in following up in the matter. I do hope you enjoy your stay in Dunlaith before you return home."

With that, Graith was led away and out of the keep. As quickly as he had gotten in, he was back outside. The whole time he was in shock. Only after he had exited the gate did he reach out to Zel.

Did you talk for me?

He could feel her seething with anger.

I did.

How?

The same way I can see out of your eyes. I'm not sure exactly. It's just a power I have.

Oh, what other powers do you have?

She was silent for a long moment, her anger still red hot to his mind. But he could feel her thinking about his question. Finally, she answered.

I don't know. I am learning them as I use them.
I see.

Graith paused, looking around at the bustling town. The night before it had been full of places for him to explore, now it felt overwhelming. He needed to get outside the city walls - as fast as he could.

Orienting himself to the east, he told Zel, *I'm on my way.*

CHAPTER NINETEEN

Nerie

There was a light knock on Myha's door, Karina entered at their acknowledgment.

"My ladies," she said while bowing, "I'm sorry to interrupt you - however, King Soren has requested Princess Nerie's presence."

Squeezing her tight, Myha helped her daughter stand.

"Get him talking about dragons and you'll be golden!" she whispered in Nerie's ear.

Bowing to Myha again, Karina led Nerie and Kiriga out the door. Nerie felt like a leashed dog as she followed Karina from room to room. She knew that it was only temporary until she learned to navigate the palace on her own, but she was growing tired of it quickly.

It wasn't long before they were faced with another set of large golden doors. At first Nerie thought that Karina had brought her back to her own room, but upon opening the door, she was greeted by an even larger suite than her own. Directly opposite the entry, the garden she remembered waking up in after the hatching ceremony faced her.

Ilex lounged like a giant snake. She saw for the first time that while he did have wings, they were as small as Kiriga's currently were. His acid-green scales glistened in the midday sun. Kiriga trotted over to him and used his nose to stand on her hind legs.

While Nerie couldn't hear an exchange, she could see

one was taking place.

Ilex says that Soren wants to eat lunch with you. I'll stay with him for now.

Looking at the two dragons it was hard to believe they were siblings. While both had Soros' smooth scales, they had drastically different body shapes.

Karina was waiting patiently to the side and ushered Nerie through the door to the right. If the first room was a lounge, this room was a private living room. There were more couches and tables scattered around. Nerie could see a study in an adjoining room.

King Soren sat at one table, a plate in front of him, with another waiting across the table from him. Seeing her, Soren got to his feet - Karina quietly shut the door behind Nerie.

"Nerie, thank you for joining me. I thought lunch would be a good chance to get to know you," he said smiling.

He gestured for her to take the seat opposite him and as she sat, he pushed her chair in, then seated himself.

"Of course, your highness," Nerie said, looking at her lap, her hands folded together tightly.

It wasn't like she had a choice in the matter. So far, her life in the palace had been a series of go here's and do that's. It was rather aggravating.

"How are your rooms? Do they suit you?"

He seemed genuinely curious, looking at her, not his food.

"They're perfect. I have never had a bathtub before."

Nerie still couldn't believe the rooms belonged to her.

He chuckled.

"I'm glad to hear." His face became sober. "However, I'm not so glad to hear how you treated Queen Alaena this morning."

Nerie looked down at her plate, avoiding his gaze. "I am sorry, your Highness. I just don't do well with criticism that I don't deserve."

"Nerie, first off, you may call me Soren - or father if you wish - when we are not in public. Second off, being ruler comes with all sorts of criticism that you don't deserve."

He laughed this time, "You can choose to make one decision, and even if it works out, some people will still criticize it. What you eat, what you wear, who you're with. It will never be enough for some people. One of the things Alaena will teach you is how to deal with those kinds of people. How to minimize the things they can comment upon."

Of course, Nerie thought to herself, feeling foolish.

She hadn't even given the queen time to teach her anything. Had her own mother been the one she had said those things to, she would have been spanked like a small child. Here, the consequences were not the same. She was crown princess - she would one day rule the kingdom.

"I should talk to Queen Alaena and apologize," she managed to say, her face burning.

"You can do so tomorrow at your daily lessons."

When he said that, she frowned.

Deciding to do something and being given a time to do so were two very different things. She looked back up at him, studying his face.

He was looking at her, smiling.

She had been right about the crow's feet at the corners of his eyes. He must smile all the time. It was still strange to look at the man who was her father. The only thing she could find that she had in common with him was his skin tone. They were both a dark golden tan.

"Sir - ah - Soren, you said I had a lot to learn about dragons. Will you tell me about them?"

Mama had said to get him talking about dragons and she did love stories.

"What would you like to know?" he asked, his eyes flicking in the direction of the garden, where the two dragons lie.

"Everything." she said in a rush.

It was true. Thinking of Kiriga filled her with joy and wonder. She wanted to know as much about the dragonling and where she came from as possible.

"All right then, I'll start from the beginning."

He took a sip of water and cleared his throat.

"Several generations ago, my and your, many times removed, great-grandfather Kyre was a general in the Great War. You know our two neighboring kingdoms, Lutesia and Etria? Well they and Situra were at war."

Nerie thought she knew where each was, but it had been a long time since she had seen a map. She nodded, having heard tales of the Great War.

"The war started when Lutesia attacked Etria, trying to kill all the dragons. They believe - even to this day - that the dragons are monsters."

Her jaw dropped. How *anyone* could want to hurt a dragon was beyond her capability to understand.

"But that's not true!" she shouted, immediately covering her mouth in embarrassment.

Soren chuckled darkly, then continued, "You're correct, it's not. Everyone but the people of Lutesia seem to know that. At first, Situra was not involved. This is our greatest shame. It was not until Eras and Soros came to the king of Situra to ask for help that our people got involved."

That man did not help us. He turned us away, Soros' voice rang angrily in their minds.

Your ancestor, Kyre, pledged to help us. High in the military, he took as many soldiers as he could recruit to our cause and marched to Etria. To get there from here, you have to go through the southern mountains. By the time they arrived, the capital had been destroyed, Eras' said somberly.

Carcasses of our loved ones littered the countryside. We found no survivors. Kyre helped regroup the humans of Etria. Reclaiming their cities, he routed the invading force from Lutesia, Soros continued the story.

Nerie could feel the two dragons' sorrow. Flashes of dragons she had never seen, lying dead before her eyes, caused tears to spill down her cheeks.

"Kyre found the heir to Etria's throne, left a force of men to defend her, and came home. The war was over. Lutesia was defeated - left to retreat to their own borders. But it was too late, they had succeeded at their goal. Eras and Soros were the only dragons to survive."

We returned here with Kyre for two reasons. First of all, we couldn't stand the sight of our homeland. Memories of those we loved, lying dead - it was too much, Soros said.

We also had a score to settle. The people of Situra were unhappy with the leadership of the man they had called king. Kyre was a better fit for that role. We gave him the throne. Not long after, we laid our first egg. When she hatched, she Chose Kyre.

Eras projected the image of a small opalescent dragon and a man who had the same golden skin, but dark hair and bright blue eyes. He reminded Nerie strongly of Soren - the strongest impression being that he was kind.

He was, a faint, voice whispered into her mind - a voice that she didn't recognize.

That would be Wyla - our eldest daughter, Eras said.

Nerie's eyes went wide.

Of course, everyone knew that dragons lived a long time - Eras and Soros were ancient - but she had forgotten about the dragons who had Chosen the previous rulers.

A chuckle came from Soros.

It's all right, dear. When their partners passed, our children spread out, choosing a city to protect. We cannot bring back those dragons we've lost, but we can continue to have children.

"Why have I never heard this story?" Nerie asked Soren.

"I don't know what your mother has or hasn't taught you. My father's dragon - Mazen - had already left the city before you were born. So, it's simply possible he was never mentioned. Eras and Soros stay here in the capitol by choice, and Ilex always stays with me."

Soren shrugged.

"How many dragons are in our kingdom?"

Nerie was mystified that she had never known there were more living dragons.

"Well, there is Ilex, Kiriga, Wyla, Soros and Eras -" He counted off with his hand, "They have four more children. Tiryn, Riya, Galean, and Mazen."

As he said each name, an image of the dragon flashed in her mind. Ilex, Kiriga, Soros, and Eras she knew. When she saw each of Kiriga's siblings however she gaped in awe.

Wyla was an opalescent-white. Tiryn was a dark-green. Riya was a purplish-red. Galean was as orange as his father. Mazen a soft-purple.

Nerie realized they were the dragons in the tapestry on her mother's wall.

They were beautiful.

Thank you, we are quite proud of them all, Eras laughed.

Nerie frowned. "You said that Wyla chose Kyre - after you'd already made him king. What does that mean?"

Dragonkind has an incredibly special connection with mankind. We have powers that are amplified through a Chosen human. We can choose at birth or later in life. The earlier a bond is formed, the stronger the powers manifest. We can also bond with more than one human; our family has just chosen not to, Soros answered.

"What kind of powers?"

Telepathy for one. That is why Wyla was able to speak to you. Never bonded with Chosen, our telepathy is weaker. I believe it's only about five miles - Wyla is at the border in Cian - far from here right now, Eras explained.

There was a soft knock at the door. Vizen, who seemed to be Soren's personal servant, opened it.

"Sir, my lady, I apologize for my interruption, however, it's nearing dinner time - also the small council is waiting for you, your Highness."

"Oh yes, well they can wait. Nerie, you'll meet them soon enough, but for now you may go back to your rooms. Karina will have your dinner brought to you."

Soren stood and motioned for Nerie to do the same.

Kiriga joined them in the antechamber, and once again it was time to follow Karina. This time, however, Nerie paid more attention to the path from her room to the king's. She expected that would be a trip she made often.

CHAPTER TWENTY

Nerie

They arrived back at Nerie's quarters - the sight of which once again hit her like a dream. The glistening jewels, the bright paint, and the soft carpet - all were overwhelming to consider as her own.

You've done so well today! Kiriga told her cheerfully.

Turning and hugging the dragonling's small head, she smiled.

Karina went to fetch their dinners, and Nerie took the opportunity to look in her wardrobe. The gown she was wearing, while sleek and soft, was not what she wanted to spend her evening lounging in.

After several minutes of searching, she found a soft shirt, which she laid on the bench in the middle of the room. Walking around, her fingers gliding over the fabrics, she frowned. Shirts, skirts, dresses, and more skirts.

Where were the breeches?

She unhappily chose a soft skirt and changed into the more comfortable clothing. Making her way back into the living area, her feet padded silently on the carpet, her toes sinking into the soft fibers.

Karina returned with an elaborate meal carried by a manservant Nerie didn't recognize. He set the tray down and promptly left.

While lunch had been a light affair of fruits and small sandwiches, the aroma wafting from the laden tray was savory. She almost started drooling, instead she turned her focus on Karina.

"Karina, will you please bring my mother here? I wish to dine with her this evening."

"Of course, your highness," accompanied by a bow, was all that was said before she left.

Taking the chance to look over the meal which had been placed on a table, Nerie saw a stew and fresh bread, steamed vegetables, a small fruit and cheese tray, and, again, a large tray of raw meat for Kiriga.

Oh good! Ilex was telling me about hunting today. Apparently when I'm big, I'll be able to get my own food!

She sounded so excited and dim images flashed through Nerie's mind.

"Did he show you those images, Kiriga? When you showed me, they were kind of dark and blurred," she told the hatchling, smiling.

She will have to learn to focus on one image at a time, Eras said as he joined the conversation.

He seemed a lot more talkative than his mate, Nerie thought. Going through her bedroom to the courtyard, Nerie found him lounging in the same spot as the night before.

This one is my favorite. I've worn quite a divot into the large rock here. Extremely comfortable.

He winked one large orange eye at her, its catlike pupil narrowing, the colors within seeming to spin and whirl, a calm green tone inside the tangerine.

I might also be more attached to my hatchlings than my mate.

I do not need to hover to know that my children are safe, mate. Though she was not present, Soros' voice was as sharp as if she was right there.

You were going to feed me? Remember? Kiriga's voice, so shrill compared to her parents, complained.

"Yes, sorry."

Nerie spun back around to their waiting meals.

Tossing a chunk into the air for Kiriga to catch quickly became a game for the two. Lobbing piece after piece in different directions across the room, Kiriga darted after them. Just as the door opened to admit Karina and Myha, the last piece Nerie had tossed reached them. Kiriga jerked herself out of her dive to avoid the two women.

"Nerie! I thought you were old enough that I didn't need to tell you not to play with your food!" Myha scolded, the meat having landed at her feet.

"It's not really *my* food," she said with a slight whine, all the while grinning at her mother. "It's Kiriga's!"

"Uh-hu." Myha rolled her eyes at her daughter. "You wanted me here?"

Straightening, Nerie nodded.

"Yes, I'd like to eat dinner with you. Karina, while we eat, will you find me some breeches to wear? They are my preferred clothing choice for evenings."

Karina bowed deeply to Nerie, but her answer when it came was unexpected.

"I'm sorry my lady, I cannot. Princesses are not to wear pants like a common man."

"But it's what I want!" Nerie looked down at her skirt unhappily, "I wear them all the time at home."

"I'm sorry, my lady. Queen Alaena forbade it several years ago with Princess Astra. Skirts and dresses are what princesses wear."

"Karina, you told me that I was to have anything I wanted, per the king. I want this."

Nerie knew she was being petulant, and her mother was frowning at her, but really? All she wanted was to wear pants in the privacy of her rooms.

Bowing even more deeply, Karina responded, "My lady, you may address the issue with Queen Alaena during your lessons tomorrow."

Seeing that the woman had not stood from her bow yet, Nerie felt bad for her, adding, "Thank you Karina, I understand you're just following your orders."

Karina straightened, her blonde hair swinging around her slightly pink face. She retreated to her preferred corner where she could observe the room.

The rest of the evening passed smoothly. Nerie and Myha talked about what was going to happen to their shop, what changes they could expect in their life, and about Soren and Myha's relationship. It was late into the evening when Myha saw her daughter's eyes start to flutter. Excusing herself from the room, she took Karina with her to serve as her guide back to her rooms.

Nerie stumbled into her bedroom where Kiriga had already curled up onto her enormous pillow.

I would not lay down yet, your brother is on his way, Soros' voice, normally so loud, whispered.

Her brother? Did Soros mean Aldis? Nerie turned back to the sitting room.

No, he's currently climbing the roof to get here, Soros sounded worried.

Nerie did an about face, quickly walking to the door that hid the courtyard from sight. Stepping outside, it was much darker than Nerie expected. Only the glowing orange and purple eyes of the two dragons lit the large space. The stars overhead were bright and the sky cloudless.

What is he doing? Kiriga asked, having followed her mistress.

"Climbing the roof. I'm not sure why though," Nerie said, looking at the dark rooftops for the young boy.

She suppressed a scream as he dropped down next to her. He immediately bent over double, panting hard.

"I wanted - to meet you. For - real - this time. Mama said - that I - needed to give you space," he wheezed out.

As soon as he'd recovered his breath, he was moving again. This time he walked over to Soros and climbed up her back to rest between her giant wings. Nerie was impressed - her brother seemed to be quite the acrobat.

I like him. A lot, Kiriga told her, then added - *But not as much as you!*

Walking over, Nerie looked up at Soros' great, purple eyes, "May I join him?"

Of course, child.

She carefully climbed her way up the dragoness. Her

skirt catching on one large scale, she apologized to the purple dragon. In the position she was sitting, Soros' shoulders towered above the roof. From here, Nerie could see many courtyards just like hers littered across the palace.

"So, do you do this often?" Nerie asked Aldis once she was situated on Soros' broad back.

"All the time. It's the easiest way to avoid the guards."

That's because we *are the guards. And we like you visiting us,* Soros said softly to them.

Nerie chuckled. Aldis seemed like a sweet boy.

He is, Soros told her.

Nerie was fairly sure that one had been said only to her.

It was, he would have made a good king. You will make a better queen.

Nerie looked at the boy again in the starlight. His dirty blond hair was dark in the night, but it blew gently in a breeze. He was smiling at her, his face just on the point of thinning from childhood into manhood. While they had only spoken briefly after Nerie had awoken after the incident with the guard, Aldis had been kind to her.

Impulsively, she reached out her hand, grabbing his.

"I'm Nerie. I've never had a brother before, but I'm glad to meet you."

She could see him light up in the dark, his blue eyes twinkling in the starlight.

"Hello Nerie - I'm Aldis. I can't wait to get to know you better!"

He pulled her from the handshake into a hug, laughing lightly.

They talked long into the night, the stars moving ever-so slowly overhead. She learned that the royal family was quite disjointed. Both the king and queen loved their children but spent extraordinarily little time with them outside of lessons.

There were no family dinners, nor did they spend time reading stories to the children. Astra and Aldis did not get along. At all. In fact, Nerie thought the boy might be afraid of Astra.

Any mention of Astra caused slight growls from the

dragons, and Aldis would change the subject quickly. That was interesting, and something Nerie would need to look into more as she became familiar with the palace.

She already knew her sister detested her. After all, Astra had slapped her just after she had awoken from unconsciousness. The glares the woman had given her at the feast had been sharper than daggers. Nerie still wanted to get to know Astra if she could - she'd never had a sister before - but she thought it would be a difficult road.

You are better off without her, Soros told her upon hearing the thought.

Eventually neither Aldis nor Nerie could keep their eyes open any longer. Soft snores from the boy made Nerie reach for him.

Do not wake him. I will take him back to his rooms. He sleeps with me quite often so it will not be out of place, Soros warned.

Nerie gently slid down the dragon's hard scales, her feet landing on the smooth rocks that created the paving in the garden.

Good night, little ones, Eras told them as Nerie and Kiriga shut the door to their room.

Good night, papa! Kiriga responded with as much enthusiasm as she could muster, her little head drooping.

They both crawled onto the large pillow and quickly fell into a deep sleep.

CHAPTER TWENTY-ONE

Nerie

Karina woke Nerie and Kiriga the following morning with breakfast ready. They bathed again this morning, but unlike yesterday, kept their antics to a minimum. Kiriga bathed first so that she could air dry while Nerie cleaned herself.

Nerie's closet had been filled overnight with a larger choice of yellow and gold dresses. She chose a light lemon-yellow dress and a pair of dark gold slippers - walking on the marble floors the day before had chilled her feet.

After dressing, she paced the sitting room waiting for Queen Alaena to arrive. She kept running her palms down her thighs as she paced. She'd spent a good bit of the morning thinking about how to apologize to the queen, since Alaena had said that royalty didn't apologize.

A knock at the door announced the queen's arrival, and Nerie bowed to her as she entered.

Alaena's first words were more criticism.

"Nerie. You do not need to bow to me, only to Soren when in public. You are bowing far too low, even for that."

Nerie stood straight, her cheeks a light pink. Before Alaena could say anything else, Nerie spoke.

"Your majesty. I am formally apologizing for my behavior yesterday. Please continue to teach me however you see fit."

Her voice was rigid, and her eyes strayed away from the

queen's.

"I told you yesterday that royalty does not apologize. However, if you *are* going to do so, it needs to be sincere. Your tone and gaze tell me otherwise." Alaena's voice was curt.

She walked to the same couch she had sat on yesterday and resumed her position.

"However, I do intend to continue your education. Today's lessons will be in etiquette. Please, have a seat."

Nerie walked to the couch opposite Queen Alaena and threw herself down.

"Stand back up," Alaena announced, doing so herself. When Nerie was standing she said, "Now watch how I sit."

Alaena kept her back straight and lowered herself down like a floating feather. The silks of her dress were fluttering, but only enough so that they were out of the way when she sat. Her ankles were crossed and tucked back. Her shoulders were level and her head held high. To Nerie, she looked every bit the regal queen that she was.

"Your turn."

She gestured slightly to Nerie with her palm upturned.

Nerie tried.

She really did.

Her dress was too long, and she got her foot tangled in the hem. She ended up falling to the floor.

Alaena did not laugh. Or criticize.

Instead she simply said, "Again."

Over and over for the next several hours they practiced sitting, and then standing, and then walking. Nerie noticed that Alaena didn't truly criticize her. No, instead she pointed out issues that a princess should not have and worked to correct them.

As the afternoon wore on, Nerie was once again summoned for a late lunch with Soren. As she prepared to leave, Alaena came over to her.

"Princess. You will have your gowns and other apparel altered to fit you better. You tripped multiple times due to the excess length. I noticed it yesterday too. I will come later tomorrow so that the seamstress has time to take your measurements."

Alaena nodded and then left without so much as a goodbye.

Nerie looked down at her dress. It *was* a little baggy in some places and tight in others. She had never had much of a chest, but she had very athletic thighs and arms from years of sprinting through the streets and lifting heavy piles of books.

As Karina led her to the king's chambers, Nerie walked next to the woman rather than behind, trying to remember the route from the night before. Noticing her interest, Karina walked at a slower pace, letting Nerie take the lead as she wanted. She only became lost twice on the way.

Taking note from Alaena, Nerie did not bow to Soren today, instead she simply thanked him as he pulled out her chair for her.

"So, Nerie, what shall we talk about today?" Soren asked as they slowly worked their way through the light lunch.

"I would like to know more about taking care of Kiriga," she answered immediately.

At three days old, Nerie was quite sure that Kiriga had already grown about six inches in her shoulders and at least a foot in length from snout to the tip of her tail.

Soren smiled.

When he smiled, Nerie couldn't help but smile too. The way his eyes crinkled, and his teeth showed, lit up a room. The only word she could think of that described him was charismatic.

"Of course. Let's finish eating and we can see Ilex and Kiriga. We shall also ask if Soros and Eras would like to join us."

They finished the rest of their meal in equable silence, then walked to the courtyard.

Kiriga had curled up into a tight ball and Ilex was resting his chin on her back. Both had their eyes closed, and their scales glittered in the sunlight. It was late summer and Nerie could feel the heat rising off of the rocks that the dragons laid on.

Without raising her head, or even opening her eyes, Kiriga spoke to Nerie.

Doesn't the heat feel nice?

"Very," Nerie said aloud.

She didn't worry about what Soren would think, in fact, he was probably the only person in the world who understood what it was like. Glancing over at him, she saw that his face was scrunched in concentration. He must be speaking to Ilex.

She giggled a little, and Soren looked over at her.

"Sorry, Queen Alaena said I look just like you when I speak to Kiriga. This is the first time I've seen you speak to Ilex."

She flushed red as she explained.

"Oh, she's teased me more than once about it over the years."

His smile fell a little. Nerie felt compelled to apologize.

"I'm sorry if I've caused you trouble by Kiriga choosing me."

She knew it had to be hard, having a bastard child show up out of nowhere. Let alone one who was suddenly chosen as heir to the kingdom.

"Nerie," he started sternly, "you have caused no trouble. My liaison with your mother was my own decision. You are the result of my actions. Do not let my actions cause you to worry."

He nodded at the two resting dragons.

"They know your every thought and emotion. Kiriga would not have chosen you if you weren't what she needed. What the kingdom needs. They are Soros and Eras' gift to our people."

Eras joined the conversation, *We have seen what makes a good ruler, and what doesn't. We impart these traits to our children as they develop in the egg. They learn to speak before they are hatched, and we teach them more with feelings than words.*

He slowly climbed over the roof of the palace to the courtyard they were in. In the bright midday sunlight, his scales looked like fire. They glittered and gleamed as he moved, like fire dancing.

Soros will not be joining us today. She is too comfortable where she is now, he told them.

"Back to our lesson, Nerie. I heard you've been bathing Kiriga? That's good. The skin between her scales can grow… *things* if you don't bathe her regularly."

"How do you bathe Ilex? Who bathes the other dragons?"

They were very large, and she could see bath time taking an entire day eventually.

Soren laughed once again.

"Once they are old enough, they can bathe themselves in lakes. You should see Ilex scrub himself in the sand. Reminds me of a dog rolling in mud."

Excuse you, Ilex spoke to both of them, *I do* not *resemble a dog in any way.*

His voice was higher than Eras' but still much deeper than Kiriga's.

Nerie giggled again, and Soren laughed outright. The afternoon flew by as she learned about caring for Kiriga's scales and talons. She learned that dragons shed their scales in a manner similar to a bird, molting several times a year. Young dragons shed frequently as they outgrew their scales.

She also learned that shed dragon scales were collected for armor. Eras, Riya, and Galean produced a harder scale - while Soros and the rest of the dragons had softer scales, that while resistant to a blade strike, were not as hard, making them penetrable.

"What kind of scales will Kiriga have?" Nerie asked, looking at her small dragon.

She was so soft right now, they felt more like snake scales than anything else.

She will likely have thicker scales like myself, Eras answered.

Kiriga had gotten up at some point and was trying to climb up his side, her talons slipping on the firm surface. That surprised Nerie, as Kiriga's claws seemed to slip into stone like butter - her bathtub was an attestation to that.

She learned that sunlight was vital to their scale health as well, and that a diet of red meat with an occasional treat of fish provided the nutrients they needed to survive and grow healthily. Eras explained that dragons continued to grow their whole - exceptionally long - lives.

When she asked him how old he was, she only got a vague answer of a few hundred years. Old enough that she had to sit down because the sheer amount of time was hard for her to imagine.

Eventually, Karina politely let her know that it was nearing dinner time and asked if Nerie would like to dine with her mother again. She agreed and this time they ate in her mother's quarters. They spent several hours talking about how they missed their shop and how they were adjusting to palace life.

Nerie spent nearly an hour examining the tapestry depicting Kiriga's parents and siblings. Wyla had not spoken to her again, and she wouldn't be surprised if she didn't hear from the dragoness again for several years. Soon after, she and Kiriga returned to their rooms.

As they lay down to sleep - the bed once again forgotten - Nerie took the chance to cuddle the little dragonling's head. It was a perfect little wedge shape and she had little stumps above her eyes that would one day harden into defined horns.

They let their love for one another flow between them as they drifted off to sleep.

And so, a pattern was set. It was a routine easy for Nerie to follow, early mornings alone, late morning to early afternoon with the queen, late afternoon until dinner with the king, followed by dinner with her mother. Every few nights, Aldis would scale the roof and they would spend long hours talking beneath the stars.

CHAPTER TWENTY-TWO

Nerie

Following a routine allowed both Nerie and Kiriga to grow comfortable with their bond and with life in the palace. Knowing who they would see, where they needed to be, and how they needed to act, relieved the stress that had arisen in the first few days.

After nearly two weeks of living in the palace, Nerie was coming to enjoy it. It was still strange to have Karina as her silent shadow - and Kiriga as her not so silent one - but she was adapting.

Queen Alaena often said that a ruler has to be able to adapt and think on their feet. Many times during their sessions, Alaena would suddenly decide they needed to stroll the halls and speak to servants that she knew were having troubles. How she knew they were having issues was beyond Nerie as of yet, but she was learning how to help handle their problems. From offering support, to suggesting ideas on how to work around their problems. Alaena seemed to approve of her responses and afterwards would offer her own ideas and suggestions.

It was one such day, when Alaena was leading Nerie towards the kitchens, that an enraged scream came from behind them. The queen didn't so much as pause, but Nerie and Kiriga both stopped to look at the source.

Astra was standing there, her dark hair hanging loosely around her pale face. Her eyes were throwing daggers at her mother's back. Seeing Nerie, Astra advanced on her half-sister, fists balled.

"How dare you."

It was all that Astra could muster. Her voice trembled and her very being quaked.

"Come now, Nerie. We are expected elsewhere."

Alaena still didn't look back.

Another wordless scream issued from Astra, and Nerie thought the princess was going to slap her again. Taking a half step back, she bumped into Kiriga mid-chest. The young dragoness had been growing like a weed recently. She was nearly as large as a horse - her head nearly a foot above Nerie's. When Nerie collided with her, Kiriga growled, looking down at Astra.

Feelings were exchanged in the moment as Nerie was momentarily terrified of the older girl. Kiriga reassured Nerie that she would be protected. Overtones let Nerie know that the dragon detested Astra.

Instead of touching Nerie, Astra lunged past them to grab her mother. Alaena simply shrugged her daughter off and took another step away. A sob broke from Astra's throat as she attached herself to her mother's waist - much like a small child.

A slap rang through the empty hallway. Alaena was looking down at her eldest coolly.

"Astra. Get to your feet. You are acting reprehensible."

Alaena's voice was soft, but her eyes were hard.

"You stopped seeing me to teach *her*?" Astra wailed, tears cascading down her face. "You don't even *look* at me anymore. Do I really not mean anything to you after not being chosen by that stupid dragon?"

"Princess Astra of house Therius, remember yourself."

The queen's words were icy as she looked down at her daughter.

This caused something to snap in the princess. Her tears stopped and her eyes became glassy. Standing in a stiff, mechanical way, she slowly turned to Nerie. The anger was gone, but a deep, terrifying nothingness shone in her eyes. In the most formal bow that Nerie had seen, Astra prostrated herself before her.

"Princess Nerie." She straightened and continued, "I have forgotten how to behave myself. Of course. I am a princess of the house of Therius. Please, excuse me."

Astra bowed again, her dark hair falling in snarls around her face.

As she stood and turned to go, Nerie's heart raced. The Astra that had stood in front of her moments before was not the same Astra as the one now. Something had broken inside the older girl, and Nerie felt that it was for the worse.

Snake. Vile, disgusting snake, Kiriga hissed in her mind.

What just happened? Nerie feared the answer but waited for it anxiously.

Growling softly, Kiriga put herself between Nerie and the retreating Princess.

She wants you dead.

Oh.

Nerie wasn't sure what else to say. She had only met her half-sister twice before now, and she honestly had wanted to get to know her. It was understandable that Astra would be jealous, but to want her dead? That was quite the leap.

Alaena cleared her throat - pulling Nerie's attention away from her sister. She turned and followed the queen on her way to the kitchens. She couldn't help but glance back at Astra's now distant form. Determination gripped her, and she decided that she would try and extend an olive branch, so to speak, to Astra. She couldn't really want Nerie dead.

***

That evening, as she lay on Eras' wide arm waiting for Aldis and Soros to appear, she thought about the incident with Astra. All day she'd wished that she could do something, *anything,* to get her sister to like her.

Soros glided gracefully - with Aldis lying along her neck - into the large courtyard. Once she was settled, Nerie made her way over to the other dragon and quickly scaled up her side. Her ascent was aided by the fact that she no longer wore a skirt in the evening. At one point, she had complained to her brother about the distinct lack of pants available to her. The very next night, he had smuggled her as many pairs as he could sneak out of his laundry without drawing any attention.

"Nerie! How was your day?"

Aldis was as lively as ever. He constantly looked for different ways to make Nerie smile. He wanted to get to know her as well as be her friend. It was a relief to be able to spend time with the younger boy every few evenings. She wished that she could see him nightly, but Aldis was exhausted most nights. They still did not see each other around the palace. Aldis had explained to her that his rigorous training took up most of his day.

Now that he had not been chosen as the next king, Aldis had been put into training to become a knight. Eventually he would become the head of Soren's guard.

"It was alright, Aldis," she told him wearily.

"It doesn't sound like it was. What happened?" he asked as he reached out to hug her.

"Astra happened," she said with a weary moan. Aldis' face fell.

"Oh. Of course, she did," his normally cheerful voice was tight and pained. He had told Nerie how horrid Astra had been to him as a child.

"She threw herself at Alaena and was rebuked. Then she became extremely formal and excused herself to me. Kiriga said that she wants to *kill* me."

Nerie was playing with the edge of her shirt as she talked. The emptiness in Astra's eyes still haunted her.

"I mean, she hates me. She's tormented me my whole life. All she's ever wanted to be is queen. Now that's been taken away from her. Of course, she'd want to take it out on you. But to want to kill you? That's low, even for her."

Aldis was busy tracing his fingers along the swirls and whirls of Soros' purple scales. He glanced up to look at Nerie, then smiled his radiant smile. She couldn't help but be a little envious of him. He would've been a perfect king.

I chose you. You will be a perfect queen, Kiriga told her sternly.

I know, but he's so kind. I'm really glad to have him as a brother. Besides you, he's been the best part of finding out that I'm Soren's daughter.

He is kind. Too kind. People would have used him. Broken him.

Kiriga was probably right. Aldis was incapable of saying no. However, it didn't stop Nerie from doubting herself and thinking about the younger boy on their father's throne.

We will rule together. You will be a strong queen. I will be the best dragoness.

Kiriga preened, or she tried to, until Eras knocked her over gently with his large head.

She tumbled and hissed at him, and a great choking noise came from him. The first time Nerie had heard one of the dragons make the noise, she had thought they were in serious trouble. She'd then been informed that they were simply laughing. Now, the noise could cheer her even when in the foulest of moods.

Won't Nerie be a good queen? Kiriga asked Aldis.

The boy's eyes lit up and his smile widened. It wasn't the first time she'd spoken to him, but she didn't do it often.

"Of course, she will, dragoness."

He tried to bow to her from his lofty position, but nearly went cascading down Soros' side. Nerie managed to grab him at the last possible moment.

"Oh, she talked to me again, Nerie!"

His excitement radiated around him and Nerie felt herself smile too.

It was strange to realize that not everyone was held in high enough esteem for the dragons to speak to them.

"Of course, she did, Aldis. She would have chosen you, had I not been there," Nerie told him playfully, tousling his hair.

"But you were."

His eyes darkened momentarily, but then he lunged forward and wrapped his arms as far around Soros as they would go.

"But I have Soros. She's my best friend."

And you are mine little one, she told the boy softly.

She turned her neck so she could look at the two small humans playing on her back.

Nerie was happy for Aldis. He deserved the kingdom's love. Besides Kiriga, and her mother, Aldis was the one who she considered family. Soren still felt like the king, and Astra - well there would probably never be a relationship there. Queen Alaena was professional, but Nerie still didn't know if she was teaching her just because Soren had commanded her to.

What about us, little one? Eras asked her.

Oh you! You know that I love all of you with my very being. You great big lizard.

She stuck her tongue out at him, and he copied, his strange forked tongue darting through the air.

You could have lain on my back, he said with false malice.

She would've too - had it not been covered in spines. She giggled as she mentally compared it to sitting on a pin cushion.

As usual, Soros ended up carrying Aldis back to his rooms after he'd fallen asleep on her back. Nerie hugged Eras's large snout and headed inside with Kiriga. After trying for several minutes to get comfortable on the large pillow with the dragoness, she gave up. The night before she'd known that their time sleeping together was ending, as Kiriga now filled the whole pillow herself. While smooth scaled like her mother, her wings still contained sharp edges and she slept restlessly.

Covering the yellow dragoness with her favorite blanket, Nerie turned to look at her bed. It hadn't moved since the day she'd arrived, but somehow, she'd forgotten it existed.

As she crawled into the silken sheets Nerie felt as if she was melting. The bed was soft down and she sank deep into the feathers. The sheets slid over her skin in a liquid motion. It was hardly moments after the nightly exchange of love with Kiriga, and she was fast asleep.

CHAPTER TWENTY-THREE

Graith

Exiting the town seemed to take twice as long as entering. Maybe it was because Graith was eager to be away from the hordes of people. He couldn't wait to be back on his own with Zel. She teased him as he sat in a line that moved at a snail's pace to the gate. Once through the gate, he flicked Mero into motion, his little cart jostling along down the road at as fast a trot as the gelding could manage.

While he traveled, he bit his lip deep, in thought. When he could think no more on the subject, he spoke to Zel.

Zel, what did we actually learn from Lord Arish?

Not much. That the men who took my eggs have been here. That they are on the move. She paused, then added, *That he thinks they can be trusted - more than a peasant off the streets.*

Graith could feel her pacing from the way her mind raced. She was putting together pieces faster than he could.

They can't be far from here, he acted as if they'd just left. Maybe tonight you should fly around and see if you can locate the group or pick up tracks. At the very least, it could help us decide where to go.

She jumped on the idea.

I could do it now!

He felt her wings stretch open.

No! Panic swept him at the thought of her being seen. *We need to keep you under cover. Otherwise the town will hunt you. They already heard you last night.*

She closed her wings, but she was still poised, ready to launch herself from the ground.

I could just come get you and fly with you until we found them.

Even as she said it, she relaxed. She could sense how bad of an idea Graith thought it was.

Gently he said, *Zel. We don't know which way they went. And we can't leave poor Mero here by himself.*

Without a moment's hesitation she said, *I could eat him.*

Oh yeah? Eat the only horse that can stand your stench? Graith knew she was bluffing.

I don't smell! He could almost hear the huff in her voice.

Well, I'm not loading you up with my stuff like a lowly pack animal, and I need my stuff.

He wouldn't. Graith had too much respect for the dragoness than to use her as nothing more than a mule. And that included carrying himself.

She didn't respond, but he knew that he had hit a nerve.

She was a *dragon*.

Much too exalted to be used as a beast of burden.

The rest of the trip back to her, he could feel her anger and tension. He tried to think of calming things and project them at her. Slowly he felt her relax, and as he approached the clearing most of the anger had abated, but she was still quite tense.

Mero's ears perked up when he saw the dragoness and he lipped at her tail which was stretched across the clearing. She looked at him coolly then lifted her tail just enough to pet his ears with the still growing tip.

"See, you couldn't eat him even if you tried."

No, but I could *eat you.*

"Uh huh. I'm sure."

She growled at him, baring her long fangs. Each was as long as his hand plus a good bit, with the exception of the front canines which were much longer. Feeling childish, he stuck his tongue out at her. She imitated him. Her tongue was long and forked at the end.

For a dragon, he expected her maw to smell of rotting flesh. Instead, it had an almost sweet smell. Her tongue flicked out and licked him on the cheek. It was a dry lick, smooth like a dog's. The action took him by surprise - she hadn't licked him since they had first left the farm.

"All right, cut it out. You win. Let's rest for now, that way we can both be awake when you go out searching tonight."

All right. I didn't rest well without you last night anyway.

He laid down in the crook of her tail and she curled around him before covering her face and his whole body with her wing. The end of her tail curled protectively around his ankle and both of them drifted off into sleep.

***

Hours later, Graith woke as Zel was having a dream. He could tell from the way her tail and wings twitched and her teeth were bared in a snarl. He laid his hand against her side, intending to wake her up. Instead he was pulled inside her dream.

Zel was pacing up and down the largest hallway Graith had ever seen. She could have easily opened her wings fully and they wouldn't have touched either wall. The ceiling was also quite high, and even as he watched, a green dragon flew above her.

His attention was drawn back down to Zel when a growl emanated deep from within her chest. As he looked at her, he saw that she was glowing a vibrant blue, brighter than he remembered her ever being before. Scales formed patterns of dark and light, a few white scales here and there, giving her the appearance of the night sky. She was growling at the biggest dragon he had ever seen.

A red dragon towered over her. So large that his wings could have almost touched both walls.

I thought I told you to leave, Azelia.

The unspoken language of dragons was thunderous in Graith's head.

I thought you *also* said you loved me, Coale.

Her tail lashed, and Graith had to jump sideways to avoid its tumultuous movement.

I *did* love you Azelia. I'm just not ready to be a father.

Oh? And yet I'm ready to be a mother? This was a decision we made *together*.

It was all fun and games, dearest.

Do not call me that. You said we would have a life together.

Dragons lie, *Azelia*. Humans lie. Everyone *lies*. You need to learn that for yourself.

Zel let out a roar that shook the dust from the high rafters. The red dragon flexed his talons and stretched like a cat.

Are you about done? I have a date.

She lunged at him, but being so much smaller, he just let her tumble past. He jumped into the air and was flying away before she was even back on her feet. She roared again but did not give chase. Instead milky tears rolled from her great eyes.

Azelia. Come here.

Zel turned, and a black dragon whose wings did *touch both sides of the hall emerged from an archway. The dragon had a pale scar running down the left side of his face, the eye that had once been there was gone. The remaining eye was a bright gold and was looking at the much smaller blue dragon.*

Papa Cimmeris! *Zel said, walking to him,* I'm a fool.

Yes, my darling, but you're my fool.

The black dragon had pulled her closer with a tail that seemed to go on forever. He then tucked her under his wing, in just the same way Zel tucked Graith under her wing every night.

We're all fools at some point in our lives. How do you think I lost my favorite eye?

She giggled. It was a noise that Graith had never heard her make before, and one that didn't seem suited for a dragon. She stuck her head out from under his wing to look at where the missing eye should be.

I think you look quite dashing. Oh Papa. How am I going to tell Father?

Like the adult you chose to be little one.

He nuzzled her head.

The dream faded and Graith found himself looking into Zel's bright blue eye, it was nearly as large as his head.

You were not invited to watch that, her tone was acidic.

"I didn't mean to Zel. It kind of just happened when I touched you. You were twitching and snarling, so I tried to wake you up…" Graith said, even as he took a step back.

Well. The past is the past.

"How did your father take the news? Was that your grandfather?"

Her eyes narrowed as she looked at him.

How do you think it went? I'm here, am I not? And yes. My mother's father, Cimmeris. A black shadow dragon.

"What is a shadow dragon?"

Zel did not answer, instead she flung herself into the air. The resulting shock wave sent Graith tumbling to the ground.

I'll be back before sunrise. I'll let you know if I see or feel any signs of my eggs.

She was already gone from sight, but Graith told her, *You know, I'm not a young man. Falling down like that could hurt me.*

Zel just laughed at him and did a cartwheel in the sky before starting her search. She had decided to spiral out from Dunlaith.

CHAPTER TWENTY-FOUR

Graith

Graith, you might want to sit down, Zel said.

That was all the warning he got before *something* happened.

It was like he was suddenly in two places. Still standing in the small clearing with Mero, but also high above the ground. He could still see around himself, but he could also see somewhere else. His vision there was altered. Colors were brighter, shapes sharper. Even though it was a moonless night, he could see as well as if it were noon.

Is this how you see all the time? he asked.

That had to be what was going on, he had to be seeing what she was seeing.

Yes. Now, you really should sit. I'm about to fly faster.

His body sank to the ground, but he couldn't stop looking around.

Graith, let me control. Moving my head too much while I fly slows me down.

How are you doing this?

The same way I controlled your body before. But – opposite? - I guess. Before I wanted to be you. This time I wanted you to be me.

Graith could feel Zel's wings strain as she climbed high into the sky, then she stopped. For a moment, they were weightless. She turned in the air, her head pointing downward, and she plummeted. Her wings snapped open and she was sailing. As she looked to her left, they drifted that way, her tail working like a rudder in the sky.

They had already made two laps around Dunlaith and were speeding up, covering a larger distance in the same amount of time each lap.

Graith couldn't believe it. Knowing that he was safe on the ground, he was exhilarated by the speed. He was able to feel the way Zel's wings sliced through the air. He saw what she saw, felt what she felt.

They were on the fourth lap now and movement parallel to the main road heading north caught their attention. Zel flew overhead, silent. Graith, however, nearly yanked her head backwards for a second look.

Zel! That's the stable boy from the city. The one who took care of Mero.

What's he doing all the way out here? He is a child correct?

Yes.

Zel made another pass overhead. The boy was running away from the city, full tilt. As she flew back towards the city, they could see why. A small group of city guardsmen were chasing him on foot.

Zel. We must help him!

How?

Bring him to me!

Graith could feel the doubt in her mind as she dove at the boy. She scooped him up in her talons. The moment his feet left the ground, he let out a blood curdling scream.

Stop it! Zel yelled into the boy's mind.

Perhaps too 'loudly' because he fell unconscious. Perhaps he had simply fainted.

The boy's screams, however, had drawn the attention of the guards. At least one of them let out a terrified shriek of his own, signaling they had spotted Zel.

Graith. I'll be there soon. I'm going to fly away from them until they can't see me, then I'll double back, but I need to focus.

Graith was back in his own body in an instant. He

jumped to his feet, running to the cart to get a blanket from his travel packs.

Then he waited.

He had prepared a fire before sleeping, but with the guards alerted to Zel's presence, it would not be a good idea to light it.

He paced back and forth from the cart to the fire ring that he could just make out in the near total darkness.

How he wished he had Zel's vision all the time.

As the minutes dragged by, Graith strained his ears, listening for any sound of the guards or for Zel's wing beats in the air.

When she landed next to him, he jumped, for he had neither seen nor heard her until her back talons touched the ground. The front talons carefully laid the boy down. Graith picked him up and wrapped him in the blanket he'd been clutching the whole time.

Both the man and the dragoness stared at the boy, wondering if he was okay. He was breathing, normal deep breaths, but when Graith shook him he did not wake.

He must have been scared witless. What did you do to him?

Normally Graith would have asked aloud, but he was still paranoid that the guards were searching for Zel.

I think I yelled at him too loudly. He doesn't seem injured though. We should rest, I'll know when he wakes, and I will wake you too.

It turned out Zel didn't need to wake him. The boy woke with the sunrise.

Screaming.

Graith was awake in an instant, his hand over the boy's mouth.

"Shh now, lad. It's all right."

Recognition of Graith flashed in the boy's eyes, however, instead of calming him, the boy started to try to get away.

"Whoa now. I'm not trying to hurt you. I'll take my hand off your mouth if you promise not to scream. The guards are still out there."

Graith didn't actually know if the guards were still looking for the boy after seeing the dragon take off with him. Honestly, they probably thought he had been the dragon's midnight snack.

The boy nodded, and Graith removed his hand and let him go. He scrambled to his feet. After a few moments of the boy just looking between the man and dragon, Graith decided to speak.

"Now, lad. Zel here saw you running from the guards. What's going on?"

"What's going on?" Outraged, he looked at Graith. "*You.* You gave me that cursed gold piece which I was accused of stealing."

His fists clenched, and he glared at Graith. He sounded a lot more mature than Graith expected. When they had spoken briefly before at the inn, all they had talked about was Mero.

"Your pa didn't stand up for you?" Graith asked, horrified.

"My pa's been dead for three years. He ain't standing up for nobody."

Graith blinked in confusion.

"Oh, I assumed that the innkeeper was your father."

"Ol' Randy? He ain't me pa. Ain't Daisy's either."

Oh.

It made more sense why Randy kept Daisy around the place, even knowing she was sleeping with the customers. Actually, it was probably *because* she was sleeping with them.

So, they just assumed you had stolen it because you had it?

The lad's eyes went wide, and the color drained from his face.

As slowly as he could, he turned to face Zel.

He had forgotten about her in his rage at Graith. All his muscles tensed, and an ever so slight shifting of his feet was all the warning Graith got that the boy was about to run.

Zel, however, already knew.

She snaked her tail out and even as the boy took his first

step, he tripped, falling to the ground.

I am not going to hurt you!

Zel's eyes whirled, an anxious yellow. Blue and silver danced inside the yellow glow in fast, little circles as she looked at the boy. He looked back at her in shocked awe. Then his focus changed, and Graith could see him really examining her for the first time.

He saw more than the talons and saber-like teeth. Her hide had darkened into a warm sky blue at some point recently, and her scars on her chest and leg were a milky-white. Even the tip of her tail had grown at least a foot since she'd had it cut off.

Graith couldn't read the lad's mind like Zel, but he didn't need to. He could see that he thought she was beautiful.

Terrifying, but beautiful.

He says his name is Alix.

Graith was surprised. They must have been speaking privately. For just an instant he felt jealous, then he remembered that he'd been the only person that Zel had talked to in months.

If not longer.

She was probably bored of him. He at least had talked to people in Dunlaith. Before that he'd had Ralph and Sarah.

I am not bored of you. But yes, speaking to someone else is… refreshing.

"Alix. I never meant for you to get in trouble. Is there anything I can do? Go back to Dunlaith and explain?"

"And what? Go back to Randy? I don't think so. He's the one who accused me of stealing. Nah. I think it's time I leave Dunlaith anyways. I'm nearly a man."

Graith chuckled. "How old are you, lad?"

"I might be puny, but I'm fourteen. What'cha doin' travelin' with a dragon?"

He's helping me find my eggs.

"Your eggs? I saw eggs!" Alix became animated, talking with his hands, "I was up late cleaning the stable when a group of men came through town a while back."

"You did?"

"Yeah, they went to the Lord's keep, then left not even an hour later, but this time Sir Braylin was with them. They left through the North gate, so I figured they were headed to Kelna." He shrugged as if he wasn't sure what to say, "It's the only city that way."

Why would they go to Kelna?

Graith answered, as he had heard of the city before. "It's the fastest way to the capital. How long ago was that, Alix?"

"It was the night before you got to town, I think, so three days ago?"

We must go. Now.

Zel was on her feet, stamping back and forth. Graith got to his feet as well and started tacking Mero up.

"Can I go, too?"

Alix was looking at the cart, and more importantly, Graith.

Don't you have anyone who will miss you? Zel asked.

"Just ol' Randy when he realizes he has to muck the stalls."

Graith wasn't sure about the company, but Zel decided for him.

Get in. We need to go. They are only three days ahead of us.

Graith noted a tinge of desperation in her tone, but he didn't say anything. Instead he just rearranged the packs and made room for Alix in the back of the cart. The boy hopped up and settled himself between the two largest ones.

Even before he was comfortable, they were crashing through the underbrush back towards the main road.

CHAPTER TWENTY-FIVE

Nerie

The days seemed to fly by, and before Nerie realized, she had been in the palace for a little over a month. Kiriga's head now loomed above her own, her scales already darkening into a smooth-gold from the pale-yellow they'd once been. Nerie had improved both her posture and gait, and her clothes now fit her like a glove - much to Alaena's approval.

Since the incident with Astra in the hallway, she'd not seen her half-sister at all. Queen Alaena did not speak of either of her children while tutoring Nerie, nor did Nerie ask after them. She knew from Aldis's late night adventures that he was training to be a knight, and that he was going to have to go away soon. Part of his training with his mentor, Sir Camran, was to travel to the different major cities of Situra.

She wished that she could go along, as there was so much of the kingdom that she hadn't even known existed before her lessons with Alaena. Situra was a large country, bordered on the west by Lutesia and to the southwest a mountain range separated it from Etria, homeland of the dragons. Along the northern and eastern sides, the country was bordered by the ocean. The only port city was Alluvial - with trading between it and Tesia, capital of Lutesia, being heavily restricted.

***

As Nerie finished her lessons with Alaena for the day and prepared for her lunch with the king, Karina rushed back in, summoned away by Vizen, Soren's personal servant.

"Nerie! We must get you changed, right now." Karina was already in the closet looking for a new dress.

"What's going on?" Nerie asked, following the woman in. Even Alaena's attention had been caught and she hovered near the door waiting to hear what the maid had to say.

"The king has requested you attend an impromptu session of the Curia Regis - the country's council. Here now, you strip out of that and put this on," she said while pulling a golden velvet dress out of the wardrobe.

Doing as she was told, Nerie changed as quickly as she could. Once the dress was over her head, it was followed by ornate jewelry and a pair of satin slippers.

"Is all this really necessary, Karina?" Nerie asked, feeling as if she was being weighed down by each piece of metal.

"Yes. While unscheduled, the king said this is to be a full gathering of the Curia. His highness also said that the queen had told him that you were ready to sit in for your first council meeting."

Karina's face was flushed as she brushed strands of hair away from Nerie's face and tugged on her gown, making it pool correctly at her feet. Nerie glanced over her shoulder in surprise at Alaena's judgment, but the woman had already left the quarters.

Once Karina was satisfied with Nerie's appearance, they were out the door. While Nerie had become quite accustomed to the halls of the palace, Karina led the way to the council hall, a place Nerie had only visited on a brief tour.

Even though she felt as if she was late, Nerie made sure not to hustle after Karina. One of Alaena's lessons had been that royalty is never late, everyone else is simply early. She had also learned there was no point in arriving out of breath and red faced. She was royalty after all and had an appearance to maintain.

Sounds could be heard echoing down the hallway as they approached, for the doors to the hall the Curia met in were open and people were filing into the room. Nerie was surprised, however, when Karina motioned to follow her down a small side hallway rather than the main entrance. This hallway ended abruptly at a door, which Karina opened, bowing Nerie inside.

Through the door lay an ornate room with a long table filling most of the interior space. Chairs lined either side, and a golden half throne stood at the head of the table. Along the walls hung charts and maps of the kingdom, as well as ornamental flags and pennants. A fireplace took up the wall opposite the throne. Standing before the flames was King Soren, who had been waiting on Nerie.

"Welcome Nerie. I see Karina was able to get you ready for the Curia Regis."

He smiled, as usual Nerie couldn't help but smile back.

"What is this room?" she asked, stepping further inside, looking closely at a large detailed map with colored pins decorating the various cities.

"This is the room for the Curia Minima - a subgroup of the full Curia Regis. I believe that Alaena has told you about how small groups of lords and ladies are responsible for different projects? Monthly, those groups meet with me here to discuss their ideas and to have funds approved from the treasury. Also, there is an entrance for our use into the Curia Regis' hall. Gives us the appearance of stateliness, or so that's what my father told me."

Soren motioned to another door that Nerie hadn't seen before on the far wall, which the noise of the hall could be heard through. Karina had left through the door that she and Nerie had entered through. While they waited for some sign, Soren spent a few minutes telling her about the items that decorated the room.

A knock from the hall door cut him off, however, and he motioned for Nerie to join him in standing before it.

"Karina or Vizen will open the door momentarily, the knock was just to signal to us that all the Curia Regis members have arrived and are ready for our entrance."

Soren smiled at Nerie with a wink. While she smiled back, she still felt a pang of anxiety about stepping through the door. The last time she had been in the public eye had been the night that Kiriga had hatched.

You will do fine, Kiriga said, her voice echoing in Nerie's mind.

I wish you were here, Nerie said as she let her anxiety bleed into the dragon.

We both know that I am getting too large to follow you around any longer. Plus, Ilex and I are using the time to bond. He's such an interesting big brother.

Someday you'll have to go meet your other brothers and sisters.

We will meet them when the time is right, Nerie. Together. However, I do talk to them on occasion.

Oh? That was something Nerie hadn't known about her young dragoness.

From time to time. They like me. Nerie could feel Kiriga preen at the statement.

Everyone likes you. But I love you, Nerie told her.

You will do fine. Vizen is about to open the door for you.

Sure enough, a heartbeat later, the door was pulled open and Soren motioned for Nerie to step into the hall before him. It took all her willpower - and not just a little bit of love from Kiriga - for Nerie to refrain from freezing before the gathered Curia Regis. So many people were in the hall, that as they stood, shifting and moving, that it was like looking upon a room full of jewels. Every shade of the rainbow seemed to be present before them, as people decorated in silks, satins, jewels, and feathers stood waiting.

Vizen's deep voice boomed across the crowded space, announcing them, "Her royal highness, heir apparent, Crown Princess Nerie. His royal highness, King Soren."

Two large thrones sat on a dais above the Curia, and Nerie and Soren sat before the waiting crowd. Nerie's heart raced as she took the practiced seat, sitting on the edge of the cushion, her back straight, her shoulders back. Managing that feat in a manner that Alaena would be proud of. Nerie wanted to relax but she couldn't. Not when every eye in the hall was on her, many of them wide. She wished that she could turn invisible, but instead, looked over at Soren.

He was relaxed, his elbows on his knees, as he leaned forward looking at his citizens.

"So, who has called a meeting of the full Curia Regis?" he asked, his voice soft, but instantly silencing the large room.

Nerie blanched. She had known this was not a regularly scheduled meeting of the Curia, but she hadn't known that Soren had not been the one to call it.

When no one spoke up, he asked again.

"No one is going to claim calling a full meeting of the Curia? A right that is normally reserved for *me* - the king - to exercise?"

A few hushed whispers floated across the room, but again no one spoke up. Nerie expected Soren to be annoyed, but instead, his smile widened, and he laughed. All she could do was keep her mouth closed, not gaping like she would have only a month ago.

"You all obviously gathered here for a reason. Dressed up in your best finery. Here at an appointed time. Well here I am, ready to listen to whatever you felt was so urgent that it needed to be addressed today."

Nerie was in awe at how calm he was. She also hadn't known that he should have been the one to call the council meeting. More whispers fluttered around the room and many people's attention returned to her. It made her uneasy, but she did her best to stay calm, focusing on Soren rather than the crowd.

Finally, a gaudy lord pushed his way to the front. He was wearing a bright red outfit that clashed horribly with his reddened face, and every one of his fingers was covered in large, jeweled rings. The rings were large enough that Nerie wondered if he could use his hands at all.

"Ah, Lord Narssus. Were you the one to call the meeting of the Curia?" Soren asked, looking at the man.

"My King, it was not I. However, I *do* know the reason for the meeting."

Narssus's voice sounded like someone with a severe cold

and an unusually high-pitched voice mixed together. It made Nerie's skin crawl.

"Oh? And what might that be?"

Soren straightened slightly, and the man took a full step back.

"Her."

Narssus pointed to Nerie.

"Many of us don't think she's your rightful heir. We don't know her. *You* don't know her. Princess Astra and Prince Aldis are your rightful heirs. She's -"

"That is *enough*, Narssus."

Soren's smile was gone and his voice a tight whisper.

Narssus seemed to choke on his words as he tried to stop them from continuing.

Soren stood, and the court collectively took a step back. Nerie remained seated. As Narssus had spoken, the blood had drained out of her face. All these people. The nobles, the knights, and the lords and ladies of the realm - all here in protest of her as their next queen.

Princess Nerie was chosen by the dragoness Kiriga as the next ruler of Situra. We shall ensure she becomes Queen, Eras' deep voice echoed through the minds of the people in the hall.

Many of the people dropped to their knees, the force of his voice overpowering their minds. Narssus was one such person. A few cried out in pain.

"Kiriga, daughter of Soros and Eras, has *Chosen* Nerie. As I, and my forefathers before me, was *Chosen*. Who are any of you to deny our divine right to rule?" Soren asked the council.

Many were whimpering apologies, but not all. Some looked at Nerie with malice. She made eye contact with each of those people - staring back at them - but inside, she was shaking.

"You will stand now and renew your fealty to myself and pledge it to Princess Nerie. Starting with you, Narssus."

The nobleman, pale in the face, walked forward and knelt before Nerie and the now reseated Soren.

"Crown Princess Nerie, Your Highness King Soren, I, Lord Narssus of house Emmed swear on my life and the life of my house that I shall be faithful to my lord, never cause him harm and will observe my homage to him completely, against all persons, in good faith and without deceit."

While he pledged himself to Soren and Nerie, the rest of the lords and ladies slowly formed a line. One after another, they repeated those words, pledging themselves to their monarch and princess.

Some couldn't get the words out fast enough, while others seemed to choke on the syllables. Nerie could feel heat rise up her neck as she sat stiffly waiting for this display of loyalty to end. Most of these people didn't mean the words they uttered, and it was obvious to her, Soren, and the dragons - who she could feel watching.

Only a few people really stood out to her. Whether it was because of their earnestness in their pledge, or their utter lack of sincerity. One of the former was Lord Sylas of house Therius, who was a perfect likeness of King Soren. Another was Lady Janai of house Callam. She was elegance incarnate to Nerie's untrained eyes.

However, more than one noble stood out for the opposite reasons. Narssus, for his initial outburst. A Lord Brodin of house Mazen made the hair on the back of her neck stand on end. While the words flowed gracefully out of his mouth, his eyes told a different story. She felt she couldn't look away fast enough. A Lady Ceilia of house Devan was one of the ones who'd had to force each word from her mouth.

Most of the lords and ladies, however, didn't stand out. Of the nearly fifty that pledged themselves to her, most were forgotten moments after their pledge. Nerie knew Queen Alaena would not be pleased with her, but Nerie figured she had plenty of time to learn their names and families.

After everyone had sworn their fealty, Soren stood once again. Nerie was awed at how he was able to command the room. As his slender frame rose from the throne, the attention of all the nobles in the hall was upon him.

"As you have all gathered for the meeting of the Curia

Regis, prepare yourselves to give me complete updates on each of your Curia Minima tasks and sessions."

He turned away, heading to the door that Vizen once again pulled open for him.

Nerie, while conscious of her effort to stand in the most ladylike fashion she could muster, followed. She arrived at the door a fraction of a moment after Lord Sylas. However, seeing her, he bowed her through the entryway. Vizen shut the door as Lord Sylas entered the room.

"Soren, brother, it's so good to see you." Sylas said.

He knelt before Soren - who immediately motioned for him to stand and embraced him.

"Nerie, I would like you to meet your uncle, Sylas. My younger brother," Soren told her.

Sylas turned and bowed before Nerie, and she flushed red. She'd known Soren had a brother, but seeing him in person was a strange disconnect. Her uncle bowing to her felt wrong.

"It's a pleasure to make your acquaintance, Lord Sylas," she told him formally.

"Soren, you've let Alaena spend too much time with the girl," Sylas complained to his brother. "Please Nerie, call me Uncle Sylas."

"It's nice to meet you Uncle Sylas."

She smiled. He had the same crooked smile and crow's feet at his eyes as his brother, and he was currently smiling at her.

"The pleasure is mine, dear niece."

He kissed her hand before turning to Soren.

"You didn't call the meeting of the Curia, brother?"

"No, I did not." Soren's face was serious.

"The summons I received were in your name, with *your* seal," Sylas told him.

"Interesting, I wonder if they all had my seal?"

"I would imagine most of them did - if not all. Why did you allow the Curia to meet if you didn't call it into session?" Sylas asked, confused.

"And waste everyone's time? While most of them have

been in the capital since the hatching, many, like yourself, had to travel quite far to get here. In the meantime, Ilex and I are going to search for the one who called the Curia. Also, we might as well get some actual work done while everyone is here." Soren shrugged, but looked uneasy.

"I do apologize for missing the hatching. There was that strange disturbance at the border. When Wyla informed me that Nerie had been chosen it was more than a little shocking."

"Well, things shall work out the way that should be." Soren turned to Nerie, "I would like you to join me in the Curia Minima sessions. You'll learn hands-on firsthand how the kingdom functions. Also, your appearance will possibly help Ilex and I gauge who is behind calling the Curia Regis."

"Of course, Your Highness."

She did a slight curtsy.

"Nerie, it's all right to call me Soren in front of my brother," Soren laughed.

***

As the day continued, small groups of five to eight nobles entered the chamber one group at a time. Many attendees seemed surprised at Nerie's presence, but she spent her time sitting quietly at the far end of the table. Vizen had left briefly and when he returned, he and another servant were carrying a large ornate chair for her to sit in. Wine was served to each group, as well as small delicacies, which were snacked upon as each group discussed their projects with the king.

One group was working on restoring older bridges throughout the kingdom, while another was responsible for collecting taxes and tithes before the harvesting season. Each group seemed to lead an important task for the kingdom, and Nerie was able to see how Soren managed the kingdom. It seemed to her like a lot of delegating and remembering what each group was doing.

She noticed more than once that Soren had a small notebook in which he kept scribbling, but she didn't know if the notes were about the groups or what he was discussing with Ilex. After the sixth group met, her stomach rumbled, and she flushed with embarrassment. The small snacks hadn't cut it. She had missed her regular lunch with Soren, and it was well past the time she normally ate with her mother.

The noise seemed to remind Soren that no one had eaten yet, and a break was called. The groups were dismissed for the day, and Nerie learned that each Lord had an estate in the city. As large as the palace was, it couldn't accommodate them all.

Sylas was invited to stay and eat with them. Nerie, Sylas, and Soren enjoyed a quiet meal together, with Sylas telling Nerie about his children, who were near her age. Learning repeatedly that her family was much larger than just her mother made her head spin, but Nerie enthusiastically told Sylas that she would love to meet her cousins in the near future.

He told her that she was welcome in Cian, which was the town that most closely bordered Lutesia, their neighboring country. Wyla, the eldest of Soros and Eras' children resided there. When Nerie asked why Sylas had chosen to live so far from the capital, he whispered in her ear conspiratorially, telling her it was for love, then laughing.

His wife's family had ruled over Cian since it was founded, and she - as an only child - refused to leave and move to the capital with him. It had left him with only one option, to leave Roria himself and live in Cian with Valria, his wife.

CHAPTER TWENTY-SIX

Nerie

Sylas had promised to stay in Roria for the following week, to get to know his niece better. Nerie was more than a little excited and Kiriga couldn't help but tease her a bit.

You're so happy to have met Sylas. Why?

You know why, silly. My whole life, it's just been me and Mom. So far, my new family has been amazing. Well, except Astra, but she's a different story.

Astra can be bitten by a snake for all I care.

I don't like her, but you shouldn't say such things, Kiriga.

You would too, if you had felt her mind last time she saw you.

The pair were in the courtyard outside of Nerie's rooms. Kiriga was starting to have trouble with doors being too small, so now she spent the majority of the time outside.

Nerie missed the constant physical companionship, however, not a moment passed when Kiriga wasn't present in her mind. Kiriga nuzzled Nerie gently with her now large snout.

Nerie had been a little surprised to find that the dragoness had not had any awkward periods of growth. Never was her tail too long or her wings too big. While constantly getting bigger, her proportions were staying nearly constant. Only the fact that she was towering over Nerie and slowly closing the gap in size with Ilex betrayed that she was indeed growing at all.

Aldis is coming, Kiriga told her.

Kiriga swung her head in the direction of his rooms. Soros was already making her way over the low rooftops - Aldis astride her wide back. Eras was absent today, but he showed Nerie an image of himself laying in the clear waters of the nearby lake.

Soros had barely stepped into the courtyards when Aldis let himself slip down her shoulder. Running to Nerie the moment his feet hit the ground, she saw that he was sobbing.

"What's wrong, Aldis?" Nerie asked, even as he ran into her arms.

As she wrapped him in a hug and Kiriga wrapped her tail around the pair, Nerie was unable to make out a cohesive sentence from his garbled words.

Kiriga however - having just laid down around them - sat up and positioned herself around them protectively. She was hissing slightly, her eyes whirling to an angry orange.

He says he's going to be taken away, Kiriga said, swinging her head around looking for the possible prince-napper.

"What? Where? *Who* is taking you?" Nerie asked, looking down at her young brother.

Her heart raced at the thought of him leaving. Even though she had known him for such a short time, her love for him was as complex and full as it was for her mother or Kiriga. Being his sister was more fulfilling than being a princess by far.

More mumbled words, but this time Soros translated.

He is being taken on a tour of Situra by Sir Camran. They will be gone for the larger part of two years.

"But why now?" Nerie's eyes quickly moistened and tears began to roll down her cheeks.

Soros curled her massive body around the three of them, mirroring Kiriga's pose.

Aldis is to be a Royal Knight one day. One of your most loyal protectors - if not the most loyal of them. His training must start now.

Soros was nearly snipping her words off as she spoke,

but Nerie was quite sure the elder dragoness was just as distraught as Nerie that the boy was leaving. They were nearly inseparable.

Will you go with him? Nerie asked Soros.

No. My place is here in the capital with Eras, Ilex, and Kiriga. Our duty is to you and Soren.

Nerie caught a glimpse of the aura that the purple dragon was emitting. Her sorrow at being unable to stay with Aldis was overwhelming.

"When do you leave?" Nerie asked Aldis through her tears.

He had soaked her shoulder with his tears. He dug his face into the wet fabric, wiping his running nose to try and manage an intelligible reply.

"Tomorrow."

Nerie felt her heart break a little bit. Who was she going to talk to when she had a difficult day? Who was going to sneak her pants when they inevitably disappeared after laundry? Kiriga might be her entire world, but Aldis had become her rock in the sea that was palace life.

With nothing more to say or ask, the two simply held one another crying. Eventually they cried themselves to sleep, surrounded by the two dragons.

***

It was night when Soros gently woke them both with her mind. She urged Aldis to climb onto her back and Nerie to go inside to her bed. Winter was approaching, and sleeping outside, even with Kiriga's heat, wasn't advisable.

The following morning, Nerie woke melancholic - she hadn't even said goodbye to Aldis last night after they had been awoken. Uninterested in her normal routine, she simply pulled her hair back with a ribbon and dressed in the least glamorous gown she could find in her oversized closet. When Karina brought her breakfast, she picked at it, uninterested in eating.

By the time Queen Alaena arrived, she was apathetic.

"What's wrong? You haven't bathed or dressed well. You have tripped on your skirt five times in the last quarter hour,"

Alaena said, exasperated.

Nerie looked at her with listless eyes, tears brimming, threatening to fall.

"Aldis is leaving."

Alaena, already sitting straight, sat up straighter - if that was possible.

"Of course, he is. He was not chosen to ascend to the throne, so he will take up the next highest role of honor available to him."

The tears started rolling slowly down Nerie's cheeks.

"Why can't he just be a lord, like Uncle Sylas?"

Alaena's expression softened slightly.

"A royal knight is an esteemed position - you should be honored that he has been chosen for this role."

"I am. I just don't understand why he has to leave. Why now?"

"It is required of all knights during their training. He will start off as Sir Camran's page and eventually will become his squire and then eventually he will be knighted himself."

Alaena looked weary even as she spoke, like she was listing off her own reasons to accept his journey.

"He has many years of understudy before him. There is much training needed before he is ready for the distinct roles he is to fill in both court and as a guardian to the throne."

Alaena pushed a lock of dark hair behind her ear, gently laying her hand upon her lap. Even sad, she was the pinnacle of ladyship.

"Now, go bathe. Take time to compose yourself. After the lunch hour, there will be a formal ceremony seeing him and Camran off. You are expected to be there, and to conduct yourself in a manner appropriate for the Crown Princess."

Nerie did so.

As she exited the large bathing room, Karina was standing next to the queen, holding a new formal gown and accessories.

It was one thing to have to attend, but Nerie did not want to wear clothing that made her look happy in any fashion. However, one look from Queen Alaena and she was slipping on the dress without a word.

They practiced sitting and standing while they waited for lunch. Karina served both of them in Nerie's quarters. They ate in silence, Alaena not commenting on any of Nerie's bad table manners, too lost in her own thoughts. Alaena was effectively losing her only son, her baby, today. Nerie doubted that Alaena was as accepting of the situation as she seemed.

Finally, they made their way down to the formal gathering hall. Nerie and Alaena were greeted with reverent bows as they joined King Soren and Lord Sylas on the raised dais. Many of the lords and ladies that Nerie had met the day before were in attendance. Another display of silks and jewels. She still didn't understand the appeal of such gaudiness.

Across the hall from the dais stood a set of large golden, double doors. Vizen stood there, and at the king's nod, opened the door. A man who looked vaguely familiar walked with Aldis towards the dais. The crowd parted like a wave, slowly moving back to where they had been standing moments before as both Sir Camran - for that's who it had to be - and Aldis passed.

As the duo stood before the waiting royalty, the courtesans grew quiet. Nerie could now clearly see Aldis's face, and while puffy from a night of crying, his eyes were currently clear of tears. His eyes darted first to her face, then to Queen Alaena's.

Ah, Nerie thought. *Alaena's training is so ingrained into him, that he can't cry in front of the nobles even if he wants to.*

"Your Majesties, Princess, your Lordship," Camran started, bowing formally to each of them before continuing, "I'm honored that you have graced me with the task of training Prince Aldis to one day become a Royal Knight."

"You have proven yourself time and again, Sir Camran," Soren said.

Nerie didn't really hear the rest of what was said. It seemed like a bunch of formal nonsense, she was more interested in the man that stood before her. The one taking Aldis away from her.

Camran looked, for lack of a better term - plain. He had short dark hair that was speckled with silver. A matching beard adorned his neither heavy nor thin face. His armor was the same as the other royal knights stationed around the room. Perhaps his shirt was of a finer quality, but it was hard for her inexperienced eye to tell.

"- as vice-captain of the guard, I do so pledge with my life to protect Prince Aldis."

Nerie's attention was finally pulled back to the proceedings at hand. Applause filled the room. Camran and Aldis turned and headed for the now open exit. Soren nodded for Nerie and the other royals to follow. Then, as more of a herd than a group, the noble lords and ladies followed the royals out the door.

They finished their procession in the largest courtyard, whose gates opened out to the city below. Two white horses, with tassels hanging from their reins and bells attached to their tails waited, along with a small regiment of men and a wagon-full of supplies.

Aldis and Camran mounted the horses. The jingle of the bells was cheerful, and the nobles cheered and waved their prince away. Only Nerie, Alaena, and Soren were not smiling as the boy and his mentor prepared to leave the palace.

As Camran took lead of the small train of men and animals, Aldis turned back to the crowd. Nerie could see the tears brimming in his eyes, waiting to fall down his pale cheeks. A glance at Alaena and a firm blink or two kept them at bay. Nerie could feel tears of her own prickle her eyes but if Aldis could hold his tears back, so could she.

Two servants that Nerie didn't recognize slowly lifted the large bar holding the outer gate shut. With a low moan, the doors swung open. More jingling, as Camran and Aldis rode their horses to the head of the caravan, signaled an increase in volume from the nobles.

One last look backwards and then they were leaving.

As Aldis's horse stepped through the gate, Soros

launched herself into the air, trumpeting her distress. From where she stood, Nerie saw a brief ray of light illuminate Aldis' face, shining off the tears now streaking down his cheeks.

And then the pomp and circumstance was over.

Soros continued wheeling in the sky as the group retreated. Her grief was potent to Nerie. Eras was still absent - noticeably at this point - and Ilex and Kiriga sat on opposing sides of the gate, watching their mother fly through the air.

The nobles were piling back inside, assuming - not incorrectly - that there would be a feast after such a gathering.

Nerie felt drained. Her one faithful friend and ally in the palace was gone. Kiriga turned to look at Nerie from her lofty position, but she didn't say anything. She was going to miss the young boy too.

***

In the days that followed, the palace was eerily silent to Nerie's ears. No clashing of swords, or giggles from down a long corridor. It was like the livelihood that came with children was suddenly gone.

Nerie hated it.

CHAPTER TWENTY-SEVEN

Graith

The cart had broken out onto the road after only a few minutes. Alix had directed them onto the road north, and they were off. Zel ghosted along parallel to them and the road, keeping to the cover of the trees.

Then there was silence. Mero's hoof-beats a sharp staccato on the paved road.

Graith was rather impressed by the young boy's silence. Perhaps it was his anger over the coin, which, if Graith remembered correctly, he'd told the boy to hide away.

A slight clinking of jarred food and rasping of fabric being pushed aside let him know the boy was going through his supplies. He didn't say anything about it, as it was unlikely the boy was going to grab it and run.

That kept Alix occupied for about an hour.

The slight clink of metal on metal told Graith that he'd found the swords. He expected questions then, but they never came.

"I need to take a leak."

That wasn't at all what Graith had been expecting the boy to say when he finally decided to speak, but he pulled the cart off to one side and Alix made a quick dash to the underbrush. Graith used the chance to stretch his old bones and to dig out a snack.

We don't have time for this! Zel's irritated voice rang through his head.

We are traveling as fast as Mero can go. The boy needed to stop. He didn't know what to expect. You *were the one who invited him along.*

He might know things that we need. He can at least recognize the men accompanying my eggs.

I'm not saying you're wrong, you just need to be patient when he needs to stop.

She didn't respond, but embarrassment and shame colored her mind. Alix reemerged and hopped back into the cart. Seeing Graith's food, he reached in and pulled out a loaf of bread for himself. The cart was moving before he had brought the first bite to his mouth.

Graith was able to eat one-handed, as Mero really didn't need much guidance. He chewed, thinking about what to ask the boy. Zel might be able to read his mind and know that she could trust him, but Graith couldn't. He wanted to know more about their young companion.

Graith was still thinking about what to ask when Alix spoke first.

"So, how'd Zel's eggs get taken? How'd you meet her? *Why* didn't you kill her? Are there more dragons?"

A chuckle echoed in Graith's mind, then the aching silence of being alone. *Oh great,* he thought, Zel was going to leave him to answer these questions by himself.

"Well, uh, it's a long story…"

"We have the time. It's a week's ride to Kelna, and that's nonstop,"

"Have you been there before?"

Alix looked over his shoulder at Graith, "Well, no. But travelers complain a lot when they first arrive at the inn. How about this. You answer one of my questions, and I'll answer one of yours! It can be a game!"

"All right then. Now, where do you want me to start? Your first question or the beginning?"

"Are they not the same?"

"No," Graith said, scratching his growing beard. "They are not."

"Well, any good story starts at the beginning."

"Now, Me and Zel, we met a little more than a month ago. She was bleeding out in my barn, you see - I'm a wheat farmer by trade. Anyway, I discovered her one morning, and I did my best to stitch her up. She'd been attacked by men sent by Lord Arish to hunt her. Before she'd even healed fully, we were out on our way back to her cave."

Graith took a sip of water from his canteen, taking the chance to glance back at the boy. Alix was short for his age, with straw blond hair and covered in dust and dirt. His ribs showed through his thin tunic, and he had finished his bread long before Graith.

"Now, what's your story?"

"Aw, but you were getting to a good part! I could tell!" His voice was still high pitched with youth, not cracking where an older boy's would have during the whine.

"Hey now, this was your game. I'm just playing by your rules!" Graith chuckled when the boy's mouth fell open in indignation.

"I am - was - a stable boy."

"Uh-huh. I want to know stuff about you I don't already know."

"Well, not much to tell. Ma died in childbirth. Pa died a few years later, drank himself to death."

Alix shrugged, feigning disinterest in his own life.

"I suppose that's good enough for this next bit."

Graith winked at Alix, who climbed over the back of the cart onto the driver's bench with Graith.

"So, Zel and I reached her cave to discover her eggs were gone. Two groups had left, one had one egg, the other had the rest. Zel discovered the lone egg group, but when she approached, they killed the egg. Smashed it open."

The blood drained from the boy's face as he listened. His breath caught in his throat as he tried to ask, "What... What happened?"

"She killed them. All of them, before I could stop her."

"I wish I was strong like Zel. I had a dog, he was just a mutt. Called him Rex. He was my only friend. Some boys beat me and choked him. I would have killed them if I could have."

He held out his arm and Graith could see a pale scar running from his wrist to his elbow, and the arm was slightly crooked.

"Took me a long time to heal from this. They broke it so bad that a fever nearly killed me."

"You can't come back from killing, boy. That's a hard lesson that Zel is learning, even if she won't admit it."

They rode along together in silence for a bit. Alix thinking over the advice, and Graith wondering what kind of life this boy had lived. It hadn't been an easy one, that he was sure about.

Alix finally broke the silence, "So, she killed them. Then what?"

"We went home to my farm. I had stuff that I needed, supplies that we didn't need for the short trip. Well I don't think I'll ever be going back. Gave the farm to a good friend. My only friend. Then we headed straight to Dunlaith. Met you, talked to Lord Arish, got this lovely black eye. We were looking for clues when we found you running."

"You mean, when Zel found me?"

"Well, she was letting me ride along."

"On her back?! Can I fly with her?" Alix twisted in his seat, trying to look for Zel among the trees.

"Easy, lad. No, she did this mind thing, where I could see through her eyes. Feel her body. It was strange. Disorienting. I'm not sure I'm looking forward to doing it again."

"Huh. Hard to believe that I thought she was a monster last night. She seems pretty nice."

Graith was looking at Alix, as it was his turn again.

"Oh, what else is there? Ol' man Randy took me in. Already had Daisy. It was a clean and warm place to sleep. He gave me food sometimes. Knights and merchants all talked about their secrets when I was around, mostly because they didn't notice me. Then you came. With your giant horse, and your too much money."

He rolled his eyes, but he was already past being mad at

Graith. Now that he was in the front seat, he was looking around. Graith was surprised at his interest in their surroundings.

Zel was suddenly back, present in his mind.

You do know he's never left Dunlaith before? That's why he's so interested in everything, she said.

You've been quiet, Graith said.

You wanted to get to know the boy - I had already learned it all. No point in listening in.

Yet you show back up, just as we finish talking.

I didn't leave you completely *alone,* she huffed.

The rest of the day passed in companionable silence. They camped for the night well after the moon had set, not bothering to hide in the underbrush. Zel crawled out, and Graith and Alix each crawled under a wing to sleep. She woke them at false dawn, and then they were back on the road.

If the men with the eggs were going to make this trip in a week, their little group would have to do it in days.

CHAPTER TWENTY-EIGHT

Graith

After the third day of travel, they stopped late in the night. Zel started a fire for them, and they got ready to sleep. Alix was sitting on the opposite side of the fire from Zel, staring at her intently.

"What's up lad?" Graith asked, while glancing at Zel. "Her color is a bit different from before, if that's what you're wondering."

She was paling again and Graith was worried about her. Hearing his thought, she rebuffed it gently, however, with not nearly as much liveliness as normal. His lips turned downward in a frown, worried.

Alix shook his head. "No, not that..."

He got up and walked over to Zel. Then around her. Graith could see the top of the boy's head as he walked on her far side.

"Is she smaller than she was last night?"

Graith stood, stepped back, and really looked at Zel. She *was* notably smaller than normal. Small enough that he could see over her with ease as he stood. He frowned.

"Zel, how long have you been changing sizes?" Graith asked, confused.

As long as you have known me. I'm just having a small day, Graith. Some days I have big days.

"Can you change your size on purpose?" Alix's voice was tinged with curiosity.

She stood, shaking out her wings. She was currently about the size of Mero, and she looked around at her body. Her form wavered for a moment and she visibly shrank. Almost so that her head was level with Graith's. Then she expanded outward so that she towered over the large horse.

"Well that answers that question," Alix said.

He giggled as she then shrunk back down to the size of a wolf. Then, she was the height of the surrounding trees.

I meant to stay small, her voice was quiet and defeated.

"So, you can change sizes at will, you just can't control it?"

Graith was curious - he also felt like a moron for not noticing that Zel's size had been changing. He had actually been quite pleased with himself for noting her color change. But honestly - he didn't *look* at her much.

When he spoke to her, it was in his mind. When he closed his eyes and thought of her, what he saw was the dark navy dragoness, like in her memory that he had seen. Her at her prime.

It's okay Graith. Zel was looking at him. *Sometimes I forget what you look like too. You are a bright point in my mind.*

Apparently, that had not been a private comment, as Alix started giggling.

I know what he looks like more than you, *little one. You are just a small human male.*

Instead of being upset, Alix started laughing so hard that he fell to the ground, rolling. Graith couldn't help but smile at the child whose life had been nothing but pain. He deserved to laugh.

Watching Zel, Graith could see that she was slowly shrinking back down. He couldn't tell by looking at her, instead he had to look at the tree next to her. He knew it wasn't getting bigger, so she must be getting smaller.

I am? The shrinking stopped as she asked.

"Well, pick a size! I'm tired and you're warm," Alix said looking up at her expectantly.

All right. I am tired too. That takes a lot of energy.

"You'll have to practice while we travel then!"

It sounded to Graith like another game of Alix's.

Zel, you know we are going to need you in Kelna if your eggs are there. These men know how to fight. I don't even know how to use a sword.

I know. We just need to get to the city. We must be catching up to them by now. A large group of men hauling dragon eggs... They are not light, you know.

They all settled down to sleep. Graith and Zel's minds heavy with the thought of trying to get her eggs back.

Zel woke them only a few hours later. She was anxious to get them back on the road.

"Alright Zel, I'm going to think of sizes, and I want you to practice being that size!" Alix told her as Graith put out the fire and handed him a small loaf of bread with jam smeared across it.

I will do my best.

Throughout the day, Graith could feel the concentration that Zel was putting into managing her size. When he tried to ask her if she was all right, she didn't even hear him.

At some point, Alix got tired of the game. Graith was driving and Alix was leaned back against the packs.

"Graith, what are dragon eggs like? How long do they take to hatch?"

"Lad, I don't know. Never saw any of Zel's eggs before they were taken."

Dragon eggs take about a year to hatch. They are incredibly soft when laid but become harder than stone as they age. It's part of the dragonling's rite of birth, escaping the egg.

"Oh, how long ago did you lay your eggs?" Alix asked aloud, he was fascinated.

About three months ago.

"How big are they?"

Well a hatchling is about the size of a large dog. So, about the same size as you. Laughter tinted Zel's mind-voice.

"Hey! I'm bigger than a dog! Time for you to practice more!"

They continued to talk and practice during the day to fill their time. Alix even took an interest in driving the cart. Once Graith showed him how to do it, they were able to alternate driving. While one drove, the other slept in the cart.

This cut down time, but Graith worried about the toll it was taking on Zel. When he saw her, she was fading back to the colorless white. Her eyes seemed to lack the luster they normally held.

Zel. We can stop if you need a break.

No, what I need are my eggs. We are so close. I can feel them.

You aren't going to leave me behind this time, are you?

She shoved her head out of the underbrush to look at him. Her eyes were sunk into her head, and her spines hung limply.

No. Not again.

Good, because we have reached Kelna.

They had crested a hill and sprawled below them was a city. Seeing it, set in Graith's mind that, no, Dunlaith was not a city. It was a large town. *This* was a city.

Split down the middle by a river, the city teemed with life up and down the banks. Graith had never seen a boat, but from their high perch he could see many floating up and down the river. Their sails reminded him of Zel's wings.

One boat seemed to have caught Zel's attention. It was moored at the farthest dock, right before the river expanded.

Graith, Alix. My eggs are there.

CHAPTER TWENTY-NINE

Graith

Even though it was the middle of the day, Zel had come to stand next to the cart. Her eyes were dark pools as she stared down at the docks at the far end of the city. Her tail lashed and her talons dug into the stones that paved the road. She roared down into the city, and even from their perch, Graith could see people stop and look around.

"Zel, we *will* get them."

Graith, they are there. I can feel them! They need me!

Graith jumped out of the cart, and grabbed at her nostrils, forcing her to look him in the eyes.

"Zel, we have caught up. We will get them! But I *need* you to stay here. You cannot enter the city."

I must, *Graith.*

"What if we hide her in the cart?"

Alix was off the driver's bench walking around Zel and looking at the small cart while eying her.

"Can you stay small long enough to get into the city? I really think we could get her curled up in the back and cover her up. As long as she doesn't move around - I think it'll work."

Graith didn't respond, instead he unhappily stepped out of the way.

Zel shrunk herself as small as she could, as small as a hatchling. She climbed into the cart carefully, folding first her tail, then her wings in. Once she was completely curled up,

Alix dug through the packs and pulled out Graith's cloak to throw over her.

He looked at the lump for a second before shoving a saddlebag next to her and draping the cloak so that it covered part of the bag too. Then, he threw himself on top of the odd pile. Zel let out a small growl as he trod on her wing.

"Hush, I have to make it look like I'm just lying on bags."

I am not a bag.

Graith looked at the pair as he climbed onto the driving bench. They were ridiculous, he hoped that they could get into the city quickly. As soon as they were all settled, he reined Mero into motion.

I want to see outside the cart, Zel complained, trying to nudge her nose out from under the tarp.

"Do you want to see, or do you want to be smuggled into the city?" Graith asked as they approached the main gate.

The guards of Kelna, unlike Dunlaith, were alert. They stopped each traveler before waving them inside the gate. Graith cleared his throat, shifting uncomfortably. The cart seemed to bounce and jostle more than it ever had before. His foot started tapping of its own accord. Alix seemed to notice his nerves because he sat upright, pulling another saddlebag to him.

"Pa! Where did that jam go? The one Ma made?" He was pulling things out of the bag left and right. Making quite the scene and causing Graith to jump.

Before Graith could respond, a guard walked over chuckling. "You and your son here to visit the Kelnar ports?"

"Aye. All the lad has talked about since before the harvest was the ships. He thinks it would be fun to travel that way."

The guard scrubbed Alix's head, as he had perked up at the mention of himself. "That it is lad. Every child in the city learns to fish from a boat at an early age."

He stepped back and waved them inside the gate. Before they were out of sight, Alix shouted, "What way to the docks? Pa gets lost walking to our own barn!"

Grinning, the guard pointed down the road they were already on.

"Just straight, you'll come 'cross the big bridge. You'll be able to find your way from there!"

Alix leaned back against the bulk that was Zel.

"That went better than I expected!"

He sounded nervous and excited, his head twisting back and forth as he took in the city. The street descended steeply towards the river, a sharp cliff rising along the western side. The city looked similar to Dunlaith, except darker. The wood and streets had the tinge of always being wet. A sheen of water slicked the roofs. Instead of clicking, Mero's hooves made more of a muffled splat.

I can't breathe.

"You'll have to hold your breath then, until we get to the docks." Graith didn't turn as he responded.

He didn't even speak very loudly. Speaking aloud was for Alix's benefit, not Zel's. She took an almost audible deep breath, and then held it.

"Oh, come on, Zel. We're almost there," Graith muttered, urging Mero onward.

Then what? I'm going to have to stay under here until you find my eggs.

Her mood was black, and it seeped into the minds of the two humans. Graith had a feeling it was exuding farther, from the way people were avoiding looking at them or the cart.

The main gate was high above the center of the city, the ground sank as they moved farther into the city. A dim roar thundered continuously in the background, growing ever louder with their passage through Kelna.

"What is that noise?" Alix asked, standing in the back of the cart looking over the heads of the people lining the streets.

Graith shrugged, looking around as well. He thought perhaps it was thunder, but the sky was cloudless in the midday sun.

The bridge came into view as they passed a large group

of citizens. A massive structure, it was nearly five carts wide and so long that the buildings on the far side looked like doll houses. As Mero pulled onto it, the strange sound nearly doubled, and the houses and shops fell away.

To their left was the source. A waterfall a hundred feet high thundered over the edge of a cliff that made up the western wall of the city. Water jettisoned into the air and shook the river far below. The largest rainbow Graith had ever seen seemed to be a permanent fixture about the dark bridge.

"No wonder the port is on the east side of Kelna! If it was any closer, the ships would fill with water from the waterfall!" Alix screamed over the deafening noise.

As they progressed across the bridge, Mero, Graith, and Alix were all soaked. Graith could only compare it to being outside in the heaviest torrential rainstorm he could imagine. So late in the autumn season, a deep chill sank into his bones and he began to shiver. Alix was crammed against Zel so hard that she was growling again - this time the noise was lost to the falls.

Graith urged Mero to speed up as the end of the bridge neared. Once back on solid ground, the horse gave a mighty shake, sending water to again coat Graith. He wanted to stop and change but knowing that Zel was relying on him to get her to the dock prevented him from doing so.

This side of the city was different from the other. Still dark and wet, the buildings were shorter and in straight lines. One building towered above the rest, like a jewel among coal. He assumed it must be the lord of Kelna's manor.

He wondered briefly if the knight that Lord Arish sent had gone there, but it didn't matter. Zel had said her eggs were at the dock. So, to the dock they would go.

A stiff breeze blew up the straight alleyway, Graith shivering doubling. He was almost there. That's what he kept telling himself. Even Mero had started to slow, his hide quivering.

A sudden flood of emotion from Zel warmed and reinvigorated them. Feelings of purpose and direction, as well as pride and caring.

We are almost there. I can feel *them. They can feel* me *too.*

Since entering the city, the trip had been all downhill, and this section was no exception. Hope flared to life in Graith's chest as masts and rigging came into view over the tops of the buildings.

They were *so* close.

Large warehouses lined the wharf and the identical buildings fell away. A strong odor of fish hung in the air and shouts could be heard over the din of the waterfall. A guard waved them over as they neared.

"Oi! What are you folks doing down here?" He eyed their wet forms, frowning. "Did no one tell you to buy oil slicked cloaks before crossing the bridge?"

"My son is interested in the ships. Promised him I would bring him down to see them after the harvest. Just got into town," Graith's voice shook as he spoke, but he hoped that the guard would think it was from the chill, not fear.

"You might want to head to an inn and get warmed up. There's only one this side of the river -"

"Oh, we will! The lad just really wants to see a ship before we get settled in," Graith cut in.

"All right then. You do you. Civilians have access to the first two thirds of the pier. After that is a military-only zone. Someone'll stop you before you get there."

Graith just nodded and Alix pulled himself up enough to wave. Urging Mero to start trotting again, they headed down the dock.

Graith's head turned rapidly as he heard Alix whisper, "Zel, stop moving, I think you're getting larger!"

The tarp was twisting and writhing. Graith slapped the reins across Mero's flank for what seemed like the first time ever. They needed to get down to the other end. Needed to get Zel to the ship with her eggs before she grew too large.

Graith! I can't stay small! Zel told him frantically.

Hearing that, Graith pulled the cart between two warehouses, hoping that they weren't noticed.

No such luck.

"Sir! I'm sorry, you can't be back here! Please back your _"

He didn't finish his statement, instead he screamed.

Graith could feel the rear axle of the cart shatter as Zel rapidly expanded. Alix jumped into the front, grabbing Graith, and they both got away from the wagon. He caught a glimpse of Zel out of the corner of his eye, as blue as the sky.

Her eyes, however, were a menacing red, and she was growling.

Before the sailor could run away, she grabbed him in her maw, instantly breaking his neck. Alix screamed, running further back into the alley. Graith understood. It was one thing to see the gentle side of the dragon, another completely to see the beast.

Alix and the sailor's screams had drawn attention. Zel was taking up most of the space between the two buildings, blocking Graith's view, but he could hear shouts and screams. He rushed to untie Mero from the wreckage of the cart. Grabbing the three saddle bags and throwing them over the horse's wide back, he led Mero away, looking for Alix.

They needed to get out of there.

CHAPTER THIRTY

Nerie

A week - it had only been a week without Aldis - to Nerie it could have already been months.

Nerie was in King Soren's study and he was talking about the main products from each region around the country. She wasn't really paying attention, slumped in her seat, knee bouncing up and down. Soren had his back to her, so he didn't know that she was less than attentive at the moment.

You know he's fine. Mother has checked in on him every two hours since he left. Kiriga's voice manifested itself inside Nerie's mind.

It's not that I'm worried about him - mostly - it's the fact that he's not here, Nerie complained.

I'm here.

Nerie felt Kiriga's mental-self wilt slightly.

Sitting upright, Nerie frowned.

Of course, you are. And I love you. But I miss Aldis.

Come see me? I'm with Ilex right now, Kiriga asked, her voice hopeful.

I can't just leave Soren in the middle of the lecture.

"Yes, you can."

Soren turned from the map and books he had been referencing.

"Huh?" Nerie's face nearly matched her scarlet hair as she wondered if he could hear her thoughts.

"Go see Kiriga. Ilex told me that she's summoning you,

and that you said you couldn't leave."

He set the book he was holding down with a thud.

"Oh."

Of course - all the dragons could hear her as she spoke to Kiriga - she had just forgotten that Ilex would then tell Soren.

"I'll go with you. Ilex says he could use some eye ridge scratches." Soren walked over and extended his hand to help her up.

They walked through multiple rooms until they reached the access door to his courtyard. The set of double doors was already open, and the two dragons were lounging in opposite corners.

Nerie walked over to Kiriga, hugging her neck. It seemed she had grown so much recently that Nerie could barely touch her fingers together from either side.

Leaning against the dragoness, she gazed over at Soren. From a distance, other than his broad shoulders, he could have been Aldis. Nerie let out a long, slow breath. She probably would have cried, but she seemed to have run out of tears three days ago.

Ilex had his head on the ground so his eyes were at just the right height for Soren to scratch. After a few minutes, both eyes were thoroughly sated so Soren walked over to Nerie and Kiriga. He gently scratched Kiriga's eye ridges while looking her over.

"You've grown quite a bit haven't you, Kiriga?" he asked, smiling.

I have! I can't wait to be big enough to carry Nerie! Her voice was clear to both Soren and Nerie.

"You'll be flying before you know it. Don't forget to do your wing exercises that Soros and Eras showed you!"

He laughed, giving her a stout pat on the shoulder.

I'll be the fastest dragon ever!

"I'm sure you will be!" he said with all seriousness.

Nerie smiled at Soren, then frowned looking at Ilex.

"Soren, why are Ilex's wings so small? He can't fly, can he?"

She'd never seen the green dragon leave the ground other than scaling sections of the palace.

"It's just the type of dragon he is. Both Soros and Eras have told me that they had ancestors who couldn't fly. Just a chance of the trait showing through."

He turned to face his dragon whose eyes were closed.

"But someday soon you'll get to see him run."

"He runs?" Nerie asked, surprised.

"Faster than a horse. And smoother too." Soren nodded. "He also likes to dig. Would spend hours underground if he could."

Nerie looked at Ilex with a newfound appreciation. Hearing her thoughts, he preened a little, turning so the sun hit his scales *just* right.

"I know you miss Aldis. I do too. So does Alaena. But time passes quickly, and he'll be back before you know it as long as you don't linger on it."

Soren's smile faded just a little.

"What can I do to keep busy? Outside of the time that I spend with you, Queen Alaena, and my mother?"

While the routine was nice, it left much to be desired in the way of variation. She'd discovered over the course of the week that it gave her plenty of time to brood about Aldis.

"Have you thought about attending the daily court session?" he asked.

"I hadn't." She frowned, looking away from Soren, "Karina told me that Astra attends daily."

"She does. However, you are the heir to the crown. It's about time you started to make public appearances." He shrugged. "It's up to you, though. I won't force you to go, but I will tell you it's in your best interest."

"Doesn't the royal court meet during lunchtime? I'm here with you."

She didn't want to go, but she didn't have a *good* reason not to.

"Yes, but we can always meet later in the day or we can start meeting on set days of the week. At this point, you're well versed in how to care for Kiriga - other than flying of course. The politics of the country, while important, you have plenty of time to learn about."

He laughed while she thought it over.

"I'll let Karina know that I would like to attend tomorrow," she said, finally.

"Good! I'll let Alaena know too. She can accompany you if you would like," Soren said.

"That's all right. I would like to go on my own the first time," Nerie said, standing from where she had slid down Kiriga's side to rest against the golden dragoness.

Soren chuckled, but didn't say what was on his mind.

"Have an enjoyable time."

I'll be in our garden, Kiriga said as she too stood.

She then lithely leapt onto the rooftop and walked away.

I'll see you there, Nerie told her.

"I'll see you in two days then," she told Soren.

He walked her to the main hallway that connected the maze that was the palace.

The next few hours were spent with Karina, choosing what to wear and how to do her hair the following day. When Myha arrived for dinner, Nerie was lost in thought. So far, the only people she'd met in the palace were the council members. Most were Soren's age or older. She didn't remember seeing anyone as young as she was.

"What's on your mind, Pumpkin?" Myha asked from the doorway.

"Mom, I'm seventeen, aren't I a bit old for you to call Pumpkin?"

Nerie turned to face her mother.

"You're never too old for me to call Pumpkin. I'm your mom."

Myha walked over and hugged her tight.

"Now, what's going on in that head of yours. I'm not Kiriga, so I can't just hear your thoughts."

"Soren -" Myha made a face as Nerie used his first name, "Soren suggested I start going to court. Daily, or at least a few times a week. I agreed and am going to go for the first time tomorrow."

"That sounds wonderful," Myha told her, sitting them both down on one of the couches.

"Only, well, Astra goes to court all the time, according to Karina," Nerie said, confiding in her mother. She hadn't actually voiced her concerns about her older half-sister before.

"I've told you before, the people who are bullies are the ones that are hurting inside." Myha hugged Nerie. "How do you think she feels? She lost the throne to a sister she had never met before, and now her brother's left."

Nerie was quite sure that Astra was glad Aldis was gone - seeing as she hadn't bothered to show up to say goodbye - but she kept this to herself.

"I know Mom. I would just rather avoid her altogether."

Nerie ran her hands over the silk of her dress. Her palms were sweating at the thought of a possible confrontation.

"Then ignore her. Prove to yourself that you're the bigger person. Anyway, you'll have a lot of fun. I've been going every now and again. I've even made a friend!"

Nerie looked at her mother in surprise.

"You did? What is she like?"

In the same manner that Nerie was known to flush, Myha turned a dark red.

"Well, *he* is quite wonderful. He's been showing me around the palace, since I can't be with you all the time."

"Oh?!" Nerie nearly squealed in excitement. Myha had dated a few men during Nerie's childhood, but nothing serious.

"Well, what's his name?"

"Sir Ahlwin," Myha mumbled, still embarrassed.

"Well, I can't wait to meet him!"

Nerie clasped her mother's hands in her own. Smiling, they continued to talk late into the evening. Long enough that Nerie only briefly ran outside to hug Kiriga good night and scratch an itch that she had been complaining about for an hour.

Sinking into the soft sheets of her bed, Nerie was asleep instantly.

***

The morning dawned earlier than she would have liked. Her eyes were gritty as she tried to blink them open, and a cold draft was hitting her face. When Karina came in, carrying her tray of breakfast foods, Nerie nearly squawked in protest because the draft was worsened by the open door. Karina didn't say anything, but Nerie knew by the way the tray was set down that it was time to get out of bed.

Walking over to the small table, Nerie surveyed her meal. Now that she had been around for a while, her favorites had been singled out. While not quite the spread it used to be, each meal filled her up more than nibbling on a dozen different things.

Kiriga's meals were no longer delivered with her own. Instead, large cuts of meat were placed outside the kitchens and she had to fetch it herself. Not that it mattered. She was large enough now that crossing the rooftop of the palace took only moments.

After eating, bathing, and dressing, she found the queen waiting for her. Lessons with Alaena were much shorter than normal. Alaena first went over the protocol of court and how Nerie should introduce herself. Apparently, there were small cliques and - while as Princess and Heir she would be announced on arrival - she should go around and introduce herself on a more private scale. They went over how she should introduce herself - as Crown Princess Nerie of house Therius - and what responses she should expect.

Knowing that there was much preparation to do before Nerie could arrive at the Solar - where court was held - Alaena left. Once she'd gone, Karina went to work getting Nerie into the gown they'd chosen the evening before. It was a soft, buttery-yellow and contrasted nicely with her red hair and freckles. Unlike most of her dresses, this one had long sleeves with golden cuffs around her forearms. The bodice had a flat and wide collar that modestly accentuated her chest. The skirt was made of several layers of fine silk, each a slightly lighter shade of gold, wrapped layer by layer and gathered at her right hip.

Then the hard part - they had decided to style her long tresses in an up-do that would be curled. A rod of metal was heated in a small brazier and then her hair wrapped around it for short periods of time. Nerie sat eerily still as Karina worked, afraid of having the hot metal touch her skin.

Then it was time.

While most of the palace was situated to the east of the kitchens, the great hall and the Solar were both to the west. Nerie had only been to the Solar once before, when she had first learned her way around the palace.

The far wall was solid glass, with doors leading out to the sprawling gardens that surrounded the palace. She still hadn't gotten a chance to explore them.

Nerie straightened her dress one last time and stepped into the large room. Every eye turned towards the princess.

"Attention Please! Welcome Her Royal Highness, Heir Apparent, Princess Nerie!" The steward said, his voice booming.

If everyone hadn't been looking at her before - they were now.

CHAPTER THIRTY-ONE

Nerie

The room was silent as everyone turned to watch Nerie enter.

Most of them were much younger than the members of the Curia, and Nerie wouldn't have been surprised to learn they were their children. She was stuck looking at everyone, as they looked like a garden of flowers. Pastels must be in fashion because Nerie didn't see a single woman in a darker color. The men, however, seemed to favor darker tones with pastel accents.

Realizing she was just standing in the doorway, Nerie stepped into the room. Immediately, everyone bowed low to her. Alaena had told her this would happen, and that they would wait for her command to rise.

"Thank you all for welcoming me. Please rise," she said, her voice thin but steady, as she commanded the large audience.

As one, they all straightened. Then it was like a dam burst. People rushing to meet her, kiss her cheek, her hand, introduce themselves. It would have been overwhelming, had she had time to think about it.

There were names. *So many* names. She hoped Alaena, or possibly even her mother, might have a list of attendees for her to review later.

She didn't know how long the introductions went on for before she heard someone clear their throat behind her.

"Come now! We will all get to meet Her Highness, as I'm sure this will not be her *only* time joining us."

Nerie looked over her shoulder to find a tall, muscular man standing there. He had pale hair and his eyes were nearly golden they were such a light shade of brown. He was smiling down at her.

He bowed slightly and then straightened.

"Allow me to introduce myself, your highness, I'm Wilm, eldest son of Lord Brodin of Mazen. You must be weary. You've hardly moved from the doorway in an hour. Please, join me for tea?"

Wilm extended his hand, and Nerie lightly placed hers atop it. He gave it the customary kiss in greeting, however, he didn't release it afterwards, instead leading her to one of the small tables that lined the room.

Nerie felt a blush slowly creeping up her neck. While she appreciated his actions, his treatment was far different than anyone else at the palace thus far.

Wilm pulled out her chair for her, then lightly pushed her in. Once he was seated, they were attended to instantly by one of the servants that always seemed to appear out of the woodwork.

A light tea was served along with finger sandwiches. She nibbled at the food, hardly looking up from her plate. This was not the way she had planned on her first court session going. Not that she minded - she hadn't seen Astra yet, and everyone seemed friendly.

"Princess, is everything all right?" Wilm asked after nearly five minutes of silence.

Shocked by the noise, Nerie jerked, nearly spilling the tea she had been about to sip. She straightened herself, feeling flustered.

"Yes, just trying to commit everyone I've met to memory."

"Would you like some help?" Wilm offered kindly.

She let out a sigh of relief. Someone who was used to court helping her would be immensely beneficial.

"Please."

Over the next twenty minutes, he pointed out people, first asking if she recognized them, then reiterating their names and ranks, sometimes adding in tidbits about who their parents were or what their claim to fame was.

Once the group started giving him dirty looks, Wilm apologized for monopolizing her time, and instead of leaving her to once again fend for herself, offered to reintroduce her to each group. However, she declined his offer.

"I think I'm just going to mosey about. Thank you for everything, Wilm. I hope to see you around," she thanked him before standing.

"I'm here just about every day, Princess," he told her, standing at the same time, and then bowing deeply one last time.

As Nerie turned back to the Solar, she saw that the small cliques that had existed when she first entered the room had been reestablished. She headed to the one hovering nearest the table she'd been sitting at.

"Princess!" A girl that seemed to be close to Aldis's age, exclaimed as Nerie approached.

"Hello Talira," Nerie said, praying that she remembered the young girl's name correctly.

"You remember me!" Talira squealed in delight. Her dark hair was curled and bounced gently as she kept herself from jumping in surprise.

"I do. I just wanted to introduce myself on a more private level." Nerie curtsied slightly to the small group.

This routine was repeated many times over the course of the next several hours. Promises of tea, or flower viewings, and even visiting family estates were made. Nerie was overwhelmed with how kind everyone was to her.

Several young men asked her to dance, but she had to decline and explained that she was unfamiliar with any court dances at the moment.

She kept reminding herself that the reason they were acting this way was only because she was the crown princess. In her heart, she knew that - but it still felt nice to have people her age so interested in her. Other than Raana, she'd not had many friends growing up.

Just before the end of the court session and the dinner hour, as she was preparing to retreat to her rooms, Nerie was surprised to see her mother approaching. Myha was in a simple light-blue gown, and she was accompanied by a man who looked to be in his early forties. His outfit was a crisp thick silk, in a midnight blue that corresponded to Myha's blue nicely.

"Nerie! This is -" Myha started before the man gently laid his hand on her shoulder.

"Princess, it is so nice to meet you in person! I am Sir Ahlwin. I suppose we met before at the council meeting, but I'm sure you don't remember me."

Nerie blushed faintly.

"I do apologize. I've been meeting so many new people recently."

He bowed, then stood and kissed Nerie's hand, before wrapping his arm around Myha's shoulder.

"It's quite all right. I've been keeping your lovely mother company. I normally don't spend much time in the capital, but this time I think I'll be staying for a while."

"Mother was just telling me how much she's enjoyed your company."

Myha grabbed Nerie's hands, leaning in close to her daughter.

"Sorry, I just really wanted you to meet him. Plus, I couldn't help myself but come see you all dressed up so nicely!"

Myha giggled and then hugged her daughter.

"It's all right, Mama. I'm happy you came. I've met so many lovely people today. *And* I haven't seen Astra," Nerie confided quietly into her mother's ear.

"I'm glad you've had an enjoyable time. Will you be back tomorrow?" Myha asked.

"I think I might. This has been fun. More fun than I imagined."

Nerie looked down at her yellow dress, as her head bowed a ruby curl fell across her face. She was enjoying being dressed up.

"While I have you here, Princess, would you mind if I stole your mother away from you for an evening? I would love to take her out to dinner, but she has told me that she eats with you every evening," Ahlwin asked.

Nerie had to admit he *was* quite charming.

Myha blushed a darker red than even Nerie could produce. Nerie grinned, overjoyed for her mother.

"Of course, you may! Anytime that you would like."

She winked at her mother, who somehow turned redder.

"I'll see you tomorrow then, Mama!"

Nerie hugged Myha close, before stepping back and waving.

In an instant, Karina was by her side. The woman had been shadowing her for the majority of the day but had, for the most part, left the princess to her own devices. As they reached the door, the same man who had announced her arrival stepped forward. Karina gently nodded back to the Solar and Nerie turned.

"Her Royal Highness, Princess Nerie." He announced her departure to the room.

As one, the occupants, for a final time that day, bowed to her. Even Myha joined Ahlwin in bowing. Nerie wanted to tell her to stand, but the moment was over, and Karina was motioning her to move again before she got the chance.

The next time she saw her mother, she would have to tell Myha that she never had to bow before her. She was her mother, for goodness sake!

As they walked slowly down the long corridors, Nerie chatted lightly with Karina about the people she had met, the outfits they had worn, and her hopes of going again tomorrow. Once they reached her room, Karina untied the lacing on the back of the dress and then excused herself while she went to collect Nerie's dinner.

Once she completed her change into comfortable evening clothing, Nerie walked through her bedroom, out to the courtyard. Kiriga was lying facing the door, waiting for her.

I missed you, she said in her most piteous tone.

You were watching the whole time. I felt you, you big baby.

Nerie walked over and leaned her body on the flat ridge between the dragon's eyes.

I am a baby. Aren't I, Father? Kiriga kept up the whining tone.

All my children are babies, Eras's voice boomed, and Nerie felt Kiriga's annoyance, knowing that hadn't been what the dragoness had meant.

As she laid against the warm hide of Kiriga's head, Nerie contemplated not eating and just falling asleep here. She started to adjust herself to be more comfortable when something touched the lower part of her back - and slowly started to slither upward.

Jumping upright and screaming, Nerie nearly climbed over Kiriga's head trying to get away. A clatter of dishes, and Kiriga's annoyance quickly followed the scream.

"My lady!" Karina yelled, running into the courtyard.

Father! Kiriga shouted.

Nerie got the courage to look behind her. Eras's long orange tail was hanging from the rooftop where he was curled. He'd obviously been slowly lowering it, trying to scare Nerie.

I was bored, he complained, but it was too late.

Nerie could hear not only Kiriga and Soros yelling at him, but also Ilex and Wyla.

You don't scare the Princess just because you are bored! Soros' voice was tinged with red anger.

Weakly, Nerie turned to Karina, "I'm fine. Eras simply frightened me."

By now, guards were filing into the courtyard, trying to surround the dragon and princess. Karina called them off.

"I'm sorry, my lady, I dropped your food when I heard you scream."

She grabbed one of the guards - who were still not quite sure what happened - and asked him to go fetch another meal from the kitchen for Nerie while she cleaned up the first.

"It's all right. It's not your fault. Eras is getting quite the earful now."

He really was, as all the dragons from their corners of the kingdom were chiming in.

A new dinner was brought, and Nerie ate quickly. She was tired, and hearing the tirade against the eldest dragon still going on was giving her a slight headache.

Good night, Kiriga, Nerie said, giving her a mental hug without going back out to the courtyard.

Good night, Nerie, Kiriga paused yelling at her father long enough to say.

Nerie climbed into bed, struggling to get comfortable. Her sheets, normally smooth against her skin, were rough. Her pillows were slightly too plump and even though she was exhausted, she couldn't find the right position to lie.

Just as she was finally drifting off, she felt something scaly brush against her feet.

Eras, did you not learn your lesson? she asked groggily.

What? she heard his distracted reply.

Your tail.

She felt it move again.

Nerie, MOVE, Kiriga suddenly screamed into her mind.

Nerie's eyes snapped open and she threw herself off the bed, even as Kiriga shoved herself through the now too small doorway.

A short battle of hissing and growling took place, and the wood frame of the bed cracked under the golden dragon's weight.

Then it was like a madhouse erupted. Karina was rushing in once again, dressed in her own nightgown. Guards were filling the room at an increased speed.

Kiriga's mind was filled with blood red anger.

What's going on? Nerie asked Kiriga, her heart racing.

Rising from the splintered wood and tangled sheets, a long, shining black snake hung limply from Kiriga's maw.

Nerie's eyes went wide as saucers. A Lutesian viper.

CHAPTER THIRTY-TWO

Nerie

Pulling herself into a sitting position, Nerie watched the snake's carcass slowly swing as Kiriga's sides heaved.

Are you all right? It didn't bite you, did it? Kiriga asked. She let the snake fall to the ground with a wet thud.

I... I'm fine. Even Nerie's mental-voice stuttered as she sat there in shock.

Karina was there, wrapping a blanket around her shoulders, helping her stand and move into the corner of the room. The guards were pulling the sheets and bed apart, looking for any other dangers. One of the royal knights had come in, and he was crouched in front of the dead snake. He was using a dagger to slowly push the thing over and examine it.

As the reality of the situation hit, Nerie started to tremble violently. Her breath came in short gasps, and her vision narrowed. Kiriga was instantly by her side, not caring who or what she trampled as she crossed the relatively small room. She sat on her hind legs, using her tail and forelegs to create a cage around Nerie.

Leaning into the warm, soft scales of Kiriga's underbelly, Nerie slowly calmed. She refused to look behind her where the snake lay. More people were still stuffing themselves into the room.

I need to go outside. I can't breathe, she told Kiriga faintly.

Kiriga lowered herself onto the ground, at the same time as she said, *Get on my back. I'll carry you outside.*

Nerie stepped from Kiriga's elbow to her shoulder, laying herself along the dragon's back. She faintly noted that even lying this way, she was still shorter than the dragon's torso now. When had Kiriga gotten so big?

You haven't noticed because you see me all the time, Kiriga told her softly.

She was carefully stepping through the crowd, trying not to jostle Nerie.

Reaching the door, Nerie saw that the frame had been cracked from Kiriga's force as she entered the room. Now, she tucked her wings in tight, trying to slide back through in the other direction. She barely fit. Nerie experienced a moment of discomfort as the hard bones of Kiriga's wings pressed together against her back.

Then they were outside. The current of fresh air was like a breath of life after the stale air in the bedroom. Soros and Eras were both lying in the courtyard, their eyes narrowed with worry. After Kiriga was between them, Eras moved himself so that he was blocking the door, the large spikes that protruded from his scales a deterrent for any who might try to push past.

Nerie was shaking again. Her mind still reeling over the brush with death - for a bite from a Lutesian Viper nearly always resulted in fire fever, which was most certainly a death sentence. If Kiriga had been any bigger or any slower, she might be dying right now.

I'm not, and you're not. We are fine, Kiriga cooed to her, sounding much more mature than her normal bright self.

Just rest, Nerie. We will protect you, Soros told her, her large, purple head hovering above her youngest child and the princess.

Climb down, Nerie. Kiriga was lowering herself to the ground again.

Complying, she was confused for a moment until Kiriga showed her what she intended. She wanted to have Nerie lay under her wing with her tail as a support.

Nothing will get to you there, Kiriga promised.

Nerie settled down in the small space. Even though it was tight and dark, Nerie was able to completely relax. She trusted Kiriga and the other dragons implicitly and knew they would give their lives to protect her. Kiriga's rhythmic breathing quickly lulled her to sleep.

***

The next morning, she woke stiffly. While she had been protected physically, she had spent most of the night tossing and turning from nightmares.

Flashes of faces staring at her angrily, people dancing around her laughing, and then darkness, being unable to find Kiriga anywhere, even in her mind. And then Astra - always staring, watching from the shadows.

I'm right here, Kiriga said, as she lifted her wing, exposing Nerie to the weak light of an early winter sun.

"I know," Nerie said as she leaned against Kiriga in a lazy version of a hug.

Good. The king and queen are waiting for you when you're ready. They want to talk about the snake.

Nerie's stomach twisted. When she thought of how close she'd come to death, she wanted to vomit. After the strange twisted nightmares she'd had the night before, she was sure that Astra had been behind the attack.

Kiriga was watching her mind as she thought, and when Nerie came to that conclusion she couldn't help but butt in.

I would have known if Astra had been anywhere near your rooms yesterday. The only people that were in them were Karina and several other servants. No one out of the ordinary.

Why would you watch for Astra? Nerie asked, curiously.

Because I know she wants you dead. But she did not enter your room.

Kiriga's tail lashed.

Nerie entered her room. It looked like an explosion had happened. Now empty of all the people from the previous night, only the destruction remained. The bed was in pieces, and the mattress, sheets, and pillows had been ripped apart.

Chairs were overturned and wall-hangings had been knocked down.

Exiting into the sitting room, she saw King Soren and Queen Alaena waiting for her.

Choosing to forgo a bath for the day, she instead entered the large wardrobe. Karina followed her in, shutting the door. Karina was quiet. Her normal chatter silent. She helped Nerie dress quickly, and then they returned to the sitting room.

Nerie curtsied to the rulers before sitting across from them. In the time she'd been in the palace, it seemed they were rarely together unless it was for a formal reason. She didn't know, however, if she was the cause of their rift or if this had been the case long before she was discovered.

"Your Majesties, good morning," she said stiffly.

She wasn't sure King Soren had ever been to her rooms before.

"Nerie, there is little reason to be so formal," Soren said smiling. Alaena's face was unreadable, so Nerie focused her attention on the king.

"I see. I assume your visit is about last night?"

Nerie really didn't want to talk about it, but she didn't think she was going to be given a choice.

"It is. Kiriga was kind enough to explain what happened last night, but I wanted to see if you were all right."

"I am. Just a little shaken."

A little might be an understatement, but Nerie didn't think that either the king or the queen needed to know that.

"I can imagine. I just wanted to let you know that while your room is being repaired, we are going to move you to an interior room. Also, along with Karina, you are going to be shadowed by two Royal Knights at all times for the foreseeable future."

His smile fell a little, and his eyes tightened. He was worried about her. Nerie glanced at Alaena, but her face was still impassive - though she thought she saw the queen's hands clench briefly.

"Of course. I'm sure all the knights are lovely people.

And Karina will help me with whatever I need to adjust. Do you have an estimate on how long it will take?"

Nerie didn't like the thought of not being able to quickly access one of the courtyards that the dragons resided in.

"Unfortunately, a couple of weeks. The structural damage to your bedroom door and the surrounding wall was… extensive," he said with a shake of his head.

In any other circumstance, Nerie was sure he would have chuckled at the dragon's antics.

"I must be going now. Why don't you attend court again today? I'll see you tomorrow at our normal time."

Soren stood and when Nerie and Alaena stood, he was already on his way out the door.

Alaena then turned to Nerie.

"As it is earlier than our normal lessons, why don't I join you for breakfast, and we will work on table manners."

As it turned out, table manners were a lot more complicated than Nerie expected. From the way she sat to how she held her fork. It seemed as though Alaena was nitpicking every detail. Throughout it all, she was expected to maintain a conversation - without talking around the food in her mouth or simply not eating.

The longer the lesson went on, the more agitated Nerie became. Seeing the queen was like seeing Astra. And every time she saw Astra she thought of the snake from the night before. Kiriga said that Astra didn't enter the room - but that didn't mean that she didn't have anything to do with it.

Looking down at her plate, Nerie set down her fork and knife. Alaena frowned but didn't say anything.

Maybe Alaena would know, and if not, she would at least understand how Nerie was feeling. She had witnessed Nerie and Astra's last encounter and knew that they were on less than friendly terms.

"Um, your highness…" Nerie started, only to be cut off by the queen.

"Princesses do not say 'um' Nerie. Also, there is no need to be formal with me during lessons." Alaena's voice was even, but Nerie couldn't bring herself to look her in the face.

"Alaena. I don't want to be disrespectful of you or the king, however, I think that Astra had something to do with the snake."

Nerie glanced up to see the queen's expression.

Alaena blanched. First white then red. Nerie could see her visibly trying to tame whatever emotions were going on in her mind.

This had been a mistake. Of course, she shouldn't have said anything to Alaena, Astra was her daughter. Her first-born child. Nerie mentally berated herself.

As the queen got her emotions under control, she spoke tightly, "Astra could not have had anything to do with the snake. She was with me the entirety of yesterday. King Soren only informed me of your decision to join the court early in the morning. I - knowing how you and Astra get along - decided that it was in everyone's best interest if she was not present during your first attendance. She simply had no time to do so."

Oh. So that's where Astra had been the day before. Nerie couldn't believe her own stupidity. Of course, there would be people who would want her dead other than her older half-sister. That must be part of being crown princess.

At the same time, Alaena hadn't said Astra wouldn't do it, just that she couldn't have been behind the snake.

A pit formed in the place that should be her stomach. Maybe it was because she didn't like Astra, maybe it was because it was easier than guessing at some unknown assailant, but Nerie still thought that Astra was somehow involved.

"Excuse me. I am going to go prepare for court. It would be unfair of me to keep Astra away for two days in a row, so instead I will be joining you today."

Alaena stood and left.

Great, Nerie thought, Astra would be there today. She hoped that her mother and Ahlwin were both in attendance. She wouldn't mind seeing Wilm again either. Karina was already picking out an outfit for today, and a secondary servant who Nerie didn't recognize had been brought in.

King Soren must not want Karina or the Royal Knight to leave her alone at any time.

Will you join me today? I know you can't enter the Solar, but would you be willing to lie in the gardens? She asked Kiriga.

Of course. You know you upset Alaena, right? She couldn't believe you would accuse Astra of trying to kill you. Nerie felt Kiriga's tail twitch. *I don't know why you brought it up anyway. I told you that she didn't enter your rooms.*

CHAPTER THIRTY-THREE

Nerie

Arriving at the Solar, Nerie was once again announced and then greeted by a mass of people bowing. While people didn't crowd around her quite the same way as the day before, there was still a constant stream of people waiting to talk to her. They seemed more aware of her needs, inviting her to sit with them and drink tea, or snack on the small delicacies.

While it kept her busy, she was constantly aware of Astra. Astra seemed to be moving in a motion that mirrored Nerie, keeping herself as far away from her half-sister as possible. Nerie felt herself relax slightly, as it seemed that she had no interest in a confrontation today.

She's just angry that you're here, Kiriga told her.

Nerie glanced over to the windows, where several courtiers stood with their noses pressed to the glass. They were looking at Kiriga who was laying in the sun, she was more than aware that she was the center of attention. She flexed her opalescent talons, and several people gasped. A smile tugged at Nerie's lips until she glanced at Astra again. Astra was watching the dragoness too, a frown crossing her face.

Nerie excused herself from her current conversation and looked around. She had hoped to see Myha, but she and Ahlwin were missing. Nerie wandered the Solar - politely nodding and greeting people as she passed, but she did not initiate any conversations.

It definitely wasn't as exciting as it had been the day before. She started towards the doors of the Solar that exited into the garden when she felt eyes on the back of her neck.

Turing, she found herself nearly nose to nose with Astra. Nerie took a half step backwards looking around for Alaena. Astra smirked.

"Mother had to take care of some urgent business. I'm sure she'll be back momentarily," Astra shrugged gracefully, noting Nerie's discomfort.

Nerie looked her half-sister up and down. It was strange - knowing that she was related to this girl - yet neither looking nor acting anything like her. Astra, unlike the rest of the court, was wearing a dark-burgundy dress that clung to her form. Her long dark hair was twisted into an elegant knot at the base of her skull, with curled tendrils hanging from her temples. Her eyes were dark, dark makeup accentuating the fact.

"Astra, it's a pleasure to see you." Nerie said, straightening her shoulders and tilting her chin slightly. She wouldn't let the older woman cow her.

Eyes narrowing, Astra's strong smirk faded slightly.

"As pleasurable as finding a serpent in your bed? I was surprised to hear that you took it so poorly. Aren't you used to sleeping with your over-sized lizard anyway?"

Nerie felt her face burn. How dare she insult Kiriga. Lowering her voice, Nerie said, "Say whatever you want about me, but leave Kiriga out of it."

"Well, I must be going. Wouldn't want to upset Mother."

Astra glided away, choosing to ignore Nerie's statement. *Why? Why does she hate me?* Nerie moaned.

She would have loved to get to know Astra, but even seeing the woman made her blood curdle.

She hates you because I Chose you over her.

Kiriga had stood and was stretching outside. Nerie once again heard gasps as people watched her in wonder.

You are a showoff.

I know.

Nerie could feel Kiriga's smile without turning to look.

I'm ready to go.

Nerie was tempted to follow Astra but knew that wasn't the greatest idea she'd ever had. It would be easier to just leave.

I know that too, Kiriga laughed.

As she left the Solar, Karina was standing by the door. Nerie ignored her, heading down the hallway to her rooms.

"Your Highness," she heard Karina say. Pausing to look back at the older woman, Karina made a formal bow.

"Your Highness, I do apologize, but as discussed with their Majesties this morning, you are being temporarily relocated to another set of rooms." Karina stood, "If you would please follow me."

Nerie let out a hiss of annoyance, and Karina paled.

"I am so sorry for the inconvenience," she repeated.

"It's not your fault Karina. Astra just took advantage of the fact that Queen Alaena had to leave the Solar to talk to me. It's left me in a rotten mood."

Nerie mentally berated herself, reminding herself that nearly everyone in the palace was dedicated to her happiness and wellbeing.

"Of course, your Highness." Karina was silent as she led Nerie to the temporary rooms.

The doors, while ornate, were of average height and width. Karina pulled them open, stepping back for Nerie to see. The sitting room was small and only had two exits, one to a bedroom and one to a bath.

Wandering inside, Nerie first went to the bath. It had a small mirror and a bronze tub that would hold her small frame but was nothing like the stone one in her suite. The tiles, while decorated, were a simple repeating pattern. Heading back through the sitting room to the bedroom, she found a bed that was as large and ornamental as her previous one. However, it took up much of the room. On the far wall was a closet, that while large enough for several of her gowns, was not large enough to change inside of.

The one thing that really stood out to Nerie, however,

was the lack of access to one of the courtyards. The lack of access to Kiriga and the other dragons.

How am I going to see you? Nerie asked Kiriga, her heart pounding.

You're being silly. I'm right here. She covered Nerie's mind in warm and loving feelings.

But I can't get to you, what if there's another snake?

There won't be, Kiriga sounded so confident.

How do you know?

Many people who've been in and out of your room today seem to think that it came in from the courtyard. Apparently, it's a local breed. It is venomous, but it is not unheard of for it to seek a warmer spot, especially since we are entering winter.

I know it's local, all children are warned away from it. But local or not, I don't think it was an accident that it ended up in my bed.

I heard Astra taunt you, however, she didn't put it there. She was simply happy that it was *there.*

Nerie threw herself onto the bed in annoyance. Even Kiriga didn't believe her. She felt the dragoness withdraw herself from her mind but ignored her. She was going to let Nerie pout about it on her own.

She heard a slight knock on the bedroom door and looked over to see Karina.

"Your Highness, I'm sure that dress isn't the most comfortable thing to lie in. Please let me help you remove it." Karina said with a slight bow.

"Did you bring my pajama pants?" Nerie asked as she stood.

Karina's face twisted into a slight frown as she answered, "No, my lady. Her highness, the queen, saw them and had them confiscated."

Of course, she did, Nerie thought angrily.

It wasn't the first time it had happened, but Aldis had always supplied her with a new pair. With him gone she would be stuck in dresses. Even sleeping ones.

"Right. Well, will you let me know when my mother

joins me for dinner?" she asked as Karina undid the intricate knots that held the dress together.

There was a slight pause, "I'm sorry my lady. She is attending dinner with Sir Ahlwin again this evening."

Nerie's mood blackened further. Astra, Queen Alaena, even her mother and Kiriga seemed to be working against her.

"I see. I'm ready for dinner whenever then. I'm going to go to sleep early. I can finish undressing myself."

She knew she was being snippy to Karina and that the poor woman hadn't done anything to earn her ire, but at the moment she didn't care.

"Of course, my lady. I'll bring it in immediately."

Karina left, closing the bedroom door behind herself.

I am not working against you. It's just that Astra didn't put the snake in your room, Kiriga's voice was quiet.

Even if she didn't do it herself, she was involved, Nerie insisted.

I'm done talking about this, Kiriga told her shortly.

Nerie was shocked. She didn't think the dragoness had ever spoken back to her before. It hurt.

I love you, Nerie. With all my being. But I am my own self, not just a reflection of you, the dragon's voice was much softer this time.

I just feel like I'm being punished. I want you here to sleep with me. To keep me safe.

Tears were welling up in the princess's eyes.

I know, Kiriga soothed. *I can feel and hear everything you think and feel. I'm sorry I'm not there. I've gotten too big to walk around inside the palace.*

Another small knock on the door drew Nerie's attention away from the conversation. Karina entered carrying a tray. Even from here Nerie could see the steam rising off a bowl of soup, and a large pile of fresh bread.

"I know that it's not going to make up for your day, but meals like this always make me feel better," Karina told her as she sat the food on a small table in the corner of the room. "If you need anything, I'll be in the sitting room."

"Thank you, Karina."

Nerie wiped at her still dewy eyes.

"You don't need to thank me, my lady," Karina said.

"Yes, I do. Royalty or not, I was a commoner most of my life. You thank people when they do things for you."

"Of course, my lady."

Nerie was feeling slightly better. She looked around the room with a fresh set of eyes. Less than two months ago, she would have been awed to be given even this suite. The bedroom was still larger than the whole second floor of their shop.

Their shop.

Nerie frowned. Who was taking care of all the books? Did Myha ever leave the royal palace to go back to their home? What about all their friends? They'd just disappeared the day after the hatching ceremony.

Nerie felt rather ashamed of herself. She'd never even let Raana know what had happened. It felt as if the life she was living now, and the life that she had always known were parts of a dream. Two things that could not possibly have ever existed in the same universe.

As she ate, she did have to give credit to Karina. She *was* feeling slightly better. Still thinking about the juxtaposition of her two lives, Nerie quickly grew tired.

As she climbed into the soft bed, she couldn't help but pull back the sheets - checking for any unwanted guests. Finding none, she quickly settled into the soft fabric.

***

The following morning, she woke to the soft knock of Karina bringing breakfast. Today's meal was light and Nerie dressed and ate slowly, chatting with Kiriga. It seemed that work was underway on her normal quarters, and Kiriga was curious about various tools. She then stole the knowledge of them from their wielders, excitedly telling Nerie about each one.

As the morning dragged on, Nerie found herself pacing the small sitting room. While Alaena had stressed royalty was never late - she also stressed that you should be mindful of the people waiting for you.

Alaena was late.

"Karina, did her majesty the queen say anything about being late today?" Nerie asked the woman.

"No, shall I send someone to see if she is coming?" Karina was already walking to the door as she asked.

"No, I'll take the morning to myself. I think that I'll go on over to the king's quarters and spend time with both Kiriga and Ilex."

Nerie also moved towards the door.

Karina moved to shadow the princess as usual, to see her to her destination. While she always accompanied Nerie through the halls, she would stay in the main sitting room of the king's suite once they arrived.

Nerie passed through several of the rooms, looking for the king to let him know she had arrived. Ilex and Kiriga were both still eating their morning meal and had yet to return to the courtyard. Reaching the king's study, she paused as she went to open the door.

She could hear raised voices from the other side.

"... cannot allow her to wear such a thing!" Alaena's voice was clear through the thin wood.

"She can't wear a dress while riding a dragon, Alaena!" Soren's voice had a hard edge to it that Nerie had only heard on a few occasions.

"Princesses do not wear pants! It's not like she'll be flying very often! You don't." Obviously, they were talking about her, and Nerie's heart raced.

"I don't because Ilex doesn't fly! Even still, I ride him like a horse."

"If you ride him like a horse, she can ride Kiriga like a horse. Sidesaddle. Like a lady." Alaena's tone was desperate.

Soren however broke into laughter. "Do you want her to fall off midair? Riding a *flying* dragon is nothing like a horse. I've ridden Soros and Eras enough to know that."

"*This* isn't acceptable. Regardless of how she will be flying."

"Alaena. This is not a matter of style but rather safety."

"I don't care! Just think of how the court would react if they saw her in such a garment."

Nerie was unsure of if she should open the door or walk away like she hadn't heard anything. She wasn't sure why she had thought that the king and queen would have separate quarters, but she hadn't imagined them sharing them.

"It's been a while since the ruler was a queen. I know that. My grandmother was the last. But the court will get used to it. I'm sure Nerie will…"

Nerie didn't get to hear what the king thought she would do, because at that moment Alaena opened the door, muttering about pants.

"Oh, Your Highness!" Nerie said, tripping on her skirt as she stepped backwards.

"Nerie. You're early for your lessons with Soren," Alaena said, steadying Nerie by her elbow.

Her face gave away no expression that she had been talking about Nerie just moments before.

"I thought I would take the morning to spend with the dragons, but they are all still eating," she stammered. "I came to let his highness know that I was here."

"Well, he will be happy to see you." Alaena let go of Nerie, walking off.

Neither of them mentioned the fact that Alaena had not shown up for Nerie's daily lessons.

Cautiously, Nerie peeked inside the doorway. Soren was standing in the middle of the room, clearly frustrated at the queen's rapid departure.

"Nerie! I'm glad you're here! Come in!" Soren waved her forward the moment he set eyes on her.

While Nerie had gotten the gist of what the argument had been about, when Soren stepped aside, Nerie could hardly believe her eyes. On a rack before her was the most luxurious outfit she had ever seen.

A jacket, pants, and a helmet hung on a rack. They were made from soft doeskin leather, lined with what looked to be warm fur. Nerie edged closer, itching to touch the fabric.

"This… is for me?" she asked slowly, her eyes lingering

on the fine buttons that made up a double row on the front of the jacket. She could understand Alaena's feelings. She could hardly imagine herself wearing it.

"Yes. You see, when you fly, it can be colder than winter, and the air just dries you out."

Soren was in teacher mode, completely oblivious to Nerie's wonder. He went on about the properties of correct air wear and seating. After finally getting the nerve up to touch the outfit, Nerie was surprised to find that there were also gloves and a face mask. Then a thought struck her, pulling her out of her reverie.

"Does this mean I'm going to learn to fly with Kiriga soon?" She could barely keep the excitement out of her voice. She suddenly felt Kiriga there watching and listening too.

"It does." Soren's smile was nearly as large as her own.

CHAPTER THIRTY-FOUR

Azelia

The sailors who had seen Zel were stuck somewhere between blind panic and determination to slay the dragon.

Pulling herself out from between the buildings, she roared so loudly that the windows on the nearest warehouses shattered. More than one man fell down screaming, clutching at their ears.

She turned to the end of the pier where the guarded section was, half leaping and half flying her way down. As she moved, her tail now nearly twenty feet long, lashed around striking anything it could reach.

The men at this end of the pier were not running and screaming. Bows and swords had been drawn. They were going to try to stop her from getting to her eggs.

She couldn't let that happen.

Breathing great gouts of flame, she mowed down soldier after soldier. One got close enough to slice open her calf before she smashed him into the ground with her taloned claw.

The ship and her eggs were in her sight.

It was a large, three-masted ship, full of more soldiers who were busily unmooring it and preparing to sail. What were they thinking? That they would be able to simply float away from her - a mighty dragon?

She snarled, black smoke billowing from her nostrils.

She jumped into the sky again, this time intending to land

on the ship. However, she was yanked back down to the ground. A large, hooked arrow had buried itself deep in her wingsail - and it was attached to a rope. Dozens of men were pulling down on it, trying to bring her to the ground. She snarled again and lunged at them. As the rope went slack, she was shot in the other side. More men pulled her in the opposite direction.

Furious, she roared again.

She summoned the forge from within her soul, and her flame burst forth, burning the men. However, the ropes attached to her, though thin, were undamaged. More men jumped to hold her down.

The ship was moving away faster than she expected. They were already shrinking in the distance. This infuriated her further. She could feel the tenuous connection with her eggs fading by the moment.

She was a dragon!

She would *not* let the humans get away with her eggs a second time.

Roaring again, she spun in a circle, knocking many of the men off their feet. Then, with a mighty thrust, she launched herself into the sky. She strained to beat her wings, the hooks tearing the fragile skin. Growing even larger to compensate, she pulled all the men who still held onto the ropes into the air with her.

Beating her wings as hard as she could, she propelled herself forward, losing several danglers in the motion. Feeling lighter, she was able to wing her way towards the now distant ship.

Reaching it in seconds, she prepared herself to land on the stern.

As she dropped, she saw a group of soldiers holding one of her eggs. Its mottled shell was undamaged, and it was so large that they had to hoist it between them. They were carrying it to the edge of the ship.

She saw her chance and lunged for them and the egg but was slowed by the few men still holding onto the ropes. They had braced themselves against the ship and were slowly pulling her backwards. Snapping her jaws, she tried to reach the men with her egg.

Her attention was momentarily pulled away from the egg when a man in metal armor shouted to get her attention.

"Dragoness!"

Seeing her eyes flicker in his direction he stepped forward.

"Come close enough for me to see you again, and this will be the fate of all your eggs!"

She couldn't react fast enough. She twisted, trying to get back towards the egg. But at the man's word, the other men threw the egg into the churning water below.

Zel dived into the rapids after the egg.

The icy water shocked Zel's hide. She could feel the bleeding in her wings slow as she thrust herself deeper after the egg. It was sinking rapidly, tumbling end over end as the strong current of the river pulled it downward.

Claws outstretched, she missed grabbing the egg by inches as a current caught her left wing and pulled her forcefully to the side. Using her tail like a rudder, she realigned herself, swiping after the egg again. This time, the egg made a quick drop downward, as it hit a spot of still water.

She passed it.

Desperately, she tried to turn herself over, like she would in midair. Instead of working as intended, she was pulled by the current farther downstream.

Righting herself, swimming with all her might up current, she saw the egg get caught in the current once again.

Zel was feet away from it when it smashed into a boulder, shell shattering.

She roared underwater, the bubbles momentarily blinding her.

She did not stop. She made it to the broken egg moments too late. A small figure hung limply out of the shell, pressed against the large rock by the strong current. Too young to have even developed a color yet but perfectly formed.

Zel had felt the hatchling die upon impact.

Carefully, she scooped up the tiny form, then she let the current pull her away.

The urge to go after the ship was hotter than the sun and burned inside her. She turned, the hatchling still in her grasp - but paused.

The look on the knight's face had told her that she would never make it before the rest of her eggs were destroyed.

She looked down at her hatchling, its blue veins visible beneath the translucent skin. Two of her five eggs - gone.

Never to take their first breath, breathe their first flame.

She was pulled out of her reverie by the worried shouting from Graith's mind. He was near. Maybe he would know what to do.

I'm coming.

CHAPTER THIRTY-FIVE

Graith

Graith tried not to look back towards all the screaming.
He *knew* Zel was killing people.

Not seeing her act made it easier to process. He knew she
was protecting herself and her eggs, and that she would do
anything in order to get them back.

Instead, he blocked out the screams and focused on
getting Mero out of the alley. He had to find Alix.

Mounting Mero, he was able to ride along the backside
of the warehouses. Petting Mero's large neck, he calmed the
horse and himself as he looked down each alley for the boy.
His heart thudded painfully in his chest as a scream pierced
his calm. Panic seized him at the thought of the lad possibly
being hurt in the mob that he could glimpse shoving itself
away from the rampaging dragon.

"Alix! Alix!" he shouted over and over, desperate to be
heard above the screaming.

When he reached the last warehouse, he turned Mero
back to the pier. Within moments they were adrift in the tide
of people.

As he sat on Mero's back, Graith towered over the men
running to and from the pier. He had forgotten how big Mero
was, having become accustomed to the horse pulling the cart
all day.

More than one person collided with the big horse. The
force of their contact nearly knocked Graith off Mero, but he

wrapped his hands tight in the horse's mane. Mero's ears were flat against his head, but he was responding to every nudge and command that Graith gave him. Graith sent a silent thanks once again to Ralph - the horse was a godsend - any other beast would have started bucking and kicking by now.

"Graith!" The young boy's scream was audible above the roar of the crowd.

Graith turned his whole body looking for Alix. He spotted him as he tried to run towards Graith from near one of the ships. The flow of the mob had pushed him to the outskirts. Graith breathed a sigh of relief that the boy hadn't been trampled.

Using Mero's large mass, he navigated his way over. The distance, while short, was filled with panicked sailors. Roars from Zel caused Graith to glance over. She had ropes hanging from her wings and men were trying to drag her to the ground. She was enormous, nearly as large as the ships in the water. Larger than Graith had ever seen her.

Another cry from Alix as he was roughly shoved aside, yanked Graith's attention back to him. Mero shoved his body between the boy and the outpouring of people. Graith leaned over and pulled the boy onto the horse's back with a single yank. Mero turned, and they were once again swept off by the mob of people.

They needed to get out of the city.

"Where are we going?" Alix asked.

His voice was muffled as he had his face tucked into Graith's shoulder blades.

"As far away from here as we can get!"

Graith desperately prayed that all the guards were busy trying to deal with Zel. Otherwise they were going to be trapped in the city. He urged Mero into a gallop, not caring about the people underfoot - they could move or be run over.

They headed back up the long hill to the wet bridge. It was full of people still trying to get as far away from the dragoness as they could, but Mero shoved his way through. His gait faltered slightly when stepping from the bridge back onto the stone street. He caught himself and kept going. Graith urged him to speed up, and somehow, he did.

People on this side of the river were just now hearing the screams and understanding what was happening down at the docks. Screams and shouts filled the air as people tried to get to their homes. Shops keepers were shoving people out of their doors, and people were stuck with nowhere to go. The cries of the women thrown out into the streets competed in cacophony with the screams of the men that still echoed up the city streets.

Another large group of soldiers ran towards the docks, swords drawn. They didn't even look in the direction of the galloping trio.

Sweat lathered Mero's hide as he continued his forward motion towards the gate. The guards there had not abandoned their posts, though they too had their swords drawn and looked like they desperately wanted to go help.

The same guard who had stopped them when they entered the city hailed them. While Graith didn't want to stop - wanted nothing more than to blow right through the gates - Mero needed to rest. He also didn't want to draw suspicion to their small group by not stopping.

"What is going on?" the guard demanded. "We can hear people screaming and saw smoke billowing up from the pier not five minutes ago."

Graith sighed in relief, the man was just worried about Kelna, and wanted to know what was going on.

"A dragon! It set fire to the docks! Destroyed our cart! We have to get out of here!" Alix's voice was fear-filled and quivering, as he spoke before Graith could.

"A dragon?! Where did it come from?" The guard seemed shocked.

"No idea, Sir, but we want to go home!" Graith let his anxiety creep into his voice. "Never coming to Kelna again. Dragons!"

He kicked Mero back in to motion, exiting the city through the gate. No one called him back, so he assumed they were free to go. He kept the horse at a brisk trot until the city was well out of sight.

"Zel, can you hear me?" Graith shouted aloud and in his mind, however, no response came.

"Is she talking to you, boy?" he asked Alix after a few moments.

This distance from the city, the only sounds were the distant roar of the river and the click of Mero's hooves on the stone road. Graith strained to hear a possible wing beat or roar but none came.

"No, I can't hear her at all. What happened back there?" Alix's voice was soft and muffled, still buried in Graith's back. Graith glanced over his shoulder and saw the boy motion back towards Kelna.

"Zel lost control," Graith said, thinking back to the moment he had heard her desperate cry, "She had to get to her eggs, Alix. What did you think was going to happen when we got to the pier?"

"I don't know. Not that. Anything but her killing -"

Alix cut off, and Graith felt a warm wetness seep through the back of his shirt. Alix was crying.

"Ah, lad. It's okay."

Graith twisted to look at Alix, and the boy started sobbing.

"I... I'd never," he said, choking the words past sobs, "I'd never seen someone *die* before!"

Graith just hugged him, patting his back gently.

"Shh, it'll be okay lad."

While still facing the boy - even in the awkward position of sitting on the horse's wide back - he turned Mero to follow the river. He hoped that they would see Zel - or the ship she had gone after.

After several long minutes of sobbing from the boy, Alix wiped his eyes and nose on his sleeve, sniffling. Graith turned awkwardly and patted Alix's back one last time before facing forward. He then navigated Mero even closer to the riverbank.

There had been no sign of Zel yet, and she still wasn't responding to his mental shouts to her.

When he saw a body that had floated to the shore, he moved them away before Alix could see. There was no need to upset the lad again.

Silently, however, he felt encouraged by it - they must be getting closer to Zel or the ship.

Desperate for a response, Graith shouted with his mind once again, *Zel, please, if you can hear me, come back.*

Like the faintest of whispers, Graith heard Zel's voice. *I'm coming.*

There was none of her usual emotion attached to it. That alarmed him, as he had expected to feel her anger. At the pier it had been overwhelming - now, there was nothing.

He scanned the surrounding section of the river for her. It looked the same as it had moments before. When she did not appear immediately, Graith wondered if he had imagined her voice, it would explain the lack of emotion attached to it.

A crashing of water pulled Graith's attention farther down the river. Zel burst forth from the churning rapids.

She was a snowy white once again.

As she landed on the ground, Graith could clearly see blood oozing from new wounds all over her body. She was holding her front claw at an odd angle, close to her body. Graith thought that perhaps she had broken it.

"Zel?" Graith asked as he approached the dragoness. Normally he could feel her presence, even hear the whispers of her thoughts at times - right now all he heard was silence, and he felt nothing from her.

He had a sick feeling in the pit of his stomach as he eased himself down from Mero's high back. His legs were weak as he staggered towards her.

Zel had only turned white for one reason before.

"Zel?" he called again, hoping that he was wrong.

She did not answer him.

Instead, she gently laid a still form on the ground in front of her. Graith's heart broke. He took a long step towards her when Alix spoke.

"Graith -" Alix's voice was shaking, "Can we, uh, stay back for a moment?"

Graith hesitated, looking between Zel and Alix. He stopped moving and turned quickly to face the boy.

"What's wrong, lad?" Graith asked, concerned. He wanted to go to Zel, but Alix needed his attention.

"I… I think I'm afraid of her."

Alix sounded surprised that he was scared of Zel.

Oh, child, Zel said. *You do not need to fear me. I was trying to save my clutch and those men were keeping me away.*

She was quiet for a moment, and they could see her look down at the pale form she had laid on the ground.

All it got me was death. Death of more humans and death of another of my children.

If Zel could cry, Graith thought she would be. When Alix spoke again, it took Graith by surprise.

"May - may I see your hatchling, Zel?" Alix's hand was now wrapped in Mero's mane, clenched as he waited for an answer.

Yes, Alix, Zel said softly.

Alix slid down from Mero's high back and slowly inched his way towards Zel. Graith could see his legs shake as he took each step.

"It's so small." he whispered when he was finally close enough to see.

Yes, she was not ready to hatch. Her egg shattering killed her.

"Oh."

Alix leaned against Zel without realizing it. She was warm, even after climbing out of the icy waters, and he was still cold and wet. Graith watched them both as she laid her head on the ground, her blue eyes closed. Her breathing was ragged, and Graith could see Zel's hot breath in the puffs of mist from her nostrils. A particular wheeze caught his attention as she spoke to him.

Graith, I don't feel right.

Graith walked over to inspect her wounds. Her right wing was in tatters and blood oozed out of it slowly.

I'll patch you up again, Zel. Let me get my kit from the

bags.

He walked back over to the horse and started pulling the bags off Mero while shouting to Alix.

"Lad, can you collect firewood? We need to get her patched up before we can move. We need to get ourselves warmed up too."

The boy jumped up from his spot against Zel. He wasn't shaking any longer. Immediately he ran along the riverbed to do just that.

CHAPTER THIRTY-SIX

Graith

Graith found it much easier to stitch up Zel this time around. Maybe it was because he knew she wasn't going to eat him or maybe it was because she was alert enough to talk during it - either way, he got the bleeding stopped within an hour.

He was proud of Alix, who had helped without question, getting wood, starting a fire, then boiling water. While Graith did the stitching and reconstruction on Zel's wing, Alix took care of Mero. The poor horse kept looking for his cart to be hitched to.

The whole time Graith worked, the three of them kept looking back towards Kelna. No one seemed to be coming after them, but they wanted to get on the road as quickly as they could.

While Graith worked on her, Zel hunched protectively over her hatchling's corpse.

Zel, I... Graith wasn't sure how to broach the subject. *I don't think that a pyre is a smart idea right now. It will draw attention from the city.*

Zel growled lightly as she said, *She deserves to be honored.*

Aye, but for now we have to not draw their attention. I don't know if, or when, they are going to come looking for you.

Zel looked down at him, her eyes glowing orange.

I will kill them if they do. She will *be honored.*

Graith sighed, putting the final stitch into place.

All right, Zel, but we must be on our way once the pyre is lit.

He rubbed Zel's snout gently.

Turning towards Alix, he said, "Alix, we need more firewood."

Standing and stretching from where he had been sitting on the ground, Graith looked around at the meager selection of trees to choose from. The boy looked at him quizzically.

"I thought we were leaving now that you've patched Zel up?"

"We are soon - but we have something important we have to do first."

Alix stood there confused until Zel spoke. *Dragon's burn their dead, Alix. My daughter deserves that honor.*

"Oh! Of course, Zel. How much wood do we need?"

Alix was already running towards the small copse of trees that lined the river.

"Enough to build a pyre." Graith said.

He grabbed a fallen sapling from the edge of the tree line, and dragged it towards Zel. Looking at her hunched form staring down at the hatchling's body, Graith's soul twisted. It wasn't fair that this was happening to her or her family - and he was powerless to do anything to help.

More for himself than her, he said, *Remember, we must go as soon as the pyre is lit.*

I know, Zel said. She sounded so resigned.

It took them about half an hour to assemble the pyre, the sun moving slowly overhead. Once complete, Zel gently laid the small form atop it.

Alix and Graith took a collective step backwards as Zel released a gout of flame. It enveloped the small pyre, and black smoke immediately billowed into the cloudless sky.

As the fire crackled, Graith and Alix mounted Mero's wide back, legs resting awkwardly on the, now properly strapped on, saddlebags. Turning and spurring Mero into a trot, Graith looked back to see Zel staring deeply into the orange flames.

Azelia. We must *go.*

She did not acknowledge him, instead she tilted back her large head. A keen, sharp and loud, pierced the air before she finally turned to follow.

Graith watched her trundle along, her tail dragging on the ground, her wings limp. Behind her, Kelna was obscured from his vision by the large column of smoke. His heart raced with every step that Mero took, moving them farther from the city. Graith wanted to get them as far away from the pyre as possible before nightfall.

***

Riding Mero was nothing like being pulled along in the cart. Bouncing more and straddling his wide back caused them to need to take several short breaks over the next few hours. It impeded their progress, and Graith worried that soldiers would show up at any moment.

In addition to their discomfort, every time they stopped Zel would stare back in the direction of the pyre. Graith's insides twisted with guilt from pulling her away from the pyre - giving her no time to grieve her loss. His curiosity also clawed at him, desperate to know what had transpired in Kelna.

Finally, he couldn't hold it back any longer. During one of their short breaks, he asked, *What happened after we were separated, Zel?*

I made it to the ship. The knight, the one Alix told us about, he was waiting *for me. Told me if he saw me again that they would kill the rest of my eggs. Then they threw my daughter overboard.*

Her voice broke and, for a second Graith, saw a vision of the egg tumbling end over end in the dark, churning waters.

I was so close, Graith. My claws missed her by inches. What if I miss them all by inches?

She was so distraught by the idea that her wings sagged again, and her tail, which had been twitching back and forth, slumped to the ground.

Graith walked over and laid himself against her head,

wrapping his arms around it as best as he could.

You won't. We *won't,* he promised.

Alix hadn't heard the exchange, but he still came over and hugged Zel's snout from the other side.

"Zel, can I ride on your back? Mero and Graith aren't as warm as you," he murmured as he rubbed his face against the soft scales of her snout. He was still wet from passing under the waterfall twice, and the cold air had him shivering.

I've never had a human ride on my back, she said, sounding thoughtful and not denying him.

Unaware of Zel's current mood, Alix perked up.

"We could have great fun! If you were the same size as Mero, we could race!"

Graith was surprised by Alix wanting to use Zel as a mount, and for a moment was rather offended by it for her, until she spoke up again.

That could be fun! she said, allowing Alix's mood to lighten her own. Anything to keep her thoughts from returning to her daughter or her other eggs.

Graith knew Alix had a competitive streak a mile wide but was surprised with Zel. Then he remembered her saying that she was young for a dragon. Not much more than a child herself. As he walked back over to Mero, he realized how little he knew about Zel. And how little about dragonkind any of them knew.

Even as Alix settled on her back and they had started moving again, Graith was lost in thought, wondering about dragons and Etria, and how exactly she had gotten into this situation.

"Zel, tell us about your family?" he asked finally, figuring that brooding on the subject would get him no answers.

She looked over at him, her eyes still not their normal blue, but no longer an anxious orange, instead they were a mint-green. She looked surprised that he had asked. Her wingtips clicked together above Alix's head.

Well, I'm the only child of my mother, Isla, and father, Corly.

She showed the image of two dragons, one a seafoam-green, the other orangish-pink. The green dragon could have been Zel with her smooth wings and soft scales. Her head was the same wedge shape too.

The coral-pink dragon, however, was different. He was covered in short spines and his head was blockier. His wings were short and wide, and his tail ended in a protrusion that looked like a mace.

Graith was fascinated. From Zel's dream and these images, all the dragons he'd seen were unique. As he thought about this, Alix spoke up.

"What determines what color a dragon will be?" Alix asked, wonder in his voice - he'd never seen another dragon before.

A hatchling can be any color that is in their bloodline.

"Why was your hatchling white?" Alix asked. Graith knew that he meant, *are there white dragons in your family?* He would have covered Alix's mouth if he could have reached. The kid had no tact - they were supposed to be keeping Zel's mind away from her lost hatchling.

She would not have been born white, she wasn't old enough to develop a color yet, Zel's voice sounded strained.

"Oh, what color would she have been?" Alix plunged forward, not noticing Zel's emotional state.

There is no way to know until shortly before they hatch. Their egg takes on a shade similar to their scales, Zel's voice was now icy.

"What color do you think your hatchlings will be?" Alix was oblivious.

Graith was considering grabbing the boy from the dragon's back at this point. Before Zel could answer, Graith intervened.

"Alix, you ready for that race?"

Graith wasn't sure what else to say to distract the boy from his current line of questions.

"Yeah! You ready Zel?" Alix leaned forward and lay nearly flat along her neck.

Yes.

She put on a fake tone of excitement, but Graith could feel her tension over the questions.

"All right, how far are we going, Alix?" Graith asked, lining Mero up shoulder to shoulder with Zel.

"Um…" He looked into the distance, "That dead tree about a quarter mile out!"

"One!" Graith counted.

"Two!" Alix shouted excitedly.

Three! Zel leapt ahead before Graith could nudge Mero into motion.

Unsure of who won, they did sprint after sprint until both Zel and Mero were panting. After Zel said she doubted she could take another step, they stopped. Both the dragon and the horse drank deeply from the river they still followed. Once sated, they resumed moving, but at a walking pace.

***

The hours passed slowly, and by nightfall Graith couldn't have pointed out Kelna if he had wanted to. He dismounted Mero and pulled off the saddle bags.

Before now, they hadn't had time to take stock of the damage. They lost a lot with the destruction of the cart, most of which had been comfort and the jars of food. They had also lost the weapons - but Graith wasn't terribly upset by that.

As he pulled the bags open, he found mostly dirty clothes and the sewing kit he had used just hours before. A large camp knife and a few loaves of stale bread were inside one bag. A blanket and his traveling cloak were buried in another.

It wasn't great, but they could survive. Especially with Zel hunting for them.

Will you be able to fly soon? he asked her silently.

While Alix was mature for his age, Graith and Zel had become his impromptu caregivers and there was no reason to worry him unless necessary.

Within a day. This was more a puncture than a rip to my mainsail. I could fly now if I needed but it would be painful.

Okay. Well, we are short on food, so once you're able we'll need you to hunt.

He packed everything back into the bags with a semblance of organization and cuddled up to Zel's left side while Alix had already done so on her right.

***

They woke the following morning to a thin layer of snow. The horse, for the first time since Graith had owned him, was in a less than pleased mood. His tail twitched in agitation, and his ears were flat against his head. He stomped restlessly as Graith cleaned the snow off him.

Zel stood and shook herself, snow coming down in small flurries. Alix shouted in glee, but Graith was more worried than ever. The boy was not dressed to be traveling in this weather. He had planned on getting him proper clothing in Kelna.

"Alix, come here," Graith called while digging the clothes out of the saddle bags.

"We need to dress you as warmly as we can. Don't know how long the trip to the capital is, and you aren't dressed for the weather. Can't have you catching a chill."

They layered as many shirts and pants onto the boy as they could and then Zel shrunk small so that he could hop on her back before increasing her size back to larger than Mero.

"You've gotten good at that!" Alix exclaimed in excitement.

Thank you. I need to continue to keep practicing. We don't know when I'll need to use it again, she said, sounding resigned. Graith knew she was thinking about how she had lost control in Kelna.

We will find your eggs, Zel, Graith told her once again.

Graith pulled the blanket on himself, followed by his cloak. The cloak, while oiled and water resistant, wasn't warm. He hoped the blanket would keep his heat in well enough. Snuggling in, he urged Mero forward, and Zel followed behind.

CHAPTER THIRTY-SEVEN

Nerie

We'll finally get to fly together! Kiriga bugled happily, her roar audible to all within the palace walls.

Soren spent the next several hours talking about the various aspects of flying and how, initially, they would work on strengthening Kiriga's wings. For the first time in what felt like weeks, Nerie was clinging to his every word.

That evening Nerie could hardly sleep. She lay in the dark room, her heartbeat pounding in her ears. She and Kiriga were going to fly - truly fly!

Kiriga's mood was happy with a bright pink and yellow aura that Nerie saw every time she closed her eyes. Soros and Eras were inordinately pleased with their offspring. Nerie had heard Eras on more than one occasion during the day instruct Kiriga on wing stretches and tail exercises.

Ilex was happy for his young sister too, but for the first time Nerie felt a slight bit of resentment from the older dragon. When Soros told him off, he mumbled something about digging a cave, and faded from Nerie's mind. She could understand him not wanting to be around the other dragons just then. It must be so frustrating for him, being stuck on the ground when his parents and all his siblings could soar through the sky.

It was Wyla who finally helped Nerie fall asleep. From her distant post, she shared the memory of her first flight with Nerie's ancestor, Kyre. Wyla did not speak, and Nerie could feel the mental strain the dragoness was under trying to clearly share her memory from so far away. The one thing that Wyla was able to crystallize in the memory for Nerie was the feeling of sheer joy that she had shared with Kyre.

Nerie thanked Wyla as the vision faded and her eyes drifted shut.

***

The next morning, Nerie was awake far earlier than normal.

Even from the confines of the dark room, she could feel the sun cresting the horizon. She wasn't sure if this knowledge came from Kiriga or her own intuition, but she knew she was right. She sprang out of bed and pulled her bedroom door open, looking for Karina.

"Karina! Please come help me dress!" she said, turning back to her small closet.

Her new outfit from Soren hung on its own rack, front and center - just waiting to be worn.

"Your highness, while it is not my place to tell you what to do, you might want to bathe first. You skipped it yesterday and your hair is quite mussed," Karina said formally, while subtly eyeing Nerie's head.

"Oh. Yes. I forgot," Nerie said sheepishly.

She really had forgotten. All her dreams the night before had been her soaring through the skies on Kiriga's back.

She ran to the waiting tub, steam rising off the water. She tested it with her hand and found it to be too hot to enter.

Tapping her bare foot impatiently, she looked around the bathroom. Seeing the pile of plush towels waiting for her, she grabbed a small one and dipped it into the hot water. She then lathered it with soap and simply scrubbed at her body. She reasoned with herself that it wasn't like she had done anything to be particularly dirty.

Her hair was another matter. She bent over the stone tub, hair hanging into the water, and quickly dunked her scalp into the tub. Hissing, she pulled it back out and started scrubbing it with her nails and palms, which were lathered with soap in preparation. A few minutes and three more dips into the scalding water, and she felt she was passably clean.

Drying off and wrapping her hair in a towel, she hurried back to her room. Karina was there, along with a golden gown she'd laid out on Nerie's bed.

Nerie let out a groan.

"Karina! Kiriga and I are flying for the first time today! I need to wear the new outfit King Soren gave me."

Nerie started to pull the outfit from the closet but stopped her motion when Karina frowned.

"My lady, you still have lessons with her majesty, the queen, this morning. She would just make you change if she saw you in pants."

Karina's voice was strained and her face pale. She didn't want to upset Nerie, but she had borne the brunt of the queen's ire about princesses wearing pants one too many times.

Nerie crossed her arms, looking at the dress. It *was* one of her favorites, but her excitement to wear the riding leathers she held was second only to her excitement to fly.

Karina spoke again, "I am afraid she might try to remove them from your possession, my lady."

Fine, she thought. She would wear the dress for the lesson.

As she dressed, Karina fetched her breakfast. Today's meal was composed of only fruit and toast. Nerie's stomach growled hungrily, and she worried it wouldn't be enough for the day.

"His highness said that you might not want much in your stomach," Karina said when Nerie looked at her in surprise.

Not that she would say it aloud, but for a split second Nerie thought that it was a comment on her weight. She wasn't afraid of heights - or at least she didn't think she was - but she could understand where Soren was coming from.

When Alaena arrived, Nerie was surprised to see that the queen's ladies in waiting had accompanied her. They were carrying multiple small baskets which they placed on the small table in the sitting room. After depositing their burdens, the two women exited the room.

Alaena opened one of the baskets and pulled out a small hoop and several skeins of brightly colored thread. Nerie felt the blood drain out of her face.

Embroidery? Really?

While she could *theoretically* darn her own socks or patch a hole in her clothes, Nerie was not a patient person. She was constantly moving, whether it was tapping her fingers or bouncing her foot. Sometimes, when she was thinking particularly hard, she even chewed on her tongue.

"Do not give me that look, Nerie," Alaena said coolly, as she looked at the pale-faced princess. "Every *true* lady knows how to embroider."

"I don't want to be a true lady then!" Nerie said, her voice tinged with panic.

"Too late. Kiriga signed you up to become the paragon of ladyship."

Alaena handed Nerie one of the hoops along with a plain white handkerchief. Then she handed her a small leather pack of needles and a simple red floss.

"We are going to start off with the different stitches. I will instruct you on a stitch, and then you will duplicate it the full width of the hoop. I will then examine your work. If it is acceptable, we will move on to the next type of stitch - if not, you will repeat the practice."

Alaena was tucking her own handkerchief into the hoop and had a green floss.

They started with the straight stitch, it was simple, into the fabric, then back out, in a line, over and over. Nerie felt confident in her work and quickly made a line of red floss and handed the hoop to the queen.

"This is unacceptable, your stitch length is wildly inconsistent and there are gaps between the end of one stitch and the start of the next. Again."

Slowing down, Nerie carefully placed stitch after stitch.

Alaena, in the meantime, pulled out a third hoop that had an elaborate scene forming on it. Nerie could make out Ilex and Eras, and from the thread still in the basket, she guessed the queen would be adding the other dragons too. More than once she pricked her finger, looking not at her own work, but the queen's.

After the straight stitch, they moved onto the backstitch, and then the buttonhole. The longer they sat there, the more that Nerie's focus wandered. The first stitch had taken three attempts before being satisfactory. The second had taken five. She was currently on the fourth round of the buttonhole, but she didn't think this one would be up to the queen's standard either.

When her stomach gave a slight growl, Nerie flushed pink.

"I'm sorry, your highness, I ate a light breakfast at the king's behest."

"Of course. He does not want you ruining that waste of leather on your first flight," Alaena said, tucking away her own hoops. "This basket is yours. I want you to start again from the beginning, in blue, for each type of stitch you learned today. Have it ready for tomorrow's lesson."

Alaena opened the door, and one of her maids came in, bowed to Nerie, and grabbed the larger basket, quickly following the queen.

Nerie looked down at her sad little handkerchief. It was spotted with droplets of her blood and the lines were woefully uneven. To complete her task meant she would either need to get up early the following morning or stay up late that night to finish it on time.

For a moment, Nerie considered not sewing the assigned stitches, but she knew that would just cause more issues between herself and the queen.

"My lady," Karina said softly, taking the hoop and placing it in the basket. "I have brought your lunch - more fruit and toast - as well as a basin of hot water for you to soak your hands in, before you eat. It will help the wounds close up."

"Then I can change?" Nerie asked hopefully.

"Of course. We wouldn't want you to be late to your lesson with his majesty."

She winked at Nerie, a small smile on her face.

The hot water stung the small punctures, but when she patted her hands dry, no blood was left on the towel. Nerie quickly ate and then made her way back to her room.

Nerie quickly discarded her dress onto the floor. She then pulled on the leather pants. They fit like a second skin. She pulled on the plain linen shirt, then slid the jacket on over it. The soft fur that lined it made her want to run her fingers through the luxurious texture.

There were pockets on the front which had flaps that buttoned down. She immediately shoved the gloves into one. The king had also ordered her a pair of stout boots. Lined with the same fur as the jacket, they went midway up her calves and buttoned up the sides. While she buttoned up one boot, Karina helped her with the other.

Standing straight, she walked to the wall where a large mirror hung. She smiled, running her hands over her hips and squatting, then leaning from one side to the other. The leather moved with her and wasn't the least bit uncomfortable. She looked at the cap that was still lying on the bed and frowned.

"Karina, do you have a leather thong to tie my hair up? I don't want it flying all over the place in the wind."

Nerie tugged at a ruby lock.

"I do, my lady."

Karina grabbed a brush off the nightstand and walked over to where Nerie stood. She quickly smoothed down the long, auburn mane, pleating it and tying off the end.

Nerie was surprised to see that the braid hung past her shoulder blades, halfway down her back. Maybe she would think about cutting it in the near future, but for now, she was ready to get to the king's chambers and the courtyard in which the dragons waited.

"Thank you, Karina!"

Nerie snatched the cap off the bed and ran out the door.

She could hear the pitter-patter of Karina's feet as she followed Nerie in a brisk walk, but the sound quickly faded. Nerie knew that if the queen saw her, she would be firmly reprimanded.

She didn't care.

Instead, she picked up her pace.

"Nerie!"

Soren was standing in the doorway to the courtyard, waiting for her.

"Soren! I'm ready to go." she panted, bending over, slightly winded.

"Hah, I can see that."

Soren's smile was crinkling the corners of his eyes.

Finally, having caught her breath, she stood. Looking past the king into the courtyard, she saw Eras, Ilex, and Kiriga.

Nerie! Look at me!

Kiriga was standing under the noonday sun, her scales gleaming golden. A leather harness had been placed upon her chest, and it wrapped around to her back where it culminated in a strange looking saddle.

No wonder you were quiet all morning! How long did it take to get that contraption on you? Nerie asked.

She laughed as she ran her hand along the strong leather straps.

Only a few hours. The first few servants didn't want to get near me, but then a nice leather worker showed up. Most of the time was spent making sure the straps fit in the right places and that they would have room to expand as I grow. What do you think?

Nerie could hear the slight twinge of nerves as Kiriga did a small pirouette for Nerie to see every side of her.

You're gorgeous, of course. Are you ready to fly for the first time?

Nerie, you know that I've been flying for a few weeks, right? Kiriga asked, confused.

But not with me! Nerie said with a giggle. *And, not very high, right? Just gliding?*

Kiriga pouted but laid on the ground in front of Nerie.

"All right, Nerie. I know you climb all over the dragons whenever you want, but there is a *proper* way to do it. You don't want to hurt yourself as you age." Turning to the great orange dragon he said, "Eras?"

Eras laid down his large body, mirroring the pose that Kiriga was in.

"I know that Eras has spikes you can climb like a ladder, but Kiriga does not. She will be Eras' size one day. So, if you first step onto her elbow like this -"

He demonstrated on the larger dragon, whose elbow was nearly as high as his head. To reach it, Soren first stepped onto a large talon, then placed his foot in the wedge of the shoulder and elbow, hoisting himself up.

"Then you move from there to the wing joint -"

Another series of steps forward, using the protruding wing as a handrail, and Soren was nearly at Eras's back.

"Finally, you should be able to reach the saddle!"

Eras was also equipped with a fine, leather network of straps and an identical large saddle. Soren swung his leg over the seat, pulling himself erect.

"Lastly, strap your legs in. If Kiriga needs to roll, or even swerve at a strong angle, you want to stay seated."

He demonstrated with his own legs, motioning Nerie over to inspect his work. She followed his steps to climb the great orange dragon.

"Your turn!" he said after he was convinced that she understood how the leg straps worked.

Nerie didn't take the same route down as she had climbed up. Instead she hopped from one spike to another, quickly lowering herself to the ground. Eras watched, amused. His eyes swirled a calm green and orange.

Nerie then stepped carefully up Kiriga's comparatively small side.

You won't hurt me! Kiriga said, turning her great head to watch her rider.

No, but you'll hurt me if you don't stay still!

Nerie had been about to step to the wing joint when the dragon wiggled dangerously.

Abashed, Kiriga muttered a quiet, *Sorry.*

It's all right, love.

Nerie settled into her own saddle, working on closing the leg straps the way Soren had shown her.

Now, Eras' voice boomed into their heads, *Kiriga, you must watch me take off. Launching from the ground is natural to you. However, a rider - even as slight a human as Nerie - throws off your natural center. You'll need to kick yourself aloft, beating downward at the same time.*

He moved to the center of the courtyard, crowding his two children. But when he stretched his massive wings, Nerie understood.

She wasn't sure he would clear the rooftops that surrounded the courtyard with his initial downbeat. His wingspan was longer than his whole considerable body. Nerie knew from experience that he could lay straight and the tip of his nose to the last spike of his tail was longer than the whole palace. As he reared back onto his hind legs and opened his large wings, he cast a dark shadow across all that she could see.

The force of him leaping into the air knocked Kiriga off balance and Nerie was instantly glad for the leg straps. The ground shook, and dust rattled out of the woodwork. He was triple the height of the palace into the sky before the first downbeat of his powerful wings. The air thundered and Nerie was left reeling, covering her ears. That reminded her of the cap and gloves. She pulled them out of her pocket and put them on as Eras gained height.

Ready? Eras asked.

He was high in the sky now, hovering, looking down upon them. The shadow he cast made the courtyard seem as if it were the middle of the night.

Of course! Kiriga told him confidently.

She walked to the middle of the courtyard, then stood on her hind legs, mimicking the large dragon's actions.

In a moment that only lasted a heartbeat, both took deep breaths. Nerie felt Kiriga's muscles coil in anticipation.

Then Kiriga launched them into the sky.

Her takeoff was a little wobbly. She pushed slightly harder with her left leg than her right. Then when her wings came down in the first beat, she tried to compensate by doing the opposite. Nerie clenched the saddle, leaning low against

Kiriga's neck.

The second wing beat was more stable, and then the third. They quickly gained altitude and Nerie looked over the dragon's side.

The entirety of the palace was visible, and Nerie had a moment of vertigo, the world spinning. Her heartbeat thudded in her ears, and the world seemed to spin. She closed her eyes tight, nauseated.

She was more than a little glad that the king had thought ahead and had her meals be light. She was not sick, but acid coursed up her throat.

She focused on breathing in through her nose. The feeling subsided and Nerie took a deep breath, opening her eyes again.

Her second look at the ground was breathtaking, but for a different reason than the first time.

It was beautiful.

She could see as far as the horizon. The palace was shrinking, and the great lake that bordered Roria to the west was glimmering in the afternoon sunlight. Taking her eyes off the ground, she looked up and saw that Soren and Eras were still far above them.

Now, my daughter, you may fly like we've been practicing. We are going to work on diving and climbing, Eras told Kiriga.

Hold on tight! she told Nerie in turn.

Then they were diving at the ground, gaining speed.

Nerie watched the trees, buildings, and even people get closer. She trusted Kiriga fully but was forced to close her eyes against the sting of the wind. Her pleated hair waved like a flag behind her, hitting her back in strange intervals as it was caught between one gust and the next.

Nerie wasn't sure when she started, but she realized she was screaming. Not in fear but pure unadulterated joy.

The same joy that Wyla had shown her the night before, that she and Kyre had shared on their first flight.

They were climbing again, this time higher than Eras. Nerie could see Soros clearly lounging on the bank of the lake to the west of the city. Eras was gleaming in the strong sunlight.

This is better than I ever dreamed, Nerie confided to her dragon.

Love for one another coursed between them, and Kiriga dove towards the ground once again.

CHAPTER THIRTY-EIGHT

Nerie

The following days were difficult for Nerie.

They were near bliss as she learned to fly with Kiriga through the skies. Then they turned hellish as the tedium that Alaena had decided to teach her continued.

Each day, by the time for her lessons with Soren, Nerie's fingers were full of pricks and sores. She may have learned the stitches, but she was by no means any good at them, as Alaena was prone to telling her.

On top of her lessons, she received word that Sir Ahlwin had taken her mother to his estate, so every night she dined alone. It was strange for Nerie not to see Myha. The night of the first flight, Nerie had been bouncing with joy as she waited to tell her mother all about it. The disappointment that had followed Karina's news of her departure stung.

She'd taken to eating in her small room alone and then working on whatever task Alaena had assigned her until she fell asleep. Karina seemed to be aware of her mood as every morning when she awoke, the hoop and threads would be returned to their basket at her bedside.

Nearly two weeks after their first flight lesson, Soren sat her down before their now daily flight.

"Nerie, and Kiriga - I know you are listening too - I think you're both ready for an extended flight. In accordance, Sylas and Wyla have extended an offer for you to stay with them."

Soren searched Nerie's face looking for any reaction to this news. Whatever he was looking for, Nerie must have done the opposite. Sitting up straight, eyes shining, Nerie's smile was large.

"Really? When? You *really* think we're ready?!"

With a chuckle, Soren patted her shoulder. It was the first time Nerie could recall him touching her in a fatherly way. If it was possible her smile grew larger.

"Yes really. As for when, I was thinking you would leave now - if you're ready? I've let Vizen and Karina know to pack for you. I'll show you how to strap your luggage onto Kiriga, and you'll do a small test flight until Eras is satisfied that she is capable of it. Then you'll be on your way to Cian."

"Really?" Nerie asked again.

She could hardly believe it. She was not only excited to see Sylas - who she still felt guilty about brushing off after Aldis's departure - but to meet his family, and to finally meet Wyla in person.

"Really, really. Now, Wyla will direct you and Kiriga as you fly, as well as help with landing once you arrive. The flight will take several hours. I expect you will arrive well after the sun has set. If you would rather wait until tomorrow to leave, you may."

Kiriga? Are you up to going now? Nerie asked. While she was excited, she would not push the young dragoness past her own limits.

I am! I want to see Wyla!

Nerie could tell the golden dragon's tail was lashing in excitement.

"No, we'll go now," Nerie told Soren, "Does Queen Alaena know?"

Nerie asked because she'd been assigned a small flower to complete for the following day, and she would not want to upset the queen.

"No, only us, Sylas, Wyla, Vizen and Karina know - Sylas invited you just this morning." Soren frowned a little, but Nerie was more focused on the upcoming flight.

"What are my cousins like?" Nerie asked after a moment

of silence.

"Wonderful children. Well, I say children - I haven't seen them in several years."

Soren chuckled softly and muttered, "Time really has flown by," before answering Nerie's question, "Karsen is only slightly younger than Astra - I want to say he's twenty by now. Kora is closer to your age, maybe fifteen? I'm ashamed that I can't recall."

Soren shook his head, flushed a slight pink and frowned at himself.

A soft knock on the door drew their attention. Vizen and Karina stood there.

"Your Highness, my Lady, everything is packed," Vizen said.

Karina was standing behind him, her hand resting on a pile of several large cases which were stacked on the floor.

"Well then, let's get everything strapped on," Soren said standing.

It took only a few minutes, as Soren showed Nerie how the saddle had not only the straps for her legs, but hooks and cords for attachments, such as luggage.

"Remember, you always want to equally distribute the weight. Otherwise it could inhibit Kiriga's ability to fly," he said, pointing to the equal number of cases.

It was only after they had all been strapped to Kiriga and Nerie was getting ready to mount the dragoness that she turned to look at Karina.

"Aren't you coming?" Nerie asked, realizing that the woman was still dressed in her normal clothing and had stepped back after everything was in place.

"No, my lady. Lord Sylas will have more than enough servants to care for you," Karina said with a bow.

"Oh -"

Nerie wasn't sure what to say. It had become so routine to have the woman following in her shadow that she felt naked without her as she mounted Kiriga.

I am not coming either, Eras said, but this did not surprise Nerie or Kiriga. *However, Kiriga, you will be flying over the cities that your siblings, Riya and Mazen, live in, on the way. I believe they would like to meet you.*

Shall I stop in their cities? Kiriga asked, unsure of the deviation in the flight path.

No, they will come to you.

Okay!

Kiriga was nearly dancing in her excitement. Nerie had to ask her to calm down, as she was trying to tighten the leg straps.

Sorry, Nerie.

Are you ready, love? Nerie asked, stroking the base of Kiriga's neck.

I am always ready to fly with you, Nerie, Kiriga said, her voice full of love.

She moved to the center of the courtyard and launched herself skyward. In the last few weeks, her legs had become stronger and she did so without wobbling to one side or the other. Soren was waving from below, leaning against Ilex. Eras was already high in the sky, doing slow twisting acrobatics.

Soros, who had kept mostly to herself since Aldis' departure, was also coasting on the updrafts high in the sky. Kiriga lit up when she saw that her mother had also come to see them off.

Be careful, my little loves, Soros said.

Always, Kiriga and Nerie both promised.

And so, they flew.

***

The wind was behind them, and Kiriga settled into a solid pace. As Eras had taught her, she let herself glide whenever possible to preserve her strength. They'd been commanded to land if Kiriga felt any strain or fatigue during the long flight.

Nerie occasionally felt chilled, as the air was below freezing this high up, but she could lay flat against Kiriga, who created enough heat that she could stay comfortable after only a few moments.

It was about two hours into their flight, and they had only

recently reached the western side of the great lake that bordered Roria, when an unfamiliar voice echoed in Nerie's head.

Sister.

A large dragon was suddenly next to them. Nerie wasn't sure where he'd come from. She'd been watching the ground that had appeared below them. The fields were no more than small squares far below, and the land was dotted with small rivers that all fed back into the lake.

His body was a soft lilac, with the scales around his large eyes darkening to nearly Soros' deep-purple. He was at least twice the length of Kiriga, and his scales were smooth and round, though his spine was covered in large spikes that ran to the tip of his tail.

Brother! Kiriga said happily, tilting herself to get a better look at her brother.

This must be Mazen, Nerie thought to herself.

She remembered the day that Soren and the elder dragons had taught her about the other dragons of the kingdom.

Mazen had been her grandfather's dragon. Soren and Sylas' father - Daviron. He'd died shortly after Ilex hatched, before even Astra had been born.

I left the capital when he died, Mazen said, responding to Nerie's thoughts. *It was too painful to be there without him. Not that it's any less painful elsewhere, but at least in Fostos I am not reminded of him wherever I look.*

He hadn't turned to look at Nerie like Ilex or Eras did when they spoke to her. Nor was it like when Kiriga spoke to her. It felt... indifferent. After a moment she realized why. She couldn't feel him - no emotions or thought - nothing.

They flew in silence for several long minutes before Mazen spoke again.

Mother and Father have hatched another fine dragoness. Be well sister, and look after your girl.

Before waiting for Kiriga to respond, Mazen roared into the air and dove straight at the ground. However, to Nerie's amazement, as he passed below Kiriga's wing he did not reappear on the other side.

Oh, he's there. He can camouflage himself. He's a rather dour one. Not my first choice for a conversation, Kiriga said, noting that Nerie was still leaning, looking for the lilac dragon.

Can you camouflage? Nerie asked with wonder.

I haven't tried. I think I'm a bit young for that anyway, Kiriga told her.

He was breathtaking, Nerie confided in Kiriga. *You each are so - different - yet similar.*

I can be "breath-taking," Kiriga said, her ego slightly bruised by Nerie's amazement with her brother, and without warning, she too dove towards the ground.

"Not funny!" Nerie screamed, tucking herself close to the dragon, the words being ripped from her mouth.

***

Nerie did not speak to Kiriga again for nearly an hour. The rhythmic beat of Kiriga's wings and the warmth of her scales made Nerie drowsy. She wasn't sure if she fell asleep or not, but the next thing she remembered was a female voice greeting them.

Sister, it is nice to meet you in person! A cheerful voice said.

Nerie glanced over Kiriga's left side, to see a good-sized city below them. Tocria, if she recalled correctly.

As she watched, a dragoness launched herself from a large courtyard. At first Nerie couldn't decide if she was red with a purple tint, or purple with a red tint, but as the sun shimmered on her scales Nerie was inclined to think she was rather a mix between the two.

She reminded Nerie of Eras more than any of the other dragons she had met. Like him, she had spines protruding from most of her scales, and was armored nearly to her teeth. Her eyes were blood-red and the veins in her translucent wings a dark-violet.

You look like you've got yourself a good one there, sister, Riya told Kiriga, ignoring Nerie.

I do, Kiriga said. *Nerie, this is my sister Riya, dragon to*

King Justan. King Justan was Queen Briya's father, who was King Daviron's mother. So, your great-great-grandfather.

It's good to meet you, Riya, Nerie said formally.

And you, little princess.

Riya turned her large head to smile at Nerie. It was... unsettling. Her large fangs were exposed, and the corners of her mouth pulled up in a strange way.

Kiriga. You don't ever need to learn how to smile, Nerie said.

Both Kiriga and Riya laughed in her mind in response.

Riya flew with them for nearly an hour. The sky darkened, and Nerie could have easily lost her in the reds and blues of the sunset. She talked with them, telling them about the kingdom and its people. She talked about her Justan, and his horde of children that had loved to climb all over her when she lived in the palace.

Apparently Briya, who'd been queen after Justan, was the third of five children. She'd gone on to have eight children of her own. Briya's reign had been short, as she had died giving birth to her youngest child, Ilana - who was closer in age to her nephews Soren and Sylas than her own brother, Daviron.

If you ever want to talk about family, just let me know, Riya said as a way of parting with them.

The sky was fully dark by then, and Nerie's stomach was rumbling. Riya had told them there was less than an hour and a half left until they would reach Cian - home of Wyla, Sylas, and his family.

The silence after she left was deafening. Not that there had been actual noise, other than her and Kiriga's wing beats, but her presence had been lively.

Riya is a gossip, Kiriga told her.

Do you talk to her often? Nerie asked.

She loved Kiriga but did not pry into the dragon's life unless she chose to share.

I do. She and Wyla are my only sisters. I speak with them most often.

It occurred to Nerie then how similar her situation was to

Kiriga. Meeting siblings for the first time - even if Kiriga had always known hers.

It was nice to meet Mazen. We have only spoken a few times, Kiriga sounded - hurt maybe? - Nerie wasn't sure. It was not the happy feelings and emotions she normally got from the dragoness.

What are your other brothers' names? Nerie asked, trying to change the subject.

Galean, who was Queen Sirah's dragon. And Tiryn, who was Queen Briya's dragon. Galean lives by the sea in Alluvia, and Tiryn lives to the south in Maltakos. We'll go to see both of them some day. I'm sure of it.

Of course, we will, love.

Nerie snuggled against the dragon's warm neck before dozing off.

***

Nerie, Kiriga woke her gently.

Blinking the sleep from her eyes, Nerie looked wearily down at the city of Cian. Even in the dark, the outline of the city was apparent. Fires glowed from the heights of the walls and from individual homes and stores. It was like looking up at the starry sky, but instead she was looking down from a dragon's back.

Few get to see the city like this, Nerie said in awe.

Only us, Kiriga replied.

As Nerie watched the city below, Wyla rose like a ghost from the tales of old. She was nearly as large as Soros and her pearly scales flashed rainbows in the firelight. Her sleek frame darted into the sky with a youth that Nerie would not have expected. Even Soros and Eras seemed to lumber into the air with their immense size.

Littlest sister, welcome to my home.

Her voice was soft and calming, and even though Nerie had spoken to Wyla more than once, something about being this close to her made it feel intimate and personal.

Wyla guided them to the courtyard they were to land in, and they were immediately surrounded by a small army of people. Someone had brought the carcass of a cow for Kiriga to eat, while others were busy unstrapping Nerie's luggage.

As Nerie lowered herself to the ground, she winced slightly at the saddle sores she had acquired from the long flight. Her legs felt numb and she stumbled, but Sylas was there to catch her.

"Welcome to Cian, your highness. Your flight was well?"

His blue eyes glittered, and Nerie smiled up at her uncle.

"Uncle Sylas! Thank you for the invitation. It was - both Riya and Mazen made sure of it."

Nerie managed to pull herself upright and looked around. The building style was similar to the palace in Roria, but more subdued in color and decorations. The courtyard was still busy with people, who were now unharnessing Kiriga as she ate.

"Come this way. We'll get you a late dinner, and then you can settle in for the night. Unless you are too tired to eat?" Sylas asked even as he led her inside.

"I'm famished. The flight was longer than I expected," Nerie told him, even as her stomach rumbled.

"Then food you shall have. You can meet everyone in the morning."

He stopped in front of a set of double doors, which he opened to reveal a modest guest room. He bowed her inside.

"It's the finest we have. I'll leave you in the hands of these very capable ladies. Don't hesitate to ask them for anything you need."

A group of three older women were waiting inside, all bowing to Sylas, then lower to Nerie.

"My Lord, My Lady," they said in unison.

"Good night, Nerie," He said with another bow to her, then saw himself out.

"Good night, Uncle!" she called after him.

CHAPTER THIRTY-NINE

Nerie

Knock. Knock. Knock.

The three loud bangs were all the warning Nerie got before the door was thrown open, and a pale and pink blur was running around her room.

As she sat up, trying to get her bearings, the blur calmed long enough to sit a tray of food on a table, and then threw itself at her. It hit her hard enough that they both went tumbling back on the bed.

"Cousin!" a feminine voice screamed from her shoulder.

Still reeling, Nerie was pulled upright by a strong grip from someone standing outside the bed. Whoever it was must have entered after the blur.

Now sitting upright, Nerie was face to face with a girl and boy who could have been twins. They had white-blond hair and fair skin. Both had sea-green eyes and matching, wicked grins.

"Cousin," the young man said formally, bowing to her.

How was she supposed to respond to those greetings? Nerie wasn't even sure she was awake yet.

They did wait for the sun to come up to greet you, Wyla's soft voice said in her mind, *That was not an easy task for them.*

"I - uh - I'm Nerie," she said finally, after the beaming smiles from their faces soaked into her sleep fogged brain.

"We know! We are *thrilled* to meet you!" the girl said,

moving slightly back so that she could get a better look at Nerie's freckled face. "I'm your cousin Kora, and this is my brother Karsen."

"We brought you breakfast. I thought you would be hungry and that we could possibly talk over the meal," Karsen said. He twisted his hands slightly behind his back, nervous.

Nerie was overwhelmed. Everyone in the palace, from the moment Kiriga had hatched, had treated her with a sort of distant respect. Even Aldis, who was her half-brother, was reserved when he first spoke to her. Only Astra had been forthright with her - and that was simply because she hated Nerie.

It had been such a long time since anyone had treated her in such an informal manner. Not since she had become a princess. Relaxing imperceptibly, Nerie realized just how much she had missed it.

The fog of sleep now fully lifted and happy to be in her cousins' presence, Nerie threw herself at Kora, hugging her back.

"I'm so glad to meet you, cousins. I would love to eat breakfast with you."

Even as she and Kora rose from the bed, the three women from the night before appeared. They clucked like a brood of hens, tugging at Karsen and Kora, trying to get them to leave the room for Nerie to change.

"His Lordship left *us* in charge..."

"You should be more respectful of the princess!"

"If your father knew you were in here..."

The two siblings ignored the pulls and prods and instead helped Nerie to the table where Karsen had set the food. The women continued to cluck and frown, grumpy that the two young adults were ignoring their demands.

"So, tell us all about your flight!" Kora said, even as they sat at the table.

"Father wouldn't let us greet you last night, we were quite annoyed," Karsen said quietly.

"Mother will want to meet you too! So, hurry and eat!"

Kora said as she loaded a plate up with food and set it before Nerie.

All Nerie could do was grin. The siblings didn't let her get a word in edgewise - even as they continued to ask her questions. In fact, she could barely get a bite in. She learned that Kora was only a few months younger than herself, just coming up on her seventeenth birthday. Karsen was a few months younger than Astra, having just turned twenty.

Kiriga was busy laughing and spending time with Wyla, only briefly sending Nerie images of them wheeling high above Cian, the feeling of the wind on her wings and the joy of being with her eldest sibling.

At some point, the gaggle of women moved out of the room and returned with Sylas and a woman in tow. She was obviously where her children had gotten their fine golden locks and sea-green eyes. She was all smiles as Nerie rose from her seat.

"You must be my aunt Valria. I am pleased to make your acquaintance," Nerie said, curtsying to her.

"I am. It is an honor to meet you Princess," Valria said, mirroring Nerie's curtsy, dipping much lower in return, however.

"Please," Nerie said with a grimace, "we are family. No need for the formality. At least, not in the privacy of my chambers?"

The small family smiled at her - Sylas winking. "I think we can manage that, Nerie," he said.

***

That was the start of the first and best vacation that Nerie had ever had. Between Kora and Karsen trying to show her the whole city, spending time with Kiriga and Wyla, and learning about running a city from her uncle, Nerie felt like her head was constantly spinning.

There was always somewhere to go or something to see.

It was fantastic.

Everywhere Nerie went, people bowed to her, screaming her name. She hadn't been allowed outside of the palace in Roria. Here in Cian, while constantly followed by an entourage of guards, cousins, and staff, the only thing limiting where she could go was her own two feet.

It was freeing, really. More like the days before Kiriga - not that she would ever trade a single of those days for a day with Kiriga in her life. It was easier.

They were currently in the Grand Market of Cian. Kora was dragging her by the hand, trying to get to her favorite stall. Something about a glassblower. Karsen was walking behind them, shaking his head at his sister's excitement. Not that Nerie was fooled - she had seen him stop at more than one stall that sold small candies that looked like gemstones.

"Look here, Nerie!" Kora whispered, her excitement palpable.

A man stood in front of a small forge; a long metal pipe stuck inside. When he pulled it out, a bright, orange glob hung loosely from the end. He drew in a deep breath, then slowly exhaled into the pipe. A second man held wads of wet paper, slowly warping the shape as it came to life. When the orange color faded, a dark azure replaced it.

Neither Nerie nor Kora could look away. Even Karsen was paying more attention to the two artisans than he had spared for the other stalls.

The shape the glass finally took was an intricate dragon. Wings spread like Kiriga or Wyla in their laziest glide, head reared and tail in a gentle wave behind it. It was still attached to the pipe by the belly, but even as they watched, enthralled, a pair of giant clippers was used, snipping off the glass before it finished hardening.

The man who had blown into the pipe finally lowered it, smiling at Kora then Nerie. He bowed low to them.

"Your Highness, My Lady Kora. It's always a treat to have your watchful eyes."

The second man stood from his crouched position, gently setting the sculpture on to a workbench. "A gift for you, your Highness. We heard you were in the city and knew it wouldn't be too long before Lady Kora brought you here."

"Please, let me pay for it." Nerie said, reaching for her less than modest coin purse.

The first man laughed waving her off, "It would do more for our patronage to have you display it in the palace or Lord Sylas's home, than for you to pay for it."

She smiled sheepishly at them, then looked at her cousins. They too smiled at her, Kora nodding gently. "We can have it shipped to the palace, so it doesn't break when you ride Kiriga home," she told Nerie, fervently.

They stayed out for several more hours, but once the light started to fade from the sky and the first hints of stars appeared, Nerie was ready to head back to the estate. Her feet were sore, the arms of her entourage laden with packages of things that she had liked or that Kora had insisted they purchase.

Nerie got the impression that while Kora and Karsen were allowed to wander the city at will, they had a moderate budget - one that they would rather save than squander. But that was not the case when their cousin was involved.

Once they returned, they were greeted by the sight of Kiriga and Wyla lying along the rooftops, wings sagging, trying to soak up the last dregs of the day's sun. Only the slow blink of eyes greeted them, and Kora couldn't help but giggle as Wyla's tail slipped slowly from its resting place, but just before it hit the ground, it twitched back up, tucking under her wing.

I like it here, Kiriga told her softly, still not moving from her spot.

I do too, Nerie said as she walked slowly to her rooms. Kora and Karsen both waved wearily to her, promising to see her in the morning.

She knew they would wake her bright and early, just as they had done every morning since she had arrived. But the smile that ghosted her lips vanished as quickly as it came because thoughts of returning home entered her mind.

I don't want to go back to the palace, she whined to the dragoness.

I don't either, Kiriga's tone echoed her own.

Father will come for you, Wyla said, her mental voice tired.

He can sleep on the roof too, Kiriga said, a little less than halfheartedly.

You know Father. I'm almost one hundred and thirty, and he still treats me like a hatchling sometimes. He was itching at the thought of you even coming here. If you don't go home on schedule, he'll be here to escort you.

Wyla chuckled at the image of her father, strangely silly looking in her mind, flapping his wings like a bird, looking down on his two daughters.

The three women, who were Nerie's maids while she stayed with her Uncle and his family, helped her undo her dress and proffered her a pair of soft pants and a loose shirt that made the perfect pajamas. Her Aunt Valria had no qualms about her daughter wearing pants and had happily found Nerie several pairs to stash away for the return trip.

While Soren hadn't given her a set deadline of when to return, Nerie knew that the king would summon them back through the elder dragons. Either Soros or Eras would contact her and Kiriga when it was time to return home.

Only, it didn't feel like home. Not in the same way that being here in Cian with Kora and Karsen did. It nearly had, when Aldis had been there, but since he had been sent away, it felt hollow. Her cousins were fun, and young, and couldn't seem to get to know her fast enough. They wanted to share their lives with her, and it was less than pleasing to think about returning to the palace where Astra lurked, Aldis was missing, and her own mother was having trouble finding time to see her.

***

Two more days flew by, Karsen showing her their library, and Kora introducing her to their stables. Kiriga had snorted derisively at the small mounts, saying they didn't even look capable of holding themselves up - let alone their riders. Each evening as their meal was served, Sylas and Valria would ask about what the young adults had done that day.

***

It was the afternoon of a cold, but sunny, day when Nerie was called back to the palace.

Kora and Karsen had been showing her the valley that separated their town from Lutesia, the neighboring country. In the distance, the city of Veles mirrored Cian, with the great maw of the valley spreading between them.

Kiriga, Nerie, Eras spoke to them. From this distance his voice sounded hollow, like someone shouting down a long corridor. *You must return to Roria at once.*

Soren finally wants me home? Nerie asked, lightheartedly sighing.

There has been an attack in Alluvia.

He said it like the name should mean something to Nerie and Kiriga, but they just couldn't place it, until Wyla's voice chimed in softly - *Galean.*

Galean was the next oldest after Wyla and lived to the north, by the sea. He was Alluvia's guardian, in the same way that Wyla was for Cian.

Is Galean all right? Wyla asked worriedly. *I didn't hear anything.*

Yes, he's fine. But Kiriga and Nerie must come home now. Soren only just got the news and that was his first reaction.

Eras' voice was tight, and Nerie had turned away from her cousins to focus on what he was saying.

We will leave within the hour, Nerie said.

She left the dragons to speak among themselves, turning to Kora and Karsen. They had quickly learned the face she made as she spoke to Kiriga and they had fallen into a conversation of their own while they waited. When Nerie turned back to them, her face was pale.

"We need to get back to the estate. There's been an attack in Alluvia. Soren wants me back in Roria - Tonight," she told her cousins as they looked at her.

"Of course," Karsen said briskly, sitting upright on his mount, turning and leading Nerie and his sister back to the manor.

Nerie kept in constant contact with Kiriga, who told her that Sylas had been informed, and packing was underway. Kiriga was ready as the three of them galloped into the courtyard. Nerie quickly dismounted and ran to her rooms to change into her riding gear.

Her dress tore slightly as she rushed to get it off, but it didn't matter. As she tugged on the leather breeches and boots, her hands shook slightly.

Situra was a peaceful country.

She had *never* heard of an attack. Sure, a riot or two from the far corners of the country over taxes a few years back, but that had ended in Soren *listening* to the people and cutting taxes in that region due to a drought.

Kora and Karsen, along with Sylas and Valria were waiting in the same courtyard where she had landed on the first night. Kiriga was in her harness and Wyla stood watch on the fire heights of the walls.

"I'll miss you," Nerie said awkwardly, looking at them. It was strange, coming into their lives and leaving with so little warning.

Kora threw herself at Nerie, starting to sob, "We'll miss you! I've already asked daddy when we can come visit you at court!"

Nerie hugged her tight, smiling. Then they were suddenly in the middle of a group hug and Nerie was more than a little warm. But it wasn't uncomfortable. This was what a family was like. They were *her* family.

Nerie, we need to go, Kiriga said, shifting her weight between her front legs. *We are already going to be flying in the dark a good part of the way home.*

Hugging each person tight then letting them go, Nerie was already climbing her way up Kiriga's side before tears started to drip down her cheeks.

The small family stepped back as Kiriga lunged into the sky, becoming small dots as Nerie watched them. Then Kora was off, running into the building, reappearing moments later, on a balcony. She scaled her way to the fire heights with Wyla. Her arm waved frantically as she reached the end of her climb. Nerie waved back just as enthusiastically, as Kiriga turned in a wide swoop, heading back towards Roria.

Wyla did not follow. Instead, she sat upright, watching

them disappear into the distance.
Goodbye, little sister. Goodbye, Nerie.

CHAPTER FORTY

Graith

Graith wasn't sure when he stopped looking back at Kelna, worried that they were being followed, but he had at some point. The road before them was quiet - desolate even. No houses or farms lined the road, only the river to the north and empty sprawling hills with occasional stands of trees to the south.

Onward they traveled - to the east and Tesia, the capital. The only possible destination for the ship carrying Zel's eggs.

Alix rode Zel like a horse, and Graith alternated between riding Mero and walking between the horse and dragon. He worried that they would be seen by travelers, but, after catching him thinking about it one too many times, Zel comforted him.

We are far from any town. If anyone sees us - I will kill them.

He wasn't sure if he was supposed to thank her or rebuke the idea, so instead, he did neither - rather he just let it go from his mind.

They traveled for two and a half days until the road took a sharp turn to the south, while the river continued to flow eastward.

Which way? Zel asked, looking over at him.

While the road had been barren thus far, it wasn't guaranteed to stay so, and there had been stretches where there hadn't been any trees for Zel to hide in, and it seemed like going south, the trees continued to thin. Far to the east, the trees became thick following the river.

Graith paused, unsure of the path to take. Then he remembered the map he had found weeks ago, in Zel's cave. Digging it out of one of the pockets of a saddlebag, he spread it out on the stone road to study.

He moaned aloud. The road from Kelna continued southeast around a giant bog before splitting into two and running to both Tesia and Veles. But the road swung wide - and Graith was unsure how long it would take to follow. Not to mention that the closer they got to the split, the more people he was sure would occupy the road - and there were a couple of small villages along the way.

"Forward," Graith announced after several quiet moments of deliberation before motioning Mero.

Within hours they knew why the road had turned south. They had entered the bog. Frozen in the frigid weather, the icy water and mud was a dangerous route to take. Slipping hooves and paws lead to mud splattered riders and grumpy horse and dragon.

Their pace was slow, and they kept as close to the river as possible. More than once, Graith wondered if they should turn around and head back for the road. But every step towards the capital was a step away from the road.

Zel went hunting that evening. She returned with a small and scraggly deer that Graith didn't think would feed the two of them, let alone leave enough to share with the dragoness. Zel heard his worry and calmed him, saying that she would hunt for herself later.

Alix tried to search for wood for a fire but found nothing but soaked logs and wet leaves. Zel stepped in, and after Graith cleaned the deer, she tried to roast it with her flames. The result being that the meat was cooked unevenly, some pieces charred to a crisp and others so rare that Alix thought the deer might just get back up and walk away.

Alix saw as Graith bit into a particularly burnt chunk and winced. The boy nudged the pile of wet leaves at his feet, then looked up and said, "It could be worse. We could have nothing to eat."

Graith flushed slightly, embarrassed that the boy had noticed, but then nodded agreeably. He turned the piece in his hand, looking for a less crunchy bit, and tried again.

"It could be worse," quickly became their motto going through the bog.

"It could be worse - we could be here without Zel."

"It could be worse - we could be frozen."

"It could be worse - we could be lost."

***

After the third day of travel through the bog, Zel left Alix with Graith and took flight in the cloudy sky. Her pale white-blue hide blended in with the overcast sky. She didn't say where she was going but promised that she would keep in touch with Graith.

Several hours later - with little progress forward - she returned. Her eyes were yellow, and her tail lashed as she landed in the clearing just ahead of them.

"Zel!" Alix shouted weakly. He had started shaking not long before, and Graith hoped to get him back on Zel's warm back shortly.

As they approached her, she told Graith, *The bog goes on for another four or five days of travel. Are you alright continuing?*

He snorted in annoyance. He was tired, hungry, and, more than anything, cold.

"Do we really have a choice? Sounds like we are already in the middle of it."

He felt Zel's anger and annoyance at his response, but Graith didn't care. Well, it wasn't that he didn't care - he simply was too tired to moderate his feelings. He knew she was trying to help, didn't want them stuck in this bog any more than he did, but it felt hopeless. What else could they do? Loop back to the road and continue south? It wasn't worth the time.

They reached her and she settled down. Alix resumed his now familiar position on her back, snuggling into the hollow just between her wings, trying to soak in some of her warmth. Graith took a minute to clean Mero's hooves of ice, mud, and stones. The big horse didn't mind the cold, the ice and snow however, he did. Graith made Mero promise after promise about clean stables and warm gruel when they got to the capital.

Graith was worried about the gelding. With little available for the horse to graze on, he had lost a lot of weight. His eyes were sunken in, and Graith could feel his ribs under thick fur. Now knowing that they still had days of travel to go, he feared for a moment that the horse wouldn't make it through.

Graith put more effort into foraging for Mero as they traveled, and that night he had Zel warm water up to body temperature for the horse. Mero ate with gusto and nosed Graith for more when he was done.

"I'll collect more tomorrow, buddy," he promised, scratching Mero's ear and looking around. The hollow they had settled into for the night was treeless and knee-deep with mud. There was nothing remotely edible for Mero.

***

The days continued on like that. Raw or burnt meat, fireless nights, and a cold so deep in their bones that Graith thought he would never get warm again. He also noted that Zel wasn't eating. The few animals she was able to catch for them really weren't enough for them all to share. Her hide faded from the sky-blue it had been to a pale, unhealthy gray.

Graith developed bright red sores on his hands from the cold and saddle sores from riding on the horse constantly. He had stopped walking, as he couldn't make it through the mud without becoming exhausted in minutes.

After the fourth day, Alix couldn't spend more than two hours on Zel's back without needing to huddle under her wing for a bit to recoup body heat. His thin frame shook like the few dead leaves that hung to the trees surrounding them.

Finally, eight days after entering, they made it out of the bog.

While all four of them would have happily gotten miles

away, Graith insisted they camp at the edge of the bog for the night. The trees thinned drastically, and he had no idea how far away the nearest town or farm would be. It would do them no good to have made it this far only to be seen now, so close to the capital.

That night, once the sun had set and the moon rose, Zel went scouting to gauge the distance remaining to Tesia. Flying as high into the air as she could, she pulled Graith's mind with her. The absolute disconnect between his body and mind terrified him, as it had the first time they had flown together, but this time he adjusted much more quickly. He imagined himself sitting still and focused on his breathing.

Even though he could feel the cold wind on her hide, and the muscles in her wings and tail burn as she flew, he tried not to interrupt.

She flew them along the river, and they could see several small farms dot the horizon. It slowly turned into a suburban area that was surrounded by low walls. A few miles in, a second, much larger, wall delineated the start of a city so large that it took Zel almost five minutes of flying to reach the far eastern side.

This must be Tesia, the capital of Lutesia, Graith said, amazed. Kelna, the largest city he'd ever seen, could have fit within the first and second wall, several times over. *We are almost there, Zel.*

He could feel her heartbeat quicken and saw as her eyes frantically searched below them.

Graith. I can feel my eggs again. What am I going to do?

I don't know, Zel. The same trick from Kelna won't work here. You can't even get close to the main city. There are no trees for you to hide in, and we don't have the cart this time.

He felt as if he were drowning and realized that Zel was struggling to breathe.

It feels like inches again, Graith. It feels like I'm going to miss each of them too.

The image of her little egg tumbling in dark water filled Zel's mind.

You must trust us Zel. Alix and I will get your eggs back, even if we have to follow them to the ends of the world.

CHAPTER FORTY-ONE

Graith

Once Zel had returned from her scouting flight, Graith and Alix quickly huddled under her wings. In the time she had been gone, they had chilled even though they had been pressed up against Mero. The large horse had lost too much weight and was barely keeping himself warm.

Alix was asleep within moments, his energy, once seemingly endless, now exhausted. Each day, Graith was reminded time and again that Alix was still a child. Alix hadn't known what he was getting himself involved in by joining the small group.

As Graith lay pressed against Zel's warm hide, he could hear Mero pacing around the large clearing they had found. Mero was gratefully eating the sparse grass that marked the end of the bog. He was shaggy and unkempt, and Graith didn't think that the large horse would have made it much further in the swamp.

You know, I think you're right, Zel said suddenly, *I wouldn't eat him.*

She was trying to be lighthearted, but it came out flat. Graith could feel her emotions in a strange cascade of interest, doubt, hope, fear, hate, and worry. They flickered back and forth, her mind restless. He was worried about her, they had lost a lot of time going through the bog. He didn't know how far away her eggs were at this point.

Zel shuffled uncomfortably, her wings clicking together

over her back. Graith could feel her ribs where he laid against her side. That worried him more than anything, if she became too weak to travel what would they do? She shifted again, heaving a sigh, as she was unable to get settled.

Would talking about your home or family help you relax? Graith asked Zel, unsure of what the dragoness needed - other than a large cow and a restful sleep.

No, she said tersely, then after a moment and realizing that Graith was only trying to help, she continued, *I was a disappointment to everyone in Etria.*

Her voice was dark, her emotions darker. Graith thought that if a dragon could cry, Zel would be sobbing.

Even Cimmeris? Graith asked, hoping that would at least stir some good memories. *He seemed to care about you deeply.*

Grandpa Cimmeris does love me, Zel said, but her mood did not lighten. *I was supposed to be his protege. I was too distracted - I let myself be led along by Coale.*

Graith could tell that thinking about her grandfather made Zel happy, but the thought of Coale, which led to thoughts of her eggs, kept her mood black.

Tell me more about Cimmeris? What kind of protege? Graith urged, slowly rubbing his cold hands on her warm scales.

Grandpa is one of the eldest and wisest of our people. He was one of the heroes of the Great War. He saved so many dragons from your people.

What war? Graith asked.

He didn't recall any lessons about a war. The three nations lived in harmony as far as he could recall.

Zel stiffened.

I may not have been alive at the time, but even as one of the youngest of my people, I know about the war. Your people - the people of Lutesia - invaded my home, Etria, and committed genocide against my people.

Graith was taken aback.

Lutesia attacked Etria? When? he asked in astonishment.

It wasn't that he didn't believe it, but he was horrified

that he hadn't known.

About 130 years ago. Every dragon and human in Etria knows about it.

We never learned about that in the history classes in the village, Graith said.

His mind was racing, wondering how they would have ever been able to commit such atrocities, but at the same time it made sense. Why dragons were so hated by his people. Why the knight had known that Zel was more intelligent than a beast.

His whole life, he had been taught that dragons were nothing more than feral monsters. After meeting and getting to know Zel, he'd learned that to be the furthest thing from the truth. It seemed like the truth about dragons had been hidden intentionally. Not only from him, but from all citizens of Lutesia.

It wasn't right.

Your king and his ancestors are not good people, Zel told him, her voice seething.

Why do they want your eggs, Zel? he asked, horrified.

If the king knew that they were more than animals - more than something tamable - what could he possibly want with the eggs? Graith felt sick.

I don't know, Zel said quietly. *If he was like his ancestors, he would have just killed them. But he wants them alive for some reason. He doesn't need them - or at least not all of them - so whatever he wants them for must be personal.*

Reaching out and laying his hand on her wing, he said for what had to be the dozenth time, *We will find them and get them back.*

***

The following morning dawned dark and cold. Snow drifted lazily down from the sky, and Mero's mood had darkened again. Promises of treats and a warm stall did nothing to cajole the horse, and he trotted at a slow pace, his head drooping nearly to the ground.

Alix could be heard shifting uncomfortably along Zel's back and muttering faint curses as he tried to warm his hands.

Graith had his hands tucked under his legs, his clothes so covered in mud that it almost created an insulating layer.

Almost.

As a stiff breeze blew across the snow-covered land, Graith frowned.

It was time.

Zel, we need to separate now. The tree cover is ending, and we are too close to the capital for you to be seen.

They stopped, and Alix climbed down from his perch upon Zel's shoulders. Graith then hoisted Alix up behind him on Mero's broad back. They looked over at Zel, only to see that her hide was an ashen gray and that she looked as exhausted as the rest of them.

Will you keep in contact with me? she asked.

Her eyes were anxious and dull. Her tail, which normally would have been twitching, was laying limply in the mud.

Of course, Graith promised. *You can always see with my eyes, hear with my ears. In the meantime, find a safe spot. Then, tonight, go hunt. You haven't eaten anything but scraps in weeks.*

I'm fine, she complained weakly, but Graith saw right through it.

No, you are not.

She walked over slowly, shrinking as she did so, until she was a little smaller than Mero. She nuzzled both Graith and Alix, and then she turned and jumped into the sky. It was early enough that her hide blended in with the slate cloud cover. She had told Graith that she would find a clearing and settle down to wait.

He didn't know how long they would be in the city. He wasn't even sure where to start looking, but he knew for now that this was as close as they would come to a goodbye.

***

Hours later, sides heaving, Mero's hooves touched the stone of the road for the first time since they had entered the bog. The slow *clack clack clack* on the snowy pavement was unnervingly loud in the silence that surrounded them.

No one was on the road on a day like today, and it left the

wide expanse feeling eerily empty. Deep winter had set in, and Graith thanked their lucky stars that they had made it this far. The city was a growing smudge on the horizon, but even from here, smoke could be seen coming from the innumerable chimneys that kept each home and store warm.

"Graith?" Alix asked after some time.

Graith had thought the boy asleep from how he was slumped against his back.

"Yes, Alix?"

"I don't care where we stay or what we eat, as long as we are warm. But… uh…" he trailed off, and Graith turned around to look at the boy.

"Yes, Alix?"

"I know I'm not your son, nor am I any relation to you. If you want me to go my own way after we get there and get warmed up, I will."

Alix was fidgeting with the back of Graith's cape and not looking him in the eye.

"Now lad, why would I want you to leave?"

Even as he said it, he knew he did *not* want Alix to leave.

In the month since he'd met the boy, he had realized something. He might have been an outcast in his village, but he had missed being around people. Having Alix around showed him what he had missed out on by not starting a family.

Before Alix answered, Graith continued.

"I would like you to stay with me, and Zel. For as long as you want, of course."

Alix's eyes got wide as he looked at Graith.

"I want to stay with you both!" he said with audible relief.

"Well then, welcome to our little, dysfunctional family."

Graith hugged Alix from his awkward position. Alix hugged back as tightly as his small arms could.

After a moment, Graith nudged Mero, trying to get the horse to move faster. He wasn't going to push the horse if he didn't respond, but Graith wanted to get them somewhere warm. Luckily, Mero seemed to have realized they were nearing their goal and picked up his pace slightly.

The sun, if it had been visible, would have moved slowly across the southern sky, but as it was, the gray clouds seemed to lighten slightly, and the snow fall eased over the course of the next two hours.

Unlike Dunlaith, there was no town surrounding the walls of the city. The wall, easily forty feet high, was a stark contrast from the plains that surrounded the city. Towers loomed at even intervals along the wall, and Graith could see large contraptions atop them. More immediately - a gate, at least twenty feet high and wide, was all that stood between them and Tesia. As they approached the portal, the guards on duty stood straighter and waved them over.

"Well, you two look like you were just dragged through the mud. What brings you to Tesia today? Not to stir trouble, I hope."

The guard, a man in his mid-thirties, eyed them both with disgust.

"No, sir. We lost our wagon and most of our supplies on the journey," Graith replied, but the words came out in a croak.

The guard gave them a second disgusted look, and Graith looked down at himself and realized how dirty and thin they really were.

"Where are you coming from then?"

The guard didn't seem hostile, but he had put himself between the gate and Mero.

"Kelna," Graith answered truthfully, but received an elbow in his back from Alix.

"Oh? Why didn't you take a boat down the river?" The guard's eyes narrowed.

"A dragon attacked! We were on the docks when it struck. Destroyed our cart. Scared us so bad, all we could do was get here. Didn't want to stay there a minute longer," Alix told him, his young voice pitched high in fear.

"A dragon? We thought those damn sailors were lying. Guess I owe Randy a drink after all."

He shook his head in disbelief but moved aside and

motioned for them to enter the city.

Mero moved forward, raising his head at the smells from the city. Right inside the gate were storehouses and military barracks. The military was made up of recruited civilians. They would head to the capital for training and then their assignment. Not many came from Graith's village, as more often than not, fathers would convince their sons to stay and help on their farms.

The river, which they had followed to the capital, ran along the northern side of the city, emptying into the largest body of water Graith had ever seen. He thought he remembered from the map that it was an inland sea. He had marveled at its expanse as Zel had flown over the city.

"Hello, Sir!" a young man called to Graith.

He was leaning against some stacked crates. Waving and smiling, he walked towards Graith and Alix. He was tall and lanky, his blue eyes sparkling as he smiled at the travelers. Graith estimated him to be in his late teens or early twenties. Graith nodded and Alix peered out from around his back. Spotting Alix, he winked at the boy.

"My! You fellows look road weary if I've ever seen such." His voice was light and cheerful, "I work at the Running Ship Inn, and I would love to escort you there! If you're so inclined of course."

As if on cue, Alix's stomach rumbled and he prodded Graith in the back, more gently this time.

Smiling, Graith nodded and said, "Well, I suppose that we should follow you then."

As they walked through the city, the man, who introduced himself as Kade, pointed out shops and sights. A large market was filled with people, even in the late afternoon of a day with such harsh weather.

They passed a theater, bakery, and several shops that had small items and trinkets. Many shops sold cloth and clothing, and Graith tried to commit them to memory so that he could get Alix and himself new gear.

However, within minutes, he couldn't even remember whether they had last taken a left or right turn. Only after he was thoroughly lost, did they stop. They were in front of a large three-story building with shuttered windows and a small stable. Both Alix and Graith nearly fell off Mero in exhaustion as they tried to dismount.

"Go on in, I'll take care of this fine fellow. Tell the proprietor, Doreen, that Kade brought you."

He waved them on, then slowly walked Mero to the stable.

Graith looked up at the place again. For an inn, it sure did look closed. Maybe it was just his imagination, or maybe it was the weather, but had Kade not led them here, he wouldn't have looked twice at the building. As he approached the door, he saw a small plaque to the right that read "Running Ship Inn" with a little painted two-sail ship.

Opening the door, they found themselves face to face with a plump woman in her early fifties. Her hair had been artificially colored an unnatural red, and her lips were a nearly identical shade.

"Oh, do look what the cat dragged in!"

Her voice was sickly sweet, and she shook her head at them, clucking. Then between one slow blink and the next, she was somehow suddenly between Alix and Graith, dragging them by their elbows to a table.

"Uh...Kade brought us," Alix told her, trying to look around her girth at Graith.

"Of course, he did! He's such a good lad. Now, what shall I be gettin' ya?"

She had plopped them both down before answering herself.

"Don't ya worry, ol' Doreen will get'cha sorted out."

She turned and made her slow way to the kitchen. Graith and Alix stared at each other in wide-eyed disbelief. They were so exhausted and hungry that they didn't care if what they were served turned out to be stale bread.

They took the moment to look around the inn. Like the outside of the building, it was rather nondescript and didn't even look open for business. An older man sat in a far corner, the only signs that he was awake were the occasional puff of smoke from his pipe and the slow rocking of his chair onto its back legs.

The building was warm, and before Doreen returned with their food, the mud, which was frozen into their clothes, had defrosted. They were in a sorry shape. Graith's hands, where he had gotten red welts from the cold, were burning, and Alix was shifting uncomfortably from the riding sores on his legs.

Doreen came waddling back out, carrying a large tray. As she placed it on the table, they saw it had two steaming mugs of tea, a small mountain of bread, and two large bowls of a soup that simmered tantalizingly.

"Now dearies, you eat up, and ol' Doreen will fish you out something to change into. I'll also heat some water for you to bathe in."

She patted Alix's head and pecked Graith on the cheek. Both flushed red and thanked her in mumbles. The moment passed and she was moving again. As soon as her back had turned, they dug into their meal.

With a sip of the tea, Graith felt his throat unstick and he realized how dehydrated he was. Alix had forgone his spoon for slices of bread dunked directly into the soup. Kade entered the inn while they ate, briefly informing them that Mero had been groomed, fed, and given a stall and blanket. He then disappeared into the kitchen after Doreen.

Doreen refilled their bowls and mugs as they emptied them, until neither could stuff another bite into their mouths. By the time they were both done eating, night had fallen, and they were struggling to keep their eyes open.

Kade and Doreen reappeared moments later and helped them both to the back of the kitchen, where a large tub of steaming water waited. Their clothes were taken, and they were left to wash themselves.

"Oh, you are handsome. We'll get you supplies to shave tomorrow, if you want," Doreen giggled at Graith. He hadn't realized his beard nearly reached the bottom of his neck.

Clean, if baggy, clothing was proffered and they were led to a room with two small beds. Their saddlebags lay on the table, and the sheets had been warmed. They crawled into bed, and Doreen pulled the door shut.

Graith thanked the gods above for having met Kade, as he lay there. He didn't care if the boy was there looking for customers daily. He had brought them here, and Graith doubted they would have been as well taken care of anywhere else in the city.

Forcing himself to stay awake for a moment longer, he sent the image of himself and Alix warm, full, and safe to Zel. She responded with an outpouring of love and thoughts of her own meal that she was hunting.

Unable to think straight and hearing small snores from Alix, Graith drifted off to sleep.

CHAPTER FORTY-TWO

Nerie

The beat of Kiriga's wings was thunderous in the quiet night. The sun had been close to setting as they departed Cian, and while they flew to the east, the sun dipped below the horizon quicker than Nerie had ever seen.

Nothing on the ground below was visible to Nerie's naked eye, but Kiriga shared with Nerie what she could see every time they flew over a town or village.

It was like looking at something in twilight, but it was all crisper - that was the only word Nerie could think of to describe the sensation. The buildings stood out sharply, with no trace of a shadow. No one was out in the streets at this late hour.

Nerie found herself unable to relax on the flight, instead constantly looking forward as if she might see Roria in the darkness. Well before they had even reached Tocria, Riya joined them. The dragoness, who had been so happy and chatty on their flight out to Cian, was now silent. Her red eyes glowed in the darkness and she took up a position above Kiriga, as if to guard the younger dragoness and the princess.

We must make better time, sister, she told Kiriga curtly.

Riya angled herself downward and the combination of gravity and her current speed caused her to race ahead.

Kiriga followed suit moments later. Nerie's heart raced at the steep dive, but once again Kiriga shared her sight, and Nerie was able to relax. They quickly settled into a pattern of alternating between diving and climbing in the sky. Nerie couldn't tell if they were actually going any faster, but Riya seemed pleased with their progress.

They were joined a few hours later by Mazen. His eyes were a luminescent purple in the darkness. Nerie could see them from her perch as they easily tracked his two sisters' movements in the dark.

I'll take it from here, Riya, he said quietly.

He positioned himself at the same high altitude that Riya had returned to.

Riya ignored him.

I can fly alone! Kiriga told her siblings in annoyance.

It was a weak argument and when both elder dragons looked at her, she dipped her head in embarrassment.

You, sister, are not our main concern, Mazen told her after a moment. *You carry the heir of the kingdom. She must make it to the capital safely.*

If we needed to be escorted home, why didn't Wyla fly with us to Tocria? Nerie asked the dragons, looking between Riya and Mazen.

Wyla must not leave her post at the border. She is our first line of defense if Lutesia were to attack, Riya answered.

Her words were clipped short, and her eyes constantly roamed the ground below them.

Especially at a time when we do not know where the attack in Alluvia came from, Mazen added.

What's going on? Nerie asked.

She understood the seriousness of an attack, but she did not understand why they were being escorted while flying through the sky at night.

No one answered her.

Kiriga growled softly, thinking of what she would do if anyone dared come near Nerie. It didn't make Nerie feel any better.

Instead, she grew more worried. She knew they had passed Fostos over an hour ago, yet Riya did not turn to head back to Tocria.

***

Roria was as dark as every other city had been. A few fires glowed dimly in the night, barely illuminating the wall that surrounded the city.

The palace, however, was alight, visible for miles from the sky. Nerie knew that it was unlikely anyone in the whole building was sleeping.

Even as they crossed over the wall of the city, Nerie could see riders leaving from the north gate. She wondered if they were headed to Alluvia or another city.

Soros was sitting in the main courtyard. Her wings were tented, and her head swept back and forth as she searched the sky for her children. Her frame towered above the palace, reminding Nerie once again just how large she and Eras really were.

Eras was flying.

He was circling the city, tail twitching as he watched for any movement in the night.

Nerie sat upright, expecting Kiriga to land in *their* courtyard - instead, she settled into the courtyard outside Soren's rooms.

Mazen and Riya both landed softly on the roof, and Nerie could hear the building creak. The five dragons present could fill the entire roof - with maybe a tail or two hanging over.

Soren is in his study. You need to join him there, Ilex told her as he watched his sister land.

Right. Of course.

Nerie was already unstrapping herself from Kiriga as a cloud of dust rose around them.

She slid to the ground and collapsed. There was no Uncle Sylas there to catch her as her weary legs gave way beneath her.

Kiriga turned her whole body, worried. Her tail whacked into Ilex with an audible thud, causing the older dragon to growl deep in his chest.

Kiriga ignored him, instead lowering her head next to Nerie, to try to give her something to pull herself up by.

"I'm fine."

Nerie waved off the dragoness, while sitting on her butt and looking down at her legs.

The left one tingled as if stuck by a thousand pins and needles. She groaned softly as she rotated her foot to the left and then the right. It burned. She then did the same for the other leg.

As blood flow slowly returned, she grasped onto one of the dozen small horns that were starting to protrude from Kiriga's face.

She had barely gotten her feet under her when the door from the room opened, and a knight of the King's Guard stepped out. Seeing her struggling to stand, he hastily bowed to her, then offered her his arm.

"This way, my lady," he said formally, nodding to the direction he had come from.

A few shaky steps later, and she was inside Soren's study. Which at the moment was more like a war room. Maps were up of the region, the city, even the streets that were affected in Alluvia. Nerie was deposited into a seat and promptly ignored.

Soren didn't even look up when she entered.

Nerie waited - patiently - but the long cold flight seemed to catch up with her, along with the long day she'd had with Kora and Karsen before. She slipped her boots off and curled her legs up under herself, trying to get comfortable in the wooden-armed chair.

***

When Nerie awoke sometime later she was disoriented. She couldn't tell how much time had passed - this was an interior room with no window and the candles seemed fresh, but she didn't remember how low they'd been when she'd drifted off.

The room was still crowded, but she didn't know if it was filled with the same people who'd been there before she'd fallen asleep. The only person she recognized was Soren, and he was still not looking at her. He was talking to a man in full armor, who held a plumed helmet under his arm. Even in the small room, their low voices were unintelligible.

Stretching, Nerie stood, recoiling slightly when her bare feet hit the cold floor. She had forgotten she'd removed her boots before falling asleep. She was still too tired to put them back on, so she padded quietly over to Soren.

Apparently neither he nor the man he was speaking to heard her, as both looked startled as she cleared her throat. The man was surprised enough that his hand reached for the sword that hung from his belt.

"My... My Lady," he stuttered as he dropped onto his right knee, head bowed.

Nerie had learned in her studies that it was an offense punishable by death to pull a weapon on any member of the royal family.

She nodded at him, still not knowing who he was. He stood, bowing quickly to Soren and left the room.

With his departure, Soren was left staring at her. His mouth was open slightly, and his face was covered in a dark stubble - either it was late enough in the day to have grown, or early enough in the morning that he hadn't yet shaved. He had dark rings under his blue eyes and his hair was disheveled, as if he'd run his hand through it more than once.

"What's going on?" Nerie asked, looking at him. As he opened his mouth further to speak, she added quickly, "I mean, I know Alluvia was attacked, but how? When? *Why?*"

Soren used his gaping mouth to gulp in a lungful of air and then another. He blinked slowly, and Nerie was inclined to think that it was closer to *too early to shave* rather than *too late in the day,* Soren had probably not slept at all that night.

"You know that Galean lives in the city?" he asked. When she nodded, he continued, "Well, yesterday afternoon there was a fire. In a grain storehouse. Of course it caught his attention and he flew overhead, trying to get an idea if anyone was inside and if the fire was going to spread."

Nerie bit her lip, worried about the dragon, but she already knew from the conversation between Kiriga and Wyla much earlier that Galean was fine.

"He saw a large group of people there, but when he flew lower, they scattered. Most were wearing long capes and hoods. No way for him to identify them." Soren shook his head at that before continuing, "But they left something behind. Something they were burning *with* the storehouse."

This, Eras said, and Nerie could nearly hear the smoke billowing from his nostrils.

The orange dragon showed her an image of two figures. They looked like dolls, except *bigger,* and one was clearly a girl with long red hair and the other was a golden dragon.

Her and Kiriga.

The blood drained from Nerie's face.

"But… Why?" she asked, her voice soft.

Soren shook his head, "We don't know. Yet."

He ran a hand through his hair, mussing it even more.

"Few enough people even know what you look like. You've done *nothing* political. Yet here they are, *burning* effigies of you and Kiriga…"

He trailed off as he spoke, his eyes darting to the maps that hung around the room. His hand reached for his hair again, shaking slightly.

"I'm back and I'm safe," Nerie said slowly.

She wasn't sure it was going to help, but Soren looked at the end of his rope.

"Yes. You're back. From now on you will always have a guard escorting you, and any food will be tested before you eat. No more flying with Kiriga for the time being…"

Horrified at the abrupt change in her freedoms, Nerie cut him off and agreed to the current terms before he limited her even further.

"I… I see. I'll head to my rooms now."

She dipped in a curtsy to Soren, then turned to go. He stopped her before she reached the door.

"While your rooms have been repaired, I would feel more comfortable if you remained in the temporary rooms that you were in before for now. Karina is already there waiting for you."

"Of course," Nerie said carefully, keeping her tone neutral. Soren was obviously under stress and she didn't want to further his paranoia by disagreeing with him.

She grabbed her boots from their haphazard position on the floor and left the room. Two of the many guards that stood in the main sitting room turned and followed her. She didn't say anything to them, picked up her step, and walked quicker.

Reaching her suite, she nearly sprinted into the bedroom and shut the door behind her. She wanted to reach out to Kiriga, but she could hear the dragons speaking and didn't feel like she could interrupt.

Instead, she disrobed. Her hands shook as she carefully folded each article of clothing. Soren had said Karina was in her rooms, but the woman had not appeared.

Nerie looked around and sighed in annoyance when she saw that her luggage had not been returned to her room yet. She searched in vain in her closet, she found that Alaena must have raided her small stash of pants while she was away.

Unhappy, Nerie donned a soft nightgown instead and she kicked at the skirt in annoyance.

While it annoyed her, it didn't matter. She was too tired from her long day. Still unsure what time it was, Nerie crawled into the soft bed, not even checking the sheets for an unwanted guest.

She was going to sleep until someone showed up to drag her out of bed.

CHAPTER FORTY-THREE

Nerie

The following days were some of Nerie's worst at the palace. The strict regulations that Soren had imposed upon her weighed heavy.

The food was cold when she got to eat it - she'd had to wait on the food tester not falling over dead before she was allowed to eat.

The guards had *tried* to follow her into the bathing room. She'd shrieked at them, slamming the door shut. They reasoned that there was the servant's passageway into the small room - only relenting when Nerie instead allowed Karina to stand in the room, facing away from the princess.

Then there was Alaena. Every time she visited Nerie, she was in a fouler mood than the day before. Like Soren, who Nerie only glimpsed every now and again - as he had completely stopped her lessons with him for the time being - Alaena had deep bags under her eyes. Even her cascade of fine dark hair had the occasional snaggle in it, something that, if she'd been more alert, would never have happened.

"No. NO. You are doing that stitch *all* wrong."

Alaena's voice was nearly shrill as she paced behind where Nerie sat, trying to make the floss work itself into a neat little flower.

Nerie jumped, unfortunately sinking the sharp needle deep into the side of her finger. A muttered curse, and she shoved it in her mouth just as the blood started to well. She glared at the older woman in anger.

There'd been no need to shout at her, besides Karina, they were alone in the room.

"Well try again," Alaena said, no sympathy in her voice. "Do it correctly this time."

Pulling the wounded finger out of her mouth, Nerie took a deep breath. It would do no good for her to escalate the issue.

"I'll do my best," she said softly, eying the silver needle with doubt.

"No." Alaena was looking for a fight. Nerie could sense it in the way she was hovering over her. "You'll do it right."

"Alaena, I don't know that I am up for this right now," Nerie said, starting to pack away the hoop and floss.

"We are not done here." The queen's voice raised a fraction.

"We are. I am," Nerie said firmly, standing.

All Nerie wanted was an ounce of control in her life, yet Alaena was unwilling to hand it over.

"Come back here," Alaena said, the barest hint of a stomped foot following her command. Nerie thought Alaena really must be exhausted, but she didn't care. If Nerie was suffering from Soren's restrictions, Alaena could suffer too.

Nerie left.

Karina and the two guards followed behind her, less than silently. Nerie didn't care. She turned down corridor after corridor, until she reached her mother's suite. She'd wanted to talk to Myha about her trip to Cian but had not found the time to do so yet.

Now would be a perfect opportunity.

However, when she pushed against the door, it didn't budge. Karina cleared her throat awkwardly.

"Your lady mother is still with Sir Ahlwin at his estate," Karina said, and Nerie could hear the trepidation in the maid's voice as she spoke.

"Still?" Nerie asked, more than a little taken aback.

"This is their third time visiting, My Lady," Karina said, looking at her feet as she spoke.

"Right. Of course. Good on her." Nerie turned back the way she had come. "Well then, I guess I want to go to court."

Nerie tried to force cheer into her voice, but she couldn't help but look back at the locked door.

"We'll make you look extra special today, Princess," Karina said, taking the lead back to the small suite.

By the time they arrived back at Nerie's rooms, Queen Alaena had departed, but Nerie wasn't the only one to notice the basket of floss strewn across the room, the failed flower laying in front of the hearth, where Alaena must have stood contemplating throwing it into the flames.

In less time that she would have imagined, Nerie found herself ready to be presented at court. Her hair was in a sophisticated twist and her dress was a golden amber that made her skin look as if it was glowing.

Nerie wasn't a petty person, but getting all dressed up did make her feel a tad bit better. Walking into the Solar and having the courtesans flock to her gave her a slight rush of endorphins.

She was surprised to see Wilm speaking to Astra as she entered the Solar. When he caught sight of her, he dropped Astra's hand with a quick bow before wading into the crowd that surrounded Nerie.

Astra's face was pale, and her eyes flashed as she watched every other person in the room beg for Nerie's attention.

Nerie couldn't believe her eyes when instead of trying to get her followers back or start a fight, Astra simply walked out of the Solar without even a backwards glance in Nerie's direction.

CHAPTER FORTY-FOUR

Astra

Astra couldn't believe it. Even Wilm, her childhood friend, had stood her up - enamored by that little bastard.

She had thought about walking over, causing yet another scene with the little *princess*, but it just wasn't worth it. Mother and Father had both put their foot down after the last time.

Astra walked to her suite, idly undressing even as she reached the door. Gayge was following her, just like the good little puppy he was. He was the guard she'd chosen to watch over her rooms - and herself - a few months before, when they'd taken away her knight from the King's Guard.

Now she had Gayge, a palace guardsman.

That had been another kick in the face. Another nod to the fact that that bumpkin of a peasant had been selected as the future ruler. That she, Astra, was worth less than a bastard.

Throwing herself down into the chair, she felt Gayge trying to rub her shoulders. Of course, he was. He would start to pout without a little physical attention every few days.

Not that she minded too much.

He was good looking and wasn't a talker. She was - but he knew better than to open his mouth when she spoke.

As she acquiesced to his massaging, she started tapping her foot. She would have been pacing, but she didn't want the man following her as she did so.

"Why couldn't you have bashed in her skull the day that yellow runt chose her?" she asked him angrily. It was how she started just about every conversation they had.

Gayge had been the soldier that had knocked Nerie unconscious right after Kiriga had selected *her* to be the next queen. Had the dragoness been older than a few minutes and not still learning to hold her head up, he would likely have lost his life. As it was, the lizard had simply bowled him over.

He gave a noncommittal grunt, kneading at her neck.

"She has not yet been proven to be my father's bastard. He can claim he slept with the whore all he wants, but she doesn't take after him in a single way. From her ugly red hair to the nasty splotches on her skin."

She stood suddenly, causing the guard to nearly fall backwards in surprise. She crossed her arms in a huff, moving to her bed. That perked the man up, and he followed suit. If anything could get him to listen, it was her body - but she wasn't in the mood, too engrossed in her complaints.

"Father spends more time with *her* than he ever spent with me. Even when he thought I would be queen." She motioned at the guard to sit on the end of the bed.

"Mother might as well have a second daughter. She stopped giving me lessons the day that bitch appeared." She shoved herself backwards on the soft cushions on the bed, and Gayge started to massage her legs. She groaned as he hit a particularly tense nerve, but she just kept talking, "All my *friends* are just sycophants. Flies following their next meal. That's all they all are. Flies."

She pushed a strand of dark hair behind her ear in annoyance, as she sat up. She studied Gayge's face, as if she was looking for some sort of answer to an unasked question.

"Aldis is just another fly. Pathetic. Thank god he's gone. Soros, fucking purple lizard, seemed so broken up about it. Not that she would tell me. Or talk to me. *None* of them talk to me."

Astra was bored and threw herself back down. She wanted Gayge to leave her bed. Not that he was an issue. She just wanted to lie back and kick her bed angrily and he was in the way.

"I lost the one person who *loved* me, and the snake didn't even bite the bastard."

"I -" he said awkwardly, "love you, princess."

She sat up and patted his cheek, "Of course you do."

Restless once again, Astra stood and wrapped a silk robe around herself and walked to her large bathroom.

Still talking, raising her voice as she moved farther from the guard, she said, "You know, it's obvious that there are some people still loyal to me. Who want to see me on the throne. Look at Alluvia. They burned a fucking effigy of the bastard and the undersized lizard."

She eased herself into her large stone tub and lazed as she washed herself slowly. She quieted while she tried to relax, but it didn't work. Before the water even cooled, she was back out of the tub. As she reentered the bedroom, her dark hair was dripping water, she picked back up where she had left off.

"All I know is that the people need to understand that the dragons aren't omniscient. They can't be trusted. Not with something like choosing the ruler of the country. Hell, look at how we got Father."

She walked over to Gayge, who was standing by the door. She patted his cheek again and said, "You'll make sure they know for me, right?"

CHAPTER FORTY-FIVE

Graith

The next morning, Graith returned to the land of the living, slowly and stiffly. He felt as if he had been trod upon by Mero, his whole-body aching. His arms and legs popped and creaked as he moved back the covers and tried to sit. Sucking in a large breath of air, he reached towards his toes, his back and hips popping.

Slowly exhaling and trying to stand, he heard a giggle from the other bed. Turning his head with another pop, he saw Alix sitting cross-legged, watching him.

"You sound like a kettle full of popping corn," he said, trying to keep his face straight. Failing, he fell over in a fit of laughter.

Graith smiled and stiffly walked over and tousled his hair.

"Well lad, we have a lot of gear to replace. And we have the eggs to locate. Zel said she felt them in the city, two nights ago."

Shrugging his shoulders with a last loud pop, he pulled on his boots, motioning for Alix to follow along.

As they reached the bottom of the stairs, they were greeted with the sight of Doreen, smiling, and carrying a large tray of breakfast foods.

"Good mornin', darlin's. Thought I heard you up and about. Eat up. You poor things are nothing more than skin and bones," she said as she laid the tray on the same table they had eaten at the night before.

Graith's stomach gave a mighty growl at the sight, and Alix nearly lunged into the seat closest to the food.

"Doreen, just a moment," Graith said, as he stepped away from the table.

"Yeah, hun?"

"I'm not sure how long we are going to be in town, but I would like to pay in advance by the week, if that's possible." Graith was pulling out his coin pouch as he spoke.

Doreen's smile faltered for a second, before she became very professional, "Of course then. A week will be fifteen gold."

Graith nodded and counted out the money before returning to the table and Alix.

"What was that about?" Alix asked around a mouthful of hot porridge.

"Just paying in advance. Don't know how long we'll be in town."

Graith reached for a scone and his own bowl. The food melted in his mouth and his eyes closed in bliss. Damn, he sure had missed hot meals.

"Oh, how much did she charge ya?" Alix continued after a few bites.

"Fifteen gold. Seems reasonable to me."

Graith shrugged and took another bite of food. Alix, however, laid his spoon down and stared at Graith. After a few moments, Graith noticed and raised an eyebrow.

"Just like a full gold seemed reasonable to give a stable boy for tending to your horse?" Alix asked, staring at Graith.

"Well... yeah?"

"Graith. That is way under charging us. Food and beds... that's a bare minimum of five gold a day. Food like this?" Alix waved his hand at the table, "I would charge another ten."

"Really?" Graith didn't see what the problem was.

"Really. Randy charged that - and you stayed there. It was much lower quality than this place."

Alix glanced towards the kitchen where Doreen was

busily sweeping.

They finished their meal in silence, Graith content to enjoy the food, Alix watching Doreen out of the corner of his eye, wary.

As if on cue, as they finished, she bustled over while calling for Kade. He sauntered down the stairs, his dark hair gleaming in the candlelight that illuminated the large room.

"Oh good, you're all ready for the day, Kade!" Doreen gave him a sugary smile and patted his cheek. "Be a dear and help Graith and Alix around the town. If I recall correctly, they have supplies to replace."

He didn't respond, just nodded, and turned around to fetch his cloak. Doreen collected the dishes and Alix and Graith stood, stretching.

"I think I need a nap," Alix complained, patting his full stomach.

"Got to get moving. Zel's counting on us," Graith said, tousling the boy's hair.

Alix grinned and stretched again. Kade returned, smiling at the duo.

"Ready to go?"

"More than ready. Please, lead the way." Graith nodded for him to take the lead.

Leaving the inn, Graith noted that all the windows remained shut, even though the morning sun would have illuminated the hall.

Kade led their small procession, with Alix right at his heels. Graith trailed along behind them, occasionally stopping to peer into a window or chat with a merchant at one of the many stalls that lined the streets. They waited for him patiently as he talked, Kade buying a sweet for Alix to suck on as they waited.

When Graith offered to repay him, Kade simply shook his head and asked where they would like to go first.

Graith looked over at Alix, who shrugged.

"Know of any good leather workers in town?" Graith asked, having decided what needed to be done first.

"Aye, it's a bit of a hike though," Kade said, turning to

face them.

"We have all day, no hurry," Graith told him, smiling.

They walked in companionable silence, their gait brisk now that they had a destination. Slowly, the smell of tanning leather and fish surrounded them, Alix tucked his nose into the collar of his shirt.

Kade knocked on the door of a small shop before leading them inside. It was dark, but not pitch black, and as a small man came out of a back room, he lit a lamp, illuminating his wares.

Belts, bags, shoes, and many others lined the walls. He was wearing a leather apron and had thrown his latest project over his shoulder as he walked into the store proper.

"Kade! Good to see you. How's Doreen?" Seeing Graith and Alix, he introduced himself. "Hello there, I'm Rand, leather worker extraordinaire," he said with a flourish, bowing to Graith.

The lump of leather that had been on his shoulder tumbled to the floor. He hurriedly picked it up then reached out to shake Graith's hand.

"Graith, nice to meet you, Rand. Kade here thinks you're the right man for my job."

"Oh? What can I be doing for ya?" Rand settled into a relaxed stance, pulling out a small notebook.

"We are in need of a few things. Primarily, Alix here needs a new set of boots. Would also like to get two bags to haul our stuff around in. We have a couple saddlebags, but we've run out of space."

He stopped and grinned at Rand as the man was scribbling notes into the book. Alix just stared up at him in amazement, but after a moment started to shake his head.

"No no no. I don't need boots."

He looked a little panicked.

"Don't be silly, of course you do. With how much we travel, you need a good pair of boots. And you're lucky you didn't lose a toe getting here," Graith said as he placed his hand on the boy's shoulder.

"Graith, really, you shouldn't spend money on me."

Alix was frowning and still shaking his head.

"Alix, I told you. That's what family does for one another." Graith pulled him into a short embrace.

"Well now, Alix, if you'll just have a seat here, I'll get you measured for your boots," Rand said, pulling over a chair with a tape measure slung over the back.

Alix sat, looking uncomfortable, but his complaints halted for the moment. After a few pulls of the measurer, and a few more scribbles in his notebook, Rand stood.

"Alright. The boots I can have done in two days. As for the bags, I have a few already made, we can look at those, and if they work you can take them now, if not, it will give me an idea of what you're looking for and I can get them made."

He nodded to the shelves to his left.

After looking through what was available, they found two bags they could carry on their backs. Rand then led them over to the counter and wrote them an invoice for their order, and the cost. Standing at the counter, Graith noticed a coin pouch and belt set that he also purchased for Alix. The boy turned a bright red but kept silent.

They left the shop, new bags hanging lightly on their backs. Stepping out onto the street, the smell of fish once again became overpowering.

"Kade, do you think you could show us around the docks?" Graith asked, seeing the riggings of ships' towers over the buildings in the distance.

"Are you looking for something in particular, Graith? Most of the stuff on the docks tends to be overpriced."

Kade smiled, but it didn't quite reach his eyes, as he too looked in the direction of the docks.

"Oh, well we - uh, had a friend arrive by boat a while back, wanted to see if the boat was still in town."

Graith chuckled and scratched at the back of his head.

"I can, don't know too much about the dockside of town myself, but we can take a peek."

Kade waved at them to follow him.

As they got closer to the docks, shouts and yells along

with the bangs and slamming of heavy objects filled their
ears. Kade's shoulders were tense as he looked side to side,
while in the center of the road he led them down. When Alix
went to peer into a window, Kade wrapped his arm around
the boy's shoulder, pulling him along.

Emerging onto the pier proper, Graith was breathless at
the sight. Water spread out along the edge of the city as far as
the eye could see. To the east, was the enormous body of
water that he had seen through Zel's eyes. From the west, the
river carved a scar into the land, clearly delineating the city's
edge. Boats were moored along the coast, while more were
specks upon the horizon. One was just beyond the city,
headed back upriver to Kelna.

Kade was standing directly behind Graith and Alix, his
head towering above Graith's.

Putting a hand on each of their shoulders he asked, "See
the ship you were looking for?"

Graith did indeed see the ship. Long furrows were dug in
the railing where Zel's talons had sunk deep into the wood.
Rigging and lines were snapped, and one of the mainsails
was scorched from her breath.

"Aye, seems he made it into town long before us," Graith
said, nodding to the ship next to the one Zel had destroyed.

Graith, please go look at the ship, Zel pleaded suddenly,
in his mind.

*Zel, I don't think I could get close to it, even if I wanted.
It's under guard,* he responded.

Just get near enough so that I can try to sense my eggs?
she begged.

All right, all right.

"Huh, I wonder what happened to that ship?" Graith
asked, feigning ignorance. He pointed to the ship that Zel had
ravished.

"No idea, heard it came into town a few days ago," Kade
said. "Did you have a plan to meet up with your friend?
Maybe I could help you find him?"

Graith just shook his head and walked forward. Kade
tightened his grip, but Graith shook him off.

"I'm just going to have a look at that ship. Looks like a monster took a bite out of it…" he said, as he walked off.

He didn't make it very far before the guards he'd told Zel about approached him.

"Sir, this ship is off limits to civilians. Please step back," one guard told him, stiffly.

"Oh, I was just surprised to see a ship so damaged. Thought I would take a look," he told the guard, still facing the ship.

"Step back now, Sir!" the other guard demanded.

Both guards were carrying short swords and small shields. The second guard drew his sword.

"We have both told you to step back, sir! Do so. Now," the first guard said, taking a step towards Graith.

They aren't there.

Zel's mental voice sounded exhausted.

Graith walked backwards, away from the ship.

"I was just taking a look! What happened?"

The second guard did not lower his sword, instead he raised it and pointed it at Graith's chest.

"What happened is King Oron's business, not yours old man. Leave."

Kade's hand was suddenly firm on Graith's shoulder.

"Excuse my father, his nose is larger than his sensibility sometimes!" he said as he dragged Graith back, away from the ship.

"Maybe you should keep a better eye on him then," the second guard said as he sheathed his sword.

"I will, sir!" Kade promised, wheeling Graith around and forcing him away from the ships.

Once they were out of sight of the guards he stopped and turned towards Graith. His face was pale and his eyes dark.

"What do you think you're doing, Graith?" he whispered, glancing over his shoulder.

"I just wanted to look!" Graith raised his hands in front of himself defensively.

"Just take a look, my ass." Kade was inches from his face. "You were looking at that ship the moment we stepped onto the pier."

"I was just surprised to see a ship so damaged!" Graith tried to step back, but Kade had him pinned between a couple of large crates.

"It's our friend. Well it's more like our *friends*," Alix said suddenly.

Kade looked over at him, frowning.

"What do you mean?"

"They actually came on *that* ship. They are in danger, and Graith just wants to help!" Alix told the young man, refusing to look at Graith.

"Alix, stop," Graith told him, but Kade's attention had shifted.

"What do you mean they came here on that ship? I heard what those guards said. No one lightly throws out the king's name, and if I recall correctly, the port was shut down when that ship came into town."

"We can't tell you about them. It's dangerous to you, and to them. But they aren't here anymore," Alix's voice cracked as he spoke quickly.

Graith stood up straighter.

"Let's get out of here then. The docks are not the safest place in town," Kade said, before he made a sharp turn on his heel and walked quickly away, back the way they had come.

Before following, Graith turned to Alix and shook his head, "Not another word from you about the eggs."

Alix just nodded and looked down at his feet. Graith ruffled his hair and they followed Kade who, noticing they were not following, had stopped and was waiting for them. He didn't mention the ship as he continued to lead them around town.

Kade took them to a few more stores where they slowly filled their packs with new clothing and supplies.

***

By late afternoon, they were back at the Running Ship Inn. They deposited their purchases in their room before coming down for an early supper. Kade had disappeared when they returned, and Doreen seemed more subdued as she served them another laden tray of food.

As they ate in silence, Graith noticed that the tavern part of the inn was empty of any other patrons. Alix ate with the same gusto he'd eaten dinner and breakfast with before, but Graith picked at his food. Zel's mood had been bleak since she'd not been able to detect her eggs on the ship. She was in no mood to talk to him, but her mood was bleeding over into his mind.

"Graith, who is King Oron?" Alix asked between bites, cutting the silence and Graith's reverie.

"King Oron is the current ruler of Lutesia. He has been in power for nearly twenty years, if I recall correctly. Why?"

"The guard and Kade mentioned him. I didn't know who he was."

Graith frowned, another piece to Alix's short life falling into place.

"You've never been to school have you, Alix?"

"Pa taught me numbers before he died, but that's about it," he said defensively.

He looked down at his plate, shoving bits of food around with his spoon.

"Well, here, a brief history lesson." Graith dug a gold coin out of his pouch and handed it to Alix. "Embossed upon the surface there, you can see a bust of our mighty king."

The profile of the face was of a heavyset man with short cropped hair and a large crown. Over his head were the words: *King Oron the Virtuous,* and under was the year it was minted. This particular coin was nearly ten years old.

"How does someone become king?" Alix asked

"By being son to the last king. That's the only way." Graith smiled, knowing that Alix's first thought was wondering if he could be king.

"Who will be the next king then?"

"If I remember correctly, Prince Brantom is King Oron's eldest son - so him, most likely. As the people, we don't hear about the daily lives of the royalty, we just feel the effects of the decisions they make. Mostly in taxes and levies. I'm a grain farmer, so each year a portion of my harvest was taken for both Lord Arish and King Oron."

Alix frowned.

"That's not very fair."

"Ah lad, life isn't fair. But some things - like the reason why we are here - are too unjust to sit by and take silently," Graith told him.

At that moment, Doreen bustled back out from the kitchen to take their dishes. Alix and Graith thanked her and bid her goodnight. She stopped Graith before he could head up the stairs.

"Graith, if you wouldn't mind, we are expecting quite the crowd tonight, you should join us after Alix is asleep," she winked at him playfully.

"I'll think about it, but I'm pretty tired." He stretched as he spoke.

"I insist, drinks are on me!"

Alix had already gone up the stairs as Graith spoke to Doreen. When Graith entered the room, Alix had laid out everything that Graith had bought for him during the day.

"Graith, here's that gold back." Alix proffered the coin to him, but he shook his head.

"Nah lad, you keep it. First thing to go in your new pouch."

"You sure? I mean, you spent so much on me today…" Alix was looking at all the clothing and items laid out on his bed.

"I'm sure. Goodnight, lad."

Alix cleared off his bed and was asleep in minutes. While Graith laid there, tired but unable to sleep.

CHAPTER FORTY-SIX

Graith

Looking over at the softly snoring form of Alix, Graith sighed and stood. Doreen had been quite insistent that he join the festivities that evening and while not wanting to be around people, he didn't want to offend their host. Scrubbing at his face and hair, he tried to push back the creeping exhaustion. It felt as though the last few months had taken only days rather than weeks and that it had been a head long sprint from the start.

As he walked slowly down the stairs, his thoughts were on the eggs. They'd already lost two. He didn't know if Zel could bear to lose another.

He shook his head. No. They wouldn't lose another. It didn't matter if they had to follow the eggs to the ends of the earth, they would find them, and get them back.

Reaching the bottom of the stairs, Graith was surprised to find that the room was already nearly filled. He knew he'd been lost in thought coming down the stairs, but the room was eerily quiet for so many guests. No music was playing, nor were people talking openly. Murmurs flew around the room, hushing around Graith as he searched for a place to sit.

Doreen appeared at his elbow, cheerily greeted him and led him to a spot near the bar. Kade was moving through the crowd with drinks, and a girl who looked similar to him in age and appearance moved in the opposite direction, also waiting on the still filling tables.

"Here, dear, be a good boy and stay here for me, alright?" Doreen said as she shoved a large pint into Graith's hands, then quickly moved back into the kitchen for more drinks.

Graith knew that he could be dense at times - hell, he'd missed a dragon changing sizes in front of him for months - but red flags were flying in his mind. Looking around at the people who surrounded him, he saw that nearly all of them were staring at him intently. He sat his ale on the small table in front of him and stood - only for a man whose face was obscured by his hood to appear at his elbow.

"Now there, Doreen just asked you so very kindly to stay here. Go ahead. Sit."

It was more of a growl than words, and a definitive command.

Graith sat uneasily. It was standing room only at this point, and people were still arriving. Nearly everyone was wearing dark clothing and over-sized cloaks, their faces hidden in the dark recesses. The volume of the crowd was still unbelievably low. Quiet enough that Graith doubted he would have woken had he been asleep upstairs.

More drinks were delivered, and the bodies finally seemed to reach an equilibrium, slowly moving in the limited space around the tables.

"Everyone here?" Doreen asked, her voice carrying across the large and quiet space.

She was standing in front of the large hearth, removing her apron. Kade and the serving girl stood on either side of her. Her tone, which up until now had been saccharine, was sharp and clear. For a short woman, her presence filled the room. Graith felt himself instinctively huddle back into his chair.

"Syla can't make it, and Reed is on watch. Other than that, I believe so, Reen," someone said from the crowd.

The man who had pushed Graith back into his chair was standing near Graith's elbow once again. His hood was pushed back, and it revealed a man not much older than Graith himself, with salt and pepper hair and stubble shadowing his cheeks. He was looking at Doreen, but Graith had no doubt that he knew where every person in the room was and who they were.

"Alright, down to business then." Doreen said.

"Reen you sure we should all be here right now? It's a work night," a young male voice complained from the far side of the room.

"Shut it, Perry," another man's voice called from near the stairs. "She never just calls us here on a whim now does she?"

"Suppose not," the first voice, Perry, replied.

"Like I said. Business," Doreen repeated.

She turned and looked at Graith. He felt himself shrink further into his chair. These were the kinds of situations he tried to avoid back home. Why he stayed in, rather than get a drink in town. When had he changed? He thought longingly of the bed upstairs that was calling his name.

"Graith, do be a dear and tell us why you were so interested in the riverboat that shut down the docks when it sailed into town, and about these friends of yours who were boarded upon it."

Doreen's soft features had taken on an edge of iron.

What did he say? Zel didn't need more people searching for her. Dragons were hated and feared in Lutesia, and these seemed to be the type of people who would hunt her down.

Before he'd figured out what to say, the man at his elbow turned and pulled out a small, wicked-looking dagger.

"Reen asked you a question. Why is a peasant like you friends with a knight and his band of mercenaries? Are they looking for you?"

"Sir Braylin? I'm not friends with *him*," Graith sputtered, angry at the thought of being associated with such a monster.

"Then who are your friends? Just some of his thugs?" Doreen asked, moving closer.

It felt like every eye in the room was on him. Graith shook his head, unable to speak. Of course, they would think that his friends were human. Why wouldn't they? They would think that he was worried about *the humans* after seeing the shape the ship was in. Why should he be worried about the dragon eggs?

Graith didn't know what to do.

Obviously being friends with any human on that ship was a dreadful thing, and these people were not friendly towards Braylin and his group. But telling them about the eggs seemed like an equally dire option. It was his responsibility to take care of Zel and her eggs.

"I must have been mistaken about the ship -" he started, unsure of what else to say.

"Graith, one thing I cannot tolerate is a liar." Doreen's voice was a whisper, but it carried loudly across the near silent space. "We know about the eggs. Why are they being taken to Oron? Did you help steal them away from their mother?"

Adrenaline shot through him at the mention of Zel's eggs. These people already knew about them.

"No. No!"

Graith waved his hands in front of himself, warding off the horrid accusations.

"She said she doesn't like liars," the man growled, and laid his dagger at the base of Graith's throat. Graith could feel the cold steel shave off a few of the day's whiskers.

He couldn't move. Couldn't breathe.

"The eggs. I'm trying to rescue the eggs," he muttered, trying not to let his Adam's apple bob in nervousness.

The dagger moved closer, pricking into the thin skin of his neck.

"Barry, that's enough," Doreen said, a strange gleam in her eye.

The dagger lowered and it took all Graith's willpower not to reach up and massage the spot where the blade had just sat.

"Now, what reason would a peasant have to rescue dragon eggs? To sell them to a higher bidder than Oron? I doubt that. We of The Market wouldn't let something like that go unchecked." She paced around the room, people moving silently out of her way. "Your own greed? The thought of taming a dragonling? You know, if that's the case, you'll just end up dead. So, what is it Graith? Why drag young Alix into this supposed rescue mission?"

"Because I promised the dragoness Azelia that I would help return her eggs to her."

Graith lowered his eyes, feeling like he was betraying Zel even though telling the truth seemed to be the only feasible option in this situation.

Murmured whispers floated around the room. Doreen was eying him with what looked like a renewed interest. Had she been about to torture him? Kill him? What if he'd said the wrong thing just then? Cold sweat trickled down his back.

"And where is the dragon Azelia now?" Doreen asked, her eyes boring into his own.

"I -" he paused, "I don't know."

"Hmm? That's not really an answer now is it, Graith?"

Doreen tapped her nails on the table she now stood before.

Zel, I need your help! What do I say?

He knew she was watching from the back of his mind as always. She was angry. Not at him, but at Doreen and her "Market".

Can you buy me time to get in range to speak through you?

I can do my best.

Click. Click. Click.

Doreen and the rest of the strange group of people were watching him. Waiting for an answer.

"Did you hear me, Graith? I really don't like to be ignored."

She smiled. A smile that chilled him to the core.

"I'm sorry Doreen. I was speaking to Zel - Azelia," he mumbled looking down at the floor once again.

"Speaking to her? How?" Doreen demanded, grabbing his chin and forcing him to look her in the eyes.

More whispers flew around the room. Graith's eyes

darted looking for likely speakers, then back to Doreen.

"She speaks into my mind, and she can hear my thoughts. I don't know how she does it, she just does."

He wrung his hands together, wondering how much time Zel needed to get into range.

"So, where is she?" Doreen repeated her earlier question.

"I don't know her exact location. East of the city, moving this way though."

Graith hoped that was a good enough answer.

"And why is she coming this way? To rescue you?" the man named Barry sneered.

"To talk to you. I - and Alix - promised to help her reclaim her eggs. But anything she says will be her choice to tell you or not."

While he didn't like the way Barry talked to him, he figured it was better to act respectful rather than rude in the precarious situation.

Doreen eyes narrowed in interest.

"How is she going to talk to us? In our minds?"

"No, she's going to use me as a vessel to speak through. She's just trying to get into range right now. She's been staying away from the city so that the guards won't know that she's nearby."

Silence filled the room for several minutes as they waited for the dragon to speak through Graith. *Who are these people?* Graith wanted to ask, but he didn't think he was in the position to do so. He could feel Zel's presence in his mind growing, and he nodded to Doreen to let her know that it would be soon.

I'm here Graith, Zel's voice sounded strained.

He felt his body sit upright in the chair, his shoulders straighten, and his head tilt up to look Doreen right in the eye as Zel took control of his body. Doreen took a small step back as she locked eyes with Zel, not Graith.

"What business do *you* have with my children, human?"

The words felt foreign coming out of his mouth, but Graith was just a puppet. A watcher from the sidelines.

"Are you the dragoness Azelia?"

Doreen seemed to have recovered her composure.

"I asked you a question first. What is your business with my children?"

"We weren't concerned about your eggs. We were concerned that Graith here had connections to one of Oron's knights. Another player so to speak, shouldering his way into *our* game."

"Then he is free to go."

Graith felt his body stand. He towered over Doreen's short frame.

"Not quite."

Doreen's eyes were sharp, and her arms had crossed.

A hiss came from his mouth, a sound he didn't even know his body could make.

"Why not?"

"Oron the moron already has your eggs. They were taken to the castle within an hour of the ship arriving. However, our sources tell us that they are being prepared to move again. A ship is preparing to leave the city soon, heading to Situra."

Zel - in Graith's body - narrowed their eyes.

"Why tell me this. Information is never free."

"Dragons are powerful. Our country believes them to be beasts. Capable of only destruction and chaos. A lie, perpetrated by the kings." Doreen took a breath, pausing before she continued, "Having an ally like that, overlooked and misunderstood, could be beneficial to our organization."

"What organization would that be?" Zel asked. Her tone - even in Graith's soft voice - was icy.

"We call ourselves the Market. We are - ah - information and procurement specialists."

"Again, information is never free. What do you want?"

"Alix. He seems like he would fit well in to our little family." Doreen smiled, "As well as the fact that I don't like to see children suffer. I took in Kade and Kali, orphans off the street."

Kade looked down, his face flushed. The girl that resembled him, who must be Kali, looked proud.

"No."

Graith wondered for a moment if Zel could make his body breath fire. The anger from that question burned in his mind. His vision was red, and his throat burned.

"We know when the eggs will leave," Doreen wheedled.

"It matters not. We will figure it out ourselves. You cannot have Alix."

Graith's body was trying to push its way towards the stairs.

"You still owe us for the information we've given you so far." Doreen seemed confident, her voice rising as Zel, in Graith's body, moved further away.

"Take his money, all of it if you want, but Graith and Alix are leaving tonight."

Doreen laughed.

"I don't want his money. I have plenty of my own. Money is worth nothing - compared to you."

Graith's body spun back around.

"You cannot threaten me. I will *eat* you, human."

"I am not trying to threaten you. In fact, I want a working relationship with *you,* Azelia. The Market could benefit from having you as an ally."

Graith could still feel Zel's anger, as well as his own, over the fact that the woman had dared ask for Alix - but he was calming down. What was important here was Zel's eggs.

He wrestled some of the control of his body away from Zel and turned them away from the watching crowd.

Zel, we need to see what they want. Other than Alix. Knowing when and where the eggs will be… that's something we haven't been able to do since we started looking for them.

He could feel her intense desire to shred Doreen to pieces.

She wanted Alix. She is a foul woman.

He soothed her, trying to not only think calmly but to feel calmly.

I don't think she is, Zel. So far, she has wanted to protect him, thinking that she could offer him a better home than with us.

So what? We give him to her? That is not an option Graith.

She sounded almost desperate to Graith and it occurred to him that losing Alix might feel like losing another child to her.

No. We see what kind of relationship she wants.

Zel was not happy, but she turned back to Doreen, and looked the small woman in her beady eyes. She pulled Graith's body up to its full height and growled, his chest rumbling at the strange sensation.

"Well? What do you want from me that could possibly be worth more than gold? Protection?" Zel asked.

Doreen smirked and walked over and put her arm around Graith's waist.

"No, but you would make for an excellent smuggler."

CHAPTER FORTY-SEVEN

Graith

Graith threw himself onto the bed. After hours of discussion, and learning more about The Market and what exactly it was that they wanted from Zel, they had finally released him. The sky was already turning a hazy gray, and a dim stream of light fell through the cracks in the shutters.

He groaned. Alix would be awake soon and Graith knew that the boy wanted to continue to explore the city. He closed his eyes and tried to force himself to sleep, but the pounding of his heart in his ears kept him awake.

Trying to let his mind drift, he immersed himself in the colors that were Zel's emotions. The ever-present spring green that felt like laying in sunlight on a warm day. That was the one that welled up when she encouraged him or thought of him or Alix. An orange and red that swirled together like fire that seemed to flare to life when she was threatened or scared. A strange blue white that constantly flowed around and through the others, Graith had come to recognize as her constant worry and fear for her eggs. It was like looking at an always changing piece of artwork, the likes of which he had only ever seen in Lord Arish's great mansion.

He could feel Zel watch him as he examined each of the emotions and thoughts, but she stayed silent. He knew that she was thinking about the deal that Doreen had offered them.

Smuggling.

At first, Zel had said that she would agree to smuggle for the group after she had reclaimed her eggs. Doreen, however, insisted that the job she wanted done needed to be completed as soon as possible. She even told them that the destination was on their way. Zel had reluctantly agreed to hear more about the job.

Graith wished she hadn't.

Doreen had asked her to carry dragon scales to a location in Situra. She promised them that the scales had come from a living dragon, but the notion that scales were being used by humans upset Zel once again. She demanded to know what they were being used for, but Doreen had just laughed, telling them that she didn't know. Her job, she said, was to procure the items for her clients, not worry about what they did with them after they were delivered.

Graith had felt Zel's tail, on her far away body, lash at the thought. Being used by humans as a pack animal infuriated her. When he had tried to reason with her that he and Alix had basically already done so, she had shaken his head, denying it. She said that they did what they had to - to survive.

Finally, Graith had put his foot down. He had told Zel to accept the job, reminding her of her eggs.

I can't believe that I lost sight of retrieving my clutch over such a matter, she whispered into his mind, horrified.

You had the honor of all dragons on your mind.

We dragons don't just give our shed scales away. I'm sure they were taken.

Zel, I know it's not okay - in any way - but we need to do whatever is necessary to reclaim your eggs.

He felt her hang her head in defeat. He hoped that she was somewhere safe. She'd had to travel close to the city to take control of his body. He was sure that the guards were on the lookout for her. Oron wanted her dead after all. She was a threat to whatever plan he had for her eggs.

That started Graith's worries anew. The Market - after he and Zel had agreed to carry the scales - divulged the information they had learned about the eggs.

Oron was planning to move the clutch to Situra. They knew he was sending a small armada to the Situran coastal city of Alluvia. The Market believed that the eggs would be on the main ship. The group was to be heavily guarded and if their sources were correct, escorted by Oron's heir, Prince Brantom, along with several knights, including Braylin.

Graith knew extraordinarily little about the politics of the world. Doreen and the man about his age, Barry, had explained that while Lutesia, Situra, and Etria - the southernmost country and Zel's home - each had their own vast economic systems, there was little to no trade between the countries. The Market however, had tendrils reaching into each country, but the movement of goods was slow.

Due to the lack of trade, little was known about the other countries. The Market, as well as Graith and Zel, were quite puzzled by the fact that Oron would send the eggs away. They thought perhaps it was an attempt to keep Zel away from the capital. Other than that, the king's motives were unclear.

***

Graith cracked his eyes open. Light now streamed into the room. Alix was up and about, fidgeting with his new bags and clothing. Graith didn't remember falling asleep, but he must have. Exhaustion still oozed out of every pore of his being.

Sitting up with a groan, Alix's attention was pulled to him.

"Morning, Graith! What time did you get to bed? It's nearly noon, and we have so much more to do!" Alix was nearly bouncing in his excitement.

"You have no idea, lad. We have a lead."

Graith was still trying to blink the sleep out of his eyes.

"We do? That's amazing!"

Alix started shoving things back into the bag.

"Aye. But it came with quite the price tag."

"What do you mean?"

Alix's motions slowed as he waited for Graith to

continue.

"Do you want the news, the bad news, or the worse news, first?" Graith asked him.

"Well, just tell me everything."

"Seems Doreen and Kade - who has a twin sister Kali by the way - are part of an underground organization, The Market. They found out the eggs are about to be moved. But in exchange for the information they wanted something." Graith took a deep breath, "They wanted you, lad."

Alix's eyes went wide in fear, and tears sprang up.

"I... I see. Anything to get Zel's eggs back. Plus, they don't seem like horrible people..."

"Oh, knock it off. I told you, we're family now. Neither Zel nor I would ever give you up. We told them that. So instead, they asked for Zel to smuggle for them. Want her to carry some dragon scales across the border. So that's our payment for the information."

Alix issued a small hiccup as he tried to stifle the flow of tears. "Oh. I... I would have stayed. For Zel."

"I know you would have, lad. But I wouldn't have let you. I won't let you." Graith got up and stiffly walked across the room to ruffle Alix's hair.

"So, what's the worst news then?" he asked quietly.

"We are going to be accompanied by Kade and Kali. We'll have little to no notice before we have to leave. We don't know for sure which ship will have the eggs. There are a lot of unknowns right now."

Graith was pacing as he spoke. The fog of sleep had finally retreated, and he was collecting the things he needed to prepare for the day. He needed a bath and a shave. He hoped they would get Alix's boots before it was time to leave.

Heading downstairs, Doreen was waiting with a table full of food, smiling.

"Late morning for you, Graith. I hope you slept well!" Her persona of a simple innkeeper was ruined for him now.

The sharp look in her eyes, the smile that was icy - she'd gotten what she wanted for the most part, and now they were no longer her patrons.

They were her employees.

"Yes, well, got business to do today -" Graith started, before Doreen cut him off.

"I do hope that you take Kade and Kali with you."

Gritting his teeth, he said quietly, "Of course. Couldn't navigate the city without Kade."

"Kali is quite talented as well," Doreen said with a wink and a smile.

Graith shuddered. How could people act one way, then flip completely and act another? For the first time in a while, he missed being all alone on his little farm.

Oh, but you would miss me! Zel joked weakly. He could tell she was still nearby.

You, Alix, the eggs. That's my family. We just don't have a home yet.

Graith - you do know that I want to return to Etria after we retrieve the eggs? Zel's voice was soft, as if she was afraid of what he might say. *Maybe wait for them to hatch, but eventually I would like to return. It's my home.*

I did not know that. I thought you were banished? Graith was surprised, he hadn't had any idea that she wanted to return to Etria. He hadn't really thought paste retrieving her eggs.

No, I was just told to leave by my father, but he can't keep me away.

Well, I'll have to ask Alix, but I would be fine going home with you. He hesitated before saying, *If that's what you want?*

Of course. You're my family too, Graith.

After eating a late brunch, Graith and Alix went to bathe. Afterwards they decided to stop and check on Mero.

Even though it had only been a couple of days since they arrived, he looked like a new horse. His coat was brushed, his mane was braided, his hooves had been trimmed and shod. His halter even had sparkling brass pins that contrasted nicely with the pale leather.

He had also put on more weight than he had lost on the

way here.

Seeing Graith and Alix, Mero flipped his head happily and perked his ears up. A light neigh, and he was standing with his chest to the half wall that kept him in the stall.

"What a good boy!" Alix said, climbing the wall and onto Mero's back. "We missed you!"

Graith proffered the large horse an apple, while Alix had stowed away several carrots. They were enjoying their time with the large gelding when Kade entered the small stable.

"Hey, Kade!" Alix greeted him from the back of the horse.

"Hello, Alix," Kade said lightly, as if he hadn't been backing Doreen the night before in taking the boy.

"I heard we are moving again soon."

"Yes. As soon as our source inside the castle lets us know."

Kade seemed surprised that Graith had told the boy, eying the older man slightly before smiling at the boy.

"Hear that, Mero? We get to travel together again!" Alix pet the horse's forelock as he spoke.

"Unfortunately, not with Mero. We'll be taking a ship to Alluvia. Once there, we will be moving with Azelia."

Kade's voice was light, but an undertone made Graith think that not everything was right in his world either.

"We can't leave Mero behind!" Alix threw his arms around the horse's wide neck.

"Alix, Mero will be safe here," Kade reassured the boy. "Anyway, I came looking for you two for a reason. While we don't know exactly when they'll be leaving, we need to be prepared. Doreen owns a boat. Of course, the hag had to name it The Running Ship. But we need to make sure it's stocked and ready to launch as soon as we get the word."

What Graith heard was that they had more running around to do. He wasn't *old* but he wasn't a spring chicken either. He wanted to rest and work on a plan - or he told himself that's what he wanted - but that had never been his thing before, so, shrugging, he followed Kade to see this ship.

***

They reached the docks, and Graith was surprised to see that the original ship that had carried the eggs was gone. Other ships had filled its place, and security, while not lax, was lowered. At the far end of the pier, a small ship awaited them. A single mast stood tall and the flag flying was a duplicate of the sign which hung outside of the inn. A ship - this ship? Graith wondered - on a field of waves. It read Running Ship, and the name was also emblazoned on the rear of the ship.

A plank was lowered from the high deck to the lower pier. Alix raced his way up the board, but immediately back peddled when he came face to face with Kali. Graith had only seen her across the room the night before, and Alix hadn't seen her at all. Up close, the resemblance to her brother was apparent. Had they had the same haircut and loose wardrobe, Graith doubted he would be able to tell them apart.

"Nice to meet you, you must be Kali! I'm Alix!"

He enthusiastically shoved his hand out towards her. She met him halfway, but her hand was limp and the shake nonexistent.

"Yes. I will be traveling with you to guarantee the client's acquisition of their goods. I am the guard on this operation."

"Really? Not Kade?" Alix asked, his eyes flickering between the siblings.

"My brother doesn't have the - ah - taste for blood that I do."

She grinned wickedly, and Alix paled slightly.

"No, I prefer to work with people who will still be alive in an hour," Kade chuckled.

Kade showed Alix around the ship while Kali and Graith spoke. Graith could hear joyful cheers from the boy as he was shown how to tie knots and was taught a few sailing basics.

"Now that those two have gone, let me reiterate the terms of this agreement per Doreen," Kali started, brushing her long hair out of her eyes. "We are currently keeping the scales onboard. We believe that the ship will take the eggs soon. Our client is in Alluvia - she is the lady of the city. Once we get one day out from shore, your dragon will land onboard, retrieve the scales, and fly them, you, and me to the meeting location."

She had been pointedly leading him around the ship thus far, showing him the crate with the scales, the space Zel would land in, and the quarters they would sleep in. Graith stopped to peer over the railing into the dark waters below.

"Why couldn't this be done without Zel? Using her seems... over the top," Graith asked, trying to carefully word his question.

"There are only two entrances to Situra from our country. One is through Alluvia, the other through Veles to Cian. All things brought into either city are searched thoroughly. The ship itself will be nearly pulled apart, board by board. Same goes for anything carried into Cian from Veles. She will allow us to bypass that."

"How long does it take to get across the sea?" Graith asked, worried about Zel flying for an extended period of time.

"Without a storm? A week. With a storm? It depends on how lost we get."

They both looked up at the currently dark sky. Graith wished they could go by land instead but knew that wouldn't happen. He hoped that whatever storm was brewing would blow over before they had to set sail.

CHAPTER FORTY-EIGHT

Graith

News came more quickly than Graith expected. A Market runner came to the ship two days after they started preparing for their voyage. He told them that their castle sources said that the eggs would be moved that night.

Kali immediately started rushing the loading of supplies onto the ship, while Kade yelled that he would be right back and sprinted off into the distance.

Graith found himself carrying barrels and boxes, and Kali directed him where to put them. Alix was told to climb the mast and sit in the crow's nest to keep an eye out for the arrival of the last of the goods that they were waiting for. While helping Graith and Alix follow the eggs, this was also a trading mission for the crew and the ship would be filled to the brim before they set sail.

Hours rolled by, and Graith's body started to ache. In the days that they had stayed at the Running Ship Inn, he'd put on more weight than he'd lost and became accustomed to sleeping in a soft bed once again. His body was protesting this sudden change in activity. At some point, the storm that had been brewing for the last few days started to set in. A small patter of rain hit the deck as they finished putting everything in place and were ready to go.

Kade had returned shortly after he had left, and Graith was surprised to see him carrying boots tied together and tossed over his shoulders. He'd gone to Rand's shop for

Alix's boots. With him were several members of the Market, including both Berry and Doreen.

Doreen pulled out an inventory list and was triple checking her wares before they could set sail. This including her precious cargo of scales.

The scales were in a hatch directly below the deck, and instructions were given for Zel to retrieve them when the ship was a day out from the Situran shore.

Doreen pulled Kade and Kali into the small captain's quarters while Graith repeated the instructions to Zel. A few minutes later, Doreen and Berry left the ship, leaving Kali, Kade, Alix, and Graith, along with a few sailors, onboard.

Graith was told to stay out of the way, and the ship was launched from the pier. Alix stayed in the crow's nest, watching the city of Tesia vanish into the distance. Graith, after checking that he was no longer needed, headed down to the sailor's bunk where he and Alix would be staying.

The motion of the ship set his hammock rocking. Between the constant motion, and the sound of the rain on the hull of the ship, Graith was lulled to sleep.

***

The rain continued late into the night, and one particularly loud peal of thunder woke Graith with a start. He was disoriented and tired, and only a single lantern by the stairs illuminated the large sleeping quarters. He could feel Zel and was surprised by how close she felt. Her mood, like the sea, was turbulent and dark.

Graith, I'm coming aboard, she said.

That was all the warning he got before the ship rocked violently as if swept up in a tidal wave.

He hastily climbed out of the net suspending him in the air and ran out to see the dragon. It was still raining, and only the brief flashes of lightning illuminated the deck. Zel's eyes glowed with a strange inner light, and her body had regained some of its dark blue coloring.

The following morning had been quite a surprise to Kade and Kali, neither had ever actually seen a dragon before. Screams from crew members had awoken Graith, who had ended up falling asleep under Zel's wing. Emerging from under her large leathery wing had made one of the sailors pass out from shock.

Kade and Kali had formally introduced themselves to Zel. They referred to her only as *The Mighty Dragoness* or Azelia. To Graith, it seemed like it was going to her head. She kept her head up and preened at her wings or tail whenever she saw someone look at her. Alix hadn't left her side - lying on her back, under her wings, or climbing along her tail.

The light rain - which Graith hadn't thought very light - had finally turned into a full-blown storm. Lightning was striking around them several times a minute, and large swells of water rocked the ship. The crew managed to bring down the mainsail before everyone, even Alix who had been reluctant to leave Zel's side, retreated to the lower levels of the ship.

Zel was the only one to remain on the deck - and she was restless.

Graith, I want to fly close enough to the ship carrying my eggs to make sure they are safe, Zel's voice filled his mind as his body swung back and forth in his hammock. The motion was making him dizzy, worried about Zel he tried to sit up, only to have to lie back down immediately.

Is it the storm? he asked. He could feel her head turning side to side, as if looking through the darkness for the other ships.

Yes. No. I... I'm not sure. Something feels wrong, she said, shifting uneasily.

He knew what she was talking about, as she'd been feeling uneasy ever since she landed on the ship. She'd been able to sense her eggs less and less the first day, until she couldn't sense them at all.

Are you sure that's the best idea? What if you're struck by lightning? Or if they see you? he asked, wishing that he could go up to her, but between the ship's motion and the raging storm, he thought he might fall overboard.

Lightning can't hurt a dragon. And I just need to get

close enough to sense my eggs. I'll be right *back,* she said, as she stood.

I can't really stop you now, can I?

Sometimes Graith wondered why she even bothered telling him.

I tell you because you are important to me. But no, you can't stop me.

In the tumultuous sea that rocked the ship side to side, Graith was unable to feel when Zel launched herself from the ship.

However, moments later, he was there, flying with her.

You can come with me though.

She sounded excited to be flying again. She'd been unhappy on the ship, but she couldn't stay in touch with Graith any other way. The sea was too large for her to comfortably fly across while following the ship. Graith supposed that lying still on a ship for two days was not her idea of fun.

Looking around, he was surprised to see that Zel was able to see clearly through the rain and lightning. He could sense that she also knew which direction they should be heading, and within moments they were racing towards an unknown point. The rain was cold on her scales, and the wind was firm beneath her wings.

Flying with her was exhilarating.

Feeling the wind on her wings, and her using her tail as a rudder, was amazing. It was completely natural to her. There was no thought in the *how* of flying, just where. Their current destination slowly came into sight - the Lutesian Armada.

There were three ships, easily as large as the Running Ship, and a fourth that dwarfed the others. All of them were of high craftsmanship, but only the largest really stood out. It was the most ornamental ship that Graith had ever seen. Gold trim, large glass windows on the rear of the ship, and flags flying even in the monstrous storm.

Graith was watching it bob like a cork in the water, not realizing that they were getting much closer than Zel had initially said.

When they made their first pass above it, Graith realized they were too close. He was going to say something to Zel but found himself surrounded by the blue-white aura of sheer panic that always related to her clutch.

Zel? What's going on?

I can't sense them, Graith. I should be able to feel them from here.

They made a second pass. Then a third.

On the third pass, Graith could see Sir Braylin standing on the deck, clear as day.

Braylin was yelling at Zel, but she couldn't hear him. When she tried to listen to what he was saying in his mind, she found she could not. She could sense him - but none of his thoughts.

She wheeled in the air, hovering over the ship, her large wings beating in time to the pounding of Graith's heart.

"Dragon! I thought we told you that approaching us again would only bring disaster for your remaining eggs!" he shouted, trying to make his voice carry over the booming thunder.

WHERE ARE THEY?

Even if she could not hear him, she would make sure he could hear her.

Graith felt her worry shifting to anger as she looked at the knight. Fear flashed in Braylin's eyes, but he motioned to a sailor who stood off to the side. The man scurried away, reappearing moments later with two others, carrying a large gray egg.

Braylin had a wicked look in his eyes as he pulled out his sword and held it above his head, preparing to swing down on the egg. Graith's heart was in his throat watching. He didn't understand why Zel was becoming angrier.

Braylin shouted one final time, "Leave now, dragoness, or I shall destroy another of your precious eggs!"

Smoke started to pour from Zel's nostrils, and Graith could feel her fire building in her chest. When she spoke, he understood.

LIAR - she landed on the ship, snapping her jaw at the

knight - *THAT IS NOT ONE OF MY EGGS.*

The fear returned to Braylin's eyes and his sword fell to the deck with a clatter. He took a half step backwards, his arms out in front of him.

Zel's vision had gone red. Her emotions were red.

Graith was forgotten, trapped watching through her eyes. When she lost her first egg, he'd only heard the screams as the first group of men died. He and Alix had retreated as fast as Mero could run in Kelna, but he'd seen the destruction dealt to the first ship.

Graith had never actually seen Zel kill.

Without the worry of protecting or losing her eggs, there was nothing holding Zel back.

A firestorm engulfed the ship in moments. The wet wood offered no resistance to the heat of her flames. Men were screaming, some jumping from the burning ship to the roiling waters below. Zel caught one in her maw, severing the man in half in one bite. The blood flowing down her throat only ignited her bloodlust further.

Sir Braylin was caught standing still, unsure of what to do.

It was too late.

Zel jumped forward and landed among the flames. They licked at her scales, warming her. She roared, and Graith, through Zel, smelled what had to be Braylin soiling himself.

Braylin turned to run, but Zel's foreclaw reached out and grabbed him around the middle. His screams were lost among her growl and a peal of thunder as lightning hit the mast of the already burning ship. He tried to escape her grasp, pulling at her claws with his small arms.

It annoyed her so she bit them off, one at a time. He screamed the first time, but Graith wasn't sure if he passed out or died before the second. She released his body, but batted it around, like a cat with a mouse. He wasn't moving, but she wasn't done. She grabbed one leg in her mouth and shook. Graith could feel the spine snap and muscles rip. The sound of the body breaking made Graith want to look away, but he was stuck in Zel's mind.

She threw the body into the air, catching it, and swallowing it whole.

Then she turned back to the ship.

Taking her anger out, she ripped it apart. Wood tore into the sensitive skin of her paws, but she took no notice. Fire raged around her, hot enough that the water below started to boil.

More sailors were killed. More wood was burned and destroyed. She was still lost to the anger that clouded her mind.

Graith watched, unable to do anything else. Her mental anguish was overwhelming. He didn't know what to do. So, he did the only thing he could think of - he reassured her and reminded her that he was there - other than that, he waited it out.

After the flagship was destroyed, she chased after the other three ships. They fled when she ignited the first ship, but they didn't get far.

The storm cleared and the sun rose before she was done.

***

Zel lay upon the burnt shell of what had once been Sir Braylin's ship. Black smoke rose into the now cloudless sky. After a few hours, the Running Ship pulled alongside the husk.

"Dragoness Azelia? Please rejoin us!" Kali yelled across the water.

Zel heard the girl but ignored her.

"Zel, please! We can't wake up Graith!" Alix screamed to her with both his voice and mind. His distress, at least, caused Zel to lift her head and look over at him.

You cannot wake Graith because I have him, Alix, she said calmly.

It was true, she had tucked all of Graith's consciousness into a corner of her mind. She needed him and the thought of being alone in her mind frightened her.

Please come back? Alix begged, *We saw the flames and were worried about you.*

Graith was still seeing through Zel's eyes, and hearing

through bother her mind and ears. When he heard Alix's plea, he was surprised by how soft the boy's mental voice was.

Not yet.

Zel didn't want to think about how much time they had wasted crossing this sea. How her eggs could be anywhere in the world right now.

Then will you at least let Graith come back? Alix sounded as if he were going to cry.

Zel, it's okay, Graith said. *Even if I'm not* here, *I'm here with you. And if you return to the ship, I will come be with you.*

Fine.

Graith wasn't sure if she was answering him or Alix, but moments later he was lying in his hammock, slowly rocking with the ship. He tried to get up, but his body was stiff and unresponsive. He managed to get to his feet and stagger up to the deck.

Kade was the first to hear his boots on the deck, but shortly, Kade, Kali, and Alix were all supporting him. They helped him walk over to the railing, where he looked out across the water at Zel.

She was black.

Graith wasn't sure if her hide had changed colors again, or if it was soot from the remnants of the ship.

Alix tugged at his sleeve, and he looked over at the boy. He looked like he'd been crying.

"What happened, Graith? Why couldn't we wake you up?"

"You know how Zel can take over my body? She can also pull me into hers. Last night she wanted to check on her eggs. She was worried about them in the storm, and about the fact she couldn't sense them." Graith's voice sounded like gravel.

"They saw you and killed the eggs?" Kali asked, trying to put the pieces together.

Graith wasn't sure if she was actually worried about the eggs, or just trying to figure out the situation and how to handle it.

"No." He shook his head slowly. "They never had the eggs. They had replicas. Fakes."

"I see. So why did Zel burn the ships?" Kade asked.

Graith stared at the young man, confused by the question. When it was apparent that he was waiting for an answer, Graith said, "Anger. Revenge. Sir Braylin was on one of the ships. He tried to threaten her. He must not have known she could sense her eggs. He was also directly responsible for destroying two of her eggs already. She wanted him dead."

"I see." Kali's voice carried across the water to Zel, who turned her eyes towards the group. "Well, we have a job to do. Our sources inside Oron's castle are reliable. If they were tricked into thinking that the eggs were being moved onto the ships, they were definitely being moved. They were going to Situra, one way or another." She started pacing as she talked.

"This just means the clutch must have traveled by land. Do you know if Prince Brantom was on board any of the ships?" she asked Graith.

"I don't think so. I would've thought he would have been on the flagship, but the only ones there were Braylin and a couple of guards and sailors." Graith shook his head as he answered.

Kali nodded, and he could see a plan forming in her mind.

"We will deliver the scales as promised, and then head south to Veles - the only city with land access to Situra. I've talked to the captain already this morning, we should dock in Alluvia by tomorrow evening." Kali looked coolly down at the dragoness. "I hope you're up to flying, Zel, it's time to fulfill your end of the deal."

CHAPTER FORTY-NINE

Graith

As the day dragged on, the Running Ship drew ever closer to the foreign shore. By the time the sun had set, the coast of Situra had become a smudge on the horizon. Graith had convinced Zel to leave the husk of the burnt ship only after the embers had cooled, which had taken nearly the full day.

She was smugly impressed with the damage she had done but grumbled more than once to Graith that she wished that she had dragged out Braylin's death. It infuriated her that the knight had thought that the faux eggs would fool them.

While waiting for night to fall, Zel tried to insist that she, Graith, and Alix leave immediately for Veles. However, both Graith and Kali immediately shot the idea down. She'd promised to deliver the scales and Graith told her firmly that she was going to hold up her end of the deal.

"What are you going to do when you get there? I thought they would kill your eggs if they spotted you?" Kali asked, arms crossed and foot tapping loudly on the deck.

That is why Graith and Alix need to go, I need help rescuing them.

Zel tried to sound like she believed herself but fell short as she tried to imagine either Graith or Alix being able to fight their way in to or out of a situation.

"Oh yes, an old man and a young boy. Neither of whom can wield a weapon?" Kade asked, joining into the conversation.

"I'm not old!" Graith muttered, while running a hand over his face, feeling for any new wrinkles.

She argued for a bit longer, but finally gave up when Graith and Alix told her flatly that even if she left, they wouldn't go with her.

Alix had climbed onto her back when she'd returned to the ship, and he'd spent several hours using an old rag to try to wipe her scales clean. Little of the smoky darkness came off.

"What did you do - char your scales?" he asked, licking his thumb and scrubbing at one spot, but it stayed black.

No, she huffed, shuffling on the deck. The boat rocked slightly, and Alix nudged her, encouraging her to shrink herself. *I just need to take a bath. But I think that it will be good cover for us anyway, flying at night.*

She looked over her body. Every inch was a sooty matte black. She stretched out her wings to look at the delicate skin of her wing sail. Even the skin was black.

***

When the shore of Situra finally became visible, activity on the ship jumped to life. Kali directed sailors to do a final inventory check. Men were running about doing her bidding. While she was giving orders, Graith and Alix tried to stay out of the way. Zel had to become airborne because the sailors were still frightened to move around her.

Kade was calmly standing to one side, leaning his back against the mast. He would be dealing with the sale of the wares when they docked. Between the two of them Kade was the merchant. Kali grumbled more than once about his ability to make friends wherever he went.

As Kali tried to give him instructions on docking for the fifth time, he grabbed her by the shoulders and spun her around, steering her to Graith and Alix.

"*This* is yours for the time being. Please don't feel hurried on returning it, but I would *much* appreciate it if you left now," he said, rolling his eyes and shoving his sister forward slightly.

Kali stomped her foot in frustration at the treatment. At the same time, she spun and swung her small fist at her brother's face. However, Kade was already moving away and laughed as she missed.

"You ass!"

She let out a small screech of annoyance before turning back around to the waiting man and boy. Her demeanor changed instantly as she looked between them and then up at Zel. She was calm, and Graith could see her thoughts churning as he watched her. She waved at Zel to get her attention.

Yes, Kali? Zel asked as she watched the girl.

"Azelia, the scales are stored in a large crate which the sailors have hoisted with a net. I think that will be the easiest way for you to carry them. Can you lift them directly out of the cargo hold, or do I need to have the men move it onto the deck?" her tone was even and mature once again.

I can try, she said, lowering herself down. to position the ropes in her foreclaws.

As Zel reached down into the hold and pulled at two looped handles, the boat rocked. After one unsuccessful wing beat, Graith saw Zel increase her size. Wood creaked as the crate slowly lifted into view.

It was larger than Graith anticipated. He could have easily stood inside it without his head touching the top and spread his arms wide without touching the sides. The net swung gently above the deck before Zel maneuvered it back down, then landed behind it.

All right, I'm ready to go. If you are ready, climb on.

She was shrinking quickly while lowering her shoulders for Graith and Kali. They would be able to ride, sitting on the smooth junction where her neck and back met just before her wings. Graith settled himself in front, and Kali slowly made her way up behind him. Her face was tight and pale, and she kept looking back at the deck. As Zel quickly grew larger, Kali let out a small squeak as the deck moved away.

"You all right? This was the Market's idea after all," Graith asked as she tried to settle in place.

Heartscale

"I'm fine." Kali shifted again, trying to find the best hand and leg holds, "Azelia, how long do you think it will take to get to shore? We are going to the far side of Alluvia, Doreen told me that there is a large shrine with a dragon statue that we should be able to see. That's our rendezvous point."

Her voice was a little thinner than normal, and Zel briefly showed Graith how scared the girl was.

Not long. I would say before the moon has fully risen.

Zel grabbed the netting once more and tensed her hind legs in preparation for lift off.

Ready?

"Ready," both Graith and Kali replied.

"Be safe, and we'll see you tomorrow!" Alix cried from the crow's nest. Graith had to chuckle, the boy did have an affinity for heights.

Spreading her wings, she gave a single mighty lunge, pulling herself and the crate into the air. The motion rocked her riders, and even Graith had a moment's hesitation on whether riding the dragoness into town was a good idea.

What if they fell?

Kali let out a single scream, and clutched tightly to Graith's waist, before burying her face in his back. He smiled, as it reminded him of Alix on their final ride out of the swamp and away from Kelna. Kali and Kade weren't that much older than the boy. He patted her arm reassuringly.

Then they were soaring. The last light of the day sparkling on the water far below. Graith was fascinated, looking left and right - even leaning a little to the side. When he did so, Kali gave a small squeak and clutched him tighter.

"Do you even have your eyes open back there?" he asked, wondering if she was seeing the beautiful sight.

"- no -"

The single syllable came out between gasps of breath.

"Well, you're missing out," he said, leaning to the right again, for a better view.

"- I'm - good -" was all Kali could manage.

Graith, Zel said, *be careful. If you fell, I would have to drop the scales to catch you.*

Graith grinned, and looked down once more, before settling into the crook of Zel's neck and facing forward.

The steady beat of Zel's wings, Kali's soft breathing, and the wind rushing past his ears were the only sounds Graith heard as the last of the light slowly faded away.

Alluvia was a pool of light below them, to their right. Zel was flying around the city, rather than directly over it. Graith understood her logic, but he wished that they didn't need to be so secretive. The architecture was drastically different from Lutesia, with low flat buildings with large openings and strange courtyards in the middle.

Since the night was still young, ethereal wisps of music carried through the chilly air, along with the noises of a city. Screams and yells, dogs barking, doors opening and closing - chaos that created a cacophony of sound.

Graith dragged his eyes forward, away from Alluvia.

As his eyes adjusted to the darkness, he blinked.

Then he blinked again.

And a third time.

Several miles outside the city, a statue of enormous size loomed. At their current altitude, they were level with the top of it.

It was a dragon.

Its wings were spread wide, and it was rearing on its hind legs with its head thrown back. It looked as if it were about to spew fire.

A dragon's ire captured perfectly in stone.

***

"We're here," Kali's faint voice floated in the wind.

She must have opened her eyes at some point.

I'll land there, Zel said, showing Graith her intended landing spot, the center of the shrine.

She immediately tilted her wings to spiral slowly around the massive dragon. There was no one at the shrine this late at night and Graith doubted that anyone could see her this far from the city. She and her two passengers were exhausted, all three more than ready to land on solid ground.

When the crate hit the ground with a *thunk,* Kali

squeezed Graith, startled by the sudden end to the long flight. The moment that Zel's feet touched the ground, Kali vaulted off the dragon. She took two large steps away, and then threw herself onto the ground, arms spread wide.

It wasn't that horrible, was it? Zel asked Graith worriedly.

No, she's exaggerating, he told the dragon.

Graith let himself slide slowly down Zel's broad shoulder, landing stiffly on his feet. The flight hadn't taken *that* long, but between Kali's death grip and the fact there had been no saddle, Graith was stiff and sore.

As he paced in front of the shrine, trying to get the blood flowing back to his extremities, Graith examined the stone dragon further. Zel barely came up to its knees and she was currently at her largest size.

While he walked, Zel gave the statue a once over, then curled up between the two massive legs. She dramatically lowered her tail - which had nearly finished healing and was looking noticeably less stubby - slowly to cover her eyes.

Graith kept staring at the stone dragon. The immense size amazed him, and he couldn't imagine anything so huge actually moving or breathing.

Is… Is this a realistically sized dragon? he finally asked Zel, looking between her and it.

Possibly? Very few dragons live long enough to reach this size. Grandpa Cimmeris is the only one even close to it that I know.

She seemed less than interested in the statue, not bothering to look at it again. Not quite getting the answer he wanted from her, Graith turned to Kali. She'd finally pulled herself into a sitting position from where she'd thrown herself onto the ground.

"So, we're here. Now how will your client know?" Graith asked as he leaned against one of the large legs and looked at the girl. The stone was warm through his clothes even though it was the middle of winter.

"See those fire pits?" she asked, as she pointed at two large cauldrons - one near each of the dragon's legs.

"Aye."

They were the only things illuminating the statue and surrounding area.

"Doreen gave me a packet to burn. Should produce a bright colored smoke for a short amount of time. Was told to do it at first light."

She pulled a small paper envelope out and waved it at him.

"And then we just hope they see it from the city? What if they don't? What if the wrong people see it?" he asked, disturbed.

The plan was a little too vague for his liking.

"Our client will have people watching for it. If someone else comes to see, we just tell them we were praying to ol' stony here." Kali shrugged. "I'm fairly sure that the Siturans consider dragons gods or something. Hell, look at this thing. You don't construct something this large to venerate your enemies."

They both looked up at the colossus again. Graith's skin crawled as he thought he saw the eye move so high above them.

Kali shrugged again, "Anyway, get some sleep. I'll keep watch."

You should sleep too, Kali. I'll keep watch, Zel told the young woman.

Kali didn't argue. Instead she leaned up against the stone dragon's tail that wrapped in front of them. It isolated the area in front of the statue, creating a private sanctuary.

"A little shut-eye never hurt, I guess," she said, eyes already closed.

Graith climbed into his usual spot under Zel's left wing, but he was unable to fall asleep right away. He hoped that Alix was all right. His mind turned, wondering what if something happened? What if the ship didn't make it into the port safely? What if...

Alix is fine. He's currently asleep. Zel's voice cut into his turmoiled thoughts.

You can sense him all the way from here? Graith asked

her, surprised.

He was quite sure they were much farther away from the ship than she had once told him she could hear.

You. Alix. You two are my family now. I can sense you much farther away than I could before.

She gave a mental shrug.

Oh. Graith was quiet for a moment, then said, *Thank you for checking on him, Zel.*

You're not the only one who worries, Graith, Zel said, squeezing him lightly with her wing.

Graith, his worry abated for the moment, finally drifted off to sleep. The last thing he remembered was the warm green tone of Zel's mental state surrounding him.

CHAPTER FIFTY

Nerie

Nerie wanted to say that going to court had made her feel better.

In fact, it had while she was there.

However, the moment she'd gotten back to her rooms the illusion she was harboring fell away. Her dinner was still cold, her mother was still gone, and the flower she had been embroidering for Alaena sat in its hoop waiting.

It's only while they search for the people who set the fire, Kiriga told her for what seemed like the hundredth time.

This time. What about the next time someone doesn't like the idea of me being queen? Am I going to be locked in a cage to keep me safe? Nerie asked angrily.

Kiriga didn't have an answer. Instead she sent waves of love and adoration to the princess, who continued to shove the cold food around on her plate.

Maybe I'll have Karina finish that flower. Then Alaena can't complain.

It was childish, but at that point, Nerie thought she might throw the hoop in the fire if she picked it up again.

Alaena will know, and I doubt Karina would do it unless you ordered her to do so.

Nerie glowered but knew that the dragoness was right. Karina seemed to be the only one on her side, so there was no point in ostracizing the maid.

I could tell you some more stories, Riya offered.

The dark dragoness had spent all of her time since she had reached the palace talking. To Soros, Eras, Ilex, Kiriga or Nerie. It didn't matter. She just chattered along, happy to be near enough that she wasn't mentally yelling across the country at her family.

Most of the stories she had told Nerie were about her great – great – grandfather Justan. Now, there was nothing *wrong* with Justan, but Nerie didn't want to hear another pointless story.

The way that Riya recoiled, her mind a dark cloud, and Kiriga's instant hiss at Nerie, let her know that her thought had been less than private.

She flushed in shame.

Of course, Riya wanted to talk about Justan. He'd been her partner, her other half. It would be like Nerie losing Kiriga and having to live the rest of her life without the dragoness.

Only through a flicker of a thought, Kiriga gently reminded her that one day she would outlive Nerie. The flush that had formed on Nerie's face drained along with all her feelings. To think that Kiriga would have to live without her… It was more horrifying than the thought of living without the dragoness.

Don't think about that. Kiriga's voice was stronger than Nerie expected. *You are here with me, now. That's what matters.*

As Nerie went to respond, a strange stillness overtook the dragons. Their thoughts, which normally buffered against Nerie's mind, stopped. She could nearly feel their heads turn in unison, to the west.

Nerie felt herself rise, and walk to the door, trying to get to Kiriga.

Something was wrong.

She couldn't even form the thought to ask *what* was wrong. She was running down the hall when her mind finally caught up with her instincts.

What's going on? she asked once, then a second time as she got no response.

As she entered Soren's quarters - the only entrance to the courtyard where all the dragons lounged - she found Soren standing in the doorway. He's face was scrunched in a frown, and his eyes were locked on Ilex.

She walked past him, laying her hand on the golden hide that was just outside the door. As her hand made contact with the warm scales, the young dragoness jumped.

Nerie, Kiriga said, her focus still elsewhere.

What's wrong? Nerie asked for a third time, her heart racing as she waited for one of the dragons to tell her what was happening.

Wyla has left Cian.

Nerie's brows furrowed. *But she protects us from invasions by Lutesia along the border?*

Yes, she's supposed to stay there.

Why has she left? Has something happened in Cian? Nerie's stomach clenched, thinking about Kora and Karsen. She would be horrified if anything happened to her cousins.

That's the thing - she won't say. Only that there hasn't been an attack.

A soft whoosh was all the notice they got before Eras launched himself into the air, and within moments was out of sight. For a dragon as large as he was, he was rocketing across the landscape.

I will find out. Do not let anyone within an hour's flight of the capital until I return.

In instant response, Riya, Mazen, and Soros all alighted from the palace rooftop.

It had only been moments, but all that were left in the courtyard were Ilex, Kiriga, Soren, and Nerie. Nerie looked around, as if coming out of a daze. She saw that at some point Soren had walked to Ilex and his frown had deepened. He seemed to not notice that Nerie was outdoors with him.

Silence hung heavy in the courtyard, and Nerie's stomach twisted. She glanced back at the palace and decided that she was going to wait with Kiriga until any news came. She climbed onto the dragon's golden back, settling herself as comfortably as she could without the harness that made it possible for them to fly together.

She closed her eyes and let herself see what the others saw as they relayed the information to Ilex and Kiriga.

Eras was flying so fast that the ground blurred beneath him. Riya was flying to the east and back. Mazen to the south. Soros to the north.

Their patrols, along with Eras's flight, lulled Nerie to sleep as she waited for something - anything to happen.

The sun had barely started to set when she was torn from her slumber.

Eras.

He'd made it all the way to Cian in less than half the time it had taken her and Kiriga. Wyla was outside the city, walking along the road. She was in the middle of a large caravan. Her wings were tented, and her scales were raised from her body, like a cat with its fur puffed out. Her eyes whirled red and orange.

She looked angry - angrier than even Eras when Alluvia had been attacked - but not distressed. She was willfully walking along. Nerie's attention was pulled to the banners that hung from each cart and wagon and the carriage at the head of the line.

She didn't recognize it - but the dragons did.

The royal coat of arms for the king of Lutesia.

CHAPTER FIFTY-ONE

Nerie

Nerie had been so caught up in riding along in Eras's mind that when he saw the banners, she felt his thorny scales rise.

She couldn't see him, but she imagined he looked like a cactus with all his spines pointed outward.

Before she could even register what she was seeing through his eyes, the free access to his mind was gone. A wall slammed down between one heartbeat and the next.

Nerie was forced back into her own body and mind. She was dazed for several long moments as she tried to get her bearings. She was still in the courtyard, lying along Kiriga's back, and it was early twilight. There was a crispness to the air that hadn't been there when she'd stopped paying attention to her surroundings, but it carried the scent of an early snow.

As she looked around, she saw Soren sitting on the ground, his back firmly against Ilex's side. He too looked as if he had left his body behind for the duration of the flight and had been kicked back into his body.

"Kiriga, can you still hear what is going on? See anything?" Nerie's voice was ragged - as though she'd not spoken in years - rather than the few hours it had been.

I... don't know. I can still feel Father and Wyla - however, they have cut themselves off from us.

She shifted from one foot to another as she spoke, her

head turned to the west and Cian. A growl could be heard from Ilex, and Nerie had a feeling that the other dragons were growling as well.

Why are they here? Riya hissed to no one in particular, but no one answered.

Nerie could hear the dragons reaching out to Eras and Wyla but getting no response. She slid down from Kiriga's back, slowly walking over to the dazed looking king. He had made it to his feet and the blood was coming back to his face.

Running her hands nervously down her thighs, she approached Soren.

She wanted to ask, 'What is going on?' but she knew she had just as much information as the king did at that moment.

Instead, she chose to ask what was, perhaps, the more pressing question, "Why would Lutesia send an envoy here?"

Soren gave his face a quick rub before focusing his eyes on her.

"I don't know. We have an ambassador in their capital Tesia - his name is Tobis. They also have one here, Myles. You've met him at least once during a gathering of the Curia Regis. Keeps to himself for the most part."

Soren was leading her into his study as they spoke, a place she hadn't been in the last few weeks.

Not since the fire.

There were new, detailed maps of Alluvia and the surrounding regions and letters from guardsmen and the nobles that lived there. Lying all around the desks were notes and a few used goblets, where Soren had clearly stayed up with a drink, going over the multitude of papers that needed his attention.

As Nerie looked around, Soren dug through one of the many piles, muttering under his breath.

After a moment, with a flourish of his hand, he waved a sheaf of paper at her.

"Tobis' latest report."

He scanned the pages, handing her each as he finished. Most of it seemed to be weather and crop reports, and the daily ins and outs of court life in Lutesia.

As Soren got to the end, he ran a quick hand through his hair with a sigh.

"Like I thought, no mention of an upcoming visit of any type. He would have said had there been even a hint of one."

He turned to the doorway where his loyal seneschal waited, "Vizen, please summon his lordship Myles."

Vizen took off before Soren had finished his sentence.

Nerie wanted to read more of the report, even if it was mostly economic, however, the dragons were getting restless.

She overheard Riya complaining more than once that she wanted to go check on Eras and Wyla, but Soros had firmly told her that she was to wait for word from Eras first. It was apparent to Nerie, however, that Soros was just as worried as her daughter and had flown to the western bounds of the city limit.

Mazen was quieter than his female kin but he had expanded his range, and was investigating every person he encountered on the road. More than one poor farmer probably had a heart attack as the massive dragon landed before them.

There was a knock at the door and Vizen bowed a harried looking man into the room. Once both were in the room, Vizen returned to his traditional place in the shadows.

Seeing his face, Nerie did recount briefly meeting the man before. However, his hair - now tussled from bed - had been stylishly done, and his clothing had been one of the many jewel tones so popular in the court and Curia. As he stood there, trying not to cross his arms in front of the king, his robe hung loosely, his night clothes exposed below.

With a deep bow, he acknowledged Soren, "Your Highness, whatever might I do for you at this late hour?"

"Myles, thank you for coming. Have you received word recently from home?" Soren's tone was light, but his eyes were cold as he stared at the man.

"My monthly correspondence, your highness, but nothing out of the ordinary. A few letters from home, my sister gave birth to a healthy boy…"

Soren cut him off, "Nothing from King Oron? Any word

of a planned visit to Situra?"

"A visit?" Myles' voice was contemptuous, "Why would any citizen of Lutesia want to visit here? I only do it as I am paid well."

"I'm sure - however, there is currently an envoy making its way from Cian to the capital. They are flying the personal crest of the king."

Nerie watched both men as they spoke, feeling out of her league.

"His Highness would *never* come here," Myles sputtered.

"Well someone is, and they are flying Oron's crest. You had no news of this?"

"No... No! When will they arrive?" He twitched his robe closed, looking around as if his kinsmen might appear out of thin air.

"It's an eight-day trip," Soren said. "It looks as if their delegation has no intention of rushing."

Myles relaxed slightly.

"They truly fly his majesty's crest?"

Soren only nodded before dismissing the man.

"If neither ambassador knew of this visit, why would it have been kept secret?" Nerie asked, pacing the large room.

"It depends. If Oron himself is for some unknown reason coming here it would be a matter of national security. If it's someone traveling in his name? It could be urgent business of some sort. But weather reports have said that Lutesia is having a mild winter, so I doubt it's anything like that..." He trailed off, shaking his head, as frustrated as she over the lack of information.

"All we can do now is prepare. Perhaps Eras will inform us who will be gracing us with their presence before they arrive. For now, you should head to bed."

Nerie wanted to go back out with the two dragons, but Vizen was shutting the door to the courtyard. With nowhere else to go but her bed, she left the king's quarters.

She walked down the quiet halls, her two guards once again at her heels. When she arrived at her rooms, she found that Karina had laid out her nightgown and heated her bedsheets. Even as she changed, Nerie felt herself dragging, the emotional energy of the last few hours draining away.

By the time her head hit the pillow she could barely keep her eyes open.

CHAPTER FIFTY-TWO

Graith

The sky was a pale gray when Graith was poked awake by Kali. She had dark rings under her eyes, and Graith wondered if she'd slept at all.

Standing and stretching with a series of pops that echoed loudly, Graith rubbed the sleep from his eyes. Kali was already over by one of the large cauldrons of fire and was motioning for him to join her. He hadn't paid much attention to the fire last night, other than the fact that it had illuminated and warmed the area - but standing there now, he saw that there was no fuel for the fires.

A bright flame seemed to burn on nothing but the bare stone of the fire pit. Kali also gave it a strange look before she tossed the envelope into the heart of the fire. A pink cloud of smoke burst to life before floating slowly into the air. It only reached halfway up the statue before it dissipated in a stiff breeze.

Kali threw herself back onto the ground against the stone tail once again, closing her eyes.

"Now we wait."

Graith shrugged and sat with his back to Zel. The sky was lightening by the minute, and Graith saw that the stone of the dragon was white marble. Zel stood out against the stone, now that the shadows from the night were fading.

"Should Zel leave?" Graith asked.

He didn't want the dragon to go - what would they do if

something happened while she was away? - but he doubted whoever the buyer was, was expecting a dragon.

I can hide on the backside of the statue, between its wings. It faces away from the city, and I can get to you in moments, Zel suggested.

Kali shrugged indifferently.

"Works for me."

***

They didn't have to wait long.

Before the sun had risen even a finger span more, Zel told them, *People are coming.*

"Good. I'm ready to meet back up with Kade and the others," Kali said as she jumped to her feet.

Graith saw her check the hilts of the knives he knew were hidden along her arms and waist. She walked over to the crate and leaned casually against it while she waited for her customers to arrive.

A few minutes later, the most beautiful woman Graith had ever seen appeared, along with an entourage of guards.

She had silky blonde hair, and dark-gray eyes. She wore a dress of red silk, and a black gossamer shawl so thin that it was transparent. Her ivory skin looked as if the sun had never touched it.

"You must be the Lady Imra?" Kali bowed to the woman.

One of the soldiers stepped forward, hand on the hilt of his sword.

"Who are you to directly address our lady?"

"Oh, Dayne, don't be so rude to our new friends."

Lady Imra's words, while harmless enough, chilled Graith to the bone. Her tone was icy, and her smile fixed in place as she spoke. She didn't even look at Dayne, but he fell to his knee, head bowed in a pose of someone who's received a lashing one too many times.

"Of course, my lady."

"We aren't your friends." Kali's tone echoed Imra's, "We're here to make a deal. We've brought your goods. Now - we want our money."

Graith had to resist the urge to turn and look at Kali. While she hadn't been out right friendly with him per say, she'd never used that tone. It sent a chill up his spine and reminded him of how Doreen had completely switched her personality after thinking he was in league with Oron.

"Once I see the scales." Imra said it dismissively, as if she doubted, they were what she had requested, and thus would be unlikely to hand over the money.

Imra motioned towards the crate, and Dayne and several other guards rushed over. Graith glanced at Kali, and saw her face was set in a frown, but she wasn't stopping them. They were opening the nearest side, using their swords to pry the wood open.

As the large wooden panel hit the ground, a cascade of glimmering, smooth red scales tumbled onto the ground. Each was as large as Graith's chest. The red of the scales was dark in the early morning light, nearly the color of fresh blood.

Zel was watching the exchange through his eyes, and when she saw the scales, he felt her anger lash out immediately. He felt her rear back from her perch on the stone dragon's wing and could faintly hear a hiss.

Ask her why she needs the scales. What she's going to do with them!

What's wrong? I know you were opposed to the scales being sold, but you act like you've just been bitten.

I know those! Those are Coale's scales!

As in, father of your eggs, Coale?

Graith did a double take and looked at them again.

Yes!

Graith cleared his throat, uncomfortably. Lady Imra had walked over to examine the scales, picking up one that was closer in size to her hand. She was paying no attention to them.

"So, what are you using the scales for?" he asked, trying to calm both his racing heart, and Zel who was contemplating flying down to them.

Her eyes narrowed as she glanced over from her bent

position. Her fine hair had cascaded in front of her face, and she brushed it back impatiently.

"Does it matter? You are the seller. I am the buyer. End of story."

Graith felt his face redden, but he also felt Zel's anger growing by the seconds. She wanted answers, and if he didn't provide them, she was going to come get them herself.

"Just curious. Not often you see dragon scales."

Graith felt Kali's eyes burning into the back of his neck. He was sure that she had her hand on at least one dagger and was considering ways to shut him up. If Zel would just tell *her* what was going on…

"More often than I would like." Imra straightened to look at him, "All the *great lords* have suits of armor made from scales. I'm having a set made as a gift."

"Oh. Where did they get the scales for their armor?"

Graith wasn't sure how far he could push the subject before Imra shut him down. Her eyes narrowed, but she let out a tinkle of laughter.

"You Lutesians really are from the boonies. They got them from their guardian dragons."

There are dragons here? Zel asked, her anger forgotten instantly.

"There are dragons here?" Graith echoed.

"Too many if you ask me." She turned to Kali, her interest in Graith immediately lost, "I find the scales to be of a suitable quality. Here is your payment. We'll take care of the scales."

It was a clear dismissal, and Kali had to nudge Graith hard in the back to get him moving. He wasn't sure where they were going, but it was away from the statue and towards Alluvia. He looked back once at the large statue where Zel hid, and then followed Kali towards the city.

Dayne was signaled to, and he escorted them around the end of the tail. Another guard waited there with a small chest sitting by his feet. With a nod from Dayne, the guard stepped back, and Kali grabbed the chest. She opened it slightly and upon inspection saw it contained a tidy amount of gold.

Zel's anger returned as she thought about the fact that it had been Coale's scales. She was half tempted to start questioning Kali on how exactly they had gotten them. She knew Doreen had said that they had been shed and sold, but honestly, she thought Coale too vain to sell them.

And the fact that there were more dragons.

Here.

In Situra.

CHAPTER FIFTY-THREE

Graith

Zel was silent as Graith and Kali rushed through the streets towards the harbor. Both were too anxious to reach The Running Ship to take time to really look around the town they were passing.

It took much longer than Graith expected to cross the city by foot. Alluvia was larger than Dunlaith and Kelna, but still dwarfed by Tesia. As the masts of ships came into sight, both picked up their pace.

"Ahoy there!" Kade shouted from the deck of the ship as they came into sight.

Kali just shook her head, but Graith could see a sliver of a smile appear on her face as she saw her brother.

"Graith! Kali! I missed you!"

Alix was shouting and waving, causing people to turn and look at them.

A wide plank had been lowered to the docks for the crew to easily unload the ship and, between two sets of busy sailors, they made their way on board. Alix was waiting for them at the top, immediately hugging both of them.

"We were only gone a day!" Graith said, ruffling the boy's hair as he hugged him back.

"A long day!" Alix said, but his attention had shifted.

He was now trying to peek into the chest that Kali carried. Swatting him off, she nodded to the captain's quarters, and the four of them filed in.

"Everything go okay?" Kade asked, once the door was closed tight.

"Mostly. Graith here got a little nosy."

"Graith?" Kade looked at the older man in surprise.

"It was Zel. The scales that we sold belonged to the father of her eggs. She was... not happy."

Graith shrugged, not sure what else to say.

"And you didn't say anything until just now - because?" Kali was looking at him in annoyance.

"They were your scales to sell. And Zel promised not to interfere."

Promise might be a bit of an exaggeration, but they didn't need to know that. They definitely didn't need to know how close they'd come to having her try to end the sale.

Kade and Kali looked at each other but let the subject drop. The two of them spent the next few minutes talking about their legal wares. What had been offloaded and what still needed to go. There were a only few items they needed to find buyers for.

Graith sat wearily in one of the few chairs in the cabin, his joints aching. While it was warmer on this side of the sea, it was still cold. Alix finally got to look inside the chest and was busy studying the strange markings on the golden coins of Situra. Graith also eyed them curiously, he'd not realized they'd have different currency.

"We can't leave Alluvia until all the goods are sold," Kade told them, looking between Alix and Graith.

"But what about Zel's eggs?" Alix asked, horrified by the thought of letting them get any farther away.

"Honestly, they are probably as safe as they can be right now. Since Prince Brantom wasn't onboard the ships, that means he and all his guards are likely with the eggs," Kali answered, shrugging.

"We can use this time to talk to our contacts and see if they know where the eggs are heading. If no one knows, we can always just head south to Veles, and follow their trail. It's not as if the prince will be hard to follow," Kade followed up.

Graith didn't care for the idea, but nothing had changed.

He still couldn't fight. The prince or his guards seeing Zel would simply put her eggs at risk. Waiting and going with Kade and Kali was honestly the best course of action.

Alix looked to Graith, clearly upset with the lack of interest and care the siblings seemed to show for the eggs.

"Alix, they're right. We can't just rush into this. We want to get the three eggs back alive."

"What does Zel think?" Alix asked impetuously.

Zel answered for herself.

They seem to want my eggs alive. So, for now, especially with that horrid knight Braylin dead, we should just follow them.

Graith nodded as Alix's face fell. It was not what the boy had wanted to hear.

In the meantime, I think that I want to know more about the dragons that live here. My people believe that both Lutesia and Situra are hostile to dragons, she told the four of them.

"There are dragon's here?" Kade and Alix asked in surprise. Graith hadn't gotten to that part yet.

"According to our client. Yes." Kali nodded as she spoke. "Also, the statue that we met her at was a giant stone dragon - you can't quite see it from the ship."

"Well, that gives us somewhere to start. People *love* to talk about their gods. I can bring it up while looking for buyers," Kade said.

He leaned against the table in the middle of the room, not quite sitting on it, but putting more weight on it than it was designed for. It gave a slight squeak as he tried to get comfortable.

Dragons aren't gods.

Zel's tone was reproachful.

"Doesn't sound like the people here know that. You don't just build a shrine to your buddy," Kade said while laughing.

"Well, we have things to do, goods to sell, and information to collect!" Kali said, even as she pulled open the door to the deck, "No point in sitting around waiting!"

Graith stood, the pops that were becoming more frequent

from his joints, making Alix laugh. He put his arm around Alix's shoulder, and they followed her out. Kade sighed once, straightened, then brought up the rear.

On the deck, the four of them stood looking out over the city of Alluvia. Graith could feel Zel watching through his eyes. He just hoped that they could find the answers they were looking for here.

We will.

Zel's current mood was green and calm. She trusted him, and Graith would do anything to protect that trust.

***

After getting directions from the harbormaster, Kade led their small band to a shop along the pier. A general wares type place, it had a cozy atmosphere, and Alix idly ran his fingertips along soft fabrics and fresh leathers. Graith followed behind the boy, turning a seasoned eye to the seeds they were offering for the coming spring and the few farm tools they had hanging on the walls.

Kade and Kali were escorted with their goods into a back room, and Graith could hear, over the general bustle of the shop patrons, their attempts at negotiation. He took their raised, but not angry tones, to mean that they were arguing for a better trade rates for some of the fabrics they had brought. Not seeing these trades being over any time soon, Graith laid a soft hand on Alix's shoulder, and motioned with his head that they could walk along the pier.

Stepping outside, the water slapped loudly against the ships and the poles that supported the pier. They were thicker around than Graith's chest and stood nearly as tall as Alix above the planking. Birds cawed loudly, and a stiff breeze blew through the open port. Graith pulled his coat a little tighter and motioned for Alix to lead the way.

Over the course of the next hour, they stopped at different stalls and stores. Each specializing in some tasty treat or craftsman's goods. They chatted idly but moved quickly. Their thick, slow accents caught the attention of the Siturans, who for the most part were polite, but brisk. A few, however, quickly became busy with other customers or tasks that needed immediate attention.

They reached the south side of the pier, then had turned around and nearly made it back to their starting point, when Kade and Kali found them in the crowd. Kali was scowling, rolling her head side to side while Kade was smirking like a dog who'd been caught rolling in shit.

"They bought everything!" he crowed excitedly when they'd finally reached Graith and Alix.

"That's amazing!" Alix bounced excitedly, while looking up at Kade.

Kali let out a loud sigh and rolled her eyes.

"It took you long enough. You couldn't have squeezed a copper more out of him - not that you didn't try."

"Trading is an art! It depends heavily on negotiations and patience. Something that *you* lack."

Kade bumped shoulders with his sister, and Graith could see her normal cool break slightly as the urge to slam her shoulder back into her brother crossed her mind.

Graith was trying to figure out how to diffuse the situation when Alix grabbed Kali's hand and dragged the girl down the pier. Graith and Kade could faintly hear Alix telling her that she just *had* to try some of the fried fish from the stall three stores down.

They looked at one another and chuckled before slowly following the two.

***

After a quick lunch, the four of them headed back to the Running Ship. They packed their few belongings, and Kade and Kali pulled the captain into the small office. They counted out their sales for the goods, as well as the small chest that had been their spoils for Coale's scales. Once the final sums were tallied, each paid out their own shares as well as portions for Graith and Alix.

With that, the ship and the money were handed back over to its captain. They headed back to the pier and into the city proper. When Kade tried to give Graith both his own and Alix's shares, Graith made a point of telling Kade that Alix had his own money purse. The younger man smiled and nodded, then made a large show of presenting Alix with his portion of the spoils.

They found an inn to stay in, but while the general attitude towards them on the pier had been of good-humored interest, here the patrons and staff seemed hostile. For a moment, as Kade requested three rooms, Graith wondered if they would be turned away. Instead, they were told that only one room was available and shown to a small room with barely enough space for the two small beds that it held.

The four of them looked at the small, hay-stuffed mattresses before Kali threw herself down on one. That left Graith, Kade, and Alix to flip for the other. When Alix was ruled out first, he pointedly told Kade that Graith was getting stiff in his old age, and that the floor wasn't the best place for him to sleep. Kade ruffled the boy's hair and agreed.

They settled in for the night and quickly fell asleep.

The following morning, Kade paid for their room, and they headed into the city. They needed to purchase supplies for traveling, and at Zel's insistence, they needed to find out more about the dragons of Situra.

As they wound their way through the city, they found that they were the center of attention, with whispers following them everywhere they went. No one seemed to want to meet their gaze, and only after multiple attempts at conversation was Kade able to get them the supplies they needed.

At one point, they turned down a road only to find that there had recently been a fire, with large sections cordoned off from the public. When Alix asked the next vendor they stopped at, what had happened, he got stony silence in return.

He asked another merchant about the large stone dragon that loomed overhead, to which he got only the response, "It's a memorial. So, visitors like you *never* forget."

Graith had moved them on before Alix could ask what it was he wasn't supposed to have forgotten.

They were never given the opportunity to ask about dragons, but something about the way the people glanced at the sky or looked around when there were arguments in the street seemed to the group like the people were looking for a guardian. The name Galean was mentioned in a few of those situations, but who or what Galean was, was never answered.

Kade confirmed with the man that he bought their horses from that Cian was the Situran city that mirrored Veles, and that they could reach it by heading south along the main road.

Zel stayed quiet for the most part, and when Graith asked her why, she told him that she was listening. He got the impression that she wasn't talking about listening to them.

When they started to ride south, she told Graith that she would catch up to them once they reached Cian. Knowing that he was leaving her behind, even temporarily, made him uneasy, but it couldn't be helped. It was still safer for her to travel at night, and Cian was only a two-day ride away.

CHAPTER FIFTY-FOUR

Nerie

The following morning, Nerie was surprised to find herself alone in her quarters. Karina was missing from her normal position, but breakfast had already been served, and a dress was lying out, ready for Nerie. It was quiet, and the fire that should have been roaring was down to the coals. A quick glance in each of the rooms revealed that Karina was not in the suite.

Nerie slipped the dress on and quickly ate her already cold breakfast. She reached out to Kiriga but was promptly rebuked by the dragoness. She was still waiting for word from Eras or Wyla and could not be distracted from her task.

Nerie's leg jiggled as she cast her mind around, wondering what was going on. While she was concerned, it *was* Eras and Wyla. They could handle themselves or reach out if something were wrong. Honestly, Nerie wondered if it was just the fact that an envoy was coming from Lutesia that had them upset and on guard.

Finished with her meal and still no Karina in sight, Nerie felt obligated to carry her dishes to the kitchen. Normally, Karina did it right after Nerie was done with her meals. She also thought that maybe she would come across her maid while she was about.

As she stepped into the hallway, she was greeted by the sight of her two guards standing outside her door. When they saw her holding the tray, both reached for it, asking if she wanted them to take care of it for her. A shake of her head and a few quick steps towards the kitchen left them following behind her.

As they left the living quarters, it quickly became apparent where Karina, as well as all the other palace staff were. The servant's quarters were like a seething ant hill with people coming and going so fast that the doors were unable to swing closed in the slightest.

No one gave Nerie a second glance as she made her way into the kitchen with the tray. Inside the kitchen was like the eye of a storm, with the Cook directing the flow. Fires roared from the ovens and stoves, the pans and dishes banging and clattering in the sinks. It was even more hectic than the hatching day, so many months before.

Karina had obviously been wrangled into service when she had come to collect Nerie's breakfast. She was covered in flour and was kneading bread with her back to the door.

Nerie had the tray taken from her hands as she approached the tub that was filled with dishes. She wanted to get out of the small space, so full of people - before she too was drafted into service. As she turned around, she found her eyes locked with Karina.

"Princess! This is *not* a place you should be," Karina said emphatically, leaving her bread station and briskly trying to pull Nerie through the door.

"Karina, I'm *fine*," Nerie said, shrugging the woman off. "You *do* know that the day of the hatching I was helping in the kitchens, right?"

Karina seemed not to hear her, instead asking her, "Your Highness, why did you bring the tray down here?"

"Because I don't like being in my room alone, and I figured you were busy. What is going on here, anyway?"

"His Majesty has announced publicly, or at least to the palace, that we will be hosting royal visitors from Lutesia. We are to prepare the palace, making sure everything is resplendent before they arrive. Cook already has menus planned out for the next month and is trying to get everything practiced before they arrive. We're also to prepare as much in advance as possible."

Karina brushed herself off, but the flour she was coated in didn't seem to be moving.

During the noticeably short conversation, Karina had managed to walk Nerie to Soren's suite. "I will be occupied for most of the week. Vizen will attend to you and the king. Please stay in the King's suite during the day."

Nerie was left gaping as Karina made her way back down the hallway as quickly as they'd come.

Turning to face the rooms, Nerie noted that Soren's office door was tightly closed and Vizen was not standing outside, meaning that he would be in the room with the king.

Frowning, Nerie turned to the garden.

She would join Kiriga and Ilex. Maybe they would hear from one of the dragons patrolling around the city or even Eras or Wyla themselves.

Kiriga was in the same position that Nerie had last seen her, facing due west. She was staring at some point beyond the wall, her eyes alert and focused. She acknowledged her other half with a sigh and lowered her still growing head for scratches on her eye ridge, but wasn't looking at the princess.

"Any word yet?" Nerie asked softly, already knowing the answer.

No. Mother is going crazy not hearing from them. But they aren't hurt or in danger, and until Father says otherwise, she, Riya, and Mazen are to continue patrolling around the city.

"Do you want to join them?" Nerie asked, watching Kiriga's tail twitch in annoyance.

No. Yes. No. She did look at Nerie then, *What I want is to know why Father and Wyla aren't speaking. That's what is bothering me the most right now.*

"I understand. But they know what they're doing. Soros is listening to Eras. Nothing would hold her back if she thought he was in any sort of danger."

That's true. Kiriga let out another great sigh. *I don't like it though.*

Nerie climbed up the now familiar set of scales to reach

Kiriga's wide back. Nestling into the small crevice there, she closed her own eyes and started to watch through the eyes of the others.

Scratching at a rough scale, eyes closed, Nerie comforted her dragon.

"It'll all be okay."

***

Nerie spent the following week laying on Kiriga's back for hours at a time. They waited together for any kind of news from either Eras or Wyla. It was mind-numbingly silent, and Nerie spent a good portion of the time seeing what Riya, Mazen, and Soros could see. At least they were moving. Their eyes roving over the ground far below them.

She could feel each of their anxieties and desire to fly to the caravan. It was an underlying fear in all the dragons that the Lutesians had done something to Eras and Wyla to keep them complicit. She didn't understand why they wouldn't speak to Soros or the others.

The morning of the seventh day after the procession of wagons and carriages had started on their journey to Roria from Cian, Eras finally spoke.

We are on our way. These humans will not increase their pace, but I believe we will be there in another three days.

His sudden communication startled Nerie, who'd been sleeping on Kiriga's back - as well as Soren - who came racing out of his study to put his hand on Ilex. He'd hardly left the small room over the course of the last week.

The cacophony of mental voices that flooded through Nerie's mind made her head spin. Everyone wanted to know why Eras and Wyla hadn't spoken. Why they were not *flying* back to Roria, but rather, walking along the road with the royal envoy.

After waiting for the questions to stop, Eras spoke quickly and urgently.

There are eggs. Three of them. We will talk when we are home. In the meantime, make sure the hatching ground is ready.

With that, he was gone again - the wall that cut him and

Wyla off from the others firmly back in place.

Nerie could hear Riya, Mazen, and Ilex talking. They were both wary and excited.

It was Soros, however, who caught her attention.

The eldest dragoness was not speaking but was emitting an oily, yellow panic. She had immediately turned her flight path toward her mate and daughter, her only thoughts to protect the eggs.

Stop! Eras roared.

The force of it startled Soros enough that it made her momentarily tumble in the sky.

We will meet you in the city, he repeated firmly.

Soros did not understand.

She flew back and forth, moving no closer to the envoy, but not heading back to Roria.

What was going on? Her instinct to take care of eggs, which should never be away from their mother, was overwhelming. Her mate knew that. Why would he keep her away?

Finally, she turned back to the city, flying directly to the hatching ground. In the time it had taken her to arrive, Soren had informed Vizen that the grounds were to be heated. While it was winter, no snow had yet fallen.

Nerie hadn't been back to the hatching ground since she'd been knocked out after Kiriga had chosen her, but as she listened to Soren and Vizen, she gathered that the ground was heated by fires from below.

Soros set herself down in the large, sand-covered area, complaining instantly that it was not warm enough. The human screams that followed shortly let Nerie know that something was wrong.

Mother just heated the sand by fire-breathing on it, Kiriga said helpfully, seeing no issue with this.

Take me over there? Nerie asked, gripping the scales before her in anticipation.

With a lithe leap, Kiriga was on the shale roof, walking towards the now visible pillar of flame.

How long until you are capable of producing flame?

Nerie asked, unable to look away from the awe-inspiring sight, unafraid of the fire.

Once I am mature, I think, Kiriga said with a shrug that almost dismounted Nerie.

Kiriga paced on the overhanging rooftop, looking for a place to hop down. She might be fireproof, but Nerie was not.

Soros was muttering to herself about the eggs and how they could have ended up in a human's care and she didn't understand why she couldn't go. She piled and repiled sand, trying to figure out how to best heat three eggs. She wondered when the last time the eggs had been heated was, disturbed by the thought. While dragonlings didn't *need* warmth or fire to hatch, it certainly helped. It produced a well-rounded hatchling, in her opinion.

Watching Soros, Nerie wasn't sure what to think.

The dragoness was understandably anxious. There were *dragon eggs* coming *here.* It had huge implications, and the chatter of the other dragons in her head was expounding upon those implications.

But why would Lutesia bring them here? Everything that Nerie had learned about the country indicated that they hated dragons.

They were the reason that dragons were nearly extinct.

Even if a few others had survived, the fact that the Lutesian royals had orphan eggs did not sit well with Nerie. Plus, the eggs hadn't come from Soros and Eras - but they must have come from somewhere?

With no signs of the others stopping their speculative chatter, and Soros constantly shifting and heating the sand, Nerie knew the next three days were going to be the longest of her short life.

CHAPTER FIFTY-FIVE

Nerie

Nerie wasn't sure how she managed to survive the wait.

Soros was beside herself, constantly furling and unfurling her wings, pushing sand around the great hatching ground, and growling with smoke issuing from her nostrils whenever someone dared to approach.

The lack of communication from Eras and Wyla continued, but it was clear that they were getting closer as Nerie, through Kiriga, could begin to sense their emotions.

They were tense and angry, making all the other dragons worry. Riya wanted to go to her father and sister, but after the direct command that Soros had received, she didn't dare approach the envoy.

Sitting upon Kiriga's back and looking out across the city, Nerie watched as the procession made its way slowly through the streets.

She could hear, even from the palace, as Wyla and Eras hiss in displeasure when they were forced into the sky. The roads were simply too narrow for their massive forms, the buildings not designed, like the palace, to hold their weight.

Their wings beat, brushing the very rooftops of the buildings as they hovered over the train of wagons and carriages. Even within the city, they were still not speaking.

Soros had risen to her hind legs, watching her eldest child and her mate as they followed the humans through the city.

Soren is telling me that you need to go inside and get ready to greet our guests, Kiriga told Nerie, as she turned away from the city and back to the garden that connected to the king's suite.

Nerie wanted to continue to watch the procession, as fascinated by Wyla and Eras's behavior as the glittering flags and tasseled horses. The flags were a brilliant purple with gold trim, and even from this distance, Nerie could make out the form of some sort of animal emblazoned upon them.

Nerie slid from Kiriga's back and hadn't even stepped through the door before Karina - finally discharged from her kitchen duties - had grabbed her by the arm and was helping her strip. An ornate ball gown was lying over the back of a couch, with laces loose and ready for Nerie to step into.

The fabric was a delicate silk, the exact golden hue of Kiriga's scales. The back was laced with a silver ribbon and the skirt hung in soft folds. Nerie's inner child screamed for her to spin around, to look like a flower straight from the royal gardens. However, anxiety from the coming envoy had her digging her nails into her sweaty palm.

They still didn't even know *who* had come to visit.

From what little she'd heard from Ilex and the other mature dragons, she didn't *think* it was King Oron. But who else had the authority to fly his royal banner? A sibling or child perhaps?

And the eggs.

Why were they bringing three eggs here? How did they even get the eggs? Nerie's head spun with questions.

Questions that would need to be answered as soon as the great procession arrived at the palace.

Riya's brassy voice let them know that their guests were minutes away, and Soren, Alaena, Nerie, and even Astra proceeded to the grand courtyard that was the entrance to the palace from the main gates. Once in place, they waited. Nerie stood to the right of Soren, Alaena to the left, with Astra to her left.

As the gates were pulled open, Eras settled onto one battlement and Wyla onto the other. Both leaning forward, creating a second arch over the gate.

As the massive doors opened, a small party of people, mounted on delicate white horses, was revealed. More tassels and bells accompanied their tack, and the musical notes rang through the silent air.

In the lead was a young man who looked to be in his early twenties. He had thick curl,y black hair, and chestnut brown eyes. He had a smile plastered to his face, but it struck Nerie as not quite reaching his eyes.

As he looked between the members of the Therius Royal family, his eyes alighted first on Astra, then Nerie. She felt like he was examining each of them thoroughly, and she blushed slightly, unused to the attention. While she couldn't see Astra's response, she was sure that her half-sister was giving him a good look.

Growls rose from the assembled dragons, but the man seemed not to notice. He was still making his way slowly towards them, having yet to dismount his horse. Seeing that he was in no hurry, Nerie spared a glance behind him where two women and a man accompanied him.

One of the two women looked as if she were the leading man's twin, but with longer hair and a younger, rounder face. Nerie thought she might be closer in age to Aldis than to herself.

The other woman looked, to Nerie's untrained eye, deadly. Her back was straight and her eyes sharp as she took in every person in the large courtyard. A thin blade hung from her side, and she had one hand resting lightly on the hilt.

The other man was older, maybe his late thirties or early forties, and he looked bored. He caught her eye and winked lazily at her. Nerie felt her face flush slightly and she looked away, back at the leader who was also looking at her.

They had reached the Therius family, and all four dismounted. The dark-haired man stood a half step back while the deadly looking woman stepped forward.

"I present to you, His Royal Highness, Crown Prince Brantom," she bowed in his direction.

"Her Royal Highness, Princess Marza," this time a nod in the direction of the girl.

"And His Royal Highness, Prince Niro," she made a final indication to the older man.

Soren stepped forward, and Nerie watched Brantom's face flicker for an instant. She wasn't sure what emotion crossed his face, but it was gone faster than it had come. Her brows furrowed slightly, but the smile was back, and this time it did seem to reach his eyes.

"Welcome to Roria, Prince Brantom, Princess Marza, Prince Niro."

Soren tilted his head forward in acknowledgment of fellow royalty.

"I am King Soren, this is my wife Queen Alaena, and my daughters Crown Princess Nerie and Princess Astra. I hope your trip was uneventful. Please, accompany us inside. We have a feast prepared in your honor."

"As eventful as having two dragons escort us," Prince Brantom said, shrugging idly.

"Yes, about that," Soren started as they headed inside, "Wyla and Eras have informed us that you travel with three dragon eggs?"

"Did they now? Yes, well, that must be why they refused to leave my caravan."

Prince Brantom's response was carefully measured, and he seemed not very interested in the fact that he had dragon eggs. His attitude annoyed Soren, who pressed the subject.

"You've been traveling with the eggs for nearly a fortnight. We have heated our hatching ground and it is ready for the eggs."

Prince Brantom stopped, causing the whole party to halt in its procession to the hall. Soren looked at the prince, who shook his head lightly. He ran a hand quickly through his dark curls, before smiling at the king.

"I apologize, it's been a long trip, and I'm quite tired. Of course, the eggs can go to the hatching ground. In my mind, it had just gone slightly differently. Mainly - I was going to present them to you later this week, at the same time I planned to ask you for Nerie's hand in marriage."

Soren took it in stride and nodded sagely while motioning for them to continue into the banquet hall. "Of course, something like that would need to be discussed at great length…"

Nerie wasn't listening. Her vision spun, and her ears rang over the prince's confession. A marriage proposal? She was much too young to get married! While she tried to force herself back to the here and now, the dragons roared from outside the hall. Both in anger and worry over Nerie's sudden anxiety.

Wyla's shrill voice cut into both Nerie and Soren's mind, *We can't hear them - any of the Lutesians.*

The dragoness had been waiting to be able to talk to them privately, but Nerie's shock forced her to speak. The distress in her tone, along with the implications that the words conveyed, nearly made Nerie trip over her elegant skirt.

Seeing her falter, Brantom stopped and cordially offered her his arm.

"Princess."

Nerie hesitated for half of a heartbeat before placing her hand on his proffered arm, even though it was the last thing she wanted to do.

They entered the great hall, and Vizen pulled out chairs for each of the nobles. Soren sat at his customary seat at the center of the table, while Brantom was placed to his right. Nerie sat to Soren's left, with Alaena and Astra to her left. Marza and Niro sat to Brantom's right. The guard woman, who remained nameless, stood behind and to the right of Brantom, her hand never leaving her sword hilt.

The royals were served even as the other members of Brantom's envoy slowly filed in.

Bread was broken and wine drank, but it sat heavily on Nerie's stomach as the night drew on. No other mention was made of the wedding proposal, but Nerie's anxiety grew.

Brantom talked of proposed trade routes and recent weather. He asked after Myles, his ambassador, who was summoned to the table, late in the feast. The man lay nearly flat upon the stone floor as he pledged himself to his prince. Nerie surmised that he had been waiting for a signal that he would be called upon, and while surprised to see the Princes and Princess, he was dressed in his most formal attire and had appeared at the table only moments after being summoned.

After the feast, the visiting royals were each shown to their own suites and bid good evening. Brantom had taken Nerie's hand and kissed it lightly, smiling his first true smile at her. That made her feel even more uneasy. He had also kissed Astra's hand in farewell, and she had squeezed his hand lightly, batting her long eyelashes at him.

With that, he had disappeared into his suite, and Astra and Nerie had gone their separate ways without speaking. Nerie, straight to Soren's quarters and her access point to the dragons, and Astra to her own rooms.

***

Once she and Soren were both in the courtyard and leaning against Kiriga and Ilex, the conversation that the dragons had been holding in exploded.

What is going on? Soros demanded.

Her haunches were still in the hatching ground, her front end was leaning on the rooftop, and her neck snaked towards the courtyard where her children and mate rested.

Why... How do they have dragon eggs? Riya asked, at the same time.

She was fanning her large wings as she sat on the far side of the courtyard.

"Why would you and Wyla not speak to us?" Soren asked Eras directly.

Wyla could not hear the prince - or any of the Lutesians. Nor could I. We were worried that shouting across the country was not the smartest way to communicate. What if they could hear us? We could talk to the prince directly - when he wanted us to hear him - but that puts us at a disadvantage.

Eras's orange scales bristled in the starlight.

And he had the eggs, Wyla said quietly.

How can they hide themselves? Nerie asked, uncertain. The mere concept of keeping the dragons out was foreign to her. Not when she was so intimately linked with Kiriga.

I don't know, Wyla's voice was quiet.

And the eggs? Soros asked.

The eggs had been delivered to the hatching ground during the feast, and Soros had clucked like a hen for the last two hours about how cold they were. How they were too quiet for eggs so close to hatching. Even now, her tail curled around them possessively.

I could sense them as soon as he entered the city. Brantom arrived in Cian, claiming he had the eggs and that he was to be escorted by me to the capital. We were scared that he would hurt the eggs if too many dragons showed up, Wyla sounded tired. She had just walked across the country and Nerie thought that the normally opalescent dragon looked pale.

But why? Mazen's lilac eyes glowed from the opposite corner of the courtyard from where Nerie sat with Kiriga.

We don't know. Eras's voice was nearly a growl. *He could* block *us from his mind, after all.*

"How is that possible?" Soren repeated Nerie's earlier question, confused.

They did it in the Great War, to hide themselves from us, Soros said, her rage palpable.

Nerie felt a shiver run down her spine. The marriage proposal, the eggs, and the ability to hide their minds were only a few of the things that frightened her about the Lutesians. Whatever their reason for coming here, Nerie felt that it would not bode well for herself, Kiriga, or Situra as a whole.

CHAPTER FIFTY-SIX

Nerie

Nerie, Soren, and the dragons were up late into the night, discussing the visiting royals, their possible motives, and their ability to block the dragons from their minds.

When Nerie finally found herself settled into bed, her mind raced, unable to sleep. She kept going back to the visiting prince.

Brantom was well bred and a good orator, however, there was something in the way that his eyes flashed that set the hair on the back of her neck to rising, and it wasn't just the fact the dragons couldn't hear his mind.

Sleep. Kiriga encouraged her, tiredly.

Nerie dutifully closed her eyes and took slow, deep breaths. She was keeping Kiriga awake with her tumultuous thoughts. Soon after, with help from the dragoness, she had calmed down and fell into a restless sleep.

***

The morning dawned bright and early, not that Nerie had a window to the outdoors, but Kiriga was awake, thus so was she.

By the time she had sat up in bed, Karina was there, ready to attend her. Another new ball gown was presented, and after Nerie bathed she was trussed up into the garment. It was much more formal than the style of dress she normally wore, with a strong shaping boning, and straight skirts.

Karina spent the time it took to lace and button up telling

her that she was to attend court for the full day. For the time being, court would be held not in the Solar but would be moved to the Grand Ballroom.

All meals were to be served there too, so she was quickly ushered out the door by her maid. As she navigated the now familiar halls, she found herself walking with both the king and queen. They too would be attending to their guests and spending the day at court.

Arriving in the grand hall, Nerie was surprised to see Astra already there, directing table arrangements and decor. Her half-sister didn't even look up as the trio entered the room but scowled deeply when Alaena started to take over the duties. Astra stormed off, leaving the room in a huff.

Soren placed an arm on Nerie's shoulders, patting them awkwardly. She glanced up at him, but his eyes were unfocused in the sightless daze of one talking to their dragon. Whatever they were saying, it was not a conversation that she could overhear.

She turned her focus outward, looking at the arriving nobles. No one wanted to miss the foreign emissaries and were acting as if their life depended upon making it to this visit.

Of course, they were, Nerie thought sourly, it was just another form of entertainment to them. They had no idea anything was off with the prince. It was no secret that Wyla and Eras had accompanied the group to the capital, but for all they knew, it could just have been for the honor due to the princes and princess.

Nerie chided herself slightly. Other than the marriage proposal, Brantom had done nothing wrong. They still didn't know why he had the dragon eggs, but he'd brought them here and given them to Situra.

Soros was still worrying herself sick about them, but they were here safe on the hatching grounds. Nerie doubted that Soros would even let her or Soren close enough to see them.

Bringing her focus back to the present, she saw that the tables were being laden with food. It was mostly pastries and fruit at this time of day, and Nerie thought about eating, but her stomach gave a sour twist, so she made her way to the dais at the head of the room which held three thrones. The center one was larger than the other two. Nerie took the right seat, as that was her traditional place as heir. Soren shortly followed, while Alaena had to be escorted away from directing the filling of the tables by Vizen. By the time Alaena was seated, the hall was teeming with nobles and merchants, the upper echelon of Roria's society.

People chatted and moved about the room, all the while Nerie fidgeted in her seat, waiting for the Lutesian royals to appear. The sun, visible through the large southern facing windows, moved slowly across the sky. Only as it approached its zenith, did the herald announce Prince Brantom, Princess Marza, and Prince Niro.

Nerie noted with slight disdain that the swordswoman once again accompanied them and remained unannounced.

Brantom swept through the milling crowd as if every person he passed were his adoring fan. He bowed and waved jauntily, a large smile crossing his face. Nerie had to school her features into an impartial nothingness.

She watched the quartet make their way slowly across the room, and the only person she felt any connection with was the young princess.

Closer in age to Aldis, Marza's eyes were large as she took in the crowd. She did not hesitate as she followed her brother, but something in the way her eyes flickered from face to face let Nerie know she was nervous to be here.

Reaching them, Brantom and Niro bowed their heads to the sitting monarch, while Marza dipped into a slight curtsy. The swordswoman also bowed, but her eyes were rapidly darting around the room, looking for any threat to her wards.

"We are so glad that you are able to join us today, Sirs -," Soren had stood and was looking down on them, "Good lady. I do hope you enjoy your visit here. We have many fertile lands to show you, and Guildhalls that are the wonder of the known world, waiting for you to grace them with your presence."

He sat once again, and Brantom stepped forward,

smiling, "Of course, Your Majesty. We will be here for the foreseeable future and will have days aplenty to visit wherever you think we might like to see."

Brantom chuckled before continuing, "We set off on our expedition when we heard that your heir had been chosen. My father, King Oron, so hopes that our countries might unite under one banner, as one people. As I mentioned briefly last night, he wants nothing more than a political alliance between our people, secured through marriage and eventually blood."

Nerie felt the blood leave her face. She couldn't believe Brantom had brought the subject up in such a public place. With all the discussion of the eggs and the fact that dragons couldn't hear the Lutesians, the marriage proposal had slipped to the back of her mind.

It took all her willpower to not look over at Soren to see if he was going to respond.

Before Soren or anyone else could say anything, Brantom continued, "We of Lutesia know how revered the dragon kind are in your land, and as such, have brought three dragon eggs, months away from hatching, as a bride price for the princess's hand in marriage."

With that announcement, the people gathered started to whisper and mumble, and Nerie could hear wisps of conversation.

"Dragon eggs!"

"But Soros and Eras are the last two breeding dragons…"

"I thought only those chosen by a dragon were worthy of ruling."

"They could be the salvation of dragon kind!"

She had known that the eggs were nothing more than a bartering chip to Brantom. But by announcing them in front of everyone even remotely important in the capital, he was guaranteeing that he and his proposal would be all that was talked about for the foreseeable future.

Soren stood, pulling Nerie from her thoughts, and her face paled. Was he going to accept the offer without even asking her? He was the king, but still - this was her life and her future.

"Prince Brantom. That is quite the bride price you have brought. However, our two nations have held animosity towards one another for several lifetimes. Something not easily forgotten, even with the future of dragon kind presented before us. You'll beg our pardon if we take some time to think this over?" Soren gave Brantom his winningest smile.

"Of course, your highness. Like I said, we are in no hurry," Brantom chuckled again. "In the meantime, I'm looking forward to getting to know Princess Nerie."

Brantom smiled endearingly at Nerie. The expression didn't quite reach his eyes - and his stare lingered on her for a heartbeat too long. He stepped back, bowing exaggeratedly low to her before turning and walking away.

Had she been standing, Nerie's knees would have been shaking. As it were, she chose to continue to sit for much longer than she normally would have. She watched Brantom make his way across the room, meeting people, talking - *laughing* - as if he belonged.

It made her stomach turn in knots.

***

The moment he started talking to Astra, she rammed herself to her feet, made a hasty goodbye and left the room. The gown she was wearing was constricting, and as she tried to draw a deeper breath, she felt the boning of the dress cut deep into her skin.

She made it to her room, ripping the dress in her haste to get it off. Karina was there, trying to help, but in her panic, Nerie batted the woman's hands away. She dug through her closet, found her riding gear, and got dressed. A short command to Karina and the woman was out the door to have someone put the riding straps and saddle on Kiriga.

Then she was running, tearing through the hallways to reach the king's quarters and her dragon. Bursting out into the courtyard, she saw Eras and Mazen sunning themselves on opposing corners of the rooftop. Ilex was in his normal spot in the center of the courtyard, and there were Wyla and Riya laying nose to tail in a tight circle. Kiriga was standing close to the door, shifting from foot to foot as she waited for her rider.

She scaled the dragoness before Kiriga could bend down for her rider, haphazardly strapping herself in.

Fly, she screamed into Kiriga's mind, and the dragon obeyed, launching herself into the sky.

Kiriga winged herself higher and higher until the palace was nothing more than a speck below them.

As she did aerial cartwheels, Nerie felt herself battle between relaxing and the anxiety the mere thought of marriage to Brantom brought her.

Nerie, Kiriga said softly. *Maybe, you should consider it. We don't know if those are the last eggs in existence. And the Lutesians gave them to us. Even if they hatch a year from now, they aren't that much younger than me. At least one of them must be a male... and even if they're no,t Mazen, Ilex, and Tiryn could mate with them.*

What... How. How could you ask me to do that, Kiriga? Nerie demanded. *You share my very soul, Kiriga.*

Nerie was sick.

The one person who could possibly understand how repulsive she found Brantom - asking her to consider marrying him.

Nerie! It's the fate of dragon kind! Kiriga said, distressed.

Land. Now.

Nerie was reaching for the straps, still wing lengths above the palace.

You might live forever, but I only have this one lifetime. I will not attach myself to someone like him.

She jumped from Kiriga's back, landing roughly on the stone. As soon as she could, she stood, and ran out of the courtyard. The great glowing eyes of all the dragons followed her as she stalked back into the palace.

CHAPTER FIFTY-SEVEN

Brantom

As the door swung shut behind him, Brantom threw himself into one of the plush couches that littered the room. Marza and Niro had already returned to their quarters, having left well before he'd finished talking with the crowd.

Well before he'd gotten to speak with the lovely Princess Astra.

Brantom sighed, disappointed that the lizards hadn't chosen Astra as heir. She was much more pleasing to the eye than the red-headed girl. More than one of the pathetic nobles clambering for his attention had made sure to mention that Princess Nerie was somewhat of a mystery - having appeared the day of the youngest lizard's hatching - and suddenly being declared not only the king's bastard, but his heir.

What a fucking backwater country. Listening to the judgment of some scaled beasts on who was *fit* to rule. Accepting, at face value, that just because the king had slept with some woman, and that the dragons had chosen the girl, that she must be the king's daughter.

And that she had more right to rule the country than the woman who'd been born and raised in the palace with every expectation of taking the throne.

He shook his head, unable to fathom the whole situation.

But it was what it was. Princess Nerie was to be queen, thus he would wed her. Even if she was the less appealing of the two.

If anything, she would be malleable. He could *help* her rule the country and - if he could win her over - do most of the work himself. The goal, after all, was to expand the Lutesian borders without violence.

Brantom groaned as he stretched, trying to make himself more comfortable on the couch. He idly kicked off his boots, each landing on the floor with a soft *thwack*.

The rooms they'd been provided were lavish and well kept - but they weren't home. There was a slight sour note to the air, an incense the Siturans used frequently, that caused his head to lightly throb. The silks throughout the palace were luscious and soft but caught easily on the thicker wool of Lutesian clothing.

That was another thing that annoyed Brantom. While it was midwinter both here and in Lutesia, the weather was much milder, and all the clothes that they'd brought were too heavy. It left him needing to bathe twice daily just to feel like the salt from his sweat was off his skin.

"What took you so long?" Niro asked, as he walked into the shared common space between their bedrooms.

Brantom cracked an eye open to look over at his uncle. The man had insisted he come, and multiple times throughout the trip had tried to act as a chaperon. It made Brantom grind his teeth in annoyance. *He* was crown prince and as such, every person on this journey should look to him for guidance in their daily responsibilities. More than once, however, plans had been spoiled, and issues arisen from him and Niro giving conflicting instructions. Other than the dragons, that had been the main cause of their slow progression from Cian to Roria.

"I was talking to the princess," Brantom said.

"I'm surprised. From the way she was glaring at you, I'd have thought she'd rather bite her own tongue out than talk to you," Niro laughed, sitting on the couch adjacent to Brantom's.

Brantom closed his eyes again, unwilling to look at his uncle.

"The other princess. Astra. She's quite the

conversationalist."

"She's not the one you're going to marry - if you get to marry either of them at all. The king seemed thrilled to have the eggs. Less than thrilled at the idea of a marriage proposal."

"The eggs were supposed to stay with us until the offer had been accepted. But things change -" he sighed, "and I don't know about you, but had we not handed the eggs over upon our arrival, I think that purple lizard would have charred us to a crisp."

"They're all terrifying!" Marza must have stepped out of her room. Her young voice pitched in just the wrong way, causing Brantom's head to pound harder.

"Terrifying or not, you had better keep up your mental block. You don't want them invading your mind or taking control of your body," Brantom snapped at her.

He knew she was genuinely scared of the thought that they could control her body, and he heard her sharp intake of breath in response. He was slightly curious what it would be like, but there were things in his mind that could put all Lutesia at risk if the dragons had free access to them.

It had been uncomfortable enough to hear the white and orange dragons. He had been deeply unsettled by the fact that he could identify their gender from their mental voice. It had also been *loud* - another of the causes of his ever-present headache. He had gotten a perverse pleasure out of how upset the dragons had been that they couldn't hear his thoughts.

Brantom pulled himself into a sitting position and opened his eyes. His head ached dully, but he worked past it. He focused on the room, his uncle, and his sister. Niro was sitting on the couch across from him, legs stretched out, arms lying along the back of the ornate cushions.

Marza sat perfectly upright, one leg tucked modestly behind the other. She was pale, uncomfortable that his attention was focused on her, but she looked back at him, nonetheless, determined to keep up the polite social norms she'd been raised with.

She glanced down at her folded hands, and he could see

her squeeze them together until the knuckles turned white. When he didn't look away, she did, awkwardly, before speaking.

"Queen Alaena's dress was quite beautiful. The fabrics they have here are so different than the ones we have at home. And the style is so strange. I wonder if I'll have to wear -"

"No one cares about the fucking fabric they use, Marza. Shut up," Brantom said, standing and moving towards his sister. "You're only here because we didn't know if the prince had been chosen as the heir. You would have been offered for the marriage in that case. As it is, I'm considering sending you home."

"Knock it off, Brantom, she's just trying to find something to talk about," Niro frowned at his nephew, crossing his arms.

"She should stay silent. She'll be lucky if I don't sell her off to one of the lords here. Strengthen our ties and all."

"If we need to secure political ties beyond your own marriage, Princess Marza will undoubtedly fulfill her role as expected," Niro said, also standing, and moving towards his niece and nephew.

Brantom turned to Niro, frowning. He crossed his arms and stared his uncle in the eye.

"Father did not send you to play guardian, Uncle. You know that if I had wanted your advice, I would have asked for it."

Niro had, however, distracted Brantom from his sister. The prince turned and walked to his private room, his bodyguard following. She'd been standing in a corner, hand resting on her sword hilt as always.

As the door shut, Brantom threw himself down on his bed. Once again, the rougher fabric of his clothes caught on the fine silk sheets, and as he shifted, they twisted around him. Annoyed, he stood back up and started pacing the room.

A quiet knock on the door drew his attention, and he motioned for his bodyguard to open it. It was one of the Situran maids, carrying a large tray of food. As she entered, she curtsied low, keeping the tray balanced. Brantom frowned. He'd not liked his first experience with their food and was not looking forward to the next.

The maid kept her eyes low, focused on her destination. She set the tray on a small table and, with a more formal bow, took her leave.

Brantom looked down at it disgusted. The food was so unappealing, that at first, he thought about not eating. But his options were limited. It was early evening, and he had no urge to spend any more time with his sister or uncle. He doubted he would be allowed to just walk the halls of the palace - not that he particularly wanted to. He couldn't even find a bedmate - not with all eyes on him and his entourage.

What forced him though, was the quiet rumbling of his stomach. He threw himself down into the chair and poked around at the food. How barbaric - most of it was meant to be eaten with your hands. Only the soup had a proper utensil. He picked at this and that but ended up only eating the fruit and a few spoonfuls of soup.

"We'll need to find a source of proper food while we're here, so I don't starve to death," he said to his guard, not bothering to look at her. He knew she was always listening to him, and their surroundings. He didn't expect a response, either.

"And as loathe as I am to say it, we'll need new clothing. The wools are too warm - I'm tired of sticking to every surface I touch."

He stood and pulled off his clothes, carelessly dumping them in a pile on the floor. As he crawled into bed he grunted in dissatisfaction, failing to get comfortable. The scent that they used for the incense must also have been in the soap they used for the sheets, because his bed reeked of it.

After several long minutes, he finally quieted and fell into a restless sleep.

CHAPTER FIFTY-EIGHT

Graith

Zel was fascinated by the city of Alluvia. Very few people came out to the large statue, and she made herself comfortable high up in the nook where its wings met its back.

She found that every mind she listened in to was worried about a fire that had occurred, and about Galean, the dragon protector of Alluvia.

Most of the people who thought about him had never seen him up close. From the images she could put together, he was larger than she, and a bright orange. He appeared high in the sky, almost like a second sun, in many of their memories.

She also found that he had left the city recently - within a day of their arrival, it seemed.

This annoyed her, as it had been months since she'd last spoken to one of her kind. She wanted to know why the dragons in Situra had isolated themselves, why they'd not returned to Etria after the war.

There was also the fact that speaking to another dragon was simply more rewarding. Graith was the only human she'd met that came close to it. She missed the ability to share what she was thinking and feeling without having to verbalize it in any way.

Zel flexed her talons in frustration.

She wanted to fly, let some of her anxiety bleed through her wings into the air. But it was daytime, and Graith and the others were only an hour outside of town. Flying to them now would only take minutes - not the extended flight she needed.

Frustration gripped her at the thought of having to travel to Cian. The Market's information had been wrong, and they'd lost so much time by ending up in the wrong place. As satisfying as killing Braylin had been, and how hot her flame had been when it burned the ships, she was angry that she was still farther than ever from what remained of her clutch.

No matter how many times Graith reassured her they would get the eggs back, it just wasn't enough. They'd been following her eggs for months. They'd be harder now, as they approached hatching - but still damageable by someone with destructive intent.

Her hatchlings must be so lonely. A large part of a dragon's upbringing is their interactions with their mother before they hatch. They'd be able to feel one another through their shells, but if they were separated by any distance they'd be quite alone - and that could be very damaging for a hatchling.

Tail lashing, Zel shifted in her temporary stone nest. Focusing on her eggs was no good. It just made her want to chase after them - and she had twice seen the repercussions of that action.

***

The horse that Graith was riding was no Mero. It had balked twice, just from Graith trying to get it to settle into a walking pace. Its ears were pinned back, and its tail swished back and forth constantly. Its gait was horrid and, after only an hour, his backside felt like it was on fire.

And it was the best behaved out of the four.

They'd had to tie Alix's mount to the back of Graith's just for it to walk forward. Kade's beast had bitten him, and Kali's had tried to buck her off when she'd first gotten into the saddle.

Their progress towards Cian was slow and hours that would have flown in Mero's saddle seemed to drag on. Kade complained constantly. The saddle was too stiff. They were barely moving. The horse was *looking* at him wrong.

After the first day, Kali would pull out one of her many knives any time her brother would open his mouth. When he noticed, he quickly stopped talking.

Alix, already bored of the trip, tried to get Kali to tell him about her knives. She declined, and Graith had to keep a close eye on the boy every time they stopped. Alix knew Kali kept even more of the small daggers in her bag, and would likely have *borrowed* one, given the chance.

The trip, which took them twice as long as locals had told them it would, led them to the gates of Cian four days after they'd left Alluvia. Zel had not followed yet, as she had briefly told Graith that she was waiting for the dragon Galean to return.

As they camped for the night, the cities of Veles and Cian visible from the rise they were on, Graith paced anxiously.

The likelihood that the eggs were still in Cian was laughably low, and the thought of riding that horse even another dragon-length was revolting. But they needed to know where the eggs had gone - to confirm that they'd ever even entered the country with Prince Brantom.

Kali and Kade didn't show it, but Graith thought that they'd been nearly as upset at the misinformation about Alluvia as he and Zel had been. They were good kids, and once they'd gotten to know Zel, they'd wanted to help her get her clutch back as badly as Graith and Alix did.

They'd built a fire, and were gathered close around it, but it wasn't as cold as Graith thought it should be. His inner farmer wondered if it would be an early spring and how the next year's crops would be.

Kade stretched and yawned before standing and walking over to his mount. He dug out his blanket and found a dry spot on the ground near the fire. Before he sat down, he looked over at Graith. The older man was slowly using his belt knife to cut a chunk of cheese into bite-sized pieces.

"I'll go into the city tomorrow, it'll be faster than the four of us all going. We need to find out what we can. I'll leave at first light, and hopefully I can be back by noon."

"That's not fair! I wanted to go to the city!" Alix said, at the same time that Kali said, "There's no way in hell that you're going there without me."

All three looked at Graith, who'd just put a sizable slice of cheese in his mouth. He frowned and chewed slowly, thinking about it. When he came to his decision, he swallowed the bite and took a swig of water before speaking.

"I think Kade is right. I don't think the eggs are still in Cian. We're good on supplies, and we saw how the Siturans responded to us in Alluvia once we'd left the docks." He took a deep breath and another swig of water, "It's to our benefit for him to be in and out without drawing attention."

"But he -" Kali started, before Graith held up a hand.

"Kali, we both know how good of a talker Kade is. Let him do his job and get back to us."

She stood, frowning, and went to retrieve her own sleeping roll. Kade laid down next to the fire, and Graith finished eating his cheese. Alix looked between Graith and the twins, not liking the atmosphere that had settled around the small fire. He got up and grabbed both his and Graith's sleeping rolls and brought them back.

As he lay down, Graith heard him say, "I miss Zel."

Topping off the fire, Graith lay down. The small campsite was quiet - the only noise, the restless movement of the four horses.

***

By the time Kade returned to the campsite, Graith, Kali and Alix had packed up their few belongings and were waiting for him.

The sun was high overhead, and Graith was feeling distinctly uncomfortable in his woolen jacket. He could feel beads of sweat forming on the back of his neck and slowly rolling down between his shoulder blades. Even if the horse was a nag, the motion of riding would create a breeze that would hopefully help cool him off.

As Kade came into view, Graith saw that the young man was frowning, his teeth gritted together. For one horrible second, Graith wondered if they'd been wrong about the eggs moving to Situra after all.

"What's the news, brother?" Kali asked, as Graith's stomach started to sink.

"Oh, they were here, all right. A procession nearly a quarter mile long, if I'm to believe the tales." He pulled his horse closer to Kali and Graith, still frowning.

"And?" Kali asked before Kade could continue.

"They're headed to Roria, the capital of Situra. Two weeks ride if we can get these ill-begotten beasts to actually move."

Graith noted that Kade had purchased a riding crop while he was in town - not that it wasn't needed, but Graith had an aversion to hitting any animal.

"We'll take the main road then?" Graith asked, pointing down into the valley below, where the white stone of the road was visible.

Kade was frowning, obviously annoyed that he'd been interrupted once again.

"Yes, but I haven't even told you the lot of it yet!" he said exasperatedly.

"What?" Alix asked, trying to move his horse closer, but it was still tied to the saddle of Graith's beast.

"Wyla - that's the dragon who lives in this city apparently - left with them. Shopkeeper I talked to couldn't stop raving about it. Apparently, she hasn't left the city in over a hundred years!" Kade sounded proud of himself for the news.

"Why?" Graith and Kali asked in near unison.

"No one seemed to know. And the day after she left, Galean showed up. They said he was the dragon from Alluvia."

"No wonder he wasn't around when we reached the port," Alix said.

Graith would have told Zel, but she was now too far away for him to easily contact. He could feel her in the back of his mind, always present, but unreachable at the moment.

Even as he motioned for his horse to turn to face the road, he hesitated. Then he turned back to the siblings.

"Kade, Kali. You don't have to go with us. This is about as close as we'll get to the Lutesian border for a long time. You've held up the Market's end of the deal, and I don't expect you to keep going."

Kade looked horrified, an expression mirrored on Alix's face. The younger boy had come to adore both Kade and Kali, and Graith hadn't mentioned them separating before.

"No!" Alix said, at the same time that Kali said, "Graith!"

Kade was the one who finally got to speak.

"Graith, Kali and I want to help Zel. We said we'd help back in Tesia, and we're going to see this through. That means Zel with her eggs in hand -" he paused, then muttered, "claw? No - whatever."

Kali cleared her throat and gave her brother a pointed look.

"What Kade means is that we keep the promises we make. Now, let's get moving. For mid-winter that sun is too damned hot."

Alix was nearly bouncing in his saddle with excitement. Graith ducked his head, embarrassed that he'd even brought it up. He was glad though. The two young people had welcomed him and Alix with open arms.

They turned to the road and immediately settled into the same slow, poking gait that had brought them from Alluvia. Each step, one closer to Zel's eggs.

CHAPTER FIFTY-NINE

Nerie

As Nerie entered the palace, her two guards joined her. She'd been about to go to her rooms, but their presence annoyed her. All she wanted was to be alone.

Away from Soren.

Away from Alaena.

Away from Karina.

Even away from Kiriga.

Exiting Soren's suite, Nerie turned down the hallway that led to her mother's quarters. Myha was absent from the palace, so her rooms would not be the first place that Nerie was looked for.

All she had to do to assure her privacy was command the two guards to stand inside the room, rather than in the hallway.

They protested at first, but she told them if they didn't come inside, she would just leave via the servants' entrance in the bathroom. That made them move quick enough. Once inside, she threw herself onto the couch in the center of the room and huffed in frustration.

Only it didn't help.

She was hot in the riding gear meant for high altitudes and shifted uncomfortably. After only a few moments she found it unbearable. Nerie stood and went to her mother's sizable closet in hopes of finding something less constrictive.

Hanging in organized rows were dresses, skirts, shirts,

and nightgowns. Not a pair of pants in sight. With a sigh, she snagged one of the nightgowns and pulled it on. As she retreated to the couch, she passed her mother's bed. Lying there, folded back and waiting for its owner, was a large, plush blanket. She grabbed the large blanket and exited the bedroom.

Back in the living room, she scooted the couch around so that she could sit facing the large tapestry of the dragons.

Soros, Eras, and the others all flying in a circle, nearly biting one another's tails.

Nerie was tired, exhausted to her very core.

How had her life ended up this way? There were armed guards standing in the same room as her, who had pledged their very lives to keep her safe. She couldn't take a single step without *someone* knowing where she was and where she was going. She hadn't seen her friends in months. She hadn't been home to *her* bed since the night before Kiriga had hatched. Hadn't stood in their bookstore since that same morning.

Here she was, in the palace.

Had a *prince* asking for her hand in marriage.

Had a dragon who was the other half of her very soul.

She wanted nothing more than for Kiriga and the other dragons to be able to repopulate their race. Even more than that, she wanted to go searching for the dragons that these eggs had to have come from.

Soros and Eras and their children *couldn't* be the last of their mighty race.

They *weren't*.

The eggs were physical proof of that.

The colors of the tapestry were starting to blur together, and Nerie felt her eyelids get heavy. She pulled the large, down blanket over her head and let herself drift off to sleep, Kiriga still blocked from her mind and shut out of her heart.

***

It was dark in the rooms when Nerie awoke. The guards were still there, but only candles had been lit, as not to disturb the princess. She felt... quiet. Only the sound of her steady heartbeat and ragged breaths could be heard.

It was when a flicker of the dim light fell on the tapestry that Nerie realized why.

Kiriga.

She'd not reentered Nerie's mind while the princess slept. A pang of fear lanced through Nerie, as she quickly reached out to the dragoness.

Kiriga was there waiting. Her normally bubbly, mood dark. She needed Nerie's love and approval as much as Nerie needed hers. Feeling Nerie's mind once again, Kiriga threw her thoughts and soul at her.

Nerie was reminded forcibly that Kiriga was not even six months old and was still a rapidly growing child. She might be physically large enough to carry Nerie, and mentally old enough to understand abstract concepts, but she was still just a babe, fresh from her shell.

I'm sorry, Kiriga. You asked me to simply consider the offer, and I shut you out. That was wrong of me, and I'm sorry, love, Nerie said, as tenderly as she could.

I thought you didn't want me anymore, Kiriga's tone was fretful.

How could I possibly give you up? I love you, and you love me, and together we are whole.

Nerie's feelings of guilt were building by the second.

Let's fly together? Kiriga asked hopefully, her voice tight.

Yes, let me get changed. What time is it? Nerie realized that without a window, and with only the little candles for light, it could have been noon or midnight, and she wouldn't have known the difference.

It's just after dawn, Kiriga told her, showing her a vision of a light sky with red clouds on the horizon.

As she started to climb out of the veritable mountain of blankets, both guards bowed diffidently to her, stiffly saying, "Princess," before turning their backs to her so that she might get changed.

Back in her rumpled riding leathers from the day before, Nerie was ready to fly as soon as she entered the hallway. As she walked quickly to the king's quarters, the tap of her boots, and those of her guards echoed loudly from the stone walls.

Soren's door was shut, but one of the guards standing to its side bowed to her before opening it for her. Soren was sitting in the small room where they had often had lunch together, eating a small breakfast. Nerie's stomach rumbled in agitation, and she realized she hadn't eaten anything the day before.

She mentally shrugged, as flying with Kiriga was much more important than a quick meal. Soren, seeing her in her riding gear, smiled and motioned her over.

"Nerie, I'm glad to see you up. Kiriga has been in quite the foul mood this morning," he said as he smiled up at her. "I know the topic of discussion yesterday was distressing, and I'm sorry that you are in this situation. However, I would like to talk to you about it."

Nerie's mouth opened to tell Soren that she couldn't talk right now, that Kiriga needed to go for a flight, but he seemed to know what she was going to say.

"It's all right, I'm not going to stop you from flying."

He handed her a muffin as he stood from the table.

"I'll ride Riya, and we can talk while we fly. Let me change while they get both dragons saddled up, and then we can go."

He motioned to the rest of the breakfast, and she was sure that he knew that she had not eaten the day before.

In fact, she was quite sure that the king knew more than he was letting on. As he left the room, Vizen disappeared, most likely to get the dragons ready to fly. Nerie looked down at the pastry in her hand, then bit into it with relish. If she had to wait on Soren, she might as well enjoy a small breakfast.

It was only a few minutes later when he came stalking back in, but by then Nerie had eaten the pastry, a piece of tender fruit, and several slices of bacon. It was heavier than she would have liked for a preflight meal, but the weakness she had felt before had dissipated.

When they walked into the courtyard, Riya was standing before the doors, her great wings tucked in close to her body. In the morning light, her scales had a wine color to them, and as Nerie tilted her head to look up at the dragoness's face, she could see streaks of red and purple race past where the light hit.

I itch, she complained, shrugging at the straps that wrapped around the spikes that protruded from her scales.

You'll itch more in a moment, once they tighten those up, Nerie said, watching as the saddle was placed in the nook at the base of her neck.

Only until I get in the air, Riya sighed.

I don't itch, Kiriga said smugly from behind her older sister.

Nerie walked over to Kiriga, who lowered her wedge-shaped head to nuzzle the girl. Nerie absently scratched at her eye ridges as they watched Riya fail to stop moving long enough to have the straps tighten.

She has not flown with a rider since Justan died, nearly sixty years ago, Kiriga told Nerie quietly. *She is anxious.*

Soren flies all the time on Eras and Soros, Nerie said, as if that should make the older dragoness relax.

It was a grunt from Eras that finally got Riya to stand still long enough for the servants to finish saddling her.

I would go, but Soros needs me to stay with her to watch the eggs, Eras said, almost apologetically, to all involved.

The eggs had not left Soros' gaze since arrival, and the hatching grounds were under constant surveillance. To prevent anyone other than herself from accessing them, Soros was currently lying in a tight circle around the eggs and would breathe fire on them and the sand every hour. She wanted Eras to stand guard and watch the corners of the hatching ground that she could not see from her position.

Everyone understood, of course. The eggs were priceless to the humans, but the dragons' survival hinged on them. Nerie mounted Kiriga as Soren mounted Riya. The older dragoness was finally calm and ready for her rider.

Nerie tightened her leg grip on Kiriga while Riya

launched herself into the air. Riya wasn't as large as her parents or some of her siblings, but she created a large gust of wind. Once she'd cleared the top of the palace Kiriga followed, two wingbeats later.

As they always did, the dragons cartwheeled through the air to stretch their wings. Nerie enjoyed the wind through her hair, which streamed behind her like a banner. Karina hadn't tied it into the plait she normally wore when flying.

Soren whooped in glee as Riya made a dizzying display of acrobatics, arching herself backwards and doing a falling loop.

Then she twisted and pumped her wings hard, trying to regain her lost altitude. Nerie and Kiriga, from their higher position, looked down on the red-purple dragoness. In her excitement, Nerie bent over Kiriga's side to get a better view of the antics.

Even from their lofty position, Nerie could hear the audible snap of leather, see the look of horror that crossed Soren's face.

Then he was falling.

Riya screamed, twisting in midair to dive after him.

Kiriga dived too, her wings tucked sharply against her body.

Soros, Eras, Wyla and Mazen all launched themselves from the palace in the same instant, sensing Riya's distress.

Only Ilex, whose small wings prevented him from joining them in the sky, was left behind at the palace. That didn't stop him though. He was running as fast as he could over the terrain towards his falling rider.

It was Ilex's scream that echoed across the still land as Soren's body hit the ground.

It was his terror, grief, and rage that echoed through the minds of all the citizens of Roria moments later.

And it was Ilex who reached the body first, as he ran across the grounds from the palace to reach Soren.

The other dragons landed in a strange semicircle around him and Soren, crooning in a hair-raising keen.

CHAPTER SIXTY

Graith

They made better time heading towards Roria than they'd made from Alluvia to Cian. Graith wasn't sure if it was because the horses were getting used to their riders, the fact that this road was better paved, or just because now that they had confirmation that Brantom, and presumably Zel's eggs, were, in fact, in the country.

They were four days into the trip when they reached the city of Tocria. It was a small city, but even as they passed through, it was abuzz with talk of Prince Brantom and his entourage. From what they could gather, not only was the dragon Wyla with him, but another dragon, Eras, had joined the procession some point after they'd left Cian.

Many residents were voicing their concern that shortly before Prince Brantom had passed through, their own dragon, Riya, had left, and had yet to return.

Graith wished, not for the first time, that Zel was closer to them. She'd left Alluvia the day after they'd made it to Cian but had taken a more direct path towards the capital. She was close enough that he could bespeak her if he needed to, but it seemed to be more of a strain at this distance.

That was four dragons they'd learned about in the short time they'd been in Situra, and it seemed like there were several more, if he could interpret the quiet whispers correctly.

They moved quickly through the city, only stopping long

enough to purchase a few supplies and ask how far until they
reached the next city on the way to Roria. Tocria, too,
seemed to be wary of them. They were stared at by nearly
every merchant along the street, and as Kade complained
later, overcharged, once again, for supplies.

That night when they stopped to make camp, Kade and
Alix took a short walk. They'd both been complaining for
hours about their legs hurting after so many days on
horseback. Graith was stiff too, but once he'd sat on the
ground, he found he couldn't muster the energy to get back
up. Only Kali hadn't complained, but Graith saw her
crossing and re-crossing her legs several times in pain and
annoyance.

Kali started a fire while the two boys walked in the dying
sunlight. Graith finally managed to stand again, with several
protesting pops from his spine. He made his way over to the
horses, intent on grooming them before the last of the light
disappeared. Foul mounts though they were, they still
deserved to be taken care of, or so Graith thought. The others
were not quite of the same mindset.

When Kade and Alix returned, not long after the sun had
fully set, they were carrying several large, round fruits.

"Look what we found, Graith!" Alix said excitedly,
handing Graith one of the slightly-hairy fruits.

"A melch?" Graith asked, frowning down at it.

"Yeah! They're my favorite," Kade said, as he sat down
to cut into his own.

Graith looked back down at the golden fruit.

Something was wrong with it.

It was a tasty summer treat, ripe around the longest day
of the year.

"Kade -" Graith started, even as the young man bit down.

"Mhm?" he asked, juice leaking down his face.

"I don't think this is melch - it's out of season."

Kali and Alix were looking at theirs doubtfully now.
Graith rubbed a hand on it again. The skin, while soft, was
fuzzy rather than smooth. The shape of it was wrong too, a
little too oblong.

Kade wiped his mouth, looking down at it.

"It tastes a little sour, but overall is good," he said, cutting off another chunk.

"You don't even know what it is then," Kali said, tossing hers behind her without another glance.

"Well, yeah?" Kade didn't see a problem with that.

"I'm not going to eat it. Sour can be a plant's way of letting you know that it shouldn't be eaten," Graith said, setting his down too.

Alix took a tentative bite out of his, but puckered his lips immediately.

"A little sour? Yuck!"

"Fine, more for me," Kade said, grabbing Alix's and Graith's before they could throw them away.

"Are you daft, brother? Graith said not to eat those," Kali said annoyed, trying to grab another of the not-melches to throw away.

"They taste fine!" Kade said, even as he finished his first and started to eat another.

Alix sat there looking disappointed until Graith handed him his small belt knife and started to show him how to whittle.

Happy to be distracted and actually allowed to hold a knife for once, Alix's attention shifted away from the loss of the fruit.

Kade made a point of eating the remaining non-melches loudly.

It wasn't even the moon's apex when Kade woke from his sleep, and rushed away from the campsite, stomach gurgling unpleasantly.

***

The following day, progress was slow for the quartet. Frequent stops were needed for Kade, whose bowels had completely given up trying to hold anything in. When he wasn't stopping to relieve himself of everything he'd ever eaten, Kade was drinking an unbelievable amount of water. They'd had to stop and find a stream at least four times over the course of the day.

Graith felt bad for him, but Kali was cackling like a crow. Every moan or uncomfortable shift on his horse set her off. Jibing him, talking about the winter-melch, and, overall, just being a sister enjoying her brother's misfortune.

By that evening, Kade was exhausted. He nearly fell off his horse trying to dismount, only the fact he got tangled in the reins kept him from hitting the dirt.

He was asleep before they even had a fire going, and when they tried to wake him the following morning, he only groaned and waved a feeble arm at them.

Unable to do anything other than wait, Graith reached out to Zel. She was closer now, as their path and hers came closer to intersecting.

We need to wait for Kade to recover before we can keep going, Zel, Graith said, letting Zel see the young man who was curled into a ball on the ground, sound asleep.

I understand. Dragons can get sick from bad foods too, you know.

She sounded as if she knew from experience.

Graith spent the day working with Alix on his whittling skills while Kali set up a rotted log which she practiced throwing daggers at from increasing distances. While he'd known she was the muscle between her and Kade, he hadn't ever seen her use her knives. It was unsettling for him to see her, accurately and consistently, hit the same five-inch square of rotting wood, over and over.

***

By the third morning, Kade had returned to the land of the living. Even before the sun had risen, he'd insisted they get back on the road to make up for lost time. He was restless and would whip his mount trying to get it to go faster. He'd get a few lengths ahead, but then the nag would become stubborn and stop moving.

"Kade," Graith said sharply after the fourth time. "Stop. You're just upsetting the poor beast more."

Kade had the good graces to flush with embarrassment and tuck the whip away.

"Sorry, Graith, I just feel responsible for delaying us."

Graith nudged his own mount next to Kade's and put a hand on the young man's shoulder.

"It's all right. We know where they are going. We're on our way, and Zel understands. All we can do is keep going, but beating your horse isn't going to get you anywhere substantially faster."

Kade nodded, and Graith gave his shoulder a brief squeeze before moving his horse into the lead.

With only the sound of the horses' shod hooves echoing off the brick road, and the sun shining from high overhead, the quartet was making swift progress towards Roria. They'd stopped long enough to fill their waterskins and dig out some lunch, when they felt a rippling scream of anguish rip through their minds. It was strong enough that Alix fell backwards onto his butt, and all four of them were overpowered with the strongest sense of grief and loss they'd ever felt.

Instinctively, Graith and Kali both had tears in their eyes, and Kade looked as if he was going to be sick once again.

For several minutes they were left reeling, not knowing what the source of the mental shockwave had been.

Graith, Zel said urgently.

What was that, Zel? Graith asked. He knew it hadn't been her, but the closest he'd ever felt to that was when she'd lost an egg.

That was a dragon keening. It came from the capital, she sounded anxious. *What if something happened to my eggs? Dragons only keen like that for extreme loss.*

Graith could feel her looking side to side, tail lashing. He wished that he could be there to soothe her, but instead said, *We're on our way, but we are still several days out from Roria.*

He felt her annoyance at that, but she kept silent. They continued onward for another hour, Zel becoming more and more restless in Graith's mind. He tried to calm her multiple times but was pushed out.

I'm coming to get you.

Zel had decided they weren't moving fast enough.

It took her an hour to reach them, even as they continued onward. Graith tried insisting that they continue on the horses, but she had made up her mind. She was stern enough that when Graith didn't tell the others, she did it herself.

When she finally landed near them, Graith's heart skipped a beat as he looked at her. She'd been snatching cows from farms since she'd learned of the other dragons in Situra. She'd filled out in the chest and her ribs were no longer quite visible. Her scales had nearly returned to their original healthy navy, but there were still splotches of both black and white.

The black is just soot I haven't been able to clean from myself, Zel said, noticing Graith was watching her.

And the white? He asked.

She craned her neck around to look at her back.

Stress, I'm sure.

Graith understood that, he had several streaks of white appearing in his hair that hadn't been there before he'd met her.

Will you be able to carry us all? he asked, as he stripped the saddle off his horse.

No matter how healthy she looked, it had been a long and hard winter for her, and he didn't want to strain her any more than necessary.

I will do anything I need to, to get to my eggs, Graith.

The look in her blue eyes was heartbreaking. It had been months since she'd seen them last.

What about the prince? Graith asked, even as Kali started compiling the absolute basics for the flight. She seemed worried about Zel as well.

There are dragons here. If they were not keening over my eggs, then they will help me protect them.

Graith worried that Zel was putting too much faith in these other dragons, but he didn't say so. Instead he climbed onto her back, with the others behind him, and held on as tightly as he could as Zel strained to get them into the air. Even at her largest, three adults and a child were heavy for her, as unaccustomed to having riders as she was.

Once they were in the air, she climbed as high as she could, and then turning herself to align with the road far below, headed for Roria.

CHAPTER SIXTY-ONE

Nerie

Nerie dismounted Kiriga the moment she landed and ran to Soren's broken body. She wasn't even within five feet of him before she could clearly make out the fact that there would be no possible recovery. The sight of blood turned her stomach, and, between sobs, she violently lost the little breakfast she had eaten less than an hour before.

A swarm of people, roused from the palace by the dragons' flight and Ilex's keen, arrived minutes after the dragons. Everyone had felt the shock wave that had resonated from Ilex and had a limited idea of what had happened. However, the shock of seeing the king dead caused many to fall to their knees moaning.

When they tried to move Soren's body, Ilex growled and crouched low, above it. They had to have Nerie ask him to let them take Soren home. When she tried to reach out to him his mind was nothing but a storm of grief and torment.

It was Soros who finally got through to him. A sharp command from her, and he let the men through.

They worked with reverence for the king, as respectful as they could be. A pallet was brought shortly after the situation had been assessed. The captain of Soren's guard directing each bearer. Soren was moved onto the pallet and prepared to be transported back to the palace.

Other than a cursory check on Nerie, everyone's attention was focused on Soren. She stood off to the side, insides shaking and mind blank. *How?* Repeated endlessly in her mind as she watched. When Nerie walked towards Kiriga to fly back to the palace, the captain of the king's guard stopped her.

"My Lady. With what has just happened to his highness, you cannot be permitted to endanger yourself at this time. Please, ride back to the palace with me."

The pain in his eyes at his failure to protect Soren was clear as he spoke. He gestured to two waiting horses. Nerie only stared at them numbly.

Go. I will meet you in the courtyard, Kiriga said, her voice muted as she too tried to deal with the king's death.

Nerie climbed on to the horse offered to her and waited. Another guard took the lead attached to the horse's halter.

And then, the procession back to the palace started.

Somehow, a ride that should have taken only minutes turned into an hour of slow progress. It felt closer to a death parade than returning to the palace. They entered the city through the Northern gate and wound their way slowly through the city.

As they passed, citizens - people who were at one point her friends and neighbors - lined the streets.

Nerie could feel the eyes of every person they passed upon her.

They knew. They all knew what had happened to Soren.

They might not be able to see his body, lying covered on the pallet, but they had felt Ilex's piercing keen. She was sure that they'd seen the dragons race through the air.

Nerie couldn't bring herself to look away from their eyes, each burning with the same unasked question. The same one still racing through her mind.

How?

She was in shock. Her mind was numb and there was no thought of, well, anything. Anything other than asking herself *how?*

When they finally entered the courtyard, however, that changed. Alaena was there, as was Astra. When they saw Soren's broken body, Astra let out a low moan, and Alaena started sobbing, holding onto her daughter and sinking to the ground.

Neither even looked at Nerie.

She was left there, sitting on the horse, while everyone moved around her. Tears slowly rolled down her face, and she failed to get her mind to work enough for her to even dismount.

It was only when Vizen offered her a hand that she was pulled back to the here and now.

The man's eyes were red rimmed, and he was barely containing the tears that threatened to fall. She took his hand shakily, and he helped her to the ground. Then she just stood there, looking at Soren's right-hand man.

He seemed to realize that she was waiting for him to speak, and he quickly dashed at his eyes and cleared his throat.

"Your highness. We must plan for what comes next. Who do you need me to assemble? What do you need right now? I am yours to command."

He bowed formally to her then rose, waiting for her response.

Her command? She didn't even fully comprehend what was going on, and he wanted her to give commands? Her mind struggled to pull itself to attention, but in her vision Soren was falling. She started to shake.

"Ma'am?" Vizen asked, his tone worried.

Nerie's green eyes focused on his brown.

"My... My uncle. Sylas. He needs to come, but... I'll send Wyla to get him. And my mother. She needs to return to the palace."

Nerie felt like she was grasping at straws as she tried to force her thoughts into a semblance of order.

"Of course, your highness," Vizen said, then hesitated a moment, his breath stiffled, "and funeral arrangements?"

He will have a dragon's funeral.

Eras' voice was soft, but from the surprised expression on Vizen's face, he had heard the great dragon too.

Turning from where he stood, Vizen found Eras roosting

on the roof to his left. With a deep bow, he addressed the dragon.

"Of course, my lord dragon."

It's all my fault, Riya moaned, laying in a pale pile on the ground of the courtyard. *Please. Please have them remove the remaining straps from me.*

Nerie relayed Riya's request to Vizen, and with a curt nod, he went to oversee this task, signaling two of the knights from the king's guard to follow him.

Wyla. I need you to fly and get Uncle Sylas, Nerie said.

She turned to the white dragoness, who in the morning sun looked gray.

I heard. I shall fly as fast as the wind can carry me.

She stretched then leaned down from the roof to touch noses with her brooding sister and grieving brother before launching herself into the sky and winging out of sight.

What does a dragon's funeral entail? Nerie asked Eras as her mind replayed the last few moments.

We burn our dead, at sundown of the day they died, he told her, voice soft.

Do I need to tell Vizen? she asked, looking for the man, who had disappeared after unharnessing Riya.

No, he was here for the last king, your grandfather, Daviron. He will know.

Nerie nodded numbly, looking around the courtyard. Kiriga was laying off to one side, her golden scales tinged green. Alaena and Astra had left at some point, and there were few people still about.

Only her personal guards were with her, and a few servants hurried across the way, not looking at her.

She walked inside slowly, dazed. Servants and nobles lined the hallways as she walked, glancing at her and whispering.

What were they thinking?

They all knew. They had to know.

Ilex's keen had been too overpowering for them not to know.

***

Karina found her standing before the doors to Soren's suite.

She'd been walking the path that she took every day and had arrived there before she was conscious of the fact. Hot tears coursed down her face, even as the older woman wrapped her arms around her shoulders and led her to her own rooms.

She helped Nerie undress from the riding leathers and muttered about getting a mourning wardrobe ready by that evening. In the meantime, she dressed Nerie in a pair of pajamas, telling the guards to let only Vizen enter the room.

Nerie just sat there, staring at the fire, breathing shallowly and not moving.

When Karina brought Nerie her midday meal, Nerie just stared at the platter listlessly. She didn't think she'd ever be hungry again.

Vizen and the captain of the king's guard knocked on the door, and Nerie was forced out of her silent contemplation.

"Your Majesty."

They both acknowledged her with a bow. The change in title, however, made her jump.

"I'm not Queen," she said. Her voice was hoarse after hours of disuse and the screaming that had left it raw.

"Your coronation will be tomorrow, at sunrise," Vizen said without a moment of hesitation. "At this moment, you are only princess in title, not action."

The captain looked uneasy, and Nerie noticed he was holding a bundle of leather straps.

"Your Majesty, I realize this is not the time that you want to talk about this, but it must be addressed immediately."

He held out the bundle and Nerie recognized it as the riding straps that Riya had worn. "Please, look here."

He pointed to several spots in the lightly tanned leather.

"The leather has been intentionally cut, not enough to fall apart, but with sufficient force…" and he pulled on the two ends of the piece and it gave out with a snap. "The whole harness is like that. Six or eight spots. It was one of those spots that caused the king's death."

Nerie just stared, running her fingers over the leather.

Then with a soft voice she asked, "Did Riya's scales do this?"

Vizen laid a hand on her shoulder, looking into her eyes, "No, your Majesty. This was human interference."

"But who -" Nerie asked, choking back a sob.

She looked back down at the straps.

Her heart sank.

"Does each dragon have their own set of riding straps?"

"For everyday riding? No, your majesty."

Vizen's eyes were dark as he understood her question.

"Check Kiriga, she is still wearing her riding straps. We'll deal with this after the funeral and the coronation. Until then," she looked at the captain with a cold determination, "I need more guards. Soren was right. I need to be protected. It is my duty to Situra to rule in his stead."

"Of course, your Majesty."

They bowed to her, each going their separate way to deal with the tasks she had given them.

Riya, she said softly, reaching out to the dragoness.

Riya, it's not your fault.

It's not? Riya asked, as if afraid to believe what Nerie was telling her.

No, Nerie confirmed, reassuring her.

She told the dragons what she'd learned, and she could hear them roaring in outrage through the palace walls. Ilex was fiercest in his grief and rage.

***

The next time Vizen returned, he confirmed that the riding straps that Kiriga wore had also been tampered with, and it was only luck that none of them had broken in the short flight. He had also brought a seamstress with him at Karina's request. The little old woman curtsied to Nerie, her arms full of red fabrics.

Karina took charge of the small woman, and the two of them worked on a gown for Nerie. They took a few rough measurements, but for the most part, Nerie was left to just sit on the couch again, waiting.

When the dress was ready to be hemmed and fitted, Nerie felt sick at the sight of the red fabric. It's shades and patterns in the dim candlelight reminded Nerie of the blood that had slowly leaked from the king's body.

When she put up her objections, she was reminded that the kingdom would look to her, and that reds were the traditional mourning colors.

Unhappy, but with no response to that truth, she stood and let them pin the gown in place.

She asked Karina if her mother had been returned yet but was told that Sir Ahlwin's estate was several hours away, and that it was too soon for riders to have returned.

The gown was removed and Nerie sent off to bathe while the corrections were set with stitches. When she returned, her hair was braided into an ornate twist, and the gown had been pressed and hung, waiting for her to be dressed.

As she waited to be told where the funeral was to be held, she caught a glance of herself in the mirror that hung on her wall. In a mind that had been empty for sake of perseverance all day, her only thoughts were that she was so pale that her freckles looked nearly black on her skin - and that her auburn hair clashed horribly with the red of the dress.

It was such a vain thought, and she wasn't even sure why it occurred to her.

Here she was, preparing for her father's funeral.

She was to be crowned as queen the following morning.

And yet she was worried that her hair didn't match her dress.

Karina led her from the room and down the corridor. Their feet tapping loudly on the floor, echoing in the now empty halls. The funeral pyre was set in the grand courtyard. When they reached the doors, Karina stepped in front of her and gave the dress a few unnecessary tugs to straighten the hem, then pushed a stray hair behind Nerie's ear.

***

As the doors were thrown open, and Nerie was announced, she felt a moment of blind panic. She didn't want to be there. She wanted to turn around and run the other way.

The courtyard was full of nobles, merchants, servants, and as many commoners as who could fit through the gate. Nerie could see Brantom, Marza, Niro, and their guard on the far side of the courtyard, directly across from where she now stood.

Alaena and Astra were standing next to the pyre. Ilex was on the wall directly behind them. He was looming overhead, his nubbed wings tented, and his eyes were whirling a burning red.

The other dragons were perched on the rooftops and walls that surrounded the courtyard. They were sitting nearly wingtip to wingtip as they watched the crowd below. More than one noble muttered uneasily, pointing upward at the dragons.

Nerie took a slow, deep breath and squared her shoulders, then she slowly walked the way that Alaena had taught her, to command the attention of the people. Within moments, all eyes were on her as she headed to the pyre to say her last goodbyes to Soren. The kind man who she'd learned was her father, too late in both of their lives.

Soren's body had been wrapped in a fine silk sheet, dyed the exact green hue of Ilex's scales. His likeness had been painted on to the silk where his face lay below. Nerie's breath caught in her throat at the thought of the broken and bloody face that she knew lay beneath.

She'd been given a prayer to say and a speech to give, but her voice froze as she turned to face those people gathered. She found herself staring into Astra's eyes, and the cold fury she saw there was disturbing.

Alaena wouldn't even look at her, and Nerie found herself thinking just how wrong it was that Aldis wasn't even here to attend his father's funeral.

She tried again to intone the traditional prayer over Soren's body, but the words wouldn't come. Instead, she stepped back and let the dragons know that it was time. People murmured slightly, waiting for her to speak. But she couldn't. She couldn't say the traditional farewell to Soren.

Ilex opened his great maw and issued forth a flame that

instantly set the pyre ablaze. It was so hot and sustained that many people took steps back and away. Nerie felt her skin redden from the heat but did not move.

Only when her dress started to smoke, did she finally retreat.

As the fire crackled, Nerie stared into the flames, her tears running freely down her cheeks, as she thought of how kind Soren had been. How she would miss the way the crow's feet crinkled at his eyes. How he'd encouraged her from the moment that Kiriga had hatched. She choked back sobs as she thought of when he'd showed her how to care for the dragonling, and the many times he'd talked about the dragons with her for hours on end.

She found herself watching the flames until they died out and only embers remained. Night was fully set, and few people were left in the courtyard. It was just her, Vizen, Karina, and her bodyguards. Astra was there, though Alaena had left not long after the flames had taken. Brantom and the delegation from Lutesia had been some of the first to leave, and the nobles had left once they realized she had nothing to say to them.

Go rest, Kiriga told her softly. *Morning comes all too soon.*

CHAPTER SIXTY-TWO

Nerie

Only a few hours after Nerie's head hit her pillow Karina gently shook her awake. There were dark rings under the woman's eyes, and Nerie knew Karina and the seamstress had stayed up late into the night to finish the gown for her coronation. When Karina informed her that it was two hours to sunrise, Nerie suspected the maid had not slept at all.

A small cold breakfast waited for her, and Karina instructed her to eat and bathe quickly, as they still needed to finish the final fit for her gown. Even doing as she was asked, Nerie found herself moving slowly and without much vigor. She was mentally exhausted. Her mind constantly was replaying the events of the horrible day before. She found it hard to forget, when today's events were a direct result of the previous day.

Kiriga was awake, as were all the dragons. They went as a group to the lake to bathe, Kiriga telling her that they, too, had roles to play in today's ceremony.

When Karina and the old seamstress helped her gently pull on the gown she would wear, Nerie gasped in shock at its beauty. It was a deep gold, once again the same color as Kiriga's scales at their brightest, and it had a gossamer layer of golden lace that lay over the top. Citrine jewels had been sewn into the bodice, and a long, golden cape of fine silk lay over her shoulders and down her back. Her hair had been left loose, in long waves, and she wanted to push them back self-consciously behind her ears but did not after a frown from Karina.

Before she really had time to take in the beauty of this gown, she was being led out the door. The coronation ceremony would start at sunrise and take place in the same courtyard that the funeral had been the night before.

This walk down the corridors was markedly different than the last, even though they were once again empty. Kiriga had been boosting Nerie's confidence since she'd awoken, and she was almost excited to enter the courtyard.

Almost.

When they reached the door, Karina pulled it open to expose an empty courtyard. Unlike the night before, when she had entered after the courtyard was already filled with spectators, this morning she would stand in the courtyard waiting ready as they entered. Karina motioned her out the door, and Nerie let the dragons tell her what needed to be done.

They were the officiants of this coronation - as they'd been since Kyre's ascent to the throne, nearly a hundred and thirty years before.

***

You are to stand on the ashes of your predecessor, Eras told her kindly, sensing her immediate denial of such blatant desecration.

She forced herself to walk slowly to the pile of ash that was all that remained from the large pyre the evening before. The hem of her gown stirred up eddies of ash, and she forced her eyes to remain on the gates, where the commoners waited to get in. As the gates opened, so did the door from the palace. As commoners poured in from one direction, nobles came from the other.

She saw the faces of people that she'd grown up with, as well as the nobles who she'd come to know over the last few months, but mostly she saw people she didn't know. Everyone wanted the opportunity to see their new queen's coronation.

Astra was there, front and center. Nerie could see the

same hatred from the night before burning brightly in her eyes.

Alaena was there, head held high, in her own gown of dark red. She would be openly mourning Soren for the foreseeable future, and Nerie wished that she too could have that opportunity. At the same time, she knew that, as queen, she would need to show the strength of her people, and as such, her own mourning would have to be a private affair.

Notably missing were her mother and her uncle. She frowned for a moment but had to assume both were still traveling to the capital.

Brantom and his entourage had also taken a spot in front, as was their right as visiting dignitaries. While he was smiling pleasantly enough, there was a slight draw to his eyebrows that made Nerie think he was deep in thought.

Now, she heard Eras say, and Vizen approached her, with a small golden coronet, balanced on a flat but ornate black pillow.

Pick up the coronet, and place it upon your head, he instructed.

She did so, the thin metal feeling so much heavier than its physical weight. The motion of moving it to her head was slow and deliberate, and she forced herself to breath evenly as the gathered crowd watched.

Now, repeat after me - I, Nerie, daughter of the house Therius, pledge myself, body and soul, to the kingdom of Situra. I shall lead my people, serving with honor and grace. I shall protect the kingdom from external and internal threats and bring it to prosperity. I will preserve both the Therius bloodline and the blood of dragon kind. I shall serve my people until my final breath, as my forefathers did before me. I am honoring the line of succession, I am Kiriga's Chosen, and I am Situra's Queen.

As the words left her mouth, she placed the coronet lightly upon her head. The sun crested the horizon just as she finished settling it in place. She looked at no one in particular, her eyes nearly glazed over in effort to repeat the words exactly as Eras spoke them to her.

Upon her declaration of being Kiriga's Chosen, Kiriga lifted herself into the air, bugling her joy and approval.

Several commoners screamed, and even a few of the nobles looked skyward in fear. She was joined shortly by Eras and Soros, their large frames casting the courtyard into darkness, even as the sun climbed its way into the sky.

Someone in the crowd cried out, "The king is dead, long live the queen!" and others joined in, screams of "Queen Nerie!" and "Your Majesty!" filled the courtyard, and cheers were screamed into the air.

It was easy to note the presence of the king's - no - queen's guard around the courtyard, as well as the faces of those who were not joining in on the celebration. Alaena and Astra both made quick escapes, and Brantom stood with his arms crossed, watching her.

A line formed, and people stood waiting to pledge themselves to her. The captain of the guard was first in line, and once he'd completed his pledge to her, he turned and started organizing his knights and the crowd. The nobles would, of course, be given the opportunity to pledge themselves first, followed by the servants of the household. Finally, until Nerie tired, commoners would be allowed to pledge themselves to her.

It seemed that the kitchens had been busy all night, as food was provided for anyone who could make it to one of the large tables that were brought out. Nerie could smell the sweet tang of glazed meat and the savory scent of herbs that garnished every dish.

She was sure she could go get food if she wanted, but she didn't want to let down anyone waiting to speak with her. These were *her* people now, after all.

***

It was several hours after the sun had fully risen when the tone of the dragon's roars changed from the happy bugling they'd continued since the coronation, to a deep growl. Nerie paused speaking with a woman who had been her neighbor in the middle city to look up at them.

What's going on? she asked Kiriga.

There is another dragon here, Kiriga's tone was excited and frightened.

Wyla? Nerie asked, unsure why Wyla returning would upset Kiriga.

No, she's crashed into the field north of the city.

Eras, Riya, and Mazen took off from the palace roof, and Kiriga, with a few screams from people in the courtyard, hopped down to be closer to Nerie. Soros had gone back to the hatching ground the moment that the coronation had finished. She was now sitting, hunched over the eggs.

Nerie looked back at the gathered crowd. Only she had reacted to the change in the dragons' tone or to the fact that three dragons had just flown off. She knew, from her own life as a commoner, that people just thought dragons did what they wanted. Which, they did to an extent, but not nearly as coordinated as they'd just been.

As she looked around, she saw Brantom, but his normally smug look had not changed. Astra was talking to the prince again, and she had glanced up at them leaving, but continued her conversation.

Uneasy, Nerie quickly said her goodbyes to the people and started walking towards the door. Vizen and the captain of the guard both met up with her before she reached it, and Karina was waiting just inside.

She was listening intently to Eras, as he directed Riya and Mazen to sweep out from the city. She could see through his eyes as he came upon a dragon not much smaller than Ilex.

She was lying on the ground, a long path of dirt carved away where she'd crashed and slid. One of her large, blue wings was tucked under her body at an unnatural angle, and to Nerie's absolute horror, she saw the bodies of four people scattered around the dragon.

Eras, so very much larger than the blue dragon, landed nearby. He called Riya and Mazen back to him, and once they too had landed, they approached the fallen dragoness. At Eras's direction, Mazen moved each human several dragon lengths away, and once they were safely away, Riya and Eras worked together to lift the dragoness off her wing.

By now, even though she was watching through Eras's eyes, Nerie had briefly informed her staff what had happened. Vizen had jumped into action, arranging for help to go out to the humans, and to bring medical supplies not only for them but for the dragoness.

Nerie could see that three of the humans, a man and woman about her age and a younger boy, had all regained consciousness and were slowly moving around. The older man, however, hadn't yet moved.

A quick word with Mazen and he relayed to them that help was on the way, but they needed to remain seated, in case they were hurt in a way they didn't know. The man and woman complied, but the young boy ran to the older man, crying.

She felt sick not knowing why the dragon had crashed, or how injured the people were. The dragoness was starting to move, and Eras was waiting for her to be able to speak.

Nerie needed somewhere to go and collect her thoughts, to focus on what was going on with this dragon. She turned first to her own quarters, but then squaring her shoulders, walked to Soren's. It was the monarch's quarters after all, and she was queen now.

She knew that, in Soren's office, there would be journals and missives she'd need to read. She also knew that there were people who still needed to reaffirm their loyalty to her.

She had inherited the kingdom, yes, but she had also inherited its problems.

CHAPTER SIXTY-THREE

Final

Graith's return to consciousness was slow. His whole body ached and his vision, even though he tried to open his eyes, was dark.

He groaned as he tried to move but found that nothing responded.

The groan, however, seemed to trigger a series of whispers, and then someone was speaking by his ear.

"Graith? Graith! Are you awake?"

It was Alix, though the young boy's throat was raw, and he sounded congested.

Then it was too bright. His eyes *had* been open, there'd just been a cloth lying over them. He blinked rapidly, trying to get his eyes to focus. At the same time, he tried to turn his head towards Alix.

Again, it didn't move.

Fear struck him then, as he came fully awake. His mind flashed with the last thing he remembered - Zel, exhausted, and unable to keep them airborne. She'd tried to land, but misjudged her speed, skipping along the land and briefly taking flight again. Then as she hit the ground a second time, she'd tumbled forward, throwing himself and the others into the empty field.

"Zel?!" he said aloud and with his mind, worried about the dragoness. He *knew* she shouldn't have carried all of them. They would have made it to the capital just fine on the horses.

"Graith, shhh, it's okay. Zel's fine. She's just sleeping," Kade said, stepping into Graith's view. He reached down and put a hand on Graith's shoulder.

"What - Where are we?" Graith managed to ask as he took in Kade's words.

"The palace in Roria," Kali said, and Graith breathed a slight sigh of relief. Not only had Zel managed to get them there, but even after crashing they were all okay.

Or at least, they were all alive.

Graith couldn't see anything other than the painted ceiling above him. He tried a third time to move his head.

Still nothing.

"Graith, you're strapped onto the bed. They didn't want you moving your neck or chest. You got pretty banged up, it seems like Zel landed on you, where as the three of us ended up with some minor scrapes and bruises," Alix said, then paused for a moment before adding, "Oh, and my broken arm."

Before Graith could respond, a fourth person spoke.

"Hello Graith, I'm Dr. Maziri. I've been taking care of you and your friends."

A woman leaned over where he could see her, and he was surprised to see she was about his age, with short-cropped, brown hair that had started to gray at the temples. She smiled down at him before speaking again.

"You seemed to have taken a hard fall. Your left arm and leg are both broken, and you've got a concussion. Because you didn't regain consciousness right away, we didn't want you to hurt yourself, so we've strapped you to the table."

She reached down and loosened something and Graith was able to move his head slightly to the sides.

"Now then Graith, can you tell me about yourself? I just want to make sure that your memory hasn't been damaged."

"What do you want me to tell you?" Graith asked, not sure that there was anything of note to tell her.

"Let's start with your name - First and last please."

"Graith Tresker," he said, feeling slightly foolish.

"How old are you, Graith?" she asked, and Graith could hear Alix giggle.

"Eh, forty-five? Maybe? Not quite sure what day," he chuckled, "or month it is. I might be forty-six by now."

He shrugged slightly and immediately let out a moan. The movement had hurt, badly.

"Shh. It'll be all right. We'll get you some pain medication here, shortly. One more," and she gave him a sympathetic smile, "What are your companions' names?"

Graith would have chuckled again, but he was still trying to catch his breath from the earlier shrug.

"Alix, Kade, and Kali."

Alix giggled again, and Graith wanted to look over at the boy, but it was too painful.

"Good, Graith, I'm going to help you sit up now, and I'm going to examine your head and neck."

Her hands were cold as they slid under his shoulders, and she helped him sit up from the waist. Then she was carefully feeling his scalp and down his neck. He turned his head as she asked, slowly stretching the muscles. As he looked to the left, he saw an ornate wall, and then as he looked right, he saw Alix, Kade, and Kali. Alix hadn't been exaggerating when he said that they'd gotten bruised up. He smiled weakly at them, and Kali gave a small wave.

"You're looking good, Graith," Dr. Maziri said, stepping into his line of sight. "Let me go get that medication, and then her Majesty would like to speak to you all."

As she walked out of the room, Alix rushed forward and sat on the end of the bed. It was a little higher than Lutesian-style beds, and the boy had a little bit of trouble lifting himself onto it with one arm strapped to his chest.

"Are you okay, Graith?" Alix asked quietly. He had been excited moments before, but as he looked at Graith's face, he sobered.

"I think so, lad. This arm is going to hurt for a while, but I'll live."

Alix's eyes welled with tears, and he scooted up the bed to hug Graith. Crying into Graith's shirt, he was just barely able to say, "I thought you were dead. I thought I was going to be alone again."

Graith wrapped his good arm around Alix's small shoulders and patted his back as he cried.

Just then Dr. Maziri returned, carrying a small mug of something steaming.

"I'll just set this here. Try and get it all down in the next half hour." She looked sternly at him, "And please stay in bed. You need rest."

She turned and left for the door again, and once she reached it, she bowed low and stepped aside. Graith watched with interest.

The queen must have arrived.

When the child entered the room, he did a double take. The golden fabric of her gown glowed, and the jewels that adorned it twinkled in the light. But she was, with no doubt, still a child - *maybe* Kali and Kade's age, but he doubted she was even out of her teens. Her face was pale. Her red hair and green eyes made her skin look sheet white, with a sprinkle of freckles that stood out like ink spots on new parchment.

She was followed closely by two guards and a man who looked to be her aide. Graith just looked at them, slack-jawed with awe. It was one thing to be told he was in the palace, another to be seen by the queen, young or not.

***

Vizen and Karina met Nerie outside the door to the infirmary. Karina pulled the door open, and Dr. Maziri bowed to her. As she stepped inside, she looked around the room. It took most of her willpower to stay composed when she saw the state of the four strangers. A man and woman, not much older than herself, were standing next to the bed, both with bruises on their faces and on what skin she could see. On the bed was a young boy with a broken arm and an older man who was staring at her. She blushed lightly but didn't acknowledge it otherwise.

She's been informed of this man, Graith. The man with the dragon. Nerie informed the captain of the Queen's Guard of this, and he told her that he would be in the room with her - no matter how injured they were, they could not be trusted to be alone with her.

Still in her coronation finery, Nerie moved slowly into the room. A chair was provided, and she seated herself as formally as she could at the bedside.

She took this moment to study Graith's face a little more. He was in his late thirties or early forties, with a dark stubble on his gaunt face. He looked as if he had taken the worst of the crash.

Other than the dragon, but Eras had assured her that she'd live. She'd need humans to help set her wing once she awoke, but it should heal fine. Karina had not followed them in immediately, but Vizen had. Now Karina returned, carrying a tray of refreshments. The man and woman shifted from foot to foot, looking uneasy. Nerie briefly wondered when they'd last eaten, she hadn't since before dawn, and it was now late afternoon. She was hungry, so she daintily picked up a cup of tea. It wouldn't sate her, but it would help curb her hunger.

She motioned for them to sit, and to join her in eating.

Then she waited.

The older man spoke first.

"Your uh, Highness," he said, as if unsure if this was the correct title to use. When she did not correct him, he went on. "My name is Graith, I am Zel - uh, the dragoness Azelia's companion." He fiddled with the sheet on the bed while he spoke. He lowered his eyes as if worried she'd be angry with him.

"I found her months ago, injured in my barn. Nursed her back to health, only to learn that she'd had a clutch of eggs that she'd been forced to leave. When we returned to her caves, men had taken them."

Nerie's stomach twisted as she figured out where this was going.

"We've been following them for months. The few times we've gotten close," he paled, clearing his throat, "they've killed eggs. There were five to start with."

A tear trailed down his cheek, and Nerie's heart broke thinking about the eggs that were currently in the hatching ground with Soros.

He fidgeted on his bed before looking at her again.

"We know the eggs are here, and all she wants is to get them back."

Nerie sat, listing. She knew that his dragon Zel, had awoken, and that she and Eras were speaking right now, but she couldn't focus on them and the man at the same time. But there was one burning question she had to ask.

"I highly doubt she is Lutesian, and I know she isn't from Situra - where is she from? Are there more dragons?"

Graith looked surprised, "Well, she told me she's from Etria. She's got a whole family and, from the few images I've seen, a whole society."

Nerie reached out to Kiriga and at the same time she felt the dragoness reaching for her.

There are more dragons! both said to the other, excitedly.
***

Nerie spoke with Graith and the others for several more hours.

She explained the situation with Prince Brantom, and how he had brought the eggs as a bride price. The first thing that she reassured, once she told them that the eggs had arrived, was that they were safe in Soros' hatching ground. She promised that as soon as Azelia was well enough to move, that she could join Soros and the eggs.

She wanted to help them completely, but she couldn't just give them the eggs. They'd been given to Soren, as a gift to encourage a marriage to Prince Brantom. She was sure that the offer still stood, but she was queen now. For a queen to marry a prince was quite different from a princess and marrying a prince.

She would have to think about her next course of action.

She apologized to Graith and told him that she didn't think it would be safe for him to stay in the palace. Not when Brantom and his father had worked so hard to keep Azelia away from her eggs.

Nerie feared some sort of retaliation if he were to find out that Graith had been working with Azelia. Instead, she told him that he and his friends could stay at her home in the middle district. They would leave the palace once cleared by Dr. Maziri and she would have supplies brought to them. If they needed anything, they just had to have Azelia bespeak any of the dragons here at the palace.

Finally, she stood and left the infirmary. Nerie's head spun, from lack of food and from the many events of the day. However, one thing stood out above all others - Kiriga and the others were not alone.

There were dragons in Etria.

Thank you for reading Heartscale.

Please look forward to Book Two of A Thunder of Dragons

Shatterscale

Set to release November 2021

To receive notifications about Shatterscale, and other works by Lola Ford, sign up for her mailing list here:
http://eepurl.com/gZLBl9

For a group dedicated to Dragons and Dragon Literature, check out
https://www.facebook.com/groups/DragonLit/

Following - A preview of
Dragonflame - Book One of The Dragon's Scion
Available on Amazon January 11th 2021
Now on pre-order
http://geni.us/Dragonflame

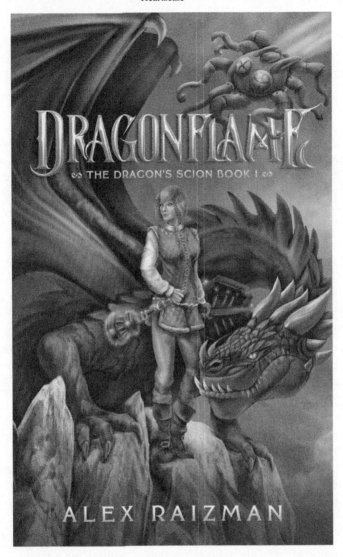

Dragonflame - Book one of The Dragon's Scion

Prologue

On the path between a dying city and a mountain, a dying guardsman rode with a precious bundle in his arms. This was not the first horse the guardsman had ridden since leaving the city. The others had perished on the journey. He hadn't even purchased this horse. Having long ago discarded his tabard and armor, this guardsman wore thick furs to keep out the bitter cold. Between that and the wild look in his eyes, he looked less like a guardsman and more like a bandit. It was fitting, in a way, the third and final horse he rode was stolen.

His name was Comber, and he had been part of the troop assigned to protect the royal family against all threats. For ten years he had stood his post, alongside the royal family's Umbrists. Comber didn't have the Shadow-infused powers of the Umbrist. He had armor that had been forged with steel mixed with light, and a sword that had been blessed millennia ago with a dragon's breath.

Had.

He had a vow to protect the royal family against any and all threats. He'd fought when the minions of a necromancer had snuck in through the sewers. He had a scar still from where an assassin's crossbow meant for the King had instead found his thigh. He was not a coward, and he had thought himself beyond fear.

Had.

Comber looked over his shoulder. His pursuers weren't there. He was alone here. There was nothing but a path through the woods, a path that had been cleared by game hunters who would head this way. It took a bold man to hunt in these woods, given what guarded them. The same being that drew Comber deeper within. His last hope for salvation.

The skies darkened, and Comber risked a glance upwards. There it was. That hole in the sky. The sun had passed behind it, casting a momentary shadow across the world. It was like the eclipse Comber remembered from when he was a child, but there was still light coming from the center. Small points showing stars unlike any he had seen before.

A few tiny dots broke off from the main circle. Comber shuddered at the sight. He'd seen what those dots could do when they got lower.

The bundle in his arms stirred when he shivered again, and looked up at him with bright green eyes. Awake now, the child's face was placid for just a moment, those beautiful eyes flickering about. Then hunger set in, and the child started to wail.

"Shhh, little one," Comber whispered, stroking the side of the child's face. "Shhh."

Still the child cried. She was just old enough to eat solid food that had been mashed together. Comber grimaced and looked around again. There was no one present. "Shhh," Comber said, pulling on the reins of the horse. He reached into his pack. He still had some berries from the last town, and got to work mashing them into a paste with a mortar and pestle. At her age, the child had just enough understanding of what that smell and sound meant, and her cries turned to excited cooing as she reached towards his hands. "Almost there, little one," Comber said. Or at least, he started to say. Halfway through the wound in his side reminded him of why he'd abandoned his sword, and Comber hissed in pain. Even the simple motion of grinding berries was too much for him.

He set the mortar down carefully. He hadn't been able to get a spoon in his mad flight. The child was able to suckle the paste off his finger, and that would have to be good enough. Once she'd been fed, Comber held her with one hand and pulled the other inside his coat. He ran his fingers over the hasty bandage. It was damp. He wanted to look at the injury, but didn't dare. He knew what he'd find. Black veins sprawling outwards from under the bandage, creeping along his skin. Last night, the veins had been halfway to his chest. Soon they would reach his heart.

He'd die then. Comber didn't need to be a Physician to know that.

The child reached up and grabbed for his nose with hands wrapped in mittens. Comber let her grab it, then pressed his forehead to hers. "Soon, you'll be safe," Comber whispered to her.

Then it was time to transition the child to the straps wrapped around his chest, freeing his hands, and Comber resumed his ride to the mountain.

***

The horse – Comber had never bothered giving it a name – came to a stop, and the jolt rocked Comber awake. He blinked around blearily. He'd fallen asleep in the saddle somehow. Everything felt like it had been coated in a layer of wool. Comber worked one of his hands free of the glove and pressed it against his forehead. In spite of the cold, heat radiated from the touch. "Fever," he muttered to the child.

"Bah-bah-bah-bah," she said, which Comber took as affirmation. He smiled down at her, then looked around again. They'd reached the mountain.

"We go no further together," he said to the horse. Comber had never been one to speak to his mounts, aside from commands. He preferred to make noises at them, reassuring ones. But in the grip of fever, Comber felt irrationally sorry for abandoning an animal he'd only had for a day. A stolen one, at that. "You'll be able to find your way back to town, won't you? Or maybe you'll be able to run free now, without the need…the need…" Comber trailed off. What had he been doing? Talking to a horse, that's what.

They were close to the base of the mountain, but not quite there. He could see it. Perhaps he could ride the horse a little bit further? He dug his heels in. The horse let out a huff of air and shook its head, instead backing up a few paces. "Of course," Comber said, shaking his head. "Of course. A horse. A horse of course." He laughed a bit. It wasn't funny, but the child joined in the laughter. He patted the side of the horse's neck again. "You smell it, don't you?"

The horse shook its head violently and took another step back. That was all the confirmation Comber needed. The horse would go no further. "You know," Comber said, getting ready to dismount. "I should have known. They eat you, don't they?"

The horse did not respond this time, for it was a horse, and all it cared about was that it didn't need to go any further.

Comber got one foot out of the stirrup, but the world started to spin. Instead of dismounting gracefully, Comber swung drunkenly, and collapsed into the snow. He had just enough presence of mind to turn around as he fell, landing on his back to keep the child safe. Comber growled in pain as the impact lanced through his back. The shock did wonders for clearing his head. The child, jostled by the fall, poked her head up and giggled.

"That's right," Comber grunted. "I'm silly, aren't I?"

The child reached up for him, grasping for him. Comber put his finger out for her to hold onto.

He'd abandoned his station, and he knew he should feel guilty about that, but…the beings that had come from that hole in the sky were beyond anything that could be fought. Arrows bounced off their gleaming carapace. Swords were deflected with swipes from their unnatural hands. He had a duty, and he could only save one person.

He'd chosen her.

Comber rose to his feet and turned the horse around. It only took a nudge to get the horse trotting away from the mountain.

It would live. The child would live. That would have to be enough.

Comber made himself walk towards the mountain. Every footstep was like lead. He spotted a trail in the snow – someone else had come this way and left. They were human, or at least walked like one. It could be an Underfolk or Sylvani. It wasn't the invaders. That much was certain. No one could mistake their skittering legs for human footsteps.

The mountain, at least, was free of snow. Impossibly free, and impossibly warm. A fire burned in the heart of this mountain. Not the molten fire of a volcano. A living flame. A hungering flame.

Had the fever started sooner than Comber realized? He'd been so certain of this plan. He'd heard tales of the flame that lived in this mountain. The tales had made it out to be one of the ones that did not feast on the flesh of Man or the other Intelligent Races. They said it had stood alongside the forces of the Light and Shadow against dread powers in the past. They said it was not to be disturbed, but would not slay – except for those that came to attack it.

But still…could he trust it?

It was too late now. There was nowhere else he was certain would be safe for the child. Not with that locket, secured carefully in a pouch in the swaddling. Even without it…would anywhere be safe from the invaders? Would anything? They hadn't been killing innocents. They'd killed armies, they'd slaughtered guards, but any who did not pick up blade or spear against them was spared their wrath. Yet… Comber didn't trust them to stop there. It was possible – nay, it seemed likely – that they were just starting with those that posed a threat to them.

"Not that we did," he said to the child, who paused in her attempts to gum his finger to look up at him. "I hope, if you remember nothing else, you remember that we tried. We tried."

"Burrrbl," the child said happily.

"We tried," Comber repeated. And they had. Nicandros, the captain of the royal guard, had commanded them perfectly. However, no strategy could overcome the fact that their weapons did no harm to the invaders. That was when Comber realized the only option was saving what he could. That there would be no victory here. Still, Comber had fought, until his wound. Then…he'd been even more useless in battle.

Time became unstable. Comber kept walking up the warm mountain and its bare stones. It was a gentle slope, which was the only reason he could progress at all. Ahead, he saw his goal.

A hole, high up the mountain. One far larger than would be needed for a man to pass through, and one too smooth and round to be the result of nature. This was not a cave. It was a lair.

Comber stumbled and dropped to his knees. The child started to wail again, startled by the jostling. Comber tried to shush its cries, but he was too late. Something was stirring in the lair, dragging itself forth from the depths. Comber saw golden eyes peering out of the darkness, followed by red scales and immense, bat-like wings.

Comber had never seen a dragon in person. Only flying overhead, and even then, such sights were rare. He'd expected them to crawl across a ground, like a lizard, but this one slunk with a cat's grace. An older cat, one that was past its prime hunting days, but still possessed with enough energy to move about. The dragon flapped its wings and took to the air, circling around Comber once before landing.

"I told Lathariel I would not be disturbed," the dragon growled, and Comber was certain he'd made a mistake. Tears started to form in his eyes, unbidden.

"Please…" Comber said, but the dragon shook its head.

"I will not fight." The dragon looked up, seeing the hole in the sky, and its nostrils flared. For a moment, Comber could see it considering…then it shook its head again. "I will not fight," it repeated. "Leave this threat for younger drakes. Ones that have hotter flames."

"Please…" Comber said again, then he coughed. Flecks of something black came with the cough, and Comber moved with speed he didn't know he still had, pulling the child free of the path of whatever those were. He groaned in pain and nearly blacked out.

"You are injured," the dragon said, leaning down. "And you are ill."

Comber nodded.

"I can heal your injuries," the dragon said, after considering for a moment. "But my flames will make the disease spread quicker."

"Not…me." Comber coughed again. "Her."

The dragon looked at the child. "She's uninjured," he said.

"Care...protect." Comber's vision grew dark. "She... she...is." Comber's vision narrowed. "She is... everything...." The dragon was barely visible now. The world was barely visible. The child stirred, looking from the dragon to Comber and back again, starting to make distressed noises. She didn't fear the dragon. That was good. But she could tell something was wrong.

"I'm sorry," Comber said to the child. He looked back up at the dragon. His vision was barely there anymore. He'd gone so far. It felt like part of his mind had been set on fire, to hold back death, and now that he was here, that flame had gone out. "Tell her..." Comber said, and then he started to cough again. "She is..."

"What should I tell her she is?" the dragon asked, after Comber had been silent for too long. When he got no response, the dragon Karjon leaned down. The man's heartbeat had been so faint when he'd approached, Karjon could barely hear it. Now, though? Now there was nothing.

And the child started to cry.

Karjon looked at it. He'd never dealt with human children before. He knew they needed more comfort than hatchlings. Uncertain, Karjon reached out with one claw and retracted his talon, then brushed his scales on the child's cheek.

Quick as a viper, the child grabbed Karjon's finger tightly, trying to seek some comfort in a world that had abandoned her.

Karjon sighed. He had not had children of his own. He hadn't planned on doing so. But...if nothing else, he could not leave this child to starve on his mountain. He carefully bit on the swaddling, making certain to only let his fangs touch the fabric.

Once these invaders had been dealt with, Karjon would take the child to the nearest humans. They would know how to handle her. He'd keep her safe until then. It shouldn't be long. There had been many threats over his nine hundred years of life. They'd always been defeated.

There was no reason to believe this would be any different.

Chapter 1

"I have lived for centuries," Karjon growled. "I dueled the Necromancer Gix and his army of undead. I was on the Council of Twelve, battling the Lichborne. When the mad Lumcaster sought to blind the world, I doused him in my flames. How is it that nothing has vexed me as much as you, little one?"

Tythel looked up at the dragon with eyes wide in feigned innocence. Sixteen years had passed since the mountain and the snow. She didn't remember it, of course. Just as she did not remember what her name had been before coming here. Tythel was a dragon's name, not a human name. For all Karjon's bluster, she was not worried. In sixteen years, Karjon had never raised a claw in anger. "Father, have you considered that it is just because you love me so dearly?"

Karjon huffed and shook his head. "That cannot be it. I think it *must* be because I did not know how *vexing* your unique subspecies of humans can be."

"Subspecies?" Tythel asked.

"Yes. Those strange beings humans call 'adolescents.' Or perhaps it is just a trait unique to daughters."

Tythel beamed at him. The expression only came through with her eyes. In her books, humans would use their mouths to do things like smile and frown. Tythel understood, in theory, what those were, but the expressions didn't come to her naturally. From what Karjon had said, she'd smiled and frowned at first…but with time, those had stopped. Now, she blinked rapidly to show her excitement. "Which would only matter because you love me. Therefore, I am still correct. And, since I *am* correct, I see no reason I should not be allowed to go."

Karjon sighed heavily. "Tythel…"

"You said I could," Tythel reminded him, trying her best not to sound sullen.

"I told you that, yes," Karjon said. "I said you could go

when it was safe."

"I want to see other humans," Tythel said. "Why can't I go?"

Karjon sighed again, a sound that filled the entire cave that was his lair and their home. "When, exactly, did 'because I said so' become insufficient?"

"When I stopped being a child," Tythel said. "You said when I was sixteen, I could go and see other humans."

"I said that you could go into the village when you were sixteen, Tythel. I did not say you could do so the very next day." Making that promise, back when she was nine, had been a mistake. He'd done it to get her to cease her incessant questions. He didn't think humans of that age could *remember* things for so long.

"You're splitting scales and you know it," she folded her arms across her chest and glowered at him.

Karjon, who weighed in at just over six tons and had battled some of the greatest foes the world had ever seen, broke the staring contest first. Tythel tried not to blink when she realized that meant she was getting through to him. For all his fury and might, Karjon had always struggled to deny her anything. Still, he was not caving like he usually did. "Tythel, there are reasons for the choices I make. They are for your safety."

"You always hide behind that, father. Are you planning on keeping me here the rest of my life? What are you hiding me *from?*"

"There are those out there that would see you dead. Is that not enough explanation?"

She again glowered at him. "You know I can't do anything if you don't tell me. But if you want me to leave it alone, you'll need to give me more than that." Her expression softened. "Please, father."

Karjon settled down onto the pile of coins that made his seat. Tythel took the cue and walked over to her own, smaller pile. She didn't have a hoard of her own. Not yet. But she would one day, although she was less than eager for that day. Dragons did not share a hoard. She'd have to leave for that day, never to live here again.

"Perhaps…" Karjon started to say, then held up a claw to forestall her before she got too excited. "It is time you know of the dangers beyond this lair. Why I keep you hidden here. And tomorrow…" he studied her critically for a moment, then nodded. "You are old enough."

"To go visit?" Tythel asked hopefully.

"Not yet," Karjon said, shaking his head. "But tomorrow, I think you are ready for the one thing I know you want more than to leave."

Tythel sat up straighter, her eyes sparkling with excitement. "You mean…you'll finish the adoption?"

Karjon nodded, and Tythel leapt up to run over and wrap her arms around her father's neck. "Thank you thank you thank you!" There were tears forming in her eyes, a human reaction she hadn't shed with age, but these were tears of joy and not sadness.

"It's past time," Karjon said. "I just worried about how your body would react to the transformation."

"I know," Tythel said, although deep in her heart, she'd worried that he wouldn't do it. That she wasn't good enough. She'd never told Karjon that. If it wasn't true, it would have broken his heart. If it was true…she couldn't have handled that. Now, though, she was practically vibrating with anticipation.

Karjon put one of his claws around her. His version of a hug. From what he'd said, dragons did not engage in touch the way humans did, but one of his books had told him a lack of touch and affection could kill human infants. Deep down, Tythel suspected he had grown to like it himself. "Now. Will you listen, and will you wait?"

Tythel nodded firmly.

"Then do so," Karjon said, and Tythel settled back onto her coins. "Sixteen years ago, just days before you were brought to me…the skies let loose monsters."

"Monsters?" Tythel asked.

Karjon nodded. "I do not know if they have a name. I know what Lathariel, the goddess of the woods, told me they were being called. 'Those From Above.' They had weapons that sucked in light and spewed forth their own, unnatural energy. Unlight, she called it."

"And you fought them?" Tythel asked, excitedly.

Karjon shook his head, and in his eyes Tythel could see sorrow she'd never imagined from her father. "I am old," Karjon said. "I thought they could be defeated without me. Even when I was told dragonflame was all that would harm them…I still thought they could be defeated. There were other dragons. By the time I realized…it was too late. Those From Above had secured power over humanity. They rule down there now. As far as I know, they only fear dragonflame."

Tythel held up a hand and focused. A ball of flame formed between her fingers. "They fear this?" she asked. Dragonflame was similar to normal fire, but more vibrant. The transition from white to yellow to orange to red that happened in a normal flame was marked by clearer lines. It was weak. Not close to the true power of a dragon. But it was not nothing.

"Yes," Karjon said, and there was a somber note to his voice Tythel couldn't ignore. "Healing you when you injured yourself…you already formed the gift. They will hunt you. For that and…for other reasons."

"What other reasons?"

Karjon shook his head. "Not yet. There is much I have kept from you. You are old enough now, but…allow me to give the information slowly. Tomorrow. I will tell you the other tomorrow. Because there's something you need to understand." He put one claw carefully on her knee. "Tythel…tomorrow, after the Ascension, the number of dragons in the world will go from one to two."

Tythel stared at her father for a long moment, processing his words. She'd never met another dragon, but the idea there had been other dragons out there…she'd just assumed it. Realizing they'd been hunted down, there was only one thing to do.

She hugged Karjon again, and her father hugged her

back.

This time, Tythel was certain it wasn't just for her benefit.